THIS BOOK IS A 'FANTASTIC ... KILLING TALE of a lifelong fri....dship, a deep...... romantic ......, daring criminal alliance, and the pretentious murderer who walks free among them.

WHAT A GREAT READ! I was lucky enough to be selected as an advance reviewer and I truly enjoyed reading *Death in a Dark Alley*. The book is a very quick, easy and relaxing read. It was full of intrigue and had its share of surprises including one especially unexpected development. The book is called a romance, but I would categorize it as a suspense novel, with an element of romance. The characters are quite engaging, making you want to continue reading on. And on. I read the book over the course of two otherwise busy days. I just couldn't put it down. I highly recommend *Death in a Dark Alley* and can't wait for the next installment in the series.

I FOUND *DEATH IN A DARK ALLEY* TO BE COMPELLING and hard to put down! The character development is well done, the settings & locations are beautifully described, and the style the authors used to weave the storyline together builds in intensity. Well done Bradley Pay...book three cannot come soon enough!!

THIS IS A WONDERFUL CONTINUATION of the Spectrum Series and I quickly saw that it can stand alone, as well! I enjoyed how the threads of characters and stories are woven and surprisingly intertwined when I was least prepared. Can't wait for the next book in the series!

THIS WAS A FANTASTIC SUMMER READ that will have you flipping pages in a flurry! Intriguing characters and lovely descriptions of places, food and relationships. Once you've flown through this one, makes sure to grab the first novel in the series, *The Killings Begin*!

Taylor —
The suspense
continues!
Be Well —
Jody

Death in a Dark Alley

Bradley Pay

First edition August 2022
Previously published as *Murder in Strasbourg*, April 2021

ISBN 978-1-7345212-6-9 (paperback)
ISBN 978-1-7345212-7-6 (e-book)

**https://BradleyPay.com
https://Facebook.com/BradleyPayBooks
https://Instagram.com/BradleyPayBooks**

For Bis Bradley and Gavin Pay

Other books in the
SPECTRUM SERIES

Book One – *The Killings Begin*
Previously published as *Murder in Zaporozhye*

Dear Reader,

Welcome to the next novel, where the Spectrum River Cruise Line once again leads Tracey Lauch to his targets. Conceived while we were traveling on a European river cruise, Spectrum itself is a figment of our very active imaginations.

The story's timeline, from December 1993 to February 2012, overlaps considerably with *The Killings Begin*. We took this opportunity to provide you with a different perspective on the murders in the first book and to peek into Tracey's tormented psyche. It includes a new group of characters, who are all affected in some way by Tracey's murderous acts, as well as cameo appearances from several of the characters in book one.

We've taken liberties with the Raleigh Police Department and the politics that influenced the work of the detectives assigned to these murder cases. We created a set of police detectives and their managers out of whole cloth and any resemblance to members of that force, living or dead, is purely coincidental.

In Raleigh, we did a bit of city planning – our warehouse district is undergoing gentrification through the addition of shops, restaurants and the Lauch Art Museum, gradually transforming this area from one of rundown buildings not too far from the city center into a vibrant new destination for locals and visitors. Emily Bissett's new office building is one more addition to that transformation. Tracey's courthouse and the plaza in front of it are also reimagined locations. All of these were designed for this novel.

Sarah's House, Shane's pawnshop, the cafe where Mari and Lydia meet, the Hotel Le Fleuve and the little bar across the street, were invented expressly for this story. The *Cathédrale Notre-Dame de Strasbourg* is a magnificent example of Gothic architecture, and we hope we have been accurate in our portrayal of the cathedral and its architectural history. The description of St Petersburg has been embellished for the purpose of Tracey and Charlotte's visit. Any errors are ours and ours alone.

Ah, so many destinations we'd love to spend time visiting, from Victor's New York City brownstone and Frank's charming 1901 apartment in Geneva to that delightful farmhouse in southern France with the fabulous guest quarters. Maybe they'll invite us there someday.

We hope you enjoy this second volume of The Spectrum Series.

Jody and Robin

Table of Contents

Prologue

August 2011, Rotterdam, The Netherlands

"Alone time with you is always nice," he replied as he looked down at her leg and ran his fingers suggestively along her silky thigh and under the edge of her skirt.

"Let's get the check, Judge," she breathed into his ear.

Tracey helped Charlotte off the barstool, watching, appreciating how her skirt slid even higher along her bare thigh.

They walked toward the exit, and he reached around her to open the door. Unexpectedly, she stopped, and they ran into each other. Charlotte turned around. "Excuse me, my love," she said as she tucked her red hair behind her ear, pressed herself hard against him and kissed him greedily on the lips.

Excuse me. Tracey froze as he felt the familiar tightening in his groin. Charlotte looked down, grinned and beckoned to him as she turned to leave. And then she was waiting for him outside, and he stepped out onto the dimly lit sidewalk and took her hand.

As they walked along, his thoughts drifted. *What would it feel like to cover her mouth and put my hand around her neck, to hear her moan like the others when their soft breathing turned to harsh panting, to feel the life drain from her? I've never killed a lover before.*

"You're awfully quiet. What are you thinking about?"

"Death."

"Poor Mari. Isn't it a shame her murder hasn't been solved? We were on that cruise with her. My God, it could have been me."

"Mmmhmm," he said, distracted by his thoughts.

Since strangling Mari last year up til now, I've had no desire to kill again. Mari was kind and sweet — like my mother was. I fought it, I fought it so, but when I bumped into her in that narrow alley, I lost control. I put my hand over her mouth and my other around her neck. I can still feel her throat, her pulse under my hand. I choked her, I choked the life out of her, and I was so aroused by the way she struggled against me, her moans against my hand, the way she slowly stopped breathing.

His heart beat faster.

I felt that arousal each time, even with Maggie, my mother. She was the first. And she deserved it for abandoning me and my sister when we were small and for rejecting me again when I finally found her years later. My anger turned to rage with those two simple words, 'excuse me'. That's what she always said when she put me in my room as punishment. My hand around her neck, the sounds she made, moaning that sounded like the sex she'd have in the next room when I was little.

Am I still killing her? – over and over again?

It took all of his energy not to show his emotions as he thought about the other murders.

Then I killed Ruth. She reminded me of my mother too – but I thought that was the end. Then Zoe tempted me with her red hair and her pitiful "excuse me", just like my mother. Her struggles, the sounds she made. I was so excited, like I am now. But I still thought I could stop. Even after Sheila, I thought I could stop. The way they all brushed their hair back from their faces, that "excuse me". They all reminded me of my mother.

Charlotte stopped and kissed him passionately, jerking him back to the present, and he took her face in his hands, his mouth hard on hers. Again, she pressed herself against him, enjoying the feeling of his arousal. "I want to be with you right now. Maybe we should just lie down here on the sidewalk and make mad, passionate love." She chuckled at the appalled look on his face and put her lips on his in another intimate kiss. "Thank goodness our hotel's right there." She pointed, her breath coming rapidly.

They lay on top of the covers on the hotel bed, gasping to catch their breath.

"Whoa, that was different, my love. I liked it. We've never had such crazy, rough sex before. I wonder why."

He looked at her. "I'm sorry. I don't know what came over me. Maybe those wanton overtures from you in public?" He gave her a sly little grin.

"We'll have to try that again if this is how it ends. I didn't realize that retired judges in their forties had that kind of stamina left in them." Charlotte stroked his face and winked at him.

Tracey grinned again and tickled her arm lightly, "And I had no idea that English professors in their *late* forties could keep up during such crazy, rough sex or would like it so much that they'd be asking for more. If I had, I might have tried it earlier."

She ran the tip of one finger over his lips, and he nibbled it gently. "Even college professors in their late forties who do Zumba and dance with flash mobs need to rest for a little while after that," she murmured and lay back against a pillow, her breathing slow and soft.

Tracey lay for a long time, thinking about her and what had just happened. He turned onto his side to look at Charlotte. *I've never killed a lover before.* He reached over to brush back a lock of tangled hair. With his left hand, he caressed her face and then stroked her throat. And then he drifted off himself.

Chapter One

March 2012

My Life is Shit

Strasbourg, France

Cinder-block walls covered in chipped and scarred grey paint. The only window, the narrow one in the door where the guard stood, chomping on his gum, occasionally glancing into the room. Bright overhead light. Hard metal table and chairs.

Frank looked at the smudged mirror. *Oh, shit. They've put me in an interrogation room. What are they going to do?* His palms grew moist. He went over and banged on the door, "Hey, hey! Is there anybody out there?"

The guard, a burly man whose shirt was neatly tucked in and his boots highly polished, entered the room and stood, towering over Frank. Very slowly, in perfect English, he asked, "Do you need a translator?"

"I speak French as well as you do."

"You need to calm down, Mr. Tomas."

"Calm down?" said Frank, his voice rising in annoyance.

"You were arrested for murder and jewelry theft, Mr. Tomas."

"I didn't murder anyone – there's a witness. You just have to find her." His voice rose another notch. "And the bracelet? I just found it on the floor and put it in my pocket. They got it back, so what's the big deal?"

"I'm only a guard. I can't answer your questions. Someone will be with you as soon as they can."

"When do I get my phone call? I get a phone call, and you haven't allowed me to make it yet." He snapped his fingers alongside his leg, and his heart was pounding.

"I don't know anything about that."

Frank clenched his hands into fists as he threatened, "If I don't get my phone call, my lawyer will go after you guys." He was almost shouting.

"Mr. Tomas, you need to calm down. Things will only be worse for you if you don't. You could be charged with disorderly conduct as well. Someone will be with you shortly." The guard turned smartly and left the room, securing the door behind him with a firm click of the lock. He turned again to watch Frank through the narrow window.

Frank sat down in the metal chair and put his face in his hands. His stomach clenched. *What if my lawyer doesn't get me off? Shit! How did my life turn into such fucking shit?*

Chapter Two

Winter 1985 to 1986

The Will

New York City

After at least the nineteenth person had jostled Victor, shoving Frank perilously close to the edge of the sidewalk at Frawley Circle, Victor looked down at his nephew. "Frankie, here, switch places with me before you end up under the wheels of some taxi." As if to emphasize his words, a taxi, crawling past, swerved close to the curb as it honked its horn, trying to get the traffic to move a little faster.

Frank twisted away from him to jump onto and off a fire hydrant, bouncing on the balls to his feet, snapping his fingers in excitement while he chattered away. "Uncle, this is taking forever, and people are being even ruder today than they usually are. And I'm starving to death. How come the lines are so long today? Why aren't these people at work, anyhow?"

With a little shrug, Victor chuckled, watching the food cart owner duck his head, first one way and then another to avoid the steam that billowed out each time he lifted a lid to serve another customer. After a quick glance at his watch, he replied, "It's always more crowded on holidays. And a lot of people have come here to Central Park today to attend the Veteran's Day speeches. We're cutting it close, so we'll need to eat our hot dogs on the go. Do you want to see Tom afterward?"

"Yes! Of course! But why do we have to listen to a bunch of old people talk about a war that has been over for ten years before we can see Tom?" Frank said petulantly. "It ended the year I was born."

"They won't only talk about the Vietnam War, son. They'll speak about other wars before that as well. I've waited to bring you to this because I wanted you to be old enough to understand."

"Dad always says, 'The commies would have taken over South Vietnam and the rest of Asia if we'd let them,' and this morning he said you were a traitor, and that *he* gave a leg for his country. Are you a commie, Uncle?"

When Frank repeated Alan's comment, Victor's face reddened

in annoyance at the way his brother consistently took the opportunity to misrepresent his political leanings. He responded tersely, "Did you know I wasn't even old enough to fight in that war? I didn't agree with it, I even protested against it, but that doesn't make me a traitor or a communist. You're smart, Frankie, and you need to understand this from another perspective besides your dad's."

When the final speaker had stepped away from the podium and the crowd had slowly begun to disperse, Frank and Victor wandered in a southwesterly direction along the paved paths that ran through the park and on past the reservoir, discussing the speeches they'd just heard that afternoon. Victor listened to his nephew, to the way his tone had changed about the war and to the thoughtful questions he was asking. He smiled to himself. *A little education. Both sides of an issue. Balance. That's all it takes.*

The afternoon air was brisk, even though the sun was still shining, and he pulled the collar to his light cashmere overcoat higher against his neck. Frank glanced over at his uncle and, reaching up, turned up the collar to his jacket and pulled it against his neck as well. *Typical mid-November weather, sometimes warm, sometimes cold, sometimes not so bad,* thought Victor as he tried not to grin at Frank's imitation of his behavior. They continued along the walkway that traced a curving line through the park toward the Great Lawn. Only a random leaf here and there hung precariously from the trees. "I'm glad we haven't had an early snow this year. As long as we're in the sunshine, it's almost comfortable." Victor looked over at Frank, "I hope Tom's on his bench. I know how much you're looking forward to talking with him." He casually threw his arm over Frank's shoulder and pulled him close for a brief moment.

Frank looked up at him, "Yeah, I wonder if he's met any new and interesting people since we saw him last."

"He always has a story, doesn't he?"

"Yep – hey, look, there he is, on his usual bench. Oh, good!" He raced ahead to greet the tall Black man seated peacefully in the sunshine. *Sometimes when we come through the park, he isn't sitting here, and if it's been a long time since we've seen him, Uncle gets a worried look in his eyes.*

Victor followed slowly to give him time alone with Tom, who

was sitting quietly with his very large, dark green backpack propped next to him, listening intently. *I'm glad nothing's happened to him.* Tom had taken off his ball cap and placed it carefully on top of the backpack. He was leaned back, his arms along the back of the bench on either side of him, his head nodding as he listened to Frank's voice that cracked now and again in excitement.

Frank sat, not too close, just like Victor had taught him. *You always need to give a man his space.* His cap was pushed back on his head, and he'd turned toward Tom, his left leg bent, his foot up on the bench and his arms wrapped around his knee. Engrossed in the conversation, he appeared not to notice his uncle's arrival as he continued, "I got an A-plus on it too."

"Congratulations." Tom reached out to high-five Frank, "Which story did ya use?"

Victor sat down on the other side of Tom. He took off his hat, balanced it on his knee and tipped back his head to the afternoon sun. It was a ritual for them. Sit on the bench and if the sun was shining, they'd take off their hats, close their eyes and lift their faces toward the sun. Then they'd take a deep breath and talk. They always talked slowly, like they had all the time in the world. That day, Victor had reached over, and smiling, he'd silently shaken hands with Tom. And then he sat and listened and watched a little squirrel run back and forth across the brown grass and up a tree. He leaned back and closed his eyes. And listened some more.

"We had to write about a famous person. So, I told the story of you meeting that guy here in the park. The one that was a famous race car driver, but no one realized it because he dressed kinda scruffy, with holes in his elbows and knees." With the ball of his foot, Frank bounced his right leg in excitement.

"Did ya include the ratty dog?"

"Of course. That was an important part – to set the scene."

"Key in storytellin'." He smiled at Frank, recalling the day when he'd told him about scene-setting.

Finally, Victor leaned forward, "Tom. How are you today?"

"Very well, Vic. What are you two up to?"

Frank jumped into the conversation between the two men, "We were at the Veteran's Day celebration," and he pointed back the way they'd come. "Why didn't you come?"

"I guess I've had my fill of seein' 'n' hearin' about war an' killin'."

Victor added, "It was very good this year."

"Tom, the best part of the speeches was when this guy read from Martin Luther King's speech at Riverside Church in April 1967." Frank then quoted, word-for-word, several minutes of the MLK speech.

Tom listened in amazement. "How d'ya remember alla that?"

"He just said it, so why wouldn't I remember it?"

"But every sentence. Every intonation. Every word."

"I've always remembered things that way."

"He has a photographic memory and can remember things, like speeches, TV programs and books," explained Victor. "His parents figured it out when he was about five."

Tom touched Frank's shoulder. "That's a very special gift ya have there, young Frank. Use it wisely."

"That's what Uncle always says to me."

After a peek at his watch, Victor said, "Tom, I hate to run, but we have an appointment with the lawyer in a little bit."

"Ah, the will."

Victor nodded and stood and motioned to Frank to stand up. "Yeah, that's today." He leaned over and shook Tom's hand. "Good seeing you, Tom."

Frank immediately followed suit. "Good seeing you, Tom."

"Good luck, Vic, Frank."

§

Victor and Frank entered the lawyer's office, chatting comfortably with one another. Alan and Patricia sat balanced on two of the beautiful, but obviously very uncomfortable chairs that were grouped around an ornate coffee table at one end of the small waiting room. Tapping his watch, Alan said in a nasty tone of voice, "You're almost late." He stood up awkwardly.

Frank muttered, "But we're not." Victor squeezed his shoulder, silently cautioning him to behave and pointed him toward his mom. Frank kissed Patricia on the cheek before she stood. "Mom, Uncle took me to the most awesome event in the park. There were all these old guys giving speeches about the Vietnam War and how wrong it was. And some of them were even soldiers wearing their uniforms, and they talked about how they felt, going over there to fight an illegal war. Other guys talked about their experiences in Korea and World War Two. And there was a really old guy who spoke about the War to End All Wars. But the wars didn't end. And the last speaker was this man who stood up and read one of Martin Luther King's speeches and," he glanced at Victor, "Uncle even got tears in his eyes during some of the speeches."

With a step toward Victor, Alan raised his hand, shaking his fist in Victor's face, his voice growing more and more strident as he spoke. "Who do you think you are, taking *my* son to hear such filth? He knows what that war was about." He tapped his prosthetic leg with his cane, "You are never to see my son again. Do you hear me? Never!"

Frank's eyes widened, and he stepped behind his mom. Patricia put her hand on Alan's arm to quieten him.

Just then, the receptionist came over, interrupting Alan's diatribe, and directed them into the conference room. Alan limped around the large table to sit with his back to the window. As Patricia moved toward the room, Victor put his hand on her shoulder and squeezed it lightly. She turned her head toward him very slightly and gave him a bleak smile. Pointing Frank to the row of chairs against the window, she gestured to him to stay quiet and then followed to sit next to Alan.

Victor took a chair opposite them facing the window. He squinted against the glare of the late afternoon sun, and turning to the receptionist, he asked, "Would you please close the shades a bit? Just enough that the sun doesn't shine in so directly."

"Of course, sir," she said with an understanding smile.

While she adjusted the shades, Alan said, "For Christ's sake, Victor, it's not that bad. It's only a little sun. God knows, we don't get enough of it at this time of year."

Refusing to let his older brother get under his skin with his barbed comments, Victor smiled at the receptionist as she left. "Thank you."

They sat in silence for a brief moment before the lawyer entered. "So, we are all here." He walked around the table, greeting each person by name as he shook their hand. Frank stood up quickly as he approached, stretched as tall as he could make himself, and with a ten-year-old's pride at being included in that little ceremony, he reached out and shook hands with the lawyer. "Frank Tomas. Nice to meet you, sir."

"Thank you, young man. It's nice to meet you too, Frank Tomas." The lawyer went to sit at the head of the table where the secretary had laid out the paperwork for him. "Shall we get started?"

At the end, the lawyer summarized, "So, Alan, you're inheriting the global international bank, and Victor, you're inheriting your father's real estate holdings in New York and Brasília. Your father shared with me that you boys have never seen eye to eye about much of anything, so he felt that this was the fairest way to divide his estate."

Victor and Alan looked at each other across the wide table before Victor said to the lawyer, "It seems like a reasonable decision to me. I don't like banking, and my father knew it. Alan does. This eliminates the possibility of any conflict between us. Please begin the process of selling all of the real estate holdings. Except for my brownstone."

"Sell? You'd sell my house out from under me and my family?"

"It's a business decision. Nothing more." Victor glanced between Alan and Patricia, and his eyes came to rest on his brother. "You're more than welcome to buy it from me. But, as I recall, neither of you, not you nor Patricia, have ever liked that house."

"I would never line your pockets with my money."

"It's up to you." In a cool voice, Victor continued, "I'm not going to tell you how to run your bank, so please don't tell me how to manage my real estate."

He turned back to the lawyer. "Patricia and Alan can take any of the silver, crystal, dishes, paintings and furniture. Anything in the house with the exception of the grand piano. That should be delivered to my brownstone. They have sixty days. I think that's more than generous. Upon their departure, we'll sell any of the remaining contents."

Alan slammed his palms on the table. "How dare you?" Frank had never seen his father lose his temper like that, and he flinched and then continued to watch in fascination. Whenever Frank did something wrong, his dad would say he was angry and disappointed, but he'd never actually lost his temper like this, and now, for the second time that day. Usually, he would just walk out of the room.

Victor gave a little shrug in acknowledgement but said nothing.

Patricia watched Alan's face turn beet red. Reaching over, she stroked her hand along his sleeve to calm him. He drew a deep breath and slowly collected himself, and then he rose abruptly, stumbling as he put weight on his artificial leg. "We're leaving. Now," he said and limped out of the conference room, leaning heavily on the dark mahogany cane with a silver lion's head that had been a gift from his father when he had returned home from rehab.

Patricia and Frank stood to follow. Frank looked longingly at Victor, and Patricia went to the door to watch Alan's progress toward the elevator. She saw the two of them, waiting for her permission, and waved him over toward his uncle. "Quickly," she said.

He wrapped his arms around Victor who held him tightly against his chest. He shut his eyes, pressed his mouth to Frank's head and drew a long breath, tightening his arms even further. And then Frank whispered, "Goodbye, Uncle."

Alan stood impatiently by the elevator, tapping his cane against his leg. With a worried glance, Patricia said, "Frank, we must go. We can't keep your father waiting any longer."

Victor looked over Frank's head at Patricia, thanking her with damp eyes, and whispered, "See you later, Frankie. Stay out of trouble." He ruffled Frank's hair and then gave him a little push toward his mother, "I hope this gives you a chance to move back home to Brasília, Patricia."

She gave him a tight smile. "I hope so."

After he had ensured they were comfortably seated in their town car, the driver quietly closed the door and walked around to his side. Alan muttered, "I'm the elder son. I should have been given the entire estate, and Victor should have received some kind of financial settlement – and maybe his old brownstone." He spoke grudgingly, "He and Dad were so different. I was always the favorite, so I don't understand why Dad would leave him all the real estate. And now, Victor is kicking us out onto the street. How dare he!"

Patricia turned to him, "Perhaps this is a blessing in disguise." Drawing a little breath, she continued hesitantly, "This could be a good time for us to go back to Brasília, Alan, where we can have a fresh start."

"But my parents' house in Scarsdale is an important part of our image. Living there has made our friends and colleagues look up to us."

"We'll have a modern house, one that *we* choose, one that's *our* style. We'll find or build something very special in the best neighborhood."

Alan gave a little sigh, "Maybe we do need a change. Now that you mention it, I think starting over in Brasília could work out well. The bank headquarters is there anyway. It would be good to be there." He sighed again, "I guess we did get the better part of the deal from my father's estate. You're right, Patricia, it's time for us to move on."

Patricia turned her head to look across Frank at the East River as the car proceeded toward their stately Scarsdale home in Westchester County. *I'd feel worse about leaving if we'd had a gracious apartment along Fifth Avenue or here with a view of the river instead of Alan's family's stuffy old house.* With a little smile, she let her thoughts drift happily. *Finally, I'm going home to a house I'll choose and furnish, one full of air and light instead of one that is dark and gloomy and old, filled with old furniture and old memories and old disagreements.*

Alan's icy voice interrupted her pleasant daydreaming, "Victor has put an end to our relationship. None of us, not me or you, not Frank, none of us will have anything to do with him ever again."

Beside her, Patricia heard Frank shift in his seat and take a deep breath. She caught his eye and with a tiny shake of her head, she mouthed, "Shhh, not now." She often gave him that warning look when she saw him preparing to argue with his father.

Angry at his father, and at his mother for giving in so easily, Frank turned away to look out the window, his face sullen. *Everybody is making decisions, and nobody is asking me what I want.*

§

Brasília, Brazil

Patricia took in a deep breath of warm air as she stepped out onto the patio through the large sliding glass doors that their staff had opened wide. The scent of *Mandeville sanderi*, that wonderful Brazilian jasmine growing along the walls surrounding their development, perfumed the air. Moonlight, soft music, guests mingling with drinks in their hands or sitting at tables around the pool or relaxing in lounge chairs. *Ah, this is my kind of party, in a home perfectly designed for entertaining.* The new house was low and modern, with the living spaces occupying the long central area and wings of bedrooms stretching off at either end forming a squared u-shaped layout. All the glass, every room opening onto the paved patio in the middle, the enormous pool, surrounded with seating for many guests, the lush green lawn stretching away from the house. It was exactly what she'd pictured that day, just a few months ago in the car when they'd agreed to move away from New York and come back home to Brazil.

I can't believe we moved and got all settled in such a short time. I adore it here. Brasília has always been home to me, even after all those years in New York.

Beatriz walked over from the bar by the pool where she'd picked up a tall, cold drink full of ice and fresh lime wedges. "Patricia, I wanted to thank you again for hosting this reception. Honestly, I should have been holding it for you, since you're the new folks on the block, but you beat me to it. I wanted to give you time to settle in before inviting the neighbors over to welcome you all."

"It all went so smoothly, the move, unpacking the little we brought with us, furnishing this place," Patricia motioned to the house. "I knew exactly what I wanted, and that made it easy. I love to entertain, especially outdoors, and I plan to hold a lot more of these parties." Patricia took a sip of her *Caipirinha.* "Mmmm – even these taste better here. Our bartender has perfected his interpretation of this drink. I don't know what he adds besides *cachaça*, sugar and lime, but it's sensational." She smiled at her friend, "But be careful, because whatever it is, they don't taste as potent as they are."

Beatriz took a small taste of hers and nodded in agreement, "It is delicious. But I'm such a lightweight, I'd better switch to soda water with lime after this."

"You'll have to have at least one more with the *feijoada* that Pedro is preparing for our midnight dinner. It's a family tradition. Even the kids get a small, weaker version." Their cook had been working hard all day, preparing for the party, and Patricia's mouth watered at the thought of his fresh bread and the black bean stew that they would all be served later that evening, accompanied by another tall, refreshing *Caipirinha*.

"Tell me about where you lived in New York," Beatriz said.

"We lived in a big, old house, north of New York City. It was Alan's family's home, but it wasn't my style. It was a sprawling old colonial, with seven fireplaces. His dad moved to New York from here when Alan and his brother were young, and they bought the house back then. But it was built in the nineteen twenties and was broken up into so many rooms. There just wasn't enough light for me." Patricia gave a shiver before continuing, "When I was in high school, my parents also moved from here to New York for my dad's job. I met Alan, and, well, we fell in love. But I never thought we'd stay there. It was dreary, and every winter, I was so cold. I was very homesick." She waved her hand back toward the house, "I'm so glad to be back here. Brasília is my home. And this house is exactly my style."

"It's a beautiful place, and you've decorated it perfectly."

Patricia reached out to touch Beatriz's arm, "Thank you." She took another sip from her glass and admired the clear evening sky. "We couldn't have asked for better weather. It's spectacular."

"I ordered it, just for you and your party. That's what good neighbors do," Beatriz said, her eyes twinkling with fun. She looked around at the large gathering of neighbors. Alan and her husband, Matheus, were talking about something that had both of them laughing and gesticulating wildly. "It looks like our hubbies are enjoying each other's company. Ever since the Souzas moved out of this house last year, Matheus has been a bit lost."

"Alan needs male friends outside of the bank. So, I'm glad

they've bonded with each other like you and I have. It's always great to be friends with your next-door neighbors."

And then Frank interrupted their conversation. "Mom, I'm so bored."

"Frank, why don't you go talk to Isabelle? She's sitting over there all by herself. She looks lonely," said Patricia, gesturing toward the young girl with braces and curly hair that bordered on frizzy in the humidity.

Beatriz joined in, "You two are in the same class in school, aren't you?"

"Yes, Mrs. Ronaldo. But she's very quiet, so I haven't gotten to know her."

"Well, this is the perfect opportunity then. This is a party, and you are one of the hosts, Frank. You need to mingle with our younger guests," Patricia told him. "Off with you now."

Frank adjusted his suit jacket and then snapped his fingers quietly, his hand next to his leg, "Right away, Mom."

"Whew, kids." Her eyes followed as he wandered slowly over toward Isabelle.

"Isabelle takes after me. She's perfectly content to be by herself for hours and hours or talking with grown-ups. She doesn't seem to need much company. I do wish she'd find a friend her age though, to hang out with. Being alone all the time, playing the piano or with her nose stuck in a book isn't healthy." Beatriz's eyes rested fondly on her daughter sitting at the table under one of the many lanterns with an open book on her lap, intent on her reading, carefully turning a page from time to time.

They watched Frank detour to the drinks table where he asked the bartender for two lemonades.

"Thanks, Patricia. It'll be a good change for her, even if they only talk for a little while."

Patricia laughed sympathetically.

Frank carried the glasses carefully toward Isabelle. *She's a mess. Wild hair, splotchy skin, braces. But Mom is right, she does look lonely, like she could use a friend.* Suddenly, he felt sorry for her and asked with a kind smile, "Do you mind if I sit here?"

Completely lost in her own world, Isabelle jumped at the sound of his voice. The book on her lap started to slip, and she grabbed at it. Her face turned red in embarrassment. She stared at Frank. "What? I beg your pardon. Were you talking to me?" Her blush deepened.

"You didn't have a drink, so I brought you a lemonade. Do you mind if I sit down?"

Isabelle recognized the good-looking, black-haired, brown-eyed boy from her class at school. She was surprised that he was bothering to pay attention to her. "Sure, I guess."

Frank handed her the glass of lemonade. It was full of ice and had a chunk of muddled lime and a long sprig of mint as garnish. He sat down and took a big swallow of his drink. Isabelle lifted her glass and took a tiny sip. "You're Isabelle, right? I'm Frank. That's my mom talking with yours over there. I've seen you around school," he said. "Do you like living here?"

Isabelle turned her head to see their mothers engaged in conversation and then back to him, "Being here, outside the city with all this space, the grass, the fresh air. I love it. Don't you?"

"It's not New York City. You can't just walk out the door and do stuff here. I used to go from Scarsdale into the city a couple of times a month to spend weekends with my Uncle Victor. We'd have great adventures. I stayed with him a lot in the summers, and I made a lot of cool friends. The kids in Scarsdale were sooo boring. I'm a city kid. Here, the chauffeur has to take me everywhere, even to the movies."

Frank looked around, trying to figure out what else to say. He looked at the candles floating in the pool. "Mom always goes overboard with these receptions. The perfect guest list, she worries about that a lot, the perfect food, the right number of candles in the pool, the perfect music."

"I think it's pretty."

"It's weird to have summer in February."

"Well, I think it's weird to have summer in July."

"Hey, the caterer has some good old American burgers and stuff as well as all those Brazilian dishes." He got up from his chair and turned toward her. "Want to get something to eat, Izzy?"

She stood up and punched him in the arm – hard.

"Owww! Why'd you do that?" he said, rubbing his arm.

"Don't ever call me Izzy. My name is Isabelle."

"Whatever."

They filled their plates – burgers and chips for Frank and a burger and raw vegetables for Isabelle – before returning to the table. He took a bite, and with his mouth full, Frank asked, "What's that you're reading?"

As she chewed, Isabelle lifted her book from the table where she'd laid it. She swallowed before she replied, "It's about riverboat captains on the Mississippi and other American rivers."

Frank gulped from his lemonade. "That sounds boring. Why are you reading that? Is it for school or something?" He crammed a handful of chips into his mouth.

His criticism didn't faze her at all. "If you haven't read it, you can't comment."

"Whatever," he muttered again.

They stopped talking when they heard a loud burst of laughter. They looked over at a group of noisy adults, and they both shrugged at the same time. They turned back to each other, and Frank asked, "What's your favorite book?"

"That's easy. The great American novel, *Huckleberry Finn*, of course."

"What's this obsession with rivers?"

"It's not an obsession. It's a passion."

"Passion for what?"

"When I grow up, I'm going to work on rivers. I want to be a riverboat captain like the ones in this book."

"Why?" He shoved the rest of his burger in his mouth and leaned back, casually crossing one leg over the other, imitating the older kids who were hanging out on the other side of the pool.

"To see the world. To meet people. To be outdoors. To not be tied down to a desk and an office." She paused, "What is this, twenty questions? Now it's my turn. What do you like to do?"

"Watch movies. Old Hitchcock movies, old action movies, the old stuff is the best. It relies on the people and not gimmicks. That's what my friend, Tom, says."

"Hmmm. I've never watched them. So, there *is* something

more to you," she tapped the side of her head and snickered, "than your looks. What's your favorite book?"

"I don't read much. I'm too busy having fun with my friends and playing tennis."

Isabelle shrugged. "I don't read all the time. I also play the piano. My teacher says I'm extremely good for my age."

Frank continued, as though she hadn't said anything, "Do you like fast cars? Do you take risks? Have you seen *The Italian Job*?"

Isabelle sat up very straight, and in her sternest adult manner said, "Driving large riverboats on crowded rivers with over a hundred people on them is a risk. Last year, we went on a river cruise, and one evening, we had dinner with the captain. He told stories from around the world that you wouldn't believe."

"Well, I would rather live in New York City. I told you, I'm a city kid. I want to live close to my uncle. Hanging out with him is the best." Frank's voice grew wistful, "We used to spend a lot of time together. Since I was really little. Until we moved here, that is. He's awesome."

"What are you going to be – in New York?"

"Either a jewel thief or a secret agent," he responded enthusiastically before adding, "I just haven't decided yet

Chapter Three

October to December 1993

Old Man

Brasília, Brazil

She was seated at their baby grand piano in the music room, her back straight, her toes resting on the pedals and her hands soft, playing Beethoven's Piano Sonata No. 8, *Pathétique*. Beatriz was relaxing on the settee in front of the fireplace with her book in her lap and a finger marking her place. Her eyes were closed as she listened, her lips curved in a gentle smile. After Isabelle played the last few notes, she placed her hands in her lap and practiced controlled deep breathing. Then she put her hands on the keyboard and started again from the beginning.

Before she left the room, Beatriz rested her hand on Isabelle's shoulder for a moment. "Your playing is lovely today. You've captured all the melancholy, all the sadness of that piece. The extra time you've been practicing is paying off now."

"Thanks, Mom." *She'll never know how upset I am. Of course, I can play what I'm feeling far better through this piece. I can't play anything light or joyful today.*

As Beatriz left, she said over her shoulder, "Please, don't get so lost in your music that you're late for dinner, dear."

I don't know what to do. Isabelle finished the Beethoven and hit random keys with her finger before picking up the sheet music for Bach's *Come, Sweet Death*. Partway through, she stopped and melodramatically crashed her fingers onto the keys and without even bothering to close the keyboard lid, ran to her bedroom. Rushing into her ensuite bathroom, she dug through the trash can, pulling out the pregnancy test, hoping she'd been wrong. *But it was positive before, so why would it be different now?*

She lay on her stomach on her big, soft bed with her head buried in her pillow, sobbing. "What am I going to do?" she cried and pounded her fist clutching the little white stick on her lacy coverlet. "Get yourself together, Isabelle. You're an adult now. You have to deal with this – by yourself." She sat up and looked at the test again. "Fuck!" Then she giggled a little hysterically. "No, you were fucked." She giggled again and burst into tears. "What the hell am I going to do?"

Standing up abruptly, she kicked the leg to the bed on her way to the window, where she stood, blindly staring out toward the immaculate gardens that surrounded their house. *Immaculate, just like Mom likes her life to be. Everything nice and orderly.* "Options. Isabelle, what are your options? Think," she urged herself.

She threw the stick toward the bed and watched it bounce onto the floor. "Should I tell Frank?" After a few seconds, she said to herself, "I can't go to Frank. He'll hate me for getting pregnant when I'm not married. All his bullshit about 'marriage is sacred'. He hated my boyfriend anyway, and he thought he was only after sex. I guess he was right, but I can't ever let him know."

Isabelle reached one hand down and touched her flat stomach. "Should I tell my mom?" She picked up a picture of her family from her dresser. "Mom, Dad, I can't go to you with this. You'll be so ashamed and disappointed in me. I can't tell you. And the school nurse and our doctor will tell you, so I can't go to them either."

She walked over, picked up the white stick and wrapped it in a tissue before stuffing it deep in her purse. "I should throw this away outside the house." Then she went back and got the rest of the packaging and thrust it into her purse as well. "So much for not having a condom. So much for pulling out in time. Should I tell him, even though we're not together anymore? Will he believe that he's the father even though I've never had sex with anyone else? Will he accuse me of sleeping around? I can't tell him, he was such a jerk at the end, and then he dumped me when I called him out for it."

She sat cross-legged on her bed for a long time, tears seeping down her face, until she heard the special light knock the housekeeper always gave before she opened the door. "Don't forget, it's Friday night, Miss Isabelle, and you're not dressed yet. You're going to be late to dinner. I know you lose track of time, but your mom doesn't like it when you're late."

"Oh, shit." She clapped her hand over her mouth and glanced over at the clock on her nightstand. "I only have a few minutes to change." She swung her feet to the floor, preparing to stand up.

The housekeeper came over and sat on the edge of the bed.

"You look so sad. You've been crying. What's wrong?" She put her arms around Isabelle.

She began to cry again in earnest. "I'm pregnant, and I don't know what to do."

"That boyfriend of yours? The one you keep sneaking out to see?"

"You haven't told Mom about him, have you? Because we broke up."

"Of course not. How far along are you? What do you plan to do?"

"I think I'm a couple of months. But this will ruin everything, all my plans for the future. I don't want children. At least not right now. I can't walk across the stage at graduation in two more months with my belly out here." Isabelle reached out in front of herself, drawing a huge, pregnant stomach with her hands. "That would be humiliating. And I can't go to the university if I have a baby. And if I can't get my degree, that will mess up my career and the rest of my life. What should I do?"

"Miss Isabelle, I know someone who can take care of it for you. If you want."

"Will you go with me?"

§

Alone in the emergency room bed a week later, Isabelle looked up at the doctor. "My abdomen hurts so badly. I'm bleeding. Oh, God, it hurts." She blinked back the tears that were threatening to spill out and humiliate her.

The doctor's examination was embarrassingly thorough. As he took off his examination gloves and tossed them into the trash, he said in a stern voice, "It looks to me like that was a very bad abortion you had. When did it happen?"

Isabelle broke down and cried softly. "It was a couple of days ago."

"Well, now, you have a severe infection."

"Can you do anything for it? Can you make it go away?"

"Antibiotics should do the trick, but I'll need to see you again in ten days to make sure that the drugs have done their job. Get dressed, and I'll be back with the prescription."

Isabelle dressed slowly and carefully, doubling over periodically as her abdomen cramped. When the doctor returned, he handed her a prescription and a clipboard. "Here you go. Now, sign here so we can release you."

Isabelle took it and signed the paperwork as he continued, "Young lady, you need to understand how very serious this is. I don't know where you got this procedure done, but it is very possible that you may never be able to have children. I'll know more when I examine you again."

§

New York City

"Oh my God, we're so spoiled." Isabelle looked around the wide body of the airplane. She shifted her position and pulled her legs up to sit yoga-fashion in her window seat, put her finger in her book to mark her place and gave a long appreciative sniff. "To me, the smell of leather seats in business class always means an adventure lies ahead. I need this adventure, Frank. Breaking up with my boyfriend was horrible, you have no idea. I just need to put all of that behind me."

"I know you've been sad, girlfriend. I told you he would break your heart. But you're really going to like New York. It'll be a good distraction. I can't wait to see Uncle Victor and my friends."

"I can't believe our parents let us visit for a whole month, and at Christmastime."

"Technically, we didn't need their permission. We're both over eighteen."

"Yeah, but they paid for it all."

"As a high school graduation gift. Everybody gets fabulous gifts for that. I can't believe my mom was able to convince my dad to let me visit Uncle Victor. But we've been arguing so much, I guess he was ready to do anything to get me out of his sight."

"Or maybe your dad finally realized how important family is."

"I doubt it. He hates my uncle. I can't believe it'll be Christmas in just a few days."

"What did you get Victor?"

"My mom sent an assortment of Brazilian coffee beans for me to give to him as a Christmas gift from her. She says Uncle always drinks Brazilian coffee. I'm getting him a shirt and tie when we get there."

"I brought him some Harald chocolates that I'll give him when we get to his house, as a thank you for letting us visit. Your mom said those were his favorites. And for Christmas, I made something for him."

"Made?"

"Christmas gifts should be personal and special."

"You don't even know the guy."

"Yeah, but we're staying with him for a month. My mom and your mom thought it was perfect."

And then the announcement came over the PA system, asking the passengers to prepare the cabin for their descent. The two of them stowed their tray tables and put their seatbacks up. Isabelle stuffed her book into her carry-on bag and shoved it under the seat with her foot.

It was clear, and the sun shone through the small window. "We'll get some snow, I bet," Frank said, noticing the dark clouds far off on the horizon as he leaned across Isabelle and pointed out the Hudson River, then the tiny Statue of Liberty standing in the harbor in the distance and finally, the two tall towers of the World Trade Center. "That's right down in the Financial District. That's downtown." He snatched her map out of her hand and pointed out each site on the map as he named it.

Excited, Isabelle bounced up and down a little in her seat before she reached out, grabbed Frank's arm and held it tightly. "Boyfriend, I've wanted to visit New York ever since you talked about it growing up. With everything you've told me, I almost feel like I've been here before."

"My uncle will make sure we see all the important and interesting stuff. I can imagine him now, waiting for us in the international arrivals area, leaning against a pillar, whistling to himself, people-watching – you'll love him, Isabelle. He's the best."

Victor stood, balanced on one foot, his other leg bent with his foot against the pillar behind him, whistling softly along with the Christmas music playing over the loudspeakers. His hands were shoved deep into the pockets of his winter coat, his blue wool scarf hung casually around his neck, and he had a matching wool cap, pulled low on his forehead, covering his dark hair. His brown eyes, twinkling with anticipation, were on the double doors, watching as they opened and closed, and passengers came out of customs and immigration.

He listened to a group of passengers as they walked past, speaking in heavy British accents. *That must be the flight from London.* Then some others came by, chattering away in German. *The flight from Frankfurt.* Finally, he heard one of the passengers greeting the man who'd come to meet him in Brazilian Portuguese. *Ah, I should see the kids any moment now.*

And then – there was Frank. *Oh, my goodness, he looks just like I did at his age. Well, well, well, that tall, gorgeous blond he's holding hands with must be Isabelle.* Victor watched them bumping shoulders and talking excitedly. *They make a handsome young couple. Patricia didn't mention they were dating.*

Frank's face lit up, he gasped and dropped Isabelle's hand. "Hey, Uncle," he called out, waving his right arm vigorously. He sprinted the last few yards to Victor, who threw his arms around Frank and gave him a huge, long hug, his eyes glistening.

"I missed you so much, Uncle." He buried his face in his uncle's neck, and Victor cupped the back of Frank's head and held onto him tightly as they rocked back and forth.

"I missed you too, Frankie. You're so tall. You're as tall as me." Victor pulled back and looked at him hard. *Is that alcohol I smell? I guess he's old enough to drink now in Brazil.* "You certainly have changed. You're a man now." Victor grabbed a pinch of his shirt. "And you've become a mighty fine dresser."

"I've grown up. Of course, I know how to dress."

Isabelle dawdled along a good distance behind Frank, letting them have their moment. *They look so much alike, that light brown skin with just a bit of gold from the sun. Frank's a little darker with more gold to his skin from all the time he spends outside, playing tennis and swimming. Those white, white smiles. If I didn't know Victor was his uncle, I'd say they were father and son.* She finally caught up with them and stepped around Frank, immediately stretching her hand out toward Victor. "Hi. I'm Isabelle."

With a warm, welcoming grin, he replied, "I'm Victor. Nice to meet you."

When their hands touched, her heart beat more quickly, and color dusted her cheeks. *Oh my, he's even more good-looking up close when I can see the way his smile shows in his eyes! And he's not as old as I thought from listening to Frank.* "Thank you for meeting us," she said quietly.

§

At the end of dinner, Isabelle asked, "Victor, do you mind if I play your piano? At home, I always play after dinner while my parents have a drink." She giggled. "They don't seem to realize that it gets me out of clearing away the dishes."

Victor smiled at her, "Sure. Some background music would be nice. Frankie'll help me clean up, right?"

Isabelle ran up the stairs, and soon, the sound of traditional Christmas carols was wafting down to them.

Frank pointed toward the ceiling, "I was gonna ask you earlier, is that the grand piano from our house? The one you took before we moved? Dad was so mad. The stupid thing was that none of us even used it. He just hired someone to play it at parties."

Victor picked up the plates from the table, laid the used utensils on top of them and handed the stack to Frank. "Yes, it is. Take these over and put them in the sink." Humming along to the music from above, he followed Frank across the room, their wine and water glasses grasped in his fingers. "I play some, but certainly not as well as Isabelle. Not even as well as my mother did. But when I sit at the piano, it brings back memories, good memories of my whole family sitting around in the evening after dinner." He paused, listening as Isabelle began to play *Good King Wenceslas,* and then he continued, "Frank, that piano has been in our family for generations. Your dad was the caretaker for a while. Now I look after it. Y'see, some things don't belong to one person. We pass them on when it's time, and we get rid of the things we don't need." He turned the water on and began to rinse the dishes.

"Like all the family real estate you sold? Like our house?"

Victor paused with a plate in his hand and tossed a damp dishcloth to Frank. "Here, son, wipe off the table with this." Thinking about how to answer Frank's question, he slowly finished filling the dishwasher, turned off the tap and wiped his hands on the soft dish towel that lay next to the sink. Then, still holding it, he turned toward Frank, leaned back against the dark granite counter and said carefully, "Awww, Frankie, when I decided to sell all the property except this house, it was purely business."

"I guess, but Dad was so angry. Every time I asked if I could come visit, he told me I could never see you again, you weren't part of our family anymore. He thought that, as the older brother, he should have inherited everything. Like he thinks we still live in the eighteen hundreds or something, and the younger brother gets nothing. He's always so angry about you. Uncle, have you two ever gotten along?"

Victor sighed, "The nine years between the two of us was just too much. We weren't close while we grew up. We didn't have the same friends or the same interests."

"What interests? All I see my dad do is work, work, work and drink too much in the evenings and yell at me."

Oh, that's no life for a kid. Victor's face saddened at Frank's words. "Your dad was always a whiz with numbers. He could figure anything out in his head. I was a little jealous about that capability. I still am. I have to get my calculator out every time I want to do the simplest math problem." He chuckled, remembering, and then he continued, "Alan liked rough sports, like football and hunting. And girls – he always had one girlfriend after another, sometimes several at one time. He didn't think much of my interest in music and photography and poetry. That was all soft stuff, not manly enough in his eyes. And in high school, I didn't date a lot. There was one girl. I don't think she even knew I existed. At least not for a long while, and by then it was too late for us." His face softened for a moment. "But in his opinion, the worst thing was that in high school, I became involved in the anti-war movement while he was over fighting in Vietnam. He lost his leg, and I opposed that war. That was the end for us. We truly had nothing in common, Frankie, except our parents and grandparents."

Victor folded the towel, put it on the counter and patted Frank on the shoulder before heading toward the stairs. Frank followed, thinking about what he'd just heard.

They went upstairs, and Frank immediately threw himself down on one of the long couches in front of the fireplace, toeing off his shoes and propping his feet up on the arm nearest the fire. He tipped one of the back cushions down and pulled it under his head.

"You play beautifully," Victor said, pausing beside the piano to watch Isabelle's slim hands as they moved confidently over the keys, listening for a moment before he went over to add a couple of logs to the fire.

She finished playing the carol and put the lid down over the keyboard. She smiled and said in her quiet voice, "Music can take you out of yourself and away from your troubles. It can reflect your sadness or make you smile and fill you with joy. Those traditional old Christmas carols do all of that to me. Playing the piano is one of my passions in life."

She stood and walked over to the couch where Frank lay, "Sit up, boyfriend, and make room for me." She gave him a nudge, and he reluctantly sat. Isabelle dropped down at the end nearest the fire and leaned against him.

"And your other passions?"

"There's only one other. She has a bit of a thing about rivers and boats, don't you Isabelle?" Frank said as he poked her in the side. She giggled.

"That sounds interesting. Are you going to make a career of it?" Victor asked.

Isabelle watched the flames for a few moments, thinking about the stories told by the captain she'd met on the river cruise and about her parents' friend who had come to dinner before she'd met Frank, how he'd described his life as a riverboat captain, how exciting that all had seemed. "As Frank said, I love rivers and boats, the fresh air, the outdoors. It's good for my soul. On the ocean, all you can see are waves for miles and miles. But rivers are more intimate. You can see the shore on both sides, but they have challenges. For starters, if you're piloting a boat, you have to know where the shallow areas are, how to navigate around the other boats – many of whom have no idea what they're doing – all that kind of stuff. Then there's the other side of it, being responsible for the passengers, making sure you stick to schedule, dealing with any problems they have. You see all of life from the bridge of a boat, from the people on it to the nature around it. And it constantly changes as you travel from one place to another, stopping off and exploring different towns and different cultures. It just has everything for me, I've been fascinated with it since I was a kid. I'm going to Texas A&M in the fall because it's the best school to study maritime science, I can't wait." She laughed at herself, "Sorry, I do tend to go on about it and be a bore – I guess that was a long way of saying I want to work on riverboats, ultimately, I would love to captain one."

After a glance at his easy chair that faced the fire directly, Victor opted instead to sit on the other overstuffed sofa across from Isabelle and Frank, his eyes resting on her face. He propped his sock-clad feet up on the large, square coffee table that stood between the two sofas and crossed his ankles. "I can see you at the helm already." Isabelle blushed at his compliment.

"Since Brazilian schools finish up six months before U.S. schools, what are the two of you going to do before you start university next fall?"

"I have an internship," said Isabelle. "My dad got me a job in the foreign ministry. Something to do with international shipping laws and regulations. I'm so excited to begin working in something even remotely connected to my field, even though it will probably be some low-level job."

"Nevertheless, it will be an excellent experience," Victor said.

"Well, I'm not going to work for my dad. I'm going to hang out with my friends and enjoy my freedom. It's the last chance we'll have before we have to be grown-ups."

Isabelle looked at him and shook her head slightly.

The three of them sat watching the fire, content to just be quiet in one another's company after the long day of travel and a pre-dinner tour of Victor's little corner of the city in the bitter cold. Finally, with a jaw-breaking yawn, Isabelle said, "I'm tired from such a busy day. I think I'll head off to bed."

She gave Frank a peck on the lips. "G' night, boyfriend." She stood up, stretched her arms up over her head and gave another prodigious yawn.

"G'night, girlfriend."

There's something there, thought Victor as he watched them.

After a moment of indecision, she went over and gave Victor a kiss on his cheek. "Good night, Victor. Thank you for making us so welcome in your home."

His eyes followed Isabelle as she went up the stairs. "She's a nice girl," he said as he turned back to Frank. "I can't believe it's been eight years since you and your parents moved away. And now, I look at you, and you're all grown up. Where did the time go?"

"I don't know. It's flown by. I've missed you so much, Uncle."

"I've missed you too, Frankie." Victor stood up from the sofa, walked over to the small bar against the wall near the stairs and poured a generous measure of cognac into a glass.

"Uncle, while you're up, would you grab me a beer?"

He can drink back home, so I guess it's okay. He took a bottle of Stella Artois out of the miniature refrigerator and handed it to Frank, who took a large gulp immediately. Then he sat in his comfortable, old chair. He put his feet up on the ottoman and crossed his ankles again. "So, Frankie, what do you think of my renovations? You haven't said much about them."

Frank flinched at the old, childhood name. "Ha-ha. You've kept us pretty busy since we got here today. I like the way you've changed it, Uncle. I like it a lot. A little bit of old, a lot of new. It suits you. I'm glad you took down that wall between the living room and the music room. And putting those floor-to-ceiling windows all the way across the back here makes this whole space so much brighter, not so gloomy. That's the coldest."

Victor took a sip of his cognac. "The coldest?"

"You know, awesome, brilliant, the best. Uncle, you need to keep up with today's slang."

"Where does it come from?"

"Here. From Harlem. When I called to tell my friends about this trip, they used it."

"Ahhh, yes, of course. The windows, here and down in the

kitchen and dining area, were definitely the *coldest* – and the most expensive – part of the renovation."

"So, you spent all the money you got from selling our house and all those other buildings on renovating this one?"

"Goodness, no. Even though this cost a lot, I was able to invest a good bit, and it's doing quite well."

Frank's eyes roved around the room, remembering all the times he'd stayed there as a child. "That brick wall sure has memories, doesn't it? I'm glad you kept it," he laughed. "Remember – how old was I anyway, about five? – when I was pretending to be an engineer whose train had gone out of control, and I ran into it headfirst? Right there," he pointed at the wall, "and here." He stroked the thin scar at his hairline.

"Phew," Victor breathed out, his lips pursed. "I had a lot of explaining to do to your parents about that one. I thought my days of quality time with you were over," he chuckled. "What do you think of my fireplace? I've always wanted one."

Frank took another drink of his beer, "It looks like it's always been here. I'm glad you added it, especially for these cold winter nights."

That had been another challenge of his expensive renovations, building the chimney all the way up through the second and third floors and making sure the brick perfectly matched the original old wall. While he was at it, Victor had added a fireplace in the third-floor master suite that occupied the entire top floor. It was a long way to carry wood, but well worth it for the ambience it added.

"How's your life down there in Brasília, Frankie?"

"We have a great house, but it's in the middle of nowhere, on a peninsula at one end of this big lake. Uncle, we live in a gated community." His voice was scathing, "Like someone is going to come in and kidnap or murder us all? Not likely. No one comes in. And we don't even have a real park in our neighborhood, not like Central Park. Just these dinky little fields where kids kick a football around. And our chauffeur has to take me everywhere. It's so confining."

"That sounds like a fine life to me. Is your mom happy?"

"Yeah, she is. She's happy to be home again. She made friends with Isabelle's mom, her family lives next door, and they do everything together. But it's not New York City, Uncle. It's not here."

Victor shook his head as he looked over and raised his eyebrows. He waited as the loud sound of a siren went by the front of the house. "What else have you been up to? What about your friends?"

"I hang out with a bunch of the jocks. We do, or did that is, the usual stuff—tennis, girls, a little drinking, a little smoking." He made the universal sign for smoking marijuana and glanced over to see what Victor's reaction would be. "I hope I can get together with my friends here. I bet we could have some fun."

Whatever happened to that sweet, curious guy that you were when you left here? Victor kept his face impassive. "I'm glad you've kept up with your tennis. You always seemed to enjoy it so much. Now, tell me about these girls. Do you have a girlfriend?"

"Oh, I play the field and date as many as I can."

"How about Isabelle? She seems charming, and you get along well."

"Isabelle? A girlfriend? That's not possible. She's like my sister."

"But you call her 'girlfriend'."

"Yeah, we started that to mess with the kids at school, and then we just kept on. But the other girls at school were all over me. I was voted the best-looking guy in my class in our yearbook."

Ah, my boy, Victor thought, *is this what you've learned down there in Brasília? Is this what Alan has taught you? That looks and money are all that matter?* "Don't let it go to your head. You're a handsome young man, but there's more than good looks to a relationship. Women are to be cherished."

"Hey, I had nothing to do with it. It's just a fact. I know how to take care of women. You adore them. And give them gifts, flowers and candy, and kisses, of course, and sweet words. That's what they want."

Victor shook his head. *He still has a lot of growing up to do.*

"So, you mentioned at dinner that you still own Tomas Rug Imports. How's it doing?"

"I sure do. It's better than ever. Hey, remember when I had that meeting, and I gave you a pretend job to take notes. You know, a way to keep you busy. You felt very important."

"You always made me feel important, Uncle."

"After the meeting, you told me everything everyone said, word for word. I was astounded."

"I had so much fun with you as a kid. I wish we could have spent more time together. Do you think maybe we could work together at some point? You know, hang out and have fun like we used to?"

"We had some great times, didn't we? But I'm sure your dad has plans for you." Victor changed the subject abruptly, "You must be glad to be through with school. How were your grades when you graduated?"

"Uncle, you sound like my old man. Why would you ask me that? It's a stupid question."

He sounded just like Alan then. He's becoming an angry, judgmental young man. That's not the boy I remember. "Easy now, son."

"Why? Isn't it good enough that I was at the top of my class? I aced everything. But it was boring."

"I'm just trying to catch up. It's been a long time, and I care about you. You're my family."

Frank took a deep breath, a trace of arrogance in his voice. "You know, Uncle – with my eidetic memory, I remember everything."

"There's more to success than just a photographic memory."

"Sheesh, there you go *again*, sounding just like my dad. That memory is what's going to make it easy when I go to Wharton in the fall. Dad has the next six years all planned out for me. Wharton for my business degree and MBA. Then to Georgetown for a PhD in international relations. And then he wants me to go to Europe to become a business liaison for the bank. I don't even know what that job is, but it sounds boring. He's got my future all figured out."

"Perhaps your dad did make that job up just for you, to help you become more familiar with how the bank is run. He only wants the best for you."

"What? What do you mean?"

"I would guess he's grooming you to take over the bank someday. You're his only heir. And all those degrees, all that education from the best schools? Those are essential in business, in banking. Take it from me, even in the import business, like mine, having that background would be helpful. Please don't fight your dad on this. I cannot believe I'm saying it, but he's right."

Frank sighed deeply, "But I don't want to work for him. I don't want to work in a stupid bank. I want my life to be full of excitement."

"You need to do what your dad wants – for now. If you do well, once you're done with school, the world will be your oyster."

"I guess."

"Does your mom agree with your dad?"

"I don't know." He shrugged. "I'm the center of her life. I can't do anything wrong. My dad's angry a lot, but she won't push back or argue with him. She just tries to keep dad happy and off my back. She spends most of her free time with Isabelle's mom."

Patricia, what happened to you? thought Victor. *What happened to that strong, self-assured, independent young woman you were when you married Alan?*

"So, what do you want to do?"

"I don't want to work hard. Like I said, I want my life to be exciting. I want to travel. I want to meet important people. I want to have a beautiful woman on my arm." *I probably shouldn't tell him what I really want to be, what I'm really planning to do.*

Oh, I'm so sad that's all you want in life, son, and so angry that your parents raised you to be so superficial. Perhaps, if I hadn't sold their home, they'd have stayed. Maybe I would have had some influence over how you turned out. Or even if they'd just let you come and visit. I hope it's not too late for you.

Victor got up and opened a drawer in the end table. He took out a box and handed it to Frank. "Frankie, I have something for you."

"Uncle, now that I'm an adult, would you please call me Frank?"

"Of course." *That's the end of an era.*

Frank opened the box and examined the Rolex. "Is this it?"

"Yep, son, it's been a lot of years, and I thought it was time to give it back to you. I hope when you look at this, you'll remember to do the right thing." Victor sat back down, recalling that day that Frank had stolen the watch.

He'd gone ahead of me, bounding up the steps from the subway, taking them two at a time. He reached the top, hardly breathing fast at all. He stopped, watching me, waiting for me, bouncing up and down on the balls of his feet the way he did when he was excited, snapping his fingers like he had since he was just a tiny kid.

"What's the hurry, Frankie?"

He looked around to make sure no one could see us, moved a little farther away from the entrance, and then he flashed that big smile of his and said, "I have something for you, Uncle." He looked around again, and then he pulled something out of his jacket pocket and handed it to me.

I weighed the cold metal object in my hand. "Where did this come from?"

He was so proud and excited as he told me, "I took it off some guy's wrist on the first train we caught. He didn't feel a thing. He had no idea it was gone."

"You stole it?"

"He was rich. He can always get another one."

I looked at it more closely, and then I put it in my pocket. "That is a Rolex, Frankie, a very old one. It's probably irreplaceable to that man. I should take it to the subway lost and found, or to the police. I need to think about this, about the consequences."

Frank's face grew pale at the word "consequences". "You won't tell my father, will you?"

I hadn't decided about that yet. "We'll talk about this later, Frank Tomas."

And then I put it away and did nothing because it seemed easier just to not deal with it.

Frank turned the watch over in his hand and tilted it so he could read the engraved message in the dim light. "*Stay out of trouble.*" And then he looked at his uncle with a question in his eyes. "How come you didn't return this? How come you didn't tell my dad?"

"I put it away for a long time, trying to figure out what to do. It wasn't my place to discipline you, that was your dad's job. Perhaps I should have told him, but it would have become unpleasant for you, and I didn't want to have anything to do with that. When your mother called me about this trip, I remembered about the watch and that's when I decided to have it engraved."

"Thanks, Uncle."

"I thought it would mean something to you now," Victor said, with an intense look at his nephew. "Can I get you something else to drink?"

"Yes, another beer, please." He kept his head down, fiddling with the watch. *I like this watch.* When Victor returned, bottle in hand, Frank smiled and slowly clasped it around his wrist.

§

Frank burst into the brownstone ahead of Isabelle, pulling off his coat and throwing it and a bag onto a nearby chair. Isabelle took off her coat and hat and put them away in the entry closet. "It's too bad Victor had to stay at work." She unwound the heavy scarf from her neck, draping it on the same hanger. Rolling her eyes at Frank, she picked up his coat and hung it next to hers.

"Uncle works so hard. I never want to do that. I want to enjoy life."

"Find something you love, Frank, and it won't seem like work. Victor obviously loves those rugs and all their history. I wonder if it's hard for him to sell them, knowing their background. I'm so glad we had a chance to visit his warehouse and hear their stories. He makes each of those rugs sound like an old friend."

"Girlfriend, do you want to lie under the Christmas tree and talk?"

"That's a great idea. It's almost dark, so we can turn on its lights and that lamp back there in the music room. It'll feel almost like Christmas Eve at home, minus our parents and their cocktails. I just adore Christmas and all its traditions. It's my very favorite holiday," Isabelle sighed.

Frank laughed, "Girlfriend, you say that every year when we start talking about Christmas traditions."

She joined in his laughter. "You're right. I do say it every year. Because I feel that way all over again every year."

The two of them sat side by side on the edge of the Turkish rug next to the tree. Isabelle looked at the vivid reds and blues in the rug's pattern and stroked the smooth blend of wool and silk. In a soft voice, she said, "I wonder where Victor found this rug. It's so beautiful. I'm sure it has a fascinating story behind it. Why else would he have it in his house? What a wonderful, interesting man your uncle is."

"Sounds like you have a crush on him."

"He is charming."

"Oh, like me?"

She shook her head and lay back beside Frank, positioned so they were barely under the branches. They looked up into the tree, and they both sighed in contentment.

Frank said quietly, "It is just like home." He turned his head toward Isabelle, "You and your traditions."

"Ummhmm. Walking through the park this afternoon, Frank, was the most amazing experience. It isn't anything like the parks near us. It's so massive. It's like being in the country in the middle of a huge city. Thank you for taking me there."

"It's too bad we didn't find Tom. You would like him."

"As you've told me a thousand times," she giggled.

Frank poked her in the side and then lay quietly, remembering his uncle's friend and the day in the park just before they moved to Brasília.

Tom was so proud of me that day. It really is too bad he wasn't there today to meet Isabelle.

They lay there and looked up through the tree for a few minutes, breathing in the spicy smell of the live fir, before Isabelle asked, "So, what's going on between you and Victor?"

"What do you mean?"

"All day when we were with him, you seemed tense, like there was something wrong between you. You weren't that way yesterday when we got here."

"I don't know what you're talking about."

"Come on, boyfriend, there's just something different."

Frank slid his hand down to hold Isabelle's. The cool metal of his watch touched her arm, and she lifted his hand so she could see what it was. "Where'd you get this watch?"

"Uncle gave it to me last night. Kind of a – uh – graduation gift."

"That was generous." Isabelle twisted his hand around so she could see it better. The colored lights from the tree reflected off the watch as she turned it, first one way and then the other. "It's very nice."

Isabelle unfastened it and pulled it off Frank's wrist. She held it up and read the engraving. "It says, '*Stay out of trouble.*' What does that mean?"

"Just what it says, stay out of trouble," he said, an edge in his voice.

Isabelle rolled her eyes. "Come on, Frank, you know what I'm asking."

"Well, I'm going off to Wharton next year, and he worries about me. He's always worried about me. Like I've told you, we have a special kind of relationship. It goes back to when I was a kid." Frank took the watch from Isabelle and put it back on.

He sat up abruptly. "Want to watch *To Catch a Thief?*"

"Of course! Good thing we found it in the video store."

Frank jumped up, snapping his fingers in anticipation and grabbed the bag from the chair near the door.

When Victor arrived home, he saw Isabelle and Frank leaning against each other on the couch by the fire, completely engrossed in the movie as they shoved popcorn into their mouths.

He stood in the doorway for a few minutes, looking on. "That's not a holiday movie, guys."

She looked up at him. "We watch this every year. That's just what we do. It's our tradition."

The firelight on Isabelle's face caught Victor's eye. *Oh, she is beautiful. I wonder if Frank sees that too.* He shook his head and then walked downstairs to start dinner.

§

Isabelle and Victor sat in the kitchen, drinking tea at the table in front of the huge glass wall to the patio, with the room illuminated only by the dim light over the stove. Isabelle inhaled deeply and stretched out her legs under the table. "Mmmm."

Victor glanced sideways at her and smiled to himself. "It is nice, isn't it?"

Isabelle nodded. "It is nice being here with you, Victor.

Everything we've done has been nice."

"You're the perfect guest."

Frank clattered down the stairs. "Why are you guys sitting in the dark?"

"So, we can watch the snow fall outside, boyfriend. Look how pretty it is against the lanterns out there on the patio. It's like the snow scenes with lampposts in fairytales. It's so different from Christmastime back home."

He gave it a quick glance and a cursory nod. "I'll probably be late. I'll be careful, Uncle. I'm off to meet the guys." Victor raised his eyebrows as Frank leaned over and gave Isabelle his usual peck on the lips. "See you, girlfriend."

Then he gave her the little finger wave they had used since they met, flashed his smile at them and ran upstairs, snapping his fingers as he went. They heard his footsteps cross the living room floor above, pause at the entry closet, and then the front door slammed loudly as he went out.

"There he goes again. I can't believe it. We come all the way here to see you, and all he does is go out with his friends. You'd think he'd have wanted to do something with you."

"You should go with him."

"If his friends here are anything like those at home, no thanks. I don't hang around his friends back home because I just don't like them. I don't want to do it here either."

"What do you think we should do tonight?"

Isabelle turned toward him, shrugging, raising her hands and shaking her head. "Surprise me."

Victor thought for a minute. "We'll have a night out together. Just you and me. We can have dinner at a restaurant right around the corner. We won't want to go far in all this snow."

Isabelle ducked her chin as she looked at Victor, shy at the thought of going out with him. "I'd like that."

"It's a little Italian place – very predictable, I know, but we are in New York, after all. Do you like Italian food?"

"Of course. When my dad was posted in Europe with the Ministry of Foreign Affairs, we lived in Rome for a while. We moved back to Brazil from there right before I met Frank. Italian food is still one of my family's favorites."

"You'll love this place. It's small and very traditional. The owner and her brother, Piero, are Italian. He's the chef. We'll have to bundle up. It's brutally cold out there tonight."

As they walked down the street, Isabelle said, "There's nothing like the feel and the sound of snow crunching under your boots."

"I know exactly what you mean."

Isabelle slipped on the snow, but Victor caught her before she fell. "Here, take my arm. I don't want you to fall and crack your head open. Then I'd have to take you to the emergency room, and we'd miss our dinner."

She giggled, "No, that wouldn't be fun," and tucked her hand under his arm. He pulled his hat lower over his eyes with his other hand as the snow continued to fall.

"Nice hat. I noticed you have a number of different ones in the front closet."

"I collect them."

"I've never known anyone who collected hats. Hardly anyone I know even wears a hat, except the gardener."

"I like them. I think they make a statement about the wearer."

"What does that one say?"

"I'm fashionable and not so old, but I hate the feel of melting snow in my hair." They laughed companionably at his answer.

Isabelle looked around. "New York is beautiful in the snow. It's so quiet and pristine."

Victor chuckled, "If it stops by tomorrow, all this pristine snow will be piles of dirty slush, and the taxis'll be honking again. Goodbye peace and quiet." He opened the door to the restaurant for her.

Isabelle noticed how close the tables were together. *Like in Europe,* she thought. They were covered with red-checkered tablecloths, a candle on each placed into an empty, straw-wrapped wine bottle with wax dripped down the sides. "It feels just like a little neighborhood restaurant we used to go to in Rome."

A petite woman in a clinging grey sweater dress and tall black boots walked up and greeted Victor with a hug and a kiss on his cheek. "*Ciao,* Victor, it's been too long."

"*Ciao,* Marina, this is Isabelle. Isabelle, this is Marina. Isabelle is visiting with my nephew from Brazil."

"*Ciao*, Isabelle."

"*Buona sera*, Marina."

Marina kissed her on the cheek and picked up two menus. "Let me get you settled at your usual spot," and they followed her to a nice quiet corner. She placed the menus next to one another at the small square table. Victor pulled out Isabelle's chair. When he sat adjacent to her, their knees touched briefly under the corner of the table, and her eyes widened slightly.

"Victor, I assume you'll want to pick out your own bottle of wine tonight?" Victor nodded, and Marina said, "Help yourself when you're ready." She walked away. *He's never brought anyone before in all the years he's come here. She's very young for him and probably too young to drink. But Victor is a good customer, so I'll look the other way.*

"Pick your own wine? From a wine list? Isn't that how you are supposed to do it?"

"Come, let me show you." He stood and pulled her chair out, tucked his hand under her elbow and guided her to the far end of the restaurant to a room lined with pale yellow stone.

She read out loud from the tiny sign over the arched entrance, "*Grotta Del Vino*, wine cave. Ahhh, is this where they store all the wine?"

He showed her around the cave, asking what kinds of wines she preferred. She confessed that she didn't know much and asked him to teach her a little. They browsed through the racks, with Victor talking intently about the different wines he picked up, until suddenly, Isabelle shivered in the cold room. Victor pulled off his sports coat, hung it around her shoulders and pulled her close, rubbing her arms briskly to warm her. Finally, with a bottle of Amarone della Valpolicella in hand, they returned to their table.

Isabelle slipped the coat off and awkwardly handed it back to him. Victor slid it back on. "Are you sure you don't need it? You're from a warm climate."

"I'm fine now. Thanks," and she blushed.

Marina gave them a shrewd look. "Good choice." She set little bowls of nuts and olives on the table and handed each of them a small glass of pale, straw-colored prosecco. "A little *aperitivo*, from me to you, to welcome dear Isabelle," she smiled at them before turning away.

Victor lifted his glass. "To you, Isabelle." His eyes caught hers, and he gave her a warm smile.

She lifted her glass with a shy smile back at him and took a sip. *I've never been toasted like that before.* Victor noticed the light blush that crept across her cheeks.

"Shall we go for the full experience? I enjoy Piero's cooking, and I think we can ask him to prepare lighter dishes for us. We have all evening to enjoy it, so there's no hurry."

Isabelle looked at the menu for a long time and then drew a deep breath, "Why not. It'll feel like being in Rome again, when we'd go out to celebrate something special."

Marina came back to the table, "So, what will you have tonight?"

They discussed the menu she would ask Piero to prepare. A small *antipasto* of cold salmon, a mushroom risotto as the *primi*, and then a single *secundi* of grilled veal, accompanied by fresh asparagus as the *contorni*. An *insalata* would follow, just some simple greens with a bit of tomato and a very light lemon vinaigrette, she assured them. The *formaggi e frutta*, only a very small amount of fruit and cheese, she promised, would precede the final course. That night's *dolce* would be a tiny *panna cotta* topped with just two berries and a sprinkling of chopped pistachios.

"Will that suit you, dear Isabelle?" asked Marina.

"It sounds wonderful. I can hardly wait."

As the waiter cleared away the bowls, Isabelle turned to Victor. "I'm such a terrible cook. Somehow, my risotto always turns out like glue or mushy and inedible. It's too bad because it's such a wonderful dish."

"I used to be terrible too, and not just with risotto." He smiled at her, "I ended up taking cooking classes and it was a revelation – I even surprised myself. Perhaps I'll cook for you before you return home – you know, I might even manage a risotto."

They continued to talk about their favorite foods – Victor confessed he was a committed carnivore, and his was simple plank steak with baked potato, while hers was butternut squash soup.

"Neither man, nor woman, can exist on soup alone," he laughed, and she joined in.

Victor reached over with his napkin and brushed a drop of salad dressing from the side of her mouth.

Their eyes met briefly, and she blushed. To hide her embarrassment, she asked, "What's your favorite book?"

He sat back and savored a sip of his wine. "Any good detective novel. I'm partial to Dorothy L. Sayers. Even though her stories are set in Britain in the first half of the twentieth century, her characters are so intelligent and sympathetic. I've always liked *The Nine Tailors*. I still do for that matter. The tailors aren't people, but I won't tell you more. That would ruin it. I hope you'll read it someday, and we can talk about it." He paused and looked at her. "But I also admire Edgar Allan Poe. Have you read any of his?"

"No. I haven't."

"You know, he wrote the very first detective story – back in the eighteen hundreds. I only know this weird little fact because of my fascination with detective stories. I've read his over and over. Poe had such a complex way of leading the reader to the solution. He was a real genius."

Isabelle giggled. "I'm afraid my reading habits are much more prosaic. I mostly read about rivers and boats – riverboats in particular. Oh, thank you again for giving me that wonderful copy of *The River's in My Blood* for Christmas. I've loved it since the first time I read it. I've checked it out from the library so many times, but I always wanted a copy for myself. How did you know?"

Victor grinned. "I didn't. It was Frank's mom who told me about how much you like that particular book."

"And autographed by Jane Curry herself – I can't believe you found an author-signed copy. That's so special. You have no idea how much it means to me. I love her descriptions of those riverboat pilots and their lives on the Mississippi and Ohio Rivers. I know it's somewhat romanticized, and it's very different nowadays, but that book's been such an inspiration for me. Thank you so much, Victor."

"You're welcome. Do you only read non-fiction?"

"Oh no, I love Mark Twain. Especially *Huck Finn* and *Innocents*

Abroad – he writes these glorious descriptions of people's lives. And his use of words – they are so evocative."

"Words? So, you must love poetry then?" he asked.

"I like to hear it read aloud, but I don't read it often myself. My mom used to read it to me every night instead of a bedtime story." She laughed, "We used to have challenges to see who could recite the most poetry. Four lines each, back and forth."

"What a delightful tradition." He looked at her with a warm smile. Then, it was his turn to be a little shy. "I write from time to time – poetry that is. Maybe I could read you some one evening?"

"I've never had anyone other than my mom read to me. That would be very special."

"Speaking of special – the picture you gave me? That was the last photo taken of Frank and me before he moved to Brazil. We had such a great time that day. That memory means a lot to me. Thank you."

"You're welcome. I found it, looking through one of Patricia's family albums. The way you two were looking at each other is what caught my eye."

They finally sat back, full of excellent food and equally good wine.

Marina watched how intimate they seemed with each other, how they mirrored one another's gestures, how they looked into each other's eyes as they spoke. She hesitated for a moment to give them their privacy before coming by to ask how they had enjoyed their meal. Victor looked at Isabelle with a raised eyebrow.

"It was perfection, *perfetto, deliziosi*. It reminded me so much of Italy," she said, "but now I understand why we only ate like this on special occasions." She rubbed her stomach, "How come kids never get full like adults? That is so unfair!"

Victor smiled at her while they relaxed and sipped their tiny cups of espresso. Isabelle immediately doctored hers with several lumps of sugar.

And then Marina came by to offer them a *digestivo*, "To accelerate digestion."

Victor said with a grin, "We'll need one after all that food, that splendid, splendid food. Do you prefer *limoncello* or *grappa*, or something more bitter?"

"I'm a wimp. *Grappa* is just too harsh for me, and I don't care for bitter drinks, so I think I'll play it safe with the *limoncello*." Isabelle watched as Marina poured a small glass for her and one of *grappa* for Victor and then placed the bottles in the center of the table so they could help themselves.

Isabelle looked across at Victor. "That watch you gave Frank for his graduation was such a generous gift. Is it something that has been in the family for generations, like the piano?"

"It wasn't a graduation gift, and, no, it isn't a family heirloom." Victor frowned to himself.

"Oh?"

"I gave the watch to Frank as a reminder to stay out of trouble."

"What kind of trouble do you mean?"

"I'm not comfortable with sharing that, Isabelle. You'll have to ask Frank."

I already did. He didn't want to talk about it. He's always up to something. Sneaking out, sleeping around with more than one girl at a time and telling them each that they're the only one, hiding things from his parents or filching things from the kids at school. I guess that's just Frank. He's bored.

After dinner, at home, while he was starting the fire, Victor looked at Isabelle, "I'm going to have a nightcap. Would you like something to drink? I'd welcome the company."

Isabelle's eyelids drooped, "Oh, I wish, Victor. It's been such a lovely evening. I hate to see it end, but all that food and wine and limoncello and then walking in the cold has made me pretty tired. I think I'll go up to bed."

"Okay. I'm going to stay up and wait up for Frank."

"Well, good night, Victor," she said awkwardly and walked over to give him a kiss on the cheek.

He held his cheek against hers for a moment and murmured, "Good night, Isabelle." And as he had the first night, he watched her climb the stairs.

He stirred the fire, and with a glass of cognac in hand, he settled into his comfortable chair facing the fireplace, put his feet up on the ottoman and crossed his ankles. He swirled the liquid in his glass, placed his nose at the top of the snifter and drew in a deep breath of appreciation. After taking the initial sip, he held the cognac on his tongue a moment before swallowing. Then he closed his eyes.

I'm worried about Frank. He never lied as a kid. Why did he lie to Isabelle about the watch? What's happened to him in the past eight years? Is there a reason for his lie? Is this a one-time thing or does he do it often? Was I wrong to give it to him and put that message on the back? Was I stirring up a past that should have been left alone?

He sighed and took another sip before he set it on the small side table and leaned back, watching the fire, troubled by his thoughts.

Victor felt a hand on his shoulder. "Uncle? Uncle?"

He squinted up at Frank. "What time is it?"

"About four."

"What were you doing out so late?"

"We fooled around, then went to a club and had a few beers. You don't need to wait up for me anymore. You shouldn't worry." *We just went back to what we used to do. Riding the subway, pilfering random little things that are easy to pawn later. Turns out my friends have been practicing too.*

"I'll always worry about you, son, no matter how old you are. This is the city, you know."

"Uncle, I've known these guys since I was young. We're going out again tomorrow night."

Frank sat on the couch and asked Victor, "What did you guys do tonight?"

"We went on a little date to Alessandro's."

"A date? What do you mean?"

"Isn't that what you call it when two people go out somewhere?"

"Uncle, sometimes you're so old fashioned. A date nowadays is when two people are dating, you know, going together."

Victor ignored him and continued, "We had a nice long dinner, and then Isabelle went off to bed as soon as we came home."

"I'm beat. You should go to bed too. Good night."

§

The sky was dark, grey with low, heavy clouds, and it was threatening to snow again. Isabelle stepped off the curb. "Frank is annoying. He was so excited to have me come with him to New York, but he keeps disappearing with his friends. We leave tomorrow, and he's spent almost no time with us. He's missed all the wonderful parts of the city you've shown me. The incredible museum exhibitions. The Broadway shows. The symphony. The side streets. The unbelievable street food. It's his loss. I've had an unforgettable time here with you."

Victor motioned with his hand to indicate which direction they were going. "That's Frank for you, and remember, he did live here when he was younger. I'm happy for him that he's reconnected with his friends. He's young and wants to be with them. I have a hunch that moving to Brasília was harder than he'll ever admit."

"It's just not right. How can you be so forgiving? I've seen more of you than he has."

"I'm happy I had this opportunity to get to know you. I'm sure, later in life, he'll be more thoughtful."

Victor settled his hat more firmly on his head and pulled his collar up to block the wind as they entered Central Park.

"I'm so glad we came here today. Do you walk here often?"

"Every day, early in the morning before you wake."

"Really?"

"We've been so busy, but I'm glad I'm finally able to share it with you."

"It's such a contrast to the rest of the city."

They walked and walked. He described the different trees they passed and told her a little of the history of the park and the landscape designer, Frederick Law Olmsted, and then he stopped in front of a man on a bench. Isabelle watched as Victor pulled off a glove to shake hands and then quickly pulled it back on. "Brrrrr, it's cold out here." He turned toward her to introduce them, "Isabelle, this is Tom."

"It's nice to finally meet you, Tom. Victor and Frank have both talked about you."

"Nice to meet you, Isabelle. Victor mentioned you were comin' up here for the holidays with young Frank. So, where is that boy, Victor? I was hopin' to see him again."

"Oh, out and about with his friends. He's very busy these days, our young man. But he'll be sorry to have missed you."

Isabelle listened as they chatted for a few minutes about how Tom was doing.

Victor pulled his hand out of his glove again, and as they shook, he slipped something into Tom's hand. "Thank you, Victor. God bless you."

"You're welcome, Tom. Stay safe. See you again soon."

Isabelle pulled off her glove and reached out to shake Tom's hand. She glanced down at her small fair hand clasped in his large dark one and then looked into his eyes and smiled. "It was so nice to meet you, Tom."

"Nice to meet you too, young lady."

While they were walking away, Isabelle looked over her shoulder to see Tom stand up and walk off in the other direction. "Frank looked for Tom when we were here. But we didn't find him. Do you see him often?"

"From time to time."

"Why can't he get a job or a home?"

Victor stopped and turned toward Isabelle. "What you did, taking off your glove to shake his hand and looking directly at him when you spoke, will have made a big impression on Tom, so, I don't think he would mind me telling you this. He says he likes the freedom of being homeless. But I have a feeling that there's more to that story. We've talked a lot during the years since we met. He always felt that war, and particularly Vietnam, was wrong. He was a good journalist, a very skilled writer. He went over there twice, first as a military correspondent and then as an independent journalist. He stayed a couple of years each time. It was a story he felt needed to be told. Not just in gruesome pictures showing the atrocity of war. He wanted to tell the stories of the civilians, the families affected by a war that he viewed as illegal. He wrote about families there and here in the United States. He wrote some award-winning pieces. You should look them up sometime. And each time he came back, the dynamic between him and his wife had changed some more. They became one of those families affected, like he wrote about. Ultimately, he left her and his little girls, his home, everything. He sees the girls sometimes, and that makes him happy. But he drifts. If he got the support I suspect he needs – housing, probably some counseling, things that would make him feel better about himself – he might do okay. But he's an independent cuss, and he won't ask for help. He doesn't like anyone to feel sorry for him or to tell him what he should do."

"That's sad."

"It is. But it's his life. So, I just listen and try to be a friend – however he wants it."

"Why did you give him money?"

"Some people give money in church, some people use money for hobbies. I give twenty dollars every day to someone in the park. That's what I do."

He's so kind and compassionate. I thought his gift to Frank was generous, but this is true generosity. What a warm, loving person he is.

Victor began walking again. "I've met some of the most interesting and unusual people this way. I can't imagine anything I would give this up for."

When they got home, Isabelle said, "I've had a spectacular visit, Victor. I've loved everything we've done since I arrived. Thanks for sharing your New York City with me." She put her hand on his arm as she looked up into his face. "I can't believe it's the last night. I'll never forget the memories we've made."

"They'll always be part of my fondest memories too." He rested his hand on top of hers briefly. "It's going to be very cold, so let's stay in and order Chinese food and eat in front of the fire."

"That sounds perfect."

After he placed the order, Victor built a big fire. Just as he stood up, brushing off his hands, the doorbell rang.

"That was quick."

"They're only around the corner."

"Everything's around the corner here."

Victor laughed, "True. That's why I like living in this neighborhood. Why don't you set out the food on the coffee table, and I'll go get a bottle of wine and some glasses."

They sat on the floor to eat – sometimes using chopsticks, and sometimes their fingers, passing the white cardboard cartons back and forth – talking non-stop the whole time. Isabelle found herself watching all his expressions, the way his eyes crinkled at the corners as he smiled, how he moved his hands while he talked. And he found himself drawn in by the animation in her voice and on her face as she told him about her life in Brasília and her hopes and dreams.

After dinner, Victor put all the debris into the bag and took it down to the kitchen garbage. Isabelle grabbed a throw, wrapped it around herself and curled up at one end of the big sofa.

He returned, another bottle of wine in hand. He grimaced lightly. "This may not be the best idea," he said as he gestured with the wine bottle, "but it is your last night, and there's no rush to get up in the morning." He sat down on the sofa next to Isabelle and poured each of them another glass of the crisp pale Sancerre.

Victor reached over with both hands to adjust the throw around her shoulders and brought it up to her neck "If your neck is warm, then you'll be warm all over." His hands smoothed the throw over her shoulders, "Better now?"

A shiver went down Isabelle's spine, "Yes, much better."

They continued to talk late into the evening. Finally warm, Isabelle pulled off the throw, and it brushed against her hair. She heard it crackle, and Victor started to laugh.

Isabelle looked at him curiously, "What?"

Victor waved his hands around his head. "Your hair. All the dry air, it's full of static."

Isabelle smoothed her hair, but it just made it worse.

He reached into the wine cooler, lifted the bottle and rubbed his hands over the moisture on the glass. "Here, I think this will help," and he smoothed his hands over her hair.

Isabelle said, "It's embarrassing. My hair always stuck out like that when I was younger. It makes me feel like the ugly duckling."

Victor's eyes scanned her face and then his gaze caught hers. "Not an ugly duckling at all. You're attractive. You're smart. You're focused. You know what you want, and you go after it."

"Frank always says I'm just boring."

"Fascinating. Anything but boring."

The fire settled, sending up a shower of sparks. He got up to put another log on it and set his glass on the mantle.

Isabelle stood and looked at him. And then she walked over, "You're a remarkable man, Victor." She put her arms around his neck and pressed her lips against his in a long, unsophisticated kiss. After the briefest hesitation, he responded, his mouth seduced hers, her lips opened and his tongue flirted with hers, and then he slipped his fingers into her hair, shaping her head with his hands, holding her to him.

She felt him respond, his kisses growing more urgent, more demanding. She moaned and stroked her hands along his back in long, leisurely movements.

Victor groaned in pleasure.

Isabelle slid her hands farther down and caressed the curve of his bottom, pressing herself against him. "Come with me – upstairs," she begged.

He stepped back, breathing hard, "I don't think that's a good idea."

"We both want this, Victor." She reached down and gently touched the front of his pants with her fingertips.

Victor groaned again. He pulled Isabelle back against him in another long kiss, and they went upstairs together.

§

Isabelle stirred. With her eyes still closed, she thought about how Victor had touched her, how exciting it had been. *It was so different from my high-school boyfriend. This was special. This is what it's like between a man and a woman when they make love. It was so wonderful. I can hardly wait* – she stretched out her hand to the other side of the bed. *He's gone downstairs to make us breakfast. I'll need to hurry with my shower, so it doesn't get cold.*

She came into the kitchen, dressed in the jeans and sweater she would wear to travel but with her feet bare. Her hair, still wet from the shower, smelled of his shampoo. She wore no makeup, and her face glowed with happiness. She poured a cup of coffee from the French press, added her usual two heaping spoons of sugar and just a touch of cream and came over to the table where Victor sat in a set of old sweats and slippers.

She dropped a quick kiss onto the top of his head. "I woke up and reached for you, but you were gone. I missed you. Is this the coffee from Mrs. Tomas? Shall I help you with breakfast?" She pulled the chair next to him away from the table and sat, lifting one foot to touch him gently on the thigh.

Victor took her foot and moved it from his leg, "Please don't." He looked at her, his eyes were tired and sad, his face drawn. "Oh, Isabelle. What I have to tell you – this is so awkward." *I don't like difficult conversations like this.*

"What do you mean, Victor? What happened?"

"Last night happened. I couldn't sleep. I've been up all night thinking about it, beating myself up over it. I made a mistake. I should have said no. It was wrong. You're beautiful, and you're very, very sexy, but I'm far too old for you. You're just eighteen. I'm almost old enough to be your father. I should never have had sex with you. It was *wrong.*"

"But – I thought – I thought you cared."

"I'm so damn sorry." He closed his eyes and rubbed his hands over his face as he drew in a harsh breath. "I shouldn't have done it. Your parents put their trust in me, sending you here. I've betrayed that trust."

"But I'm an adult. You knew I wasn't a virgin. I wanted you. You wanted me. We both wanted to make love—"

"It wasn't love, Isabelle, it was sex. We drank too much wine, and we had sex. Nothing more. Nothing."

Isabelle gasped and stood up. She bit back tears of betrayal that made her voice shake. "You used me? I thought something special had grown between us in all the time we spent together this month. We laughed and talked and enjoyed the same things. We were so close. You read your poetry to me. The way you've looked at me this month. The way you've constantly found reasons to touch me. And you certainly wanted me last night. You kissed me back right away. I thought we—"

"Oh, my dear, sometimes there's more to life than just wanting. I'm sorry I let it happen. You need to experience your life, Isabelle, and meet someone who's your age. You have dreams. You have your whole life in front of you. You have so much to look forward to. You start your internship with your dad next week. You'll go on to the university in the fall. You need to get your degree, be your own person."

Her face reddened, and her voice grew louder. "How could you do that to me? How could you lead me to believe—? You might as well have raped me." Her voice broke.

Victor's face turned white, but in a strained voice, he just said, "I made a dreadful mistake last night. I'll never forgive myself. But you'll find someone. You'll fall in love. You'll have a family, and I'll be an old man by then. You'll forget about me."

"Oh, you, you were nothing but a rebound from my boyfriend. And by the way, I've already forgotten about you, *Old Man*. I'll get myself to the airport." Isabelle spun around and stormed across the room, tears of hurt and embarrassment pouring down her face. She shoved past Frank, who had just come down the stairs.

He watched her go and then turned toward Victor. "What's wrong with her, Uncle?"

"Go with her. Make sure she gets to the airport and onto that plane safely."

"Well, what did you do to her? What did you do?"

"You'll have to ask her about that."

Chapter Four

August 1994 to March 1998

Lifelong Friends

College Station, Texas

"That's the last of them," Frank called out as he walked into the common area with a suitcase in each hand. "I'm not sure where you plan to put all this stuff." He crossed the shared living room and kitchenette, where the smell of fresh paint and new carpet still lingered in the air. There were four bedrooms, two on each side. He entered the second room on the right, where the door was propped open.

While all the rooms in the new dorm were spacious, Isabelle's corner room felt even larger because of the extra windows, and the pale-yellow walls lent a cheerful air to the space. She had been left with the bed under the windows since her roommate had already claimed the one along the inner wall. Each girl had her own desk, nightstand and a spacious closet with built-in shelves and drawers, freeing up the space that would have been occupied by dressers for a couple of petite upholstered chairs for reading.

"Nice digs," said Frank, looking around appreciatively at the decidedly undorm-like space. "Now that all your things are out of the car, I was finally able to move my bags into the trunk."

"Girls always have more stuff," Isabelle defended herself. "I can't believe you came off to college with only a carry-on and two suitcases. And one is probably full of your body wash and lotions."

"Ha-ha. I can buy that stuff when I get to Wharton. And anything else I need, for that matter. Those two cases are full of what I need for my summer adventures." He shrugged, "And, well, yeah, there is a little body lotion to use when I come in off the beach."

"I've always been amazed at how you obsess about taking care of your skin, and then you eat crap."

"Hey—"

Isabelle giggled at Frank as she pulled another suitcase onto her bed, opened it up and began to hang more clothes in the large closet. He walked over to look out the window. "Wow, check out this view. You're gonna be so happy looking at all this green space."

"Mmmhmm. It's a great view, isn't it? And I'm so glad this room faces east so I don't get all that hot Texas afternoon sun. It's perfect." She continued to unpack. "Have you figured out how long you think you'll stay in Nashville?"

"At least a week. There are a lot of shows that I want to see. After that, I'll head off to the beach. You know, we could've just stayed there on Galveston Island for at least another week, maybe two, if you hadn't signed up for this summer session."

"Are you planning to go back there?"

"No, I'll probably head to the East Coast, probably to the Outer Banks. Apparently, there's a lot of cute coeds who hang out there at the end of the summer, working on the ultimate tan."

"You'll be in good company then." She walked over to the window and bumped her shoulder against his, "Frank on the prowl."

"You bet," he said with an excited little snap of his fingers.

After leaning against him for a few moments, Isabelle returned to her suitcase. She shook the folds out of a summer top and hung it carefully in the closet. "This seminar has lots of wonderful guest lecturers."

"Right. But it's like school or work or something."

Other than raising an eyebrow, Isabelle ignored him and went on, "I'm so excited that I'll have the chance to meet some of the leading scientists in maritime studies. Someday, I hope you find something that's as exciting to you."

"Thanks, girlfriend." The door opened as Frank replied. He turned to watch a young woman enter the room — *short, well endowed, dressed perfectly, immaculate make-up, very dark brown hair*, Frank noted to himself as he looked her over with interest.

She bounced over to Isabelle. "Hi! I'm Chloe Rose Johnson. I'm so excited to meet you and to be your roommate! I just know we're going to become lifelong friends," she said in a heavy Texas drawl.

"I'm Isabelle Ronaldo. It's nice to meet you."

"I love your accent. Are you from England or Australia?"

"No. I was born in Paris, but my family lived in London from the time I was three until I was six. That's where I learned to speak English, and that's where I got my accent. I live in Brazil now, or I did until I came here. My parents are from there."

"Oh my *gosh*, my wish has come true. I decided to live in the dorms because in sororities, all the girls are the same. I want to meet different people. They're so interesting. I'm studying sociolinguistics because that's about people. You're so international, you've lived all over the world. I was born and raised in Houston, and here I am at a Texas university. At least, now I get to live with someone with world experience. Where else have you lived? Why did you come to Texas? Have you ever been here before?"

"Well, after London, my family moved to Rome. We were there until I was nine when we moved back to Brazil. My dad works for Brazil's Ministry of Foreign Affairs. Until I got here today, I'd never been to Texas in my life. I'm in the maritime science program. I applied to come here because the course has such a good reputation."

Frank interjected, "Best in the world, apparently."

"Well, bless your heart." Chloe looked between them, and then she turned to Frank, "Hello, handsome, who are you?"

"I'm Frank."

"Ohhh, an accent too. Where are you from?"

"New York City."

"Ahhh, the tall, quiet type."

Chloe turned away and picked up the picture on the nightstand next to Isabelle's bed. "Are these your friends? Will I get to meet them? She's beautiful. And he's so hot."

Isabelle blushed. "They're my parents." Nodding her head, she added, "You'll probably meet them at some point."

Chloe looked at the photo and then at Isabelle, "But you have such – light skin. Were you adopted?"

"No, we're *Afro-Brasileiros*."

Chloe looked at her quizzically.

"Afro-Brazilians. My parents are of African and Portuguese heritage. It's a weird quirk of genetics. We can have fair skin or very dark skin or be somewhere in between. Apparently, generations ago, my dad's side came from mostly white Portuguese colonists and some indigenous people, while my mom's side of the family is African. You can see how *Preto* my mom is." Seeing the look of confusion on Chloe's face, she explained, "That is one way we describe dark-skinned people. My dad's skin color is *Pardo*, or brown. In Brazil, we usually describe ourselves by color, not race, since nearly everyone there is mixed. There are a lot of families where one child is dark and one is fair, depending on how the genes work out. As you can see, I got fair skin and blond hair. It's purely a roll of the genetic dice."

Chloe gushed, "That's so romantic and even more international than I would have ever imagined. I'm so glad we're roommates."

Frank glanced at Isabelle and rolled his eyes. "I need to check into my hotel. I'll swing by in the morning to get you." He turned to Chloe, "Nice to meet you, Chloe Rose Johnson."

"Nice to meet you too, Frank. You're welcome here anytime. I'll step out while you two, ahem, say goodbye." She closed the door behind her.

Frank and Isabelle grinned at each other.

"Well, you won't have a quiet moment with her around."

"Oh, be nice, Frank. I like her. She's different. I think she'll be fun."

"Better that she's your roommate than mine. I'm so glad I have a private room at Wharton."

"I don't think you'd be a very good roommate anyway," teased Isabelle.

"Hey."

After they'd chatted for a few more minutes about their plans for the following day, they walked through the common area together to the suite door. Frank held it open and gave Isabelle a peck on the lips. "See you in the morning, boyfriend," she said, giving him their special finger wave, and as she closed the door behind him, she heard him snapping his fingers while he walked away down the hallway.

Chloe was standing in the kitchen area making a cup of tea, pretending not to listen. "Isabelle, would you like some?" She held up a box of herbal tea bags.

As they walked into their room with their steaming mugs, Chloe said, "We need to see if our bedspreads go together. If not, we definitely have to do some shopping. We want the best room in this suite. I hope you don't mind that I took the bed over here."

"Not at all. I prefer this corner with all the light." Isabelle set her mug on the floor next to the nightstand and flopped, stomach down, onto her bed with her chin propped on her hands.

Chloe slid down onto the floor, pulled the pillows off her bed, shoved them behind her back and picked her mug up from the lower shelf of her nightstand where she'd put it so she wouldn't knock it over. "Tell me about your yummy boyfriend. Are you going to spend the night with him?" She took a tentative sip of the hot tea and waved her hand in front of her mouth. "Ohhh, hot, hot, hot!"

"Boyfriend? Oh, Frank. Frank's not my boyfriend."

"Is he available?"

"Frank's always available. He thinks he's God's gift to women. But that's Frank for you. Don't you have a boyfriend?" She picked her tea up from the floor and blew on it gently before taking a sip.

"I'm in between right now," Chloe sighed. "My last boyfriend is going to a different university, so I broke it off. Men. I like to flirt with them, even if we don't sleep together. There's something about them that just makes me all warm and tingly. Hey, maybe we can hook up with Frank tonight?"

"Mmmm," Isabelle wrinkled her nose and gave a little shake of her head. "I think Frank already has someone in mind for tonight. He was talking to this girl at lunch. I'm not sure what they said to each other while I went to pick up our order, but I bet he got her number. He always does."

"You know him really well, don't you?"

§

Bryan, Texas

The next day, Isabelle was strolling along the main street of Bryan's rejuvenated historic district, admiring the old brick-and-stone block buildings that lined Main Street, challenging herself to pick out the oldest ones before referring to the brochure she'd grabbed from the visitors' bureau. They were sturdy buildings, two and three stories high. The red-brick Carnegie History Center, with its tall white pillars, was set on just a little more land than the buildings lining the several blocks of Main Street that she'd explored. She paused briefly to examine it before she wandered on, stopping periodically, sometimes to admire a building up close and sometimes to look into the artfully decorated display windows. It was so different from the modern shopping districts she frequented in Brasília.

She and Frank had browsed up one side of the street, Isabelle, pausing every now and then to look in the enticing shop windows. Then he'd gone off exploring when she'd ducked into that charming little boutique to try on a sweet top she'd spotted. He hadn't reappeared, so she crossed to the other side and continued to entertain herself, rummaging through a second-hand store and then popped into the glass gallery to look for something fun and different to add to her dorm room. Her phone vibrated in her pocket.

"Hi, Frank. This downtown area is wonderful, and the shopping is fabulous. They have an amazing farmer's market. I'll be back here a lot, I think. I finished trying on that blouse, and I've explored the other side of Main Street. Where are you? How about you buy me that pistachio ice cream now?"

"Isabelle, I'm being arrested for stealing. I need you. Where are you?"

"What? Where are *you*? What do you mean stealing? What happened?"

"Come meet me at the jewelry store, you know, that one where you liked the pearl earrings in the window?" Frank hung up abruptly.

With her phone clutched in her hand, Isabelle ran to the next corner and crossed over. Her heart pounding, she dashed the last few yards and stopped in front of the plate-glass window. Frank was standing inside, talking to a police officer. *Oh, no! I can't call his parents. His dad will be furious. The only other person I can call is Victor. Phew, that won't be fun! But Frank might need a good lawyer. Here goes.*

She lifted her phone and dialed his number. When she heard his voicemail recording, Isabelle panicked and hung up. *I can't do it. I just can't do it. I'll figure out what to do later, after I find out what's up with Frank.*

As she put her hand on the door to open it, she saw Frank being handcuffed by the police, and she burst into the store. "What's going on?" she demanded. *What am I going to do?* Next to the police officers stood an elderly couple with white hair and twinkly eyes. *They look just like my grandparents.*

The woman said in a quavering voice, "I can't believe it. He tried to steal a pair of earrings."

Isabelle watched the old man put his handgun back in the drawer beneath the cash register counter. She spun around to look at Frank, "Oh, my God, Frank. The ones I was looking at earlier?"

The old woman went on, "He said they were for you, honey."

Ready to lead him away, the policeman took Frank by the arm, "Come along, now, young man. Excuse me, sir, ma'am." He tipped his hat to the old couple and then to Isabelle.

Looking back over his shoulder, Frank asked, "Isabelle, do you have my other set of car keys?"

She nodded, "I'll meet you at the police station." Then she began to cry as though she was devastated. "It's all my fault. I wanted those earrings so badly," she sobbed dramatically to the elderly owners.

The old man said in a matter-of-fact voice, "Then he should have paid for them before he walked out the door."

Isabelle stood in front of them and cried harder, "You have the earrings. Can't we figure something out?" She clasped her hands in front of her chest. "I love him so much," she wailed. "He's my best friend in the whole world. My birthday is coming up, and he must have wanted to get me something special."

The woman took Isabelle's hand and patted it. She sniffled pathetically, and the woman patted her hand again. "Come on into the back room, honey. We'll talk about this and have a little tea."

Isabelle left the shop an hour later shaking her head in disappointment. *Now I've stooped to his level. Now I'm lying for him.*

She sat waiting in the police station, looking down at her hands twisted in her lap, one foot tapping on the floor. Her eyes were puffy and red from all the crying. Then Frank's voice in the hall caught her attention, and she looked up. He came through the door with the same policeman who'd taken him away.

"You're a very lucky young man to have a woman like this as your fiancée," he said sternly.

Isabelle jumped up, "Darling, I was so worried about you. Let's go. Let's get you out of here." She threw her arms around him and whispered in his ear, "You're a piece of crap. You know that? Total crap!" Isabelle dug the keys out of her pocket and slapped them in his hand. "Here, you drive."

Before they pulled out of the police station parking lot, Frank tried to placate her, "Let's go get your pistachio ice cream, girlfriend." He touched her leg.

Isabelle smacked his hand away. "Get off me. Ice cream? Now? I'm not going downtown. I'm humiliated, Frank. I've only just arrived here, and now, I can never go back there. I'm so done with you. Take me back to my dorm right now," she said, her voice shaking with anger.

Frank looked at her in shock and, wisely, said nothing.

Finally, she broke the silence, "*What* were you thinking?"

"How did you get the owners to drop the charges?"

Isabelle looked at Frank, her face flushed with anger. "I cried. A lot. I put on a massive act that I was sooo upset. I *lied* for you, Frank. I told them how in love we were. I told them it was an act of crazy-in-love madness that made you do it. I told them we were going to be married."

"Wow, you never tell lies. That was good thinking, Isabelle."

Isabelle glared at him, "I also made a generous donation to the humane society. I saw a jar on the counter and offered to donate the value of the earrings. I had to spend *my* money on *your* stupidity. And as a result, now you owe me seven hundred dollars. You can afford to buy every piece of jewelry in that store. How could you do something so stupid? *What* were you thinking?"

Shit, I've never seen her this angry. "I didn't think those old folks were watching. They seemed like an easy target. I'm sure they'd have had insurance to cover them. I was just doing it because you liked those earrings so much."

"Don't put this on me, Frank." She jabbed her finger at his face, "*What* were you thinking?"

"I just did it for the thrill."

Isabelle pointed at the Rolex, "Like the watch?"

"What did Victor tell you, anyhow?" he snapped.

"Calm down Frank. He didn't tell me anything. But you just

did. I was so hoping I was wrong."

His voice was cocky. "That was the only other time I was caught. And I wasn't really caught because I gave the watch to my uncle. I thought he would be proud of me. I took it right off that guy's wrist while Uncle and I were on the subway. But nooooo, he was angry too."

Isabelle said, her disappointment obvious even to him, "Of course he would be. So, that's what 'Stay out of trouble' is all about."

"I got careless in there. I won't underestimate anyone again. I just do it for the thrill, Isabelle."

"I just don't know what you're thinking. I called Victor—"

"What? Why would you call him?" he said, his voice rising in anger.

"You got arrested. I didn't want to call your parents. Who else would I call?"

"What did you tell my uncle? What are you doing, butting in with my family business, anyhow?"

"Butting in? Don't even think about claiming the higher ground, Frank. You called me! Lucky for you, Victor didn't answer, and I hung up and didn't leave a voicemail. Lucky for you."

"I'm nineteen years old. I don't need anyone's help."

"You needed *my* help." She tapped her chest with her finger. "*I* convinced that sweet couple to drop the charges. If it weren't for *me*," she thumped her finger against her chest again, "you'd still be in jail, and because you're nineteen, you'd have a record. *What* were you thinking?"

"It would have never come to that."

"You don't know. You just don't know."

They finished the short drive to her dorm in silence. He stopped the car in front of the entrance, and turning slightly in her seat, she glared at him. "Frank, don't ever do that again. You're my best friend. You're like a brother to me."

"I'll be careful, girlfriend."

"Careful's not enough." She shook her head sadly as she climbed out of the car.

Frank lowered the window and continued, "You're a good person, Isabelle. I'm out of here in the morning, and I'm gonna miss you so much. I'll be in touch. You're coming to Uncle Victor's for Thanksgiving, right?"

Isabelle looked away as she blushed. "No, I'm not. Why don't you come here? Maybe I won't be so mad at you by then."

"But I thought you had such a good time in New York."

"I did, but – it'll be warmer here."

"It's a date." Frank flashed one of his big smiles and gave her a finger wave.

I'll miss you too, boyfriend. But what were you thinking? Furious that he'd put her in such an uncomfortable position, Isabelle ignored Frank's grin and his wave and said in a low voice, "You behave yourself – and stay out of trouble."

§

College Station, Texas

Chloe and Isabelle stood in a long line in the campus bookstore, waiting to pay for the notebooks, pens and other supplies that they'd piled into their hand-held shopping baskets.

"I'm all set. I got everything on my list." After a final glance, Isabelle tucked the paper into the front pocket of her jean shorts.

"You even got a Texas A&M sweatshirt, Isabelle? What? Are you feeling okay?"

"I'm giving in to your constant nagging from last year." She grinned at her roommate. "I just decided that it's time to show off my school spirit." She held up the sweatshirt and admired the colors. "Besides, I think this maroon and white looks exceptionally good on me."

The line inched forward slowly as Chloe continued to tease Isabelle. Suddenly, she reached out and tapped the shoulder of the tall, lanky, blond guy in front of them. "Hey, Rick."

He turned around in surprise and looked at the two coeds, a short, dark-haired girl and a tall blonde standing next to her. They were both wearing shorts and t-shirts in deference to the summer afternoon heat, and Rick couldn't help noticing their nipples showing through. They had their hair pulled up on top of their heads. Chloe's hair was a sleek knot, while Isabelle's was a messy jumble of curls, barely held in place by a thick, bright green elastic. Little tendrils had escaped and clung annoyingly to her damp neck.

"Hey. I don't remember your name, but you're in my history lecture, right?"

"Yeah, I'm the one who dropped my books in front of you when I came in late the first day of class. I'm Chloe Rose Johnson."

"Nice to meet you." Rick took a step as the line moved forward a little.

Chloe nudged Isabelle and jerked her head toward him in an exaggerated movement. Isabelle gulped nervously, "Nice tennis bag, Rick." She touched the bag slung over his shoulder.

He turned back toward them. Isabelle moved the basket to her other arm and stuck her hand out. "Hi, I'm Isabelle Ronaldo. I'm Chloe Rose's roommate."

"Hello there," he said, a big white smile lighting up his face.

"My best friend has a bag just like that."

"Do you play?"

"No, I'm a runner. Those are some nice balls, Rick."

Chloe began giggling hysterically and squeaked out between gasps for air, "Isabelle, your mind is in the gutter." Tears of laughter ran down her face. She reached over and grabbed the back of Isabelle's t-shirt and wiped her eyes.

Isabelle's face turned bright red. "Oh! God – no, no. I meant the can of – tennis balls – in your hand." She turned to look at Chloe. "It's your mind that's in the gutter, Chloe Rose." Isabelle pointed at the can Rick was holding, "I happen to know they're a great brand. Yikes, talk about putting my foot in my mouth."

"If you did that, you would fall on your ass, Isabelle." Chloe continued to laugh, and then the others joined in, howling until tears poured down their faces.

The line moved ever so slowly as they continued to laugh and joke.

Ahead of them in the line, Rick finally sobered up enough to ask Isabelle, "Would you like to go out sometime?"

"I'd like that, Rick," she replied before she had time to think it over. *Oh my! He's older than me, and he's so hot and sexy.*

§

"Frank's arrived. He came into the house, said hello, gave me a kiss and then dragged Chloe into her bedroom." Stepping over the books that were scattered across the floor, Isabelle nudged Rick's leg aside with her foot and stood looking around at the mess. "Are you done studying yet? You've taken over our entire bedroom. I still don't understand why you don't use the den to study. There's that big desk in there so you wouldn't have to sit on the floor."

"There's no room in the office with your shit spread all over. Besides, I like to sit on the floor to study." He grinned and pulled Isabelle down onto his lap, "Or do other stuff." He gave her a vigorous kiss.

"Oh!" she said as she came up for air.

Deliberately making his voice low and sexy, Rick said, "If you're offering something better than this," he pointed at the books, "then I'm done." He pulled her against him, kissing her again for a very long time.

She was breathing hard when she stood and took Rick's hands, pulling him up. She looked suggestively at him and then over at the bed. "I was hoping you were ready to study me," she said with one hand on the hip she'd thrust forward, vamping a little for him.

"Oh yes, I do need to study you," Rick hooked his finger into the V-neck of Isabelle's sundress and pulled her toward him to look down the front. Reaching around her, he deftly slid the zipper down. Isabelle wiggled her shoulders, and her dress fell to the floor.

They lay close together on the bed, noses almost touching, Isabelle slowly running one finger back and forth along his collarbone. "My God, Rick, you're so sexy. Out of all the places we've made love, which did you like best? The dorms where we always worried about your roommate walking in on us? On top of that big rock during the lake hike when we put on a show for the deer? The backseat of your old blue Pontiac?"

Rick kissed her – her hair, her eyes and then her mouth. "It's hard to pick just one place."

"Then, we'll do it anywhere and everywhere we can – always."

"That's one of the things about you that I fell in love with, Isabelle." Suddenly, Rick propped himself up on his elbow, "How do you think Frank and Chloe do it? How have they kept their relationship so casual for all this time? This whole thing Chloe says, 'When we see each other, we're a couple, but when we don't, we're not.' I could never do that. I could never share you, Isabelle."

"I don't want to share you either."

They both jumped when they heard a loud knock on the door. Frank shouted, "Hey, birthday boy. Let's get dinner started."

Freshly showered and dressed in their usual shorts and light-weight shirts, the four of them were relaxing in the backyard in the shade of a tall oak. The men had poured beers for themselves and wine for the women. Chloe had perched on the wide arm of the sectional sofa that stood in the center of the huge flagstone patio at the back of the house, her feet on the seat cushions, her glass in one hand and her chin propped in the other as she chatted with her friends. Isabelle and Frank sat in the middle section, and she leaned against him, happy that he'd made it back to Texas for the birthday party. She sipped from her glass of wine and sighed with contentment. Rick stood on duty at the barbeque, periodically checking the ribs and the corn-on-the-cob that he'd coated with butter and soy sauce and placed off to one side of the coals to roast slowly. A little breeze came through every now and then, rustling the leaves overhead, and the pair of blue jays that had a nest high up in the tree fought over an old acorn one of them had found lying on the ground.

Isabelle sat up and glared at the birds, "They are noisy neighbors. But not as noisy as you, Frank, when you banged on our bedroom door." She nudged her shoulder against his.

"Ha-ha, girlfriend. I've missed you. It's been months since our trip to Brazil." Frank bumped her back and took a swallow of his beer. "What do you have planned for dinner, Rick?"

"We have barbequed ribs and corn. And I got some potato salad as a side and chips with salsa to munch on while we grill."

"To balance all those carbs, Chloe and I've made a veggie tray."

Frank snickered, "So you cook now, girlfriend?"

"No, I only chop vegetables. Rick is the head chef at this address." She toasted Rick with her stemless wine glass that she'd brought home the previous summer from her Spectrum river cruise internship in Europe. She drained her glass.

Chloe pointed at the sun as it sank lower in the sky. "It's going to be a beautiful sunset tonight. It's too bad, it usually means there's a lot of dust or pollution in the air."

Turning to look at her in surprise, Isabelle asked, "When did you start to care about that kind of stuff?"

"During our Christmas break, while you and Frank were in Brazil. Rick decided, since I was between boyfriends, I might be lonely, so he kept dragging me off to hear all these environmentalists speak, and to hike and get back to nature." She grinned at Isabelle, who stared at her friend, taken aback by this new Chloe.

"Chloe, the tree hugger?" Frank reached out and tugged on one of her braids.

She bent forward to tug his hair in return, "I can take or leave all those trails and that back-to-nature hoo-hah, but the environmental part was pretty fascinating."

"I'm glad I didn't totally waste your time, Chloe," Rick smiled.

"Awww, shucks, Rick," she said, leaning over to pick up the bottle from the coffee table. "Hey, Isabelle, we're out of wine. We need to go get some more before we're all too over the limit to drive." Chloe put her hands on Frank's shoulders and kissed him. "I've had my time with you, Frank. This will give you and Rick some time for your little love affair."

As Chloe backed out of the driveway, Isabelle could scarcely contain herself and gave a little bounce in the passenger seat. "Chloe Rose, I'm so excited. This afternoon, Rick was asking me about my ring size."

"You know what that means. I can tell from the way he looks at you and the way he talks about you, he's totally smitten. I just know he's going to ask you to marry him."

Grinning from ear to ear, Isabelle said, "We've been together for two and a half years. I hope he does ask. He's so sensitive and kind and really, really smart. Ever since I slept with him that first time, I knew he was the one." *Victor, you were right,* she thought. *I did meet the love of my life.*

"You two make a great couple."

"I still have a long way to go to finish my education. But I want to be with him. The plan is to live together for the next couple of years until we finish our master's degrees. Then after we graduate, we'll get married."

"Whose plan is this, my friend?"

"Ummm, mine," she grinned. "We'll get married in Brasília, of course. I'll have a lot of help from my mom. She's going to be so excited about helping me pull it all together."

"Tell me about it," said Chloe excitedly. "I can't believe we've never talked about it before."

"Maybe because Rick never asked about my ring size before?" said Isabelle with a little giggle.

Even though she was focusing on the road, from the corner of her eye, Chloe could see Isabelle's face light up as she continued, "My wedding dress will be a long, simple, white dress, lightly flared from the waist, cut to here in the front, like this." She drew a curving neckline that ended where her cleavage began. "The bodice will be covered in Belgian lace, and the overskirt will be made of silk chiffon. I'll write '*Chloe Rose*' inside, on the hem of my skirt, to provide you with good luck in your own love life. It's one of our traditions."

"Awww, that's sweet."

"And the shoes," Isabelle raised her feet just a little and pointed her toes. "In my country, it's conventional to wear shiny gold shoes, the brighter the better. I can already see myself, walking down the aisle wearing very high heels with peep toes and a sweet little bow on top. Maybe, I'll find ones with a sexy ankle strap. You'll be my maid of honor, right?"

"Of course," she nodded vigorously. "Yes, of course I will."

"I've already picked out the venue. The wedding will be held at a wonderful restaurant on Lago Paranoá – that's a huge lake in Brasília. It has a beautiful patio at the back, surrounded by grass and trees, that can easily hold a couple hundred guests." She turned toward her friend. "We'll have a live band, and after all the other guests leave, the four of us will party into the wee hours of the morning. We'll dance all night under the stars, Chloe Rose, you and me and Rick and Frank. It'll be perfect."

Chloe parked the car, and after she'd switched off the engine, she turned toward Isabelle. She lifted an imaginary glass. "Here's to your perfect wedding and to the four amigos. We're going to have a spectacular time, just like we always do and always will."

They clinked their imaginary glasses as Isabelle said, "To the four amigos." She took a deep breath, and as she opened the door, she said, "I need to calm down. I'm not even engaged yet."

Isabelle carefully set the case of wine they'd just bought inside the trunk. "I can't believe how much time you took to pick out twelve bottles of wine," said Chloe.

"Last year, I started with a list of a hundred different wines I want to try before we graduate in May. I've tried the more popular ones, and now I'm down to the wines that are harder to find."

Chloe shook her head with a little smile. After they got back into the car, she said, "Now that we're in the cone of silence, finish your story about Victor. Tell me why you never want to go to New York with Frank. He keeps asking you."

Chloe carefully maneuvered the car out of its space, through the lot and onto the main road before Isabelle answered. "I've never told anyone this, Chloe Rose. And you mustn't tell anyone, either. Not Frank. Not Rick."

"I don't tell Frank anything."

"Well, it was the winter that Frank and I visited Victor, when I was eighteen, before I started here. On our last night in New York, before we went back home, Victor and I had Chinese take-out and we ended up drinking a lot of wine, and then I threw myself at him. And we made love." She cleared her throat, "I mean, we had sex."

"So, you went for it?"

Isabelle blushed. "Just once, that night."

"Well, bless your heart, Isabelle. We've all had one-night stands. I'm certainly not one to judge you. But I can't believe you slept with Frank's Uncle Victor. He must be way older than you."

"Sixteen years, actually. And now I'm with Rick. He's seven years older than me. Obviously, I like older men."

"This is true."

Isabelle told her the rest of the story, "I was so hurt back then when he said it had just been sex. I practically accused him of raping me."

"Did he?"

"Oh, no, no, no. And now I'm just embarrassed by the whole thing." She buried her face in her hands.

"I'm so sorry, Isabelle. I'm *so* sorry." Chloe reached over and stroked her arm. "I've been there and done that. We're young. We're supposed to make mistakes and get them out of our systems. But no wonder you won't go back to New York. Now, I finally understand."

"I just can't. The whole trip was fantastic, and then I ruined it all at the end." In an attempt to lighten the tone, Isabelle lifted her head, "But God, I jumped his bones, Chloe Rose."

"You brazen hussy."

"I can laugh about it now. But I can't go back, even now that I've fallen head over heels with Rick. I was so mad before. I said such dreadful things."

§

With the ribs in place, Rick closed the grill top and Frank lifted his mug, "Happy birthday, Rick. I can't believe you're thirty. That's almost middle-aged!"

"I don't feel that old. And besides, I can still beat you in tennis any time – junior. Age is just a number."

Frank picked up a tennis ball and bounced it on the ground. "When you turn forty and you're wildly successful in your career, we're going to take the trip of a lifetime to celebrate. Hey, we could take a tennis trip anywhere in the world."

"That would be exceptional. You know, every year, I look forward to celebrating our birthdays together," said Rick. "To brothers," and they drained their mugs.

"Are you ready for our little tennis challenge this weekend – to get whipped by me again? Don't think I'm going to let you win just because you're the birthday boy," Frank jeered.

"I'll kick your ass back to Pennsylvania. My dad's been giving me pointers on how to beat you."

"Well, I doubt that will happen. I have some new moves myself."

Rick took the growler out of the cooler and poured them another round, "Man, this brewpub is the best. They make an IPA like nobody else."

"Remember when we found it last year? When we tried all of their beers to celebrate our birthdays and barely made it back here? And how mad the girls were when we came in singing *Happy Birthday* to each other and woke them up? I thought they were going to make us share a room." Frank bumped Rick's upper arm. "You can share my bed anytime as long as you don't spoon me."

"Ha-ha," Rick laughed. "This house is so great. There's plenty of room for when you visit, Frank, and for Chloe's get-togethers with her friends." Rick opened the heavy metal lid to baste the ribs, and they squinted against the smoke. "You know, I'm glad the girls chipped in to get us this barbeque."

"It's a very manly grill – like us." Frank bent over, grabbed an acorn from the patio, "Take this, you noisy old birds," and he pitched it at the raucous jays who ignored him and continued their fight. "They just don't stop, do they?"

"They are always at it. Chloe hates sitting out here at this time of the day because this is when they seem to fight the most." After a few more swigs of beer, they stared into the yard.

"Isabelle and Chloe sure are taking their time. I thought she was just grabbing a bottle of wine."

"Jeez, Frank, you should know by now that Isabelle gets lost in the big liquor stores. Too many choices. That's why Chloe went along, to keep her focused and make sure she gets back in time for dinner."

"I didn't realize Isabelle had become such a wine aficionado."

"Yeah, she's so into it now. She talks non-stop about all these French and Italian and Portuguese wines she wants to try. Pinot this and sauvignon that. No more box wine for her. Me, now, just give me a good brewsky every time." Rick dropped the basting brush back into the empty bowl. "Hey, I'll be right back. I need to get some more sauce."

When he came back, he basted the ribs again. "I have a question for you." He closed the lid to the grill, turned around and took a big swallow of his beer. He dug into his shorts pocket and slowly handed Frank a little black box. "What do you think?"

Frank opened it. "Oh honey, you shouldn't have." He opened

his eyes wide and batted his lashes at Rick and burst out laughing.

Rick ignored him. "Do you think she'll like it? Do you think she'll say yes?"

"Of course she will, my friend. You're all she talks about." Frank leaned over and gave him a loud smooch on his neck.

Rick shoved him away, rubbing at the spot Frank had kissed.

Frank tilted the box and examined the small, square-cut stone in a white gold setting. He took it out and held it to the light. "This diamond has great clarity and color. And the cut is quite nice. You have a good eye." *If it were me buying Isabelle an engagement ring, I would have gotten something people would sit up and notice, something with some flash, to match her beauty. But I know this is all he can afford.*

"Thanks. You know a lot about jewelry, man. But I picked this because it's classy, like her."

"You two're a perfect match."

"You're like her brother. I wanted your blessing before I popped the question."

Frank flashed one of his huge smiles at Rick. "When are you gonna ask her?"

"Next weekend."

"How?"

Rick opened the grill and moved the ribs and corn to the top rack. "I'm taking her to our favorite restaurant. We'll start with champagne, and she can pick out a great bottle of wine to have with our dinner, and the ring will be part of the dessert at the end. When she sees it, I'll go down on one knee and propose."

"Are you kidding?"

"No, I think it will be romantic. It'll be just like they do in the movies. You know how she is about old movies, especially old romances."

"Oh no, my friend, you're in trouble. Biiiiig trouble."

"What do you mean?"

"When we were about eleven, she told me about her dream proposal."

"So? Tell me, what does she want? How should I do it? I just want her to say yes. I don't want to screw this up." Rick walked over to the picnic table and sat down. Frank straddled the bench across from him.

"She wants to be proposed to outdoors, near the water. You know how Isabelle is about the outdoors – and water – and fresh air. She says it's good for her soul."

"I know." He frowned. "So, I should propose to her on a beach?"

"That could work, or you could do it in the mountains next to a beautiful stream or river."

Rick picked up a slice of cucumber and dunked it into the dip he'd made that morning. Frank teased, "So, she has you eating your veggies now? You're already like an old, married couple."

"Yeah, but veggies also make a good vehicle for this dip." Rick grinned and held up the piece of cucumber, dripping with aioli mayonnaise, before popping it whole into his mouth. Frank looked at him, and then, holding his gaze as though it was a challenge, he took a big tortilla chip, loaded it up with salsa and crammed it into his mouth.

"Hmmm. Outdoors. Water." Rick pointed a carrot stick at Frank, "I know the perfect place. It's on a river, not too far from here. I've never taken her there, but it's a great place to stop for a rest when I'm hiking in that area." He took a bite and crunched thoughtfully.

Frank picked up the box and admired the ring. "Isabelle's getting married. I can't believe it's happening. And I can't wait to become Uncle Frank."

I wish Isabelle would finally tell him about her abortion and the fact that she can't have kids. He'll be so disappointed.

Chapter Five

April 1998

In a Dark Parking Lot

Raleigh, North Carolina

"Bye, guys. That was fun. We'll have to do it again," Penelope said, hugging each of her friends in turn.

"Let's make it sooner rather than later."

"Let me know, and I'll be there." Penelope waved and walked away. *This parking lot is always creepy after dark. Especially when it's windy like tonight. There just aren't enough lights, and there are too many shadows.* She brushed her hair out of her face, noticing that the lot was much emptier than when she'd arrived earlier that evening. A light in the middle caught her eye, and she glanced over a few rows toward it. *Someone else likes the cheap rates here. I wonder if they're coming or going.*

She put her hand over her mouth and gave a quiet belch. *The burgers and beer in that place are always good. I'm so full. Why do I always eat too much there?* She sighed. *I guess I'll have to run some extra miles tomorrow.*

She'd almost reached the back of her Jeep when she realized she hadn't heard the car with the light on start up or the beep of a lock engaging and footsteps as someone left. She looked over at the car again. A '97 Toyota Camry. It was still sitting there – with the interior light on and the driver's side door standing open. *I should at least close it, so the battery doesn't run down.*

She walked toward the center of the lot so she could see the car more clearly. What appeared to be a woman's feet were sticking out of the driver's door. She watched for a moment, and they didn't move. *Guess I should check on her. She's probably drunk – or maybe it's a medical issue.*

Penelope walked toward the car. *Like I told my new partner yesterday, police officers are always on duty. I'll have to tell her about this example on our next shift.* As she passed the trunk, she called out, "Hey. Hello. Are you okay? Do you need anything?" And when she got to the open door, she saw a woman lying slouched over, with her head tipped against the side of the passenger's seat. *She probably overdid it at happy hour tonight.* Penelope gently pushed the woman's foot with the top of her shoe, but she didn't move.

Boy, she's really out. She raised her voice, "Are you okay?" and pushed her foot harder to wake her up.

The woman didn't stir. Penelope took off her glove as she crouched down beside the open door and looked across the woman to see if her chest was rising and falling. Nothing. Still crouched down, she moved her eyes over the woman's body and up toward her face. That was when she noticed red marks on her neck. "Looks like you ran into some trouble, lady." She touched her ankle, and her skin was cool. "Yeah, looks like you lost the battle."

Penelope stood up, pulled her phone out of her jacket pocket and dialed 911. While she was on the phone, she looked around the lot and saw no one, nothing suspicious. "This is Officer Huber of the Raleigh PD, and I'm off duty. I'm at the downtown self-park lot at Fifth Street and Columbia Drive. I've found a woman in a car. I think she's deceased."

Then the commotion began. A patrol car came screaming into the lot with sirens blaring and lights flashing. A few minutes later, a couple more patrol cars arrived, followed by an ambulance. Suddenly, the dark parking lot was filled with lights – headlights, spotlights, flashing red and blue lights – from all the emergency vehicles.

To keep onlookers away, the patrol officers worked quickly to secure the scene with yellow tape, strung around the lot. Penelope watched the controlled chaos, *People are drawn to police sirens and lights like bugs are drawn to a porch light.* She stepped aside as the EMTs, equipment in hand, approached the body.

Then another car arrived, and the on-duty patrol supervisor got out, hooked her thumbs into her belt, just like cops in all the TV shows, and swaggered over to Penelope. "What do you have here, Huber?"

Penelope described the situation while she watched the EMTs put leads from the monitor on the victim's ankles. The reading showed that the victim was clearly no longer alive. As they were packing up their equipment, Penelope overheard one technician say to the other, "Since we won't be taking anyone back, wanna stop and get a sandwich?"

The supervisor said sarcastically, "Looks like she's onto her next life." She turned to Penelope and looked over the top of her glasses, saying in the condescending tone she always used, "Of course, you know you have to stick around, Huber, to speak to the detectives?"

"Yes, ma'am," she replied as she turned away.

Penelope heard her call the detective supervisor. *Like I would leave. After all these years, she still treats me like a rookie, like an idiot. As a matter of fact, she treats all of us women this way. Like she's the supervisor of a group of dummies.*

She watched the ambulance leave the lot, and shortly after, Detective Bissett and her partner arrived.

"Hey, Em. I'm glad you're here tonight."

She didn't recognize Emily's partner and stuck out her hand. "I'm Officer Penelope Huber. I'm the one who found this body." She pointed to the woman in the car.

He shook her hand. "Detective Eric Daniel."

"Nice to finally meet you. Em mentioned she had a new partner."

"I thought you were going out tonight with friends. Wasn't that enough for you? Now you're out looking for more fun?" Emily chuckled. "What've you got for us, Pens?"

"Yeah, I did go out with'em for a burger and a beer. But a dead body is double the fun." Penelope gave a grim little smile and carefully described what she'd seen and what she'd done. Emily and Eric stopped her from time to time to ask for additional information or to clarify a point.

Emily tapped Penelope's shoulder. "Hey, want to shadow me? Nothing like a real crime scene." She turned to the other detective, "Eric, I'm going to have Penelope tag along on this one. Ten years ago, when she was a rookie, I trained her. She'd make a dynamite detective, but I haven't been able to convince her to let go of patrol."

"Whatever you want, boss." He walked away to begin working the scene.

Penelope leaned close and whispered to Emily, "With supervisors like numb-nuts over there," she jerked her thumb toward the on-duty patrol supervisor, who was speaking to the officers at the scene, "I'm closer every day to letting it go."

"I'm happy to hear that."

"You know the crap she pulls, the things she says."

"Mmmhmm. So, of course you know the procedure – in *theory* – but before the medical examiner gets here to take her away, let me show you how it works in practice," Emily said. "We'll start with the body and the car. C'mon, let's get our protective gear and the camera—

Eric cleared his throat to get their attention. "The car registration says Maggie Wilson. I thought I recognized her – I've met this woman. She owns the MJW Expressions art gallery. I've been there with my wife, Morgan. It's not far from here. She was probably on her way home. Morgan goes to the gallery regularly, and she's told me how wonderful Maggie is. Apparently, she'd been teaching classes for underprivileged women. She'll be devastated to find out that Maggie has been killed."

Chapter Six

July 1999

Sarah's House

Raleigh, North Carolina

ANNOUNCING THE GRAND OPENING OF

Sarah's House

Where Siblings Stay Together

Sarah's House is a new, privately-owned foster home in Raleigh, committed to keeping siblings together for as long as needed. The new facility was established by Tracey Lauch in honor of his sister, Sarah, and was made possible by a generous donation from the Lauch family estate by his adoptive grandparents, Mason and Ava. After an extensive eighteen-month renovation, the property has been transformed into a comfortable, safe, educational environment for children.

Please come celebrate with us. The grand opening is on Saturday, July 10, at 10AM, and tours will be given until 3PM.

431 N McCaleb Lane, Raleigh, NC

"I wanted to give you a personal tour before the opening," Tracey said to his grandparents. "But you were in the hospital, Granddad. I want the two of you to see how your old house has changed and is being put to use for these kids." He pushed the elevator button for the third floor. "We'll start at the top and work our way down."

"You've put in an elevator? Oh, my," said Grams, "this old house has come up in the world."

"We needed it for children with disabilities. We're part of the state foster system, even though our funding is largely private. It was either install the elevator or create additional accessible living quarters on the ground floor for kids with physical disabilities. We chose to add the elevator and to do slight modifications to the rooms, so these kids have access to the same sleeping, recreation and study areas, all the same privileges as their able-bodied counterparts. And an elevator certainly makes housekeeping much easier," he said with a grin at his grandmother. "This one isn't high-speed, and it's only designed to hold three or four people, but it does the job."

Granddad looked over his shoulder at Tracey as the elevator rose. "You're so busy, young man. Are you sure you have time for this?"

Tracey wheeled his grandfather off the elevator. "Of course I have time, Granddad. Now, this floor is where the kids sleep." They continued down the hall. "We've set it up so we can reallocate the spaces depending on how many kids we have of each age and gender."

"How many children can you have here?"

From behind Tracey, Grams said, "Didn't you say about twenty, dear?"

"Yes, we wanted to keep the facility small enough to be intimate, so the kids would feel at home, like they are part of a family while they are waiting for adoption or to return to their parents."

They looked into a couple of bedrooms. Grams commented on the beds with chests of drawers at the foot of each and the narrow nightstand near the head that had sufficient room for a small lamp and a book. "They're just like bedrooms you'd find at home. In fact, this reminds me of the room you used to stay in when you'd spend the night with us, Tracey. Those kids sure keep them neat."

"We focus on responsibility, on keeping the commitments they make to others and to themselves and on taking care of the space they live in. They have to keep their rooms clean and tidy, and when they use the common spaces on the first or second floor, they have to straighten up after themselves. And the older ones learn how to do laundry, take turns setting the table and clearing away after dinner and helping the cook in the kitchen. Just because this is a group home that has a lot of staff, it doesn't mean they're waited on hand and foot."

Granddad said, "They need to grow up to be self-sufficient."

"Exactly. This is their home. It's not just a temporary place before they're adopted. They have to feel like they belong, that they have a role and that there are consequences when they don't follow the rules. We have a responsibility to set boundaries, just as parents should."

Grams rested her hand on top of Tracey's on the wheelchair handle. "You would make a good father, Tracey."

On their way to the second floor, Granddad said, "This is pretty nice. Maybe we should just move back in here, Grams."

"Dearie, you know we need more care these days. We're not spring chickens anymore." She laughed, "Besides, who would adopt us?"

Tracey listened to their banter with an affectionate smile.

Once they'd finished their tour of the upper levels, they took the elevator back to the main floor.

"Who takes care of these kids?"

"Granddad, we have live-in staff here seven days a week, twenty-four hours a day. They have separate quarters in that other wing. They're part of the Sarah's House family too."

Tracey picked up a small Siamese cat that had wandered into the wide hallway near the elevator and held her so he could look her in the face. "What are you doing in here, little kitten?" He tucked her into his elbow and petted her for a moment and then set her on his grandfather's lap, and he began to stroke the kitten's fur with his gnarled hand. She tolerated it for a few seconds and then jumped down and vanished.

Tracey led them along the hall into the spacious living areas and the huge dining room. "We combined the old, formal dining room with the parlor that was next to it. Now, it's big enough for all the kids and staff to sit down to eat together," he said. They came to the kitchen and poked their heads in to see all the changes that had been made – lots of counters with hard surfaces, two huge stainless-steel sinks, an enormous walk-in pantry and glass-fronted storage for dishes to keep the room from feeling too industrial. And then they moved on to a bright, airy exercise room with windows that looked out onto the gardens. "Everyone is allowed to use this room, though we do have separate hours for staff and the children."

"Where's the pinball machine? You and I could have a tournament, Grandson," asked Granddad, looking around at all the modern exercise equipment.

"There's no pinball machine here, anymore. We wore it out. But wouldn't that be fun to play again?"

From the exercise room, they went out the door onto a large, shaded patio that ran the entire width of the house. While Tracey was settling his grandparents at the table, the kitten came back to rub against his legs. He picked her up. "Holy smokes, little one, you're adorable but very persistent," he said and gave her a gentle scratch behind the ears.

A woman came out from the kitchen with a tray of salads and saw the cat in his arms. "That kitten keeps coming back. Every time we put her outside, she sneaks back in. She's searching for her person, I guess."

"Doesn't she belong to anybody?"

"No. The kids don't even like her because her meow sounds like a baby crying."

He walked out onto the lawn and set her down before joining his grandparents at the table.

As the woman put their salads on the placemats in front of each of them, she asked, "Mrs. Lauch is joining you, isn't she? Shall I put her salad out?" She walked over to turn on the patio ceiling fan over the table. "It's sure warm today. Would you like ice water, tea or lemonade?"

"We'll have iced tea with a slice of lemon." Grams pointed to Granddad and herself.

"I'll just stick with ice water, also with a slice of lemon. I don't need any more caffeine after that delicious coffee you served at the beginning of our tour," said Tracey.

His mother walked out to the patio. "Here you all are. I'm sorry I kept you waiting." She kissed her parents-in-law on the cheek. "Hello, Ava. You look lovely today." She smiled at Granddad, "You're not overdoing it, are you, Mason?"

"I'm strong as a horse."

She caressed Tracey's shoulder in passing before she sat down.

"Darling."

"Hello, Mom."

Grams said, "You're just in time for lunch, Natalie."

"I'll have iced tea as well, please," she said with a gentle smile to the woman who stood waiting, "but no lemon."

After lunch, they relaxed over decaffeinated coffee served in thin porcelain cups with tiny violets scattered around the rims and on the saucers. A plate of the delicate orange cookies that Grams adored had been placed in the center of the table. Granddad lifted his coffee and cleared his throat, "Here's to you, young man. This is the last year your age will begin with a two. Happy birthday."

"Dearie, that was a couple of weeks ago."

"I know, I know, but I was still in the hospital and never got to wish my successful grandson a happy birthday."

"Thanks, Granddad."

A set of twins ran past the table and into the backyard to play. "Those two are about the same age I was when you adopted me. I've noticed they're inseparable, just like we were."

"They are. How fortunate those children are to have been able to stay together."

"Exactly. You know that's why I'm so passionate about this house, Mom." He pointed at the two children, "Siblings shouldn't be separated like Sarah and I were. I know it's early days still, but if this model is successful, in a few years, I plan to build more houses like this on the grounds."

Tracey leaned over to pet the kitten that had returned to him, her tiny paws on his leg, kneading very gently. "You just don't give up, do you?"

"Granddad, I couldn't have done all this without you and Grams. Donating your house, the financial support, all the ideas you helped me flesh out." He reached over and gave his grandfather's hand a light squeeze.

"And that's a lot of work on top of being a lawyer here in town," said Grams.

Tracey picked up the kitten who wouldn't leave him alone and talked to her. "Hey, little one. Do you think I'm your person? Would you like to come home with me?"

"She'll be good company for you, rattling around in that big house by yourself."

"You're right, Mom. I think I will take her home. Maybe I'll call her Mrs. Whiskers." He looked over at his grandmother. "Grams, being a lawyer is just a job. This place is my dream."

Natalie added tenderly, "Your sister, wherever she is, would be honored that you named this place after her. It's too bad you all got separated by the system and that the adoption records were sealed. If we'd known about her in time, we would have adopted you together."

"That's why I have to do this, Mom. We both felt abandoned when we were taken away from our mother. Sarah and I used to talk for hours and hours about what we were going to do when we saw her again, how much fun it would be. But when our mother never came back and they took Sarah away, I felt like I had been abandoned all over again. I don't want any other kids to feel like that." Tracey's eyes glistened.

Granddad said gruffly, "That damn fire. If it hadn't burned all the adoption records, perhaps we could have found a way to locate your sister for you."

Natalie reached over to hold Tracey's hand. "You don't need to relive that anymore, darling, now that you've done all of this for other children."

"If she knew about it, I think my birth mother would be proud of Sarah's House too."

"Now, that's a pity," Grams said sadly, "that no one ever found her either."

Tracey thought, *They'll never know — when I finally found my mother, she had a new family and a new life. Maybe if I had found her after Sarah's House opened, she would have been proud of me. Maybe she would have said, 'Hello, Tracey, I'm Maggie Wilson. I'm your mother, and I'm so proud of you. I want to take you home to meet my family — my husband and my son. They'll be excited to meet you.' Then I could have been part of that family too. But she didn't even recognize me. When we stood in that dark parking lot and I told her I was her son, she didn't want me. She rejected me — again. That was the third time she'd abandoned me. And I was devastated. I was so angry. So, I killed her.*

Chapter Seven

May to November 2002

The Rendezvous

Washington DC

Isabelle opened the taxi door and swung her legs out. Her hand rested on the roof, and she stood still in the warm spring air, looking at the exclusive restaurant on Capitol Hill. *Victor will probably be here. I shouldn't have come.* She straightened her shoulders and scolded herself, *Don't be such a coward. That was eight years ago. You're here for Frank,* and she paid the driver.

The maître d' showed her to the private room and held the door for her with a slight inclination of his head. "Ma'am." Isabelle took a deep breath before entering. Soft classical music was playing in the background as she glanced around.

An enormous bouquet of spring flowers sat on a round table in the window facing the street. Six upholstered chairs were arranged at a rectangular table, each set at a forty-five-degree angle to the table's edge. Crisp napkins folded to resemble roses sat atop the charger at each place, and there were enough knives, forks and spoons for a royal banquet. Against the back wall, a long, antique table stood between two doors, doubling as a bar and a serving station. A waiter stood quietly at one end of the table, his hands held loosely behind his back.

I'm glad I made it before lunch was served. Isabelle's eyes drifted across the room, and she saw Frank just as he saw her. She gave him a finger wave. He returned it and flashed his huge white smile. He touched his mom's shoulder and pointed at Isabelle. "Mom, she made it."

She walked over to the two of them and gave Patricia a kiss on each cheek. "Hello, Mrs. Tomas."

Patricia's eyes lit up. "Hello, my dear. You look lovely. I can't believe you just stepped off a plane from Europe a few hours ago. Thank you for coming all this way. It means so much to Frank – to all of us. It's a shame that Rick had to stay on in Hamburg."

"Yeah, I miss my brother," Frank added.

"I know. He's been very busy with work, and he's defending

his dissertation this week. They are slave drivers at his school."

"He works too hard. When I get to Europe that'll change," Frank snickered.

Patricia said, "Dear, not everyone has had your advantages. Isabelle, it's too bad you'll be here and not with Rick for your anniversary."

"Working on a cruise line means I'm gone six weeks at a shot. I can't count how many special days I've missed," Isabelle said. "We're always celebrating things a little early or a little late."

"I hear from your mom that your job is everything you had hoped for."

"It is. I can't imagine doing anything else. How are you? How's my mom?"

"I'm fine. And everyone back home is doing well." Patricia put her arms around Isabelle and said, "Beatriz asked me to give you a hug when I saw you."

On the far side of the room, Victor stood alone with his drink in one hand as he watched the two women talk quietly. He looked at Isabelle in her stylish, black summer dress with a square neck and large covered buttons down the front, light, tastefully applied makeup, her blond hair pulled up in a simple French twist, her high, tan heels accentuating her long legs. She carried a small clutch in her hand and a light shawl hung over one arm. *My, she's grown into a beautiful, confident, elegant woman.* He watched her walk over to the table in the window and drop the tiny purse and shawl on a delicate chair standing next to it. He thought back to the way she'd been eight years ago, when she was growing out of her awkward teenage body with an uncertain sense of her presence.

Patricia went over to talk to Alan as Isabelle returned to Frank and threw her arms around his neck.

"Girlfriend, you made it." Frank gave her a peck on the mouth and wrapped his arms around her in a long hug.

"I'm so sorry I missed your graduation ceremony. My flight was delayed out of Frankfurt, and so we were late arriving at Dulles, and the traffic was horrendous. I had to stop at my hotel for a quick shower and to change."

"I'm just happy you got here."

It felt so right, having his arms around her again. "I wouldn't have missed seeing you today, boyfriend."

Frank let her go and reached out his hand. "Mindy, I need to introduce you to my best friend, Isabelle."

Mindy came over to them. "I've heard so much about you. Frank is very fond of you. He tells endless stories about when the two of you were growing up." She looked at him and back to Isabelle, "He says you were inseparable."

Isabelle reached out to shake her hand, "It's so nice to meet you too. Frank told me about you the last time we talked. He said he had met the most wonderful woman."

Mindy turned to Frank and put her hand on the back of his neck. "You're so sweet, honey." Isabelle looked at her, big eyes accentuated with just a light coat of mascara and long, wavy blond hair. *She's so his type.*

Frank's father stood in the middle of the room talking with Patricia. "Excuse me," Isabelle said to them, "I need to go say hello to your dad," and she walked over to Alan with her hand outstretched.

"Mr. Tomas, thank you for inviting me to this celebration." She shook his hand.

Alan pulled her in, giving her a kiss on the cheek, "You don't need to stand on ceremony with me, Isabelle." He grimaced as his phone vibrated. With a brief glance at the screen, he excused himself, "I'm sorry, I have to take this call." Already talking, he left the room. Patricia raised her eyebrows and shook her head as she watched him walk away.

Isabelle overheard Frank say, "Uncle, look who's here! I told you she would make it."

Victor came over, and with both of her hands in his, he gave her a kiss on each cheek. "It's good to see you again, Isabelle."

Isabelle breathed a small sigh of relief at the warmth in his voice. *Perhaps this won't be so awkward after all.* "Victor, you look well."

Patricia said, "You don't have a drink. What will you have, my dear?"

"A pinot grigio, please. A *very* large glass. It's been a long, long day."

Patricia nodded in agreement. "We'll have two pinot grigios. Very large," she said to the waiter as she gestured to herself and Isabelle.

Alan returned and looked around to make sure everyone had a drink in their hand. "I would like to make a toast." The room grew quiet. "Frank, or should I call you *Doctor* Tomas now?" Frank stood up tall, and Mindy reached over for his hand. "You worked hard, and all that work has paid off. *Summa cum laude.* Your mother and I are very proud. But now, with your education out of the way, it's time for you to enter the real world and put that expensive PhD to use. I'm looking forward to having you come to work for me at the bank. I have great plans for you."

"Thanks, Dad. I have great plans for the future too." Frank rested his hand on his wrist briefly.

Isabelle raised her glass and added, "Here's to Frank. The smartest man I know. Congratulations, boyfriend."

The group continued to chat for a while, and then the waiter came over to Patricia. "The first course is ready to serve, ma'am." He motioned to the table.

Patricia turned to them. "You all must be very hungry. Let's sit down and relax and enjoy this meal. Alan and I have always found the food here to be very good."

As they began to move toward the table, Victor came up behind Frank and put his hand on his shoulder. In a low voice, he said, "Son, I'm so proud of you. I didn't want to make a toast and antagonize your dad, but I want you to know that. I know you found school boring, and it wasn't easy to study for all those years, but you did it."

Frank turned toward Victor. "Your support was what kept me going, Uncle. I'm glad I was close to New York and able to see you so often over the years."

"Me too. Come on, I'm starving. Let's not keep everyone waiting."

Alan was moving toward Isabelle's chair when Victor stepped in and pulled it out instead. He leaned over and said quietly, "You look stunning, Isabelle."

Alan glared at Victor as though he had no place at the table and certainly no right to pull out the chair for Isabelle. Victor said to him in a calm voice, "It's not about us today, Alan, it's about your son." Alan's face reddened with anger, and he abruptly took the chair to Isabelle's left and sat.

"Thank you, Victor," Isabelle said as he seated her.

Once Victor had taken his seat to Isabelle's right, Patricia touched him on the arm to get his attention. Isabelle noticed and quickly turned toward Alan. "Mr. Tomas, how long will you be in the States?" she asked. They chatted comfortably, catching up on the years since she'd last been home, about what was happening in Brasília, about the places she'd visited in Europe.

Patricia said to Victor, "I'm so sorry about that. I was hoping that Alan would have given up his grudge. We're both so happy in Brasília and have been for years. When you sold our place in New York, it was a blessing in disguise. I realize you did it partly as a favor to me, so I could return home, and I'm very grateful. It's very late in coming but thank you. And Alan likes it there, more so than the States, I'd say. I just wish he would admit it." Patricia shook her head sadly.

"You know, for some people, it just takes longer," Victor said matter-of-factly. "It's okay." His voice warmed and he looked into her eyes, "It's good to finally see you again."

"Victor, you haven't changed one bit in all these years. You're still a flirt. And you're as handsome as ever."

"You've always been the most attractive woman in the room, Patricia. I'm only sorry that Alan got you first," and he put his hand over hers for a brief moment.

She touched his hand as she gave him a little smile. "We'll talk later," and she turned to talk with Frank.

As afternoon turned to evening, following their long meal, they all stood outside the restaurant saying goodbye.

Isabelle hugged Frank's parents. "Thanks, Mr. Tomas, Mrs. Tomas. What a wonderful way to celebrate Frank's graduation."

Patricia asked, "Can we give you a ride to your hotel, Isabelle?"

"Thank you, but I think I'm going to go for a walk to work off some of that fabulous meal."

After saying goodbye, Isabelle, Victor, Frank and Mindy watched as Frank's parents climbed into their town car. They all stood waving as the Tomases pulled away into the traffic.

"Congratulations again, Doctor, I knew you'd come through with flying colors. Welcome to the world of those of us who work for a living." Isabelle gave Frank a quick hug.

"I'll see you in Europe next month after I get settled."

"Before you go, boyfriend, can I talk to you over here?" She took his hand and led him several yards away.

"What's up, girlfriend?" Frank frowned as Isabelle's voice grew intense.

Mindy tilted her head toward them. "Looks serious," she said to Victor.

"Mmmhmm, they are like brother and sister, always going on about something," he responded, and they watched. Frank's complexion turned beet red, and he began jabbing his finger in her face. *Just like his father. All that anger.*

Isabelle knocked Frank's hand away and continued speaking in a low tone. She put her hands on her hips and raised her voice, "I'm through. You don't understand, Frank. You have no idea what you're talking about."

He said something and then shook his head vigorously, stepped back from her and raised his hand with his palm facing her. "I'm done, Isabelle." Without saying another word, he turned on his heel, stomped over to Mindy and grabbed her hand. "Come on. We're fucking outta here." He pulled her down the street. Isabelle watched them walk away, Mindy's hair swinging, her long legs trying to keep pace with Frank's.

Victor raised his hand to wave goodbye to Frank, but there was no one there to say goodbye to.

Isabelle took a deep breath, tugged her wedding band off her finger and dropped it into her purse. "Whew. Now, I *really* need that walk."

"May I join you?" he said.

Isabelle swallowed, suddenly nervous at being alone with him, and then, regaining her equanimity, she said, "I'm heading down to the Mall. I remember it being peaceful at this time of the evening. I would welcome your company, Victor."

They wandered down through the neighborhood toward the

majestic Capitol building. Finally, Isabelle broke the silence. "I have to vent. All I wanted was to let Frank know about my divorce. I thought he would support me, or, at least, be able to see both sides. Instead, he lost his temper and defended Rick. I suppose he sees it as a betrayal of his relationship with Rick. He's snapped at me in the past sometimes, but he was very angry this time. His outbursts make me uncomfortable."

"Me too. He came up to see me a lot while he was at Georgetown, after you all got your master's degrees and went your separate ways. During that time, he began to lose his temper more and more easily. Usually, it was over something his father had done."

"Between my marriage and career, I haven't had much time for him since I graduated. But hopefully he'll get over this once we spend some time together when he moves to Europe."

They came around the Capitol building to the side facing the Mall, and Isabelle sat down on the steps. Victor sat beside her. Slipping her feet from her shoes, Isabelle wiggled her toes. She looked down the length of the Mall toward the Washington monument and sighed heavily. "I promised Rick I would tell Frank while I was here. I know they're close, but I didn't expect him to take it so badly."

"But Frank can be friends with both of you, whether or not you're married. Why do you think he was so angry?"

"There was more – he thought Rick and I should have kids right away. He has an image in his head of what marriage ought to be. And he wanted to be Uncle Frank so badly."

"Those decisions were for you and Rick to make. Frank doesn't get a vote. And besides, someday you may have kids, and he still could become Uncle Frank."

"Well, probably not." Isabelle looked down at her hands, embarrassed to continue. "I had an abortion, Victor, a badly botched one when I was eighteen. It wasn't long before we came to visit you in New York. They told me that I probably wouldn't be able to have kids. It seems like they were right because Rick and I never used any protection, and I never got pregnant."

"I'm so sorry, Isabelle."

"Rick said it didn't matter, but it seems it did. Rick does want to have kids, after all. I never told Frank before, but he kept pushing and pushing me back there. I was so frustrated, and finally, I just blurted it out."

"Ouch! Frank's beliefs – marriage is for life and abortion is murder – those come from his father."

"Exactly. That's why I've kept it to myself all these years. But honestly, I don't know if he's angrier about my divorce or my abortion. Regardless, I'm just glad it's finally out in the open." Isabelle stared up at the clear sky that had begun to deepen to sapphire. "Let's walk some more."

They strolled down the Mall, on past the reflecting pool and then by the Washington Monument, enjoying the warm May evening. Isabelle was surprised by how easy it was, how much she was enjoying his company again.

They stopped at the Vietnam Veterans Memorial, and Isabelle watched as Victor searched for and found a name, tracing it with his fingers, reading it silently. Tears gathered in his eyes, and he said, to himself as much as to Isabelle, "He was the older brother of my high-school girlfriend. He wasn't even walking point that day. They just popped up out of the jungle and started firing at them. He was hit. He didn't stand a chance." His voice choked, "Then his lieutenant had to go back to his tent and write a letter telling his parents and family that Bobby was gone. It was so close to the end of the war. But he didn't make it. He was such a good guy. They were a wonderful family, but they weren't ever the same after that. There was always something – someone – missing. It really tested them. Damn war, anyhow!" Tears seeped down his cheeks.

Isabelle stretched out her hand to comfort him and then dropped it to her side. She stood silently as he pulled out his handkerchief and wiped his eyes. He cleared his throat. "I'm sorry. I guess it was seeing his name on that wall. It makes it so personal. I don't usually get that emotional."

"Is that why Tom and the others you talk to in Central Park are important to you?"

One corner of his mouth turned up in that little smile that she still remembered after all those years. He gave a short nod, "It is, and so, a few years back, when I began growing my business, I hired Tom and gradually, he helped me bring on a small handful of veterans from the park. The guys I hired were ready for change. Not all of them are. So many are still too damaged by what they experienced in the war. It makes me angry and sad, but at least I can help a few."

"That's splendid, Victor."

"I learned about a program called Housing First. It starts by providing people with basic necessities, like food and a place to live. With those needs taken care of, they can look toward the next steps – personal goals, quality-of-life issues, jobs, dealing with substance abuse and so on. When I volunteered for them, I saw how successful their program could be, what change it can bring about.

"So, I took part of the second floor of my warehouse and converted it into small apartments. Somewhere these guys can live, side by side with others who understand what they're going through. So now, they have a place to live and a job to provide for other necessities."

"You're so kind and generous."

"No, no, I wanted to do more than just hand out twenty-dollar bills. It was time for me to become involved."

They paused in front of the Lincoln Memorial to pay their respects and read some of the words engraved into the walls. And then Isabelle began to recite quietly, "'*that the government of the people by the people for the people shall not perish from this earth.*' Frank made me memorize The Gettysburg Address in its entirety when I was in high school, and we were studying different governments, their histories and political systems. That language is beautiful, like poetry." She gave Victor a sideways glance.

He caught her eye and smiled, remembering how he'd read his own poetry to Isabelle so long ago.

"Let me take you to my favorite monument." They wandered a little farther to the Korean War Memorial. "Rick and I came to see Frank one winter. We visited all the monuments. It was beautiful."

As they stood in front of the field of nineteen soldiers made of stainless steel, Isabelle described the scene. "There was about a foot of snow on the ground, the air was misty, it was just dusk, and these ghostly soldiers were walking toward us out of the mist, out of the past." She beckoned with her hands, as though inviting them to her.

"They felt so real, it gave me goosebumps." She rubbed her arms, recalling that evening.

Victor watched her closely as she spoke. Then they made their way to the Pool of Remembrance and sat on a bench, looking silently across the water at the United Nations wall, etched with figures of armed forces from that same war.

"Shall we walk on around the Tidal Basin and visit a different Tom? There's a beautiful view of the Mall from old Tom Jefferson's monument."

"That's quite a hike," replied Isabelle as she looked down at her stylish but impractical shoes. "I'm not sure my feet can take it, and the city isn't the place to take these off and walk barefoot. I think we'll need to save old Tom for another time."

As they walked past the Ellipse and toward Lafayette Square, Victor asked, "Where are you staying?"

"A block this way."

"I'm a block this other way."

They laughed.

"What if we split the difference and have a nightcap here before we head back?" She pointed to a small bar, and they found a quiet table outside in the mild evening.

Victor pulled out a chair for her. *That young girl I knew is all grown up now. The little black dress that clings in all the right places. I'm glad she still doesn't wear a lot of makeup. Not a lot of jewelry, just that silver chain and simple silver earrings.*

Victor took a sip of his drink. He looked down at the table and then at Isabelle. He leaned toward her. "I need to say this – I'm so sorry about—"

"Victor, I'm the one who should be apologizing. I behaved like a spoiled child."

"Let's put it behind us, shall we?"

"Thank you." She breathed a small sigh of relief. *A lot has happened in those eight years.*

They fell into comfortable conversation, like when she'd visited him in New York. While they talked, Isabelle caught Victor looking at her intently. Her eyes met his, and they held each other's gaze for a long moment before he looked away down the street and then back at her. His eyes followed the neckline of her dress, resting on her smooth skin, noticing the sheen of perspiration on her chest, the way it rose as she took a long breath.

"It's warm this evening," he said.

Isabelle watched him loosen his tie and unbutton the top button of his shirt. She watched the pulse beating in his throat. She watched how he swallowed. And she watched the movement of the muscle in his jaw. Strains of Puccini floated out from the bar, and she said, "I remember this was playing at your house the day we arrived in New York. For me, I remember that visit whenever I hear this piece."

Victor smiled. "Shall we have another?" he asked, pointing at their glasses.

"Why not? I have nowhere to be tonight. And it's been too nice an evening to end early."

With one finger, Victor stroked the pale line against the tan on her ring finger and said, "Tell me about you and Rick."

She drew a sharp breath at his touch. And then she told him how good it had been in the beginning, before they got married. How they'd gradually grown apart. He was going to school to finish his PhD and working the rest of the time, while Isabelle traveled six weeks at a stretch.

"That's not an easy life."

"At the end, we both realized that – all through college, right until our marriage – it had always been four of us, the four amigos. And when we were just two, it wasn't as good anymore."

Isabelle went on to tell him how Rick had been so happy in Germany, in the bustling port city of Hamburg where they'd lived – that German beer had been his favorite. But the planned parks there weren't enough for her. How she longed for greenery and open space and the temperature and pace of life in southern France. Ironically, she told him, she'd fallen in love with it while on her honeymoon. She told him how she had finally found the house there that she had always wanted, a place to spend time between cruises, but that Rick didn't want to go there to live. And then he had decided that he did want to have children, but it never happened. Finally, they both agreed it wasn't working, and they separated and then divorced.

Victor took her hand between his, "I'm so sorry."

"Don't be. I feel a great sense of relief."

Victor looked into her eyes again, and she didn't look away. He put some cash for their drinks under a glass, and then they got up to leave.

They stood on the corner, and she swallowed hard when she heard his breath catch in his throat. A shiver ran along her spine.

He took another breath. *One night together?* "Your hotel or mine?"

"Yours."

Victor hooked her little finger with his, and without talking, they walked toward his hotel. They walked, their arms pressed against each other, in silence, their thoughts on what lay ahead.

I've never felt this way with anyone else, she thought.

They reached his floor, and he led her down the hallway to his room, their little fingers still linked, only their arms touching.

She put her purse and wrap on the small table in the entry to his suite and turned to watch him while she reached up and took the pins out of her hair and put them in her purse, as she combed through it with her fingers, and it returned to her natural curls. She watched – as Victor prolonged his anticipation, taking his wallet from the inner pocket of his suit coat and laying the wallet and key card on the table, aligning them precisely with the edge. As he slid his arms from his suit coat and hung it carefully in the closet. As he bent over and untied and removed his shoes, setting them side by side and closed the closet door. As his fingers carefully unknotted his tie and removed it and folded it in half and then in half again and laid it on the table.

And as he put his hand on the strap to his watch, preparing to unfasten it, Isabelle couldn't stand it any longer, "Victor."

Then she was in front of him, and her arms were around his neck, pulling him to her. Her mouth pressed against his, and their world narrowed – to touch and sensation, to memories of one night, eight years earlier – he backed her against the wall, his fingers tangled in her hair, his hands remembering the shape of her head, his mouth remembering the taste of her, overlaid now with the flavor of their nightcaps, his body remembering hers as she pressed against him in eagerness – mouths, lips, tongues, a world framed by their desire.

Victor growled softly with pleasure.

Isabelle murmured against his mouth, "I want you – now."

He rested his mouth against the sensitive skin below her jaw, her pulse pounding under his lips. His breath came harder as he felt her fingers at his waist, unfastening his belt, the button on his trousers, the zipper, finding, touching him through the silk of his boxers.

His fingers slid her soft knit dress up her thighs in a long, slow caress. As he lifted her leg over his hip, Isabelle's tan shoe fell to the carpet with a soft thud. With her leg around his waist, he slipped aside the wisp of lace that covered her and paused against her for a moment, waiting. "Yes," she gasped, and he entered her with an urgency neither of them had expected.

§

Isabelle slept with her head on Victor's shoulder, one hand tucked beneath him, and her other arm flung across his chest. He held her hand in his. Her leg was thrown over his thigh, and her toes rested on top of his foot. His lips softened in pleasure as he woke and buried his face in her long hair, inhaling the smell of her. "I love you, Izzy. There's never been anyone else since you," he whispered softly.

He felt her toes curl against the top of his foot. "I love you too, Old Man," she murmured, her lips against his skin.

And in the thin watery light before dawn, they made slow morning love.

They ordered breakfast from room service and talked and talked and talked.

Then Isabelle explained that she had shopping to do. Her attempt to do a ten-piece wardrobe after her divorce had been an abject failure. So, she desperately needed to buy clothes – and shoes, of course. "What was I thinking, getting rid of all my shoes when Rick and I separated?"

The sheet wrapped around her legs, Isabelle reached over and snagged the last triangle of toast from the plate, smeared it with a thick layer of damson plum jam and took a huge bite.

"Why do you take such enormous bites, Izzy?"

"Because when something tastes so good, you have to fill your mouth with it," she said and broke off a small bite, and then another, and then another and fed them to him.

He put the empty tray on the floor beside the bed, and they made love again in a tangle of sheets and arms and legs, with mouths that tasted of toast and coffee.

"Come back to Manhattan with me. You can shop there."

§

Southern France

Isabelle reached for the glass from Victor, "Thank you." Her face glowed. "I didn't want to get out of bed, but I was gasping for something to drink." She took a gulp. "There's nothing like sparkling water over ice to quench your thirst." With one toe, she rocked her chair slightly, a look of complete satisfaction on her face.

Before taking a seat next to her, with a glass in his right hand, Victor reached out to stroke Isabelle's reddened cheek, "Whisker burn."

"Six weeks is a long time. My face got out of practice," she turned her face into his palm and kissed it.

He sat down, looking around, taking it all in. The wide planks of the porch creaked slightly as he pushed his chair back and forth on its rockers. "This place is much better than I pictured when you described it to me in New York."

"I feel so peaceful, Victor, so at home when I'm here."

"I can see the attraction for you. I can see why you say it feeds your soul. I only wish I could have arrived with you yesterday."

"But that gave me time to sign the paperwork and close on this house and take care of a long list of little tasks, like grocery shopping, making up the bed, settling in, so now, we can spend the rest of my break focusing on us. Oh, I'm so excited to finally share this little place with you."

"Little? My word, you could sleep at least six or eight people here comfortably."

"I know. Isn't that great?" She waggled her fingers toward the orchard that began not far from the other side of the driveway. "The pears over there aren't ripe yet, but when we come back in September, we'll be able to eat them right from the trees. We will come back in September, won't we? We'll keep a couple of bushels in the cellar, and the rest will go off to market. Just imagine all the delicious things we can do with them."

"We? Unless you've learned to cook, I think that 'we' is going to be me."

Isabelle gave a delighted giggle. "You're right. Imagine all the wonderful things *you* can make for me with those lovely, lovely pears."

Isabelle glanced over at him as he took a sip of his water. And then she pulled a sprig of lavender from the vase on the table between them and crushed it between her fingers, holding it close to her nose with a long intake of breath. "There's nothing like fresh lavender. Oh, smell this, Victor." She reached her hand over toward his face and waved it gently. "Close your eyes and breathe in."

"Mmmm. That is wonderful."

Isabelle began to fidget, running her finger up and down the arm rest. *I guess I should just jump in and tell him.* "Sooo, Victor—"

"Mmmhmm." Victor had leaned his head against the chair back, and he looked at her fondly, thinking about how happy he was to be there with her. "Now, I have a place to stay here, and you have a place to stay in New York. We should be drinking champagne to celebrate. After all, we are in France. I'll get it, shall I?" He stood up and went into the house.

Isabelle put her elbows on the arms of the chair and tipped her head forward, holding it with her fingertips. Closing her eyes, she took a deep breath. *He has no idea what's coming. This is so hard. I don't even know how to start. I have no idea how he's going to react. Maybe he'll leave me, and that would be the end after we've barely started again.*

Victor came back out with two champagne flutes and the bottle perched on a tray. Isabelle moved their water glasses and the vase, and he carefully set the tarnished silver tray down on the table between them.

Delaying, she touched the silver tray. "This will clean up nicely, I think."

He nodded as he sat down and began to pour from the bottle. "Victor—"

He stopped and looked at her.

"I don't know where to begin. This is so difficult for me. It's personal, and—"

"I have the same problem, talking about personal things, especially the difficult ones. But this is me, Izzy, I'm not just people, I'm the man who is head over heels for you."

Isabelle let out the breath she was holding.

Victor continued to pour the champagne. "So, just tell me. I won't bite. I promise."

She took another deep breath and her eyes moistened, "Don't be so kind. I might cry."

Now that she has this place, is she breaking up with me? So soon. Don't jump to conclusions, Victor. Wait to hear what she has to say.

Isabelle pressed the heels of her hands against her eyes, took a deep breath and blurted out, "I'm pregnant."

"With me?"

"Of course. Yes." Then Isabelle quickly recited the script she'd written in her head. "I hadn't been feeling well. I was throwing up in the mornings. I took a pregnancy test yesterday and couldn't believe it. So, after I did the paperwork for the farmhouse, I took a second test. It was the same. We made this baby in New York, Victor, but we've never talked about kids. We haven't even talked about whether or not we want a permanent relationship. We're just getting to know each other again. I don't know how you feel about this baby. I would never tie you down or force you into any arrangement that you're not comfortable with. But I'm keeping it. I'll never have another abortion. And I won't put it up for adoption. My mom can come help. Chloe Rose can help me. She can write from here. I can hire a nanny or whatever. Lots of single women raise children."

"You've thought this through, haven't you?"

"Of course. Yes. All night."

His face softened. "I could help, you know."

"What do you mean? With money? I don't understand."

Victor took her hand and pulled her over onto his lap and kissed her. "Izzy, I love you." He kissed her again. "I want to be the father of our child."

Isabelle pulled away and wrinkled her forehead. *How is this going to work? I'm not going to live in a big city. I've tried city life before and hated it. I'll visit but not live there.*

Victor saw the uncertainty on her face. "What's wrong? I told you I wouldn't bite."

"Where would we live? I need to live here, but your business and your whole life are in New York. And we hardly know each other."

"You're my life now. When I sent you away, all those years ago, I knew it was the right thing to do then, but I regretted it so. I thought I had ruined any opportunity for us, that I'd lost you forever. So, I filled my time with work, trying to forget." He tightened his arms around her. "Ah, my Izzy."

"Old Man, if we could live here, I would be the happiest person on earth."

"We can live anywhere we want. We'll figure that out." Victor stroked her hair and then pulled back to look at her. "To be honest, I'm nervous about being a father. I watched Alan raise Frank, and it was so toxic between them. Over the years, I've seen the impact it has had on him. He's becoming more and more angry. I don't want to be that kind of father."

"You aren't Alan, and we'll do it together." Isabelle took Victor's face in her hands, happy tears glistening in her eyes and rested her lips against his in a soft kiss. "We'll be a team," she said, her voice barely a whisper.

"Should we get married?"

"I don't want marriage again. I want a partner. Someone who is a friend and a lover and a parent to our child. Someone who will make decisions with me about life events – *with* me. I was gone so much that Rick made critical decisions for us – and I wasn't included."

"Marriage isn't what's important to me either. It's you and this child. I want to be the best father possible and to be there for you, however you need me."

Isabelle tucked her head into his shoulder. "Thank you," she murmured and gave a happy sigh.

He buried his head in her hair and said, "I love you, Izzy."

"I love you too."

§

Is loving each other enough to make this work? We haven't talked about any arrangements since I told him I was pregnant. He's had days to think. Why hasn't he said anything about where he wants to live? There are so many things we have to plan for. Do I need to begin looking for someone to help me raise this child when he's in New York? Should I call Chloe Rose to talk to her about this? Isabelle's hormones surged as she moved about the kitchen. Teetering on the verge of tears, she began to make tea while she waited for Victor to come downstairs. "I miss my coffee. This herbal tea isn't going to make me feel any better." She fumbled with the cup, and it fell to the floor and shattered into pieces.

Victor heard the kettle whistling and noticed that it hadn't stopped. *Where did she go?*

He rushed down the stairs, buttoning his shirt as he went, to find Isabelle sitting on the floor with her face in her hands, crying, shards of her broken cup spread around her. He reached over to turn off the burner and then leaned down. "Hold onto my neck. I don't want you to cut your bare feet." With her in his arms, he backed through the screen door onto the porch and sat in the rocking chair with her on his lap.

Isabelle continued to sob. Her head tucked into his shoulder and his cheek against her hair, Victor rocked her slowly, "Shhh. Shhh. Whatever is wrong, we'll figure it out."

Isabelle looked up, hiccupping and sniffling and said in a small voice, "I want coffee, and you won't talk to me," and she put her head on his shoulder, sobbing pitifully again.

Completely bewildered, he continued to rock her. "I don't know what you mean. We talk day and night."

She raised her wet face again. "But we don't talk about anything important. We don't talk about our plans. We need to have a plan. I have to go back to work and quit my job. A baby can't grow up without a mother. I'll have to abandon all my career plans that I've worked so hard for – for such a long time. How are you going to manage with a business in New York and a baby in southern France

– that's an ocean apart? Victor, I'm so scared. I don't know what I'm going to do," she wailed.

"I told you, we'll figure it out. I've been doing a lot of thinking about it."

She jumped off his lap, walked down to the end of the porch and then came back and stood in front of him with her hands on her hips, her face stormy. "Victor, I told you I want to have a partnership. Didn't you hear me? We have to talk about what you're thinking. You can't keep it all in your head and then just give me your final decision. I told you I won't have that. We have to do this together or there's no us."

Victor stood up and pulled her to him in a long hug. Isabelle stood there, still angry, with her hands by her side. "Come on, Izzy, let's go for a walk."

They paused at the edge of the orchard, and Victor looked back at the sprawling stone house, the smaller outbuildings of the same light grey stone and the wall joining it all together. His eyes paused at the sagging blue gate. *That needs to be rehung. I'll need to get some basic tools and paint. I can see that this house, as charming as it is, is going to be quite a project. But we'll just do a little bit here and there until it's exactly the way we want it.*

They walked on into the orchard, in the shade beneath the pear trees. "What are you thinking? I can't read your mind. This place," and she gestured at the property, "the peace and quiet, the smell of the orchard and the grass, the air. The people in town. *Here* is where I'm raising this baby."

"It is nice," he agreed as he reached up and plucked a leaf from a nearby branch.

He took Isabelle's hand and put the leaf in it. As he closed her fingers around it, she calmed down a little. "Victor, this place feeds my soul." She looked up into his face. "But is nice going to be enough for you?"

"I don't know." Victor lifted her hand holding the leaf and pressed it to his lips. Then, with his eyes watching hers, he went on, "The other day I told you I was nervous about being a father. But in reality, I'm terrified, and I've been in complete emotional paralysis for the last few days thinking about it. My dad wasn't a good role model. Alan is a horrible father. What if I'm just like them? I'm so afraid, Izzy."

"Ah, Victor." She reached up and caressed his cheek.

"That's been my dilemma – my fear versus my love for you." He closed his eyes for a moment and then looked at her again. "What I do know is that I love you more than New York City. More than Central Park, even."

A tiny smile pulled at the corners of her mouth as she asked, "That much?"

"Mmmhmm."

"Then, we'll figure it out, Victor – somehow. But I need a plan. At least, I need to feel like we'll have a plan. How are we going to do this? Your rug business – I know how much you love it, the way you know the history of each one that passes through, how you tell your customers the stories behind them all. You can't give it up."

"That's part of what I've been thinking about." He looked around and out to the mountains off in the distance. "But this place is beautiful. I'd like to give being here with you a try."

"Can you really be happy here?"

"In truth, I don't know. I've lived in New York City almost my entire life. Maybe it's time for a change. Over the past few days, I've been imagining living here, you, me, our baby. It could work. I promise you, we'll make whatever we decide work – together."

§

Isabelle reached over and hooked her little finger through Victor's. They swung their arms back and forth as they ambled along the street in the small market town. The hem to her bright, poppy-covered sundress brushed against her calves, and the autumn sun reflecting off the weathered grey stone of the buildings that lined the street warmed her arms. Every now and then, she'd lean over to rest her cheek against the shoulder of Victor's soft, old linen shirt and breath in the scent of him. Then she'd exhale a small happy breath, and Victor would glance at her, a smile crinkling the corners of his eyes.

She paused in front of a pile of luscious-looking red apples, stacked in the display in front of the grocer's shop. "Victor, don't these look delicious? Let's buy a few. I have such a craving for apples these days."

"That's a much healthier craving than peanut M&Ms."

"Or ice cream? Or dill pickles?" she added with a grin and sighed, "I guess you found my little chocolate stash."

Victor chuckled deep in his throat. "Little stash? You could survive for two years on a desert island with as much chocolate as you have tucked away in that cabinet. By all means, let's buy lots of those apples. I want you and our little one to be healthy." He glanced down with a fond look at the curve of her stomach that was just beginning to show.

Isabelle picked through the pile to find the ripest and best apples, carefully placing them, one by one, into her net shopping bag, and took them inside to pay. She came back through the door with an apple in her hand and crunched a huge bite from it as she handed the bag to Victor. He smiled at her, shook his head gently and reached over to wipe the juice from the side of her chin with his thumb and licked it thoughtfully.

"No one is going to take it from you," he said as he reached over to swipe the apple from her hand and took a large bite himself.

"No one except you, Old Man," said Isabelle, reaching for the apple that Victor waggled back and forth. "Please, may I have my apple back?"

Victor took another enormous bite and handed it to her. "Good thing you bought so many. This bunch might just get us home before we run out." They looked at each other with a laugh as they munched away, passing the piece of fruit back and forth between them.

They strolled on, their fingers linked again, Isabelle happily finishing the last of the apple, and Victor swinging the net bag in his other hand. Finally, she sighed with contentment and tossed the well-gnawed core into a trash bin along the curb.

An empty storefront caught Victor's eye, and he walked over to the dirty window. He cupped his hands around his eyes to peer inside. His face lit up, and he turned to Isabelle, "I could open a rug shop here. It's a perfect location." He looked up and down the street. "It looks like it gets good traffic, so there'd be a steady flow of passing trade, and I could do some aggressive advertising throughout the region."

She stood beside him, looking in the window and then turned around. "I can just see it, Victor, you here every day – grabbing a coffee from the shop down there," she gestured, 'having lunch in the café over there, and within weeks, you'll know all the other shopkeepers and their stories. I think it's perfect!"

"We would have to hire someone to help with the baby and the housework."

"I'm sure we can find someone, and some days, you can just bring the baby along to the shop."

Victor lifted her hand to his mouth and kissed her fingers. *Maybe this will be enough for him to want to stay*

They made quick stops for meat, butter and a baguette – and a much longer one as they lingered over which cheeses they would buy. With their shopping completed, they returned to where they'd left their bicycles locked to a railing and piled their packages into the baskets on the back.

Isabelle adjusted her straw hat with the ragged brim so it sat more securely on her head, put her leg through to the far pedal of her bicycle and tucked her dress down so it wouldn't blow around as she rode. Victor gave his smart new straw hat a little tug and swung his leg over the seat of his bike.

"I think I like that hat best of all the ones in your collection."

"You know, I think I do too. Ready?" he asked, and at her nod, they cycled down the main street and onto the narrow road that led to their little farm.

"Oh, Victor," called out Isabelle once they were out of town. "You probably should know that I have nothing on under this dress." She flashed a grin at him and pedaled hard, pulling ahead.

"Nothing?" he asked, turning his head as he caught up with her. His bike wobbled for a moment.

"Absolutely nothing. Not a single stitch!" giggled Isabelle and bent over the handlebars, pedaling even harder, panting a little at the exertion.

Victor caught up with her. "Perhaps we should stop over there under those trees so I can verify that." He pointed toward them with his thumb.

Isabelle laughed at him, her white teeth flashing, and rode off with a wave. "No way, Old Man. Race you home!"

They rode into the kitchen courtyard, side by side, their breathing heavy, and propped the bicycles against the wall of the house. Isabelle kicked off her leather sandals and walked across the smooth paving stones to the oversized fountain set in the middle of the space. She hiked her dress up above her knees, sat on the wall and swung her legs over to bathe her feet in the cool water. "Now, that is heaven. I'm so glad the previous owner put this fountain here. We have to bring Chloe Rose to visit. She would think it was very international," Isabelle said with a laugh.

"I can't wait to meet her."

He rolled up the legs to his worn khaki pants, stepped into the fountain basin and sat beside her on the wide stone wall.

Victor reached down into the water and rinsed the dust from her legs and then his, and then he stroked his cool, wet hand over her shoulder blades. Little goosebumps raised on her arms at the chill, and Isabelle leaned against him. "We have a good life here, don't we?"

"Yes, we do," he said as he tipped her face to his and kissed her. "Now, let's get that food inside. Because I need to see what all this 'nothing' is about." He chuckled as Isabelle scooped a handful of water and threw it at him before she ran into the house. Victor splashed water on his face, wiped it against his sleeve and followed, the string handles of the shopping bags looped over his fingers. He set them on the kitchen island and then, with another kiss, lifted Isabelle and sat her at the other end. "You rest there while I put these things away," he said, hanging their hats on the hooks beside the door, moving back and forth from the counter to the pantry and the ice box. Isabelle leaned back on her hands, her bare feet dangling, and watched his economical movements, waiting for what would come next.

He enjoys the anticipation of things, and so he does all these little tasks, stretching out the time, thinking about what's to come. But that's the way he is. Just watching him, being with him makes me happy.

With everything put away in its place, he came over to the island

and asked with a low growl of pleasure, "Nothing at all? What's that about?"

"Oh, nothing," she said and began to laugh. "Nothing at all."

"Mmmm – nothing, eh?"

"Nope. Nothing," and she laughed harder.

Victor stepped between her knees and slid his fingers into her hair, untangling her long dark-blond braid, and felt the familiar shape of her head in his hands. He pulled her forward, stifling her laughter with a long kiss, one she immediately returned with growing intensity. Her arms slid around his shoulders, and he picked her up and stood her in front of him. His hands caressed her back in lengthy, unhurried stokes as he moved his mouth to that spot where her neck met her shoulder. Her pulse pounded in her throat as he bit down gently.

"Ahhh, when you do that—" she moaned and tipped her head to the side. His mouth rested on her neck, his breath coming faster, while her fingers unfastened his belt, the button on his trousers, slid down the zipper and cradled him in the silk of his boxer shorts. Gently, he bit down again and then turned her around to face the island.

"Nothing?" whispered Victor against the back of her neck. "Bend over, my Izzy."

Isabelle leaned forward, and the skirt of her dress tickled her legs. She bent one arm, so her cheek rested on her hand and slid the other low on her belly to cradle the mound growing there.

His fingers slipped her dress up her thighs and over her hips. "Ahhh, nothing at all."

§

"We finally have a plan," Isabelle said in a bright voice, filled with laughter. "Now we can tell people. We're shacking up in southern France, we're having a baby out of wedlock and you're keeping the business and the brownstone in New York. We'll visit when we can. It's perfect." She began to laugh out loud at her silliness.

Victor joined in her laughter. "Yes, Izzy. It's a perfect plan. It will be even more perfect when I open my rug shop here."

"I'm just a planning kinda gal. And that makes it an even more perfect plan."

"Oh? I hadn't noticed." Victor wrapped his arms around Isabelle and spun her around, "Shall I call Tom?"

"Yep, go for it."

A few minutes later, Victor was pacing around the living room with the phone in one hand and the receiver in the other. Every time he crossed the room, he kicked the cord out of his way so he wouldn't trip over it.

The weather was still mild, and they'd thrown all the farmhouse windows wide open. Isabelle was perched on the deep windowsill with her toes hooked over the rung of the chair in front of her, and her hair was blowing in the cross-draft.

"Tom, I shared our idea with Izzy. She doesn't want you to feel pressured into running the business when I'm over here, especially once the little one is born." She heard Victor's voice slow down, and she remembered how they'd talked that day in the park, like they had all the time in the world.

Victor gave Isabelle a wink as he listened to Tom's reply. "Mmhmm. That's right. I told her you were all in, but she worries for you." He nodded, "I'll tell her again that you've thought this over for months, and you do want to do it." Sitting down in the chair in front of Isabelle, he placed the telephone on his lap.

He took a sip of water from Isabelle's glass that she'd set on the table next to the chair. "She had another idea – I know, she's always thinking," he chuckled. "We want to offer you a percentage of Tomas Rug Imports – yes, seriously. Listen, Tom, she and I have talked this over, and we want to offer you thirty percent. We insist. You're going to be running the business in my absence, and that frees me to be here with Izzy and the baby and concentrate on opening a second shop without having to worry about what's going on back there in New York. We both agree it's the right thing to do."

Victor covered the receiver and said to Isabelle, "He's so overwhelmed, he's crying."

Leaning over, she rested her hands on his shoulders and whispered into his free ear, "I told you so." Victor reached up and patted her hand.

"Tom, you've earned this. You work hard every day, and

everyone admires you. Since you've started helping me buy the rugs, you've become better at telling their stories than I ever was. You have such a gift with words."

Victor wrapped the receiver's coiled cord around one of his fingers, fiddling with it. "You are very welcome, and yes, I'll pass on your thanks to Izzy. I'll be back in New York in two weeks. No, I'm staying on here for a few days to paint the nursery. We want it to be completely ready when she comes back after her next set of cruises, just in case the baby's early. Yeah, I guess you can never tell, especially with the first one. Mmmhmm, we decided on a light green color. It's called *Pale Summer Pear*." Victor chuckled. "Yes, it's very appropriate with the orchard here. And yes, I can paint. Not very well, but the baby will never know."

He listened for a minute. Shaking his head, he replied, "No, we haven't told him anything yet." Isabelle knew he was talking about Frank. "We wanted to sort out all the details first. You know, it's an easy trip from here to Geneva, and I know he will be excited about Izzy and me and the baby. Okay. Next time we see him, I'll tell him you send your regards – I'll let you go – oh, Izzy sends you her love, Tom – I will. Bye now."

Isabelle smiled at Victor, "Let's go visit Frank next week before I go back to work. Except for Tom, I want him to be the first to know. Even though he'll technically be her cousin, he'll be excited about finally becoming 'Uncle Frank'."

§

Geneva, Switzerland

Frank handed Victor a cold bottle of Stella Artois. "Here you go, Uncle."

"Thanks, son. It's been too long, mmm?"

"Remember that first time you gave me a beer at your house when Isabelle and I visited? That was a Stella. These always bring back good memories." He lifted his bottle toward his uncle. They were standing shoulder to shoulder in front of the huge living room windows, looking out at the lake, and Victor put his arm around Frank's shoulders in a quick hug.

"I'm so excited you're here. When Dad came to Geneva, he didn't even come by. He didn't care about seeing my place. He didn't want to spend any time with me. He just invited me to dinner at his hotel, and we were done in under two hours."

Talking to Frank had become so difficult. It always seemed to end in whining and complaining – or anger. "I talked to Tom earlier this week. He said to say 'hello' to you. He asks about you all the time."

"I still don't understand why he would want to work for you. He had all the freedom in the world. He could have done whatever he wanted whenever he wanted. Now, he's tied down. I bet he hates it."

"He's a hard worker, he is well respected by his coworkers and he likes what he's doing." *Why can't Frank just be happy for Tom?* "So, how are you settling in?"

"Geneva isn't New York City, but I'm getting used to it."

"You're expanding your horizons. Change is good."

"I guess."

Victor took a sip of his beer. "So – have you seen Rick, now that you're in Europe?"

Frank's face lit up, "We've been texting a lot. We're going to have a tennis vacation for a week over New Year's. He just found the perfect tennis resort in Greece. He'll send me all the details later this week."

"That sounds like a lot of fun. I'm glad you two are staying in touch."

"Now that we're both on the same continent and he's done with school, it'll be easier. Did you know he got several good offers last summer after he finally earned his PhD? We're both doctors now, can you believe it? And neither of us have to deal with sick people," Frank snickered. "Anyway, now that he's settled into his new job, he's ready to have some fun. It will be a great trip because we plan to celebrate heavily. In between matches, of course."

"You guys always were like a couple of brothers." Victor looked around. "This apartment is spectacular, Frank. And the view," he shook his head in admiration.

"Personally, I'd prefer to live in a modern high rise downtown, but you can't beat the location of this place. I can do my long-distance runs along the lake, I'm close to my tennis club and I can walk to work."

"New job, new life, new apartment. Seems like a lot's happened since your graduation. Show me around, Frank."

"This building dates back to 1901 but even though it's been renovated a lot since, you'll see quite a bit of period stuff that they left alone." He pointed out the high ceilings. The intricate detail on the plaster molding. The wide arches separating spacious rooms. The floor that squeaked slightly as they walked down the hall. He told Victor about the way the parquet floors were laid in a chevron pattern that is more challenging to install than the more common herringbone. He showed him the balcony off the kitchen with intricate iron railings and a small café table with two chairs.

"This balcony isn't very big, but it's quiet because it faces the courtyard instead of the street. And it is outdoor space," Frank said with a sarcastic laugh. "I sound like Isabelle. Maybe I should grow some flowers."

Frank ended their tour there in the kitchen, pointing out the modern features that had been added during the most recent remodel. He tossed their empty beer bottles into his recycling bin, took two more from his sub-zero, popped the tops and handed one to his uncle. They went back into the living room and sat close to the fireplace.

With his feet propped on the brass fireplace surround, Frank leaned back and closed his eyes. *How am I going to tell Uncle about my other business? Maybe I shouldn't be too worried about it.* He put his hand over the watch on his wrist. *After all, he didn't tell the police about this.*

"Are you still bored, son?"

"I keep myself busy."

"You've been working for your dad for what, four or five months now? How's it going?"

"Just over five months. It's okay. As the European liaison for Dad's bank, I have access to so many events and people."

"That must be fascinating."

"It is." Frank took another swig. *It's not a big deal, I think he'll be okay with it.* He went on after a lengthy pause, "It's great for my other business too."

Puzzled, Victor cocked his head, "Other business? You have time for a second job? I thought your dad would keep you too busy for that."

"My bank job doesn't take a lot of time or effort. I just travel around and attend meetings. I'm supposed to be my dad's eyes and ears over here and to make sure the clients are happy. To be honest, I think he just made up the role. There isn't much to it."

Victor took a slow swallow of his beer. *It's unfortunate. Alan has no idea what Frank is capable of. He should be challenging this boy.*

"You know, Uncle," his voice was cautious, "I've had time to become an entrepreneur. And the work I do for my dad helps with my own business." He glanced sideways at Victor, "It's a win-win."

"What do you mean?"

"I do procurement."

"What do you mean," Victor repeated. "What do you procure?" *I hope it's not what I'm thinking.*

"You procure rugs. I procure – other things people are looking for." Frank gave him a self-satisfied smile.

Victor raised his eyebrows and looked at Frank, a question in his eyes. *Oh, dear.*

"It's quite clever, really. I meet businessmen, their wives and their friends at the events I attend on behalf of the bank. You know, networking parties, holiday gatherings and whatnot. I conduct business for my dad – but I also take notes, mental notes."

"Notes on what?"

"What jewelry the women are wearing. I've been studying jewelry, designers and stones for years and years. I know all the cuts and values, what's in vogue and what's fallen out of fashion, what's real versus fake. I've spent decades improving my skills and knowledge. I'm serious about this, Uncle. It's not just a hobby."

Victor shook his head in disappointment. *Decades? It's too bad he doesn't put that kind of effort into his banking job.* "Why do you do that? Don't tell me—"

"Then I get myself invited to other parties that the same people are going to. I wouldn't steal during a bank event. I wait and go to other affairs to take the jewels."

"Awww, son. You're still stealing? I hoped after you took this watch, that was it." He lifted Frank's wrist and tapped on the Rolex.

Frank snatched his hand away, "You set the precedent when you didn't turn this into the police, when you gave it back to me engraved. I've never stopped. I've been practicing, honing my skills, you might say. I'm very good now. It's what I live for."

Distressed, Victor stared into the fire. *He's a grown man, but this? I can't believe it. He was a good kid, and he's turned into this?*

Oblivious to his reaction, Frank's words tumbled out excitedly, "I've been thinking about you a lot. I'm trying to expand my business. You could join me. I'm already using the inter-office mail in the bank here to get the items," he cleared his throat, "that I procure to brokers in different locations. It's easier than having to go to the post office. And far cheaper. I could send you some of the goods. You could sell them to someone in New York City. It would be a perfect way to get them out of Europe."

Victor leaned toward Frank, and his voice was quiet and cold, "You want me to become involved in this madness, in your thievery? Are you serious?"

"It's good money. And you wouldn't be involved with the stealing."

In disbelief, Victor asked, "Become an accomplice to this illegal, harebrained scheme of yours?"

"Well, you're a bit of a hypocrite, aren't you, Uncle?" he said with a tinge of arrogance in his voice.

Victor narrowed his eyes and tilted his head to one side again. "Hypocrite? What do you mean, Frank?"

"Well, you, with your gambling. Cards, dice, you know, what you and your buddies do at night in your kitchen. I saw them all the time. I saw the money when I stayed with you as a kid. You take risks. This is nothing more than a gamble – on a larger scale, of course."

Victor looked hard at Frank and shook his head. "And you think that is the same. That was just friends having fun. And if there's no cheating, gambling isn't stealing."

He's just like my dad. Always telling me I'm not good enough. "I thought you'd want to do it. We've talked about working together for years.

This is our chance, and all you're doing is putting me down." Frank began pulling the paper off the bottle in his hand. *Why doesn't he want to work with me? He's changed so much. He said maybe we could work together.*

"Frank, the answer is no. Maybe if what you were proposing was legal and above board, I'd want to collaborate with you, but there's no way I'm interested in this. I don't want to take that kind of risk."

"Well, do you know anyone who would want to work with me? Someone you trust? I'm looking for another person in the States – to keep my options open."

"The answer is no. I never imagined you'd get involved in this type of business." Victor took a series of deep breaths, tamping down his anger. *God, I want to turn him in. But I can't, I just can't – he's my nephew.*

"Oh, come on. You've got connections. You must know someone who can handle the big stuff." *My New York buddies are too small fry for what I want.*

"You have so much more potential, son." He shook his head sadly. *I worry about you.* He took another swallow of his beer.

He's fucking passing up the chance of a lifetime and pissing on my plans too. Frank took a long gulp, finishing the last of the beer from his bottle. He held it up. "Want another?"

Victor shook his head.

"Well, I'll be right back." He vanished into the kitchen. The bottle clinked into the recycling, and then Frank reappeared, a fresh beer in his hand. "So, what brings you to Europe, Uncle?"

"I've moved to southern France. I wanted to stop and visit you since I'm so close now."

"Really? There's no big city there, not like New York. What made you do that?"

"My life has changed. Tom is running the business for me. It's early days, but I think it will do quite well with him at the helm."

Frank looked sideways at his uncle. "Why? Your business is what you live for."

"Why don't you and Tom run my New York business together instead of this little sideline of yours. You like Tom, and it could be a good change for you. You'd be able to stop working for your dad.

You could live there. You could live in my brownstone."

Frank looked at his uncle as though he were crazy. "That would make Dad so angry – taking over your business and living in your house. But as tempting as that is, no thanks." *That's like a real job. I don't want to have anything to do with that.*

The doorbell rang.

Victor's face lit up. "I have a surprise for you. I think it's just arrived."

They stood, and Frank went over to the door and pulled it open. He beamed, "Girlfriend! It's been so long. I've missed you."

Isabelle sighed. *Well, he could have reached out to me when he got over his temper tantrum. But that's Frank. It's all about him.*

He gave her a peck on the mouth and a big hug, lifting her off the floor.

Isabelle giggled. "Boyfriend! How have you been?"

He set her down and touched her belly. "What is this?"

"I'm six months pregnant, Frank! I'm due in February. We're having a girl, and we've decided to name her Frankie – after you!"

"Wait. You and Rick got divorced. You guys are back together? You didn't tell me anything. Rick hasn't told me. That sly devil. I'm so happy for the two of you. You are going to be such great parents. Wait, a girl named Frankie? It's not a boy? But Rick said he wanted enough boys for a baseball team. Is Rick parking the car?" He glanced behind her expectantly.

Isabelle closed the door and looked at Frank for a long moment before she said, "No," and touched her stomach. She looked over to Victor and made a little face, "I don't think we did this the right way."

Frank turned his head back and forth, from one to the other with a confused expression on his face. "Wha – what do you mean? What are you talking about?"

Victor walked over to stand beside Isabelle and took her hand. "Isabelle and I have been together since your Georgetown graduation. This is our baby." He stroked her belly affectionately.

"What? That can't be." Frank turned away, thinking about what he had just heard before turning back. "Well, you should have told me at my graduation. We were all there. You could have said you were together then. When you told me that you left Rick, when—"

"We didn't get together until after your graduation luncheon." Isabelle tried to calm him down, "Frank, we want you to be happy for us. Victor and I have moved to southern France together. We're close now, so you can spend a lot of time with us. You can come and spend time with little Frankie. You'll get to be Cousin Frank. Isn't that great?"

Frank shook his head and said to Isabelle, "This isn't right. You're moving in with Victor? You'll regret it."

"Frank, let's sit down and talk about it," Victor said.

Frank swung toward him, "What did you do?" His eyes narrowed, "Seduce Isabelle and steal her from Rick? He's the best person anyone could be with, he *sooo* doesn't deserve to be treated like this!" Frank turned abruptly toward Isabelle. "How could you let him do that? I thought you were better than that."

Isabelle defended herself in a quiet voice. "Frank, there was no seduction. It was mutual. We fell in love."

Frank took a couple of steps back. He opened his mouth, but no words came out. Finally, he said to Isabelle, "Love? I never thought you were fickle, flitting from one man to another so easily."

"You know I'm not like that, Frank. You're being mean."

Spitting slightly in indignation, he went on, "And you're a *liar*. Fickle and a liar. You told all of us you couldn't have kids. You told me. You told Rick. You even told Chloe. And now this?" Frank pointed at Isabelle's stomach. "How could you lie to us? We were the four amigos. How could you lie to *us*?"

"Frank, I didn't lie. Once we got engaged, Rick and I didn't use birth control. I never got pregnant. But with Victor, this... just happened."

"So, Isabelle," he sneered, jabbing a finger toward Victor, "he's just a rebound, then. It'll never last. And he's so much older than you, he's so much older than us. *Frankie*," his voice had taken on a nasty tone, "is going to have an old man as a father."

Old Man. Isabelle was overcome by an inappropriate urge to giggle. She bit her lip as she struggled to suppress it because she knew Frank would misunderstand and think she was laughing at him. She breathed deeply a few times and finally said, "Rick's moved on with his life. We both agreed that we weren't right together. We tried and tried, but it just didn't work out. It wasn't good anymore. Rick's happy for me. He's happy I found the right person. He's happy I can have children, even though I couldn't with him."

Frank exploded, "You told *Rick*, and you didn't tell me?"

Isabelle tried to answer, "We're here now to tell—"

"But you're having a baby with *him*. He's my *uncle*. He was like a father to me. It's just wrong." Turning to look at Victor and then back at Isabelle, Frank's mouth turned down in distaste. "How could you be with *him*? Eeeeeew," he shuddered.

Victor shook his head sadly, "Oh, Frank—"

"You're not right for each other. It won't last," Frank said. And then he looked back at Victor, "She's my best friend, and you've come between us like that? Why didn't you tell me? I should have known."

"Frank, I thought you would be happy for us. Victor isn't coming between us. You're both special to me. This is the happiest time of my life. I thought you would want to share it."

He shook his head petulantly, "But you could have told me about your relationship sooner."

Victor looked at his seething nephew, "You're right. We should have told you sooner. We were trying to figure it out ourselves. It all happened so quickly. We didn't expect to fall in love or to get pregnant, but we did, and we want to spend the rest of our lives together. We're going to be a family. We want you to be part of it, son."

Victor reached out toward him, but outraged, Frank jerked back. "I'm not your son! You have your *own* child now. No wonder you don't want to help me. Well, I won't be any part of this." His voice quavered as he jabbed his finger, first at Victor and then at Isabelle. "This isn't right."

"Please don't say anything you'll regret, Frank."

Isabelle stepped forward and stretched out one hand, "Boyfriend, please, it'll be okay."

He slapped away her hand. And when he spoke, his voice was loud and furious. "I'm not your boyfriend anymore. You're not my girlfriend."

Victor's eyes narrowed as he stepped between them and leaned close to Frank's face. "You crossed the line there. Don't you *ever* touch her again, Frank."

Frank stepped back, intimidated by Victor's threatening stance. His eyes darted between Victor and Isabelle. "You used to be like a father to me – and you, Isabelle, you had an abortion, you betrayed your marriage vows, you betrayed me and our relationship." He opened the door. "I'm done with you both. Fuck you and get out of my house. Get out of my life."

Isabelle pleaded, "Please, Frank. Please don't do this. We—"

"Get out. Get out. Both of you and your bastard child." Frank shoved the two of them out the door and slammed it behind them. *He's taken her away from me.* He struck the door over and over again with his fists, "Fuck. Fuck. Fuck."

Isabelle recoiled at the sound and turned her face into Victor's shoulder at the angry pounding on the door. She sobbed, tears pouring down her cheeks, "He hates us. I've never seen him so angry."

"That's his father talking, Izzy. That's Alan. When Frank calms down, when he's ready, he'll be back in our lives." Victor put his arm around her shoulders and held her close as they walked to the elevator.

Frank changed into his tennis clothes and grabbed his racket. He threw his bag into the trunk of his car and screeched out of his parking spot.

Thwack! – "Fuck you, Victor!" he yelled as he hit the first ball against the wall at his tennis club.

It came flying back at him. He hit it again. *Thwack!* – "Fuck you, Isabelle!"

He settled into an angry routine. *Thwack!* – "Fuck you!" – *Thwack!*

Chapter Eight

January 2005

Flashback to Murder

Raleigh, North Carolina

RALEIGH WEEKLY NEWS   SATURDAY, JANUARY 8, 2005

The Society Scene
by EDGAR SPRING

The Perfect Fundraising Gala

The Lauch Art Museum gala was the premier fundraising event of the holiday season. The annual New Year's Eve affair included a tribute to the museum's founders, Mason and Ava Lauch, by their son and daughter-in-law, Jonathan and Natalie Lauch. Their grandson, Judge Tracey Lauch, also attended, along with the most powerful and successful members of Raleigh's society.

The stunning art museum is in Raleigh's former warehouse district, now a vibrant area filled with shops, galleries and artist studios. Once inside the building, you couldn't miss the newest addition to the decor, the large Chihuly glass chandeliers hanging from the rafters. The grand tree stood proudly in the huge curve of the staircase, its decorations complimenting the new lighting with glass balls that sparkled in the same greens, blues, creams and reds from the chandeliers overhead.

North Carolina Supreme Court Judge Maxwell Johnson talked, smiled and laughed with other patrons, apparently enjoying himself. Tall, slim and fit, he looked as dapper as always in his classically simple tuxedo. Mayor Jan Erkes was glowing as she danced all night. Her mermaid-cut evening dress in dark blue, with its sweep train, shimmered against her flawless skin. Governor David Whitehaus, and former Raleigh mayor, a long-time friend of the Lauch family, attended again this year to show his continued support of the arts. It was a tender moment when, at midnight, he gave his wife a kiss and a long, warm embrace to welcome in the new year.

At the end of the evening, donations totaled in excess of a half million dollars. Continuing a twenty-year tradition, these funds will be awarded to local, underprivileged art students. A special thank you goes out to actress Jessica Lynn for her very generous donation.

If you haven't visited the Lauch Art Museum, you should. The art and the building's architecture are worth seeing.

Tracey carefully backed his car into the best space – between two large pillars. He always arrived very early to get that particular spot at the back of the parking garage. Six months before, on the very first day after he was appointed to his position on the court, he'd found it, the perfect place, where no one could park on either side of him.

He took the key and locked his vintage Mercedes. Then he chuckled to himself about the running debates he and his golf buddy, Cal, had over what to call the car. *No matter what he says about vintage versus antique versus classic cars, I still think of my baby as vintage, even though she's only forty-three years old.* Tracey stopped to brush a fleck of dust off the flawless silver paint.

That was a nice vacation, but I'm ready to go back to work now. My parents and I got to spend a relaxing Christmas together and enjoy the afternoon with all those kids at Sarah's House instead of dashing off to some other obligation. For me, that was the highlight, more than all our other holiday rituals, even the gala.

Walking toward the exit, he paused. In just a moment, for the first time since the night of the gala, he'd pass the spot where he'd killed the bartender, a little more than a week ago. He looked in the other direction. *If I continue to park back here, every day on my way to work, I'll have to go past the place where I strangled Zoe.* He shuddered and picked up his pace, in a hurry to get out of the garage. *I may need to find another location for my car, one where I won't need to see where she died.* The echo of his footsteps faded as he exited into the plaza where the courthouse presided, surrounded by white office buildings with red-tiled roofs and gracious trees spaced evenly around the perimeter. Wooden benches were positioned beneath them to catch the shade when the afternoon sun flooded the area.

Tracey crossed the open plaza and then stopped to read the words above the tall, white pillars of the imposing building. *Wake County Courthouse.* Each morning, he paused to read those words, and each morning, he felt again the solemnity of the position he held. He bounded up the eight steps, eager to begin his day. And then there was another ritual, to remind himself why he was there. The bronze plaque to the left of the entry door, *Family Court.* He reached out and ran his fingers over it in a light caress before he opened the heavy wooden doors and entered.

He walked briskly down the empty corridor to his chambers. This quiet time, early in the morning, when there was no one there but the cleaning staff and maybe a clerk or two hidden away, preparing a brief or organizing another judge's calendar, this was the time he used to get his day started right, the time to make sure everything was in order.

He looked at his name on the plaque screwed to the door. "Judge Tracey Lauch," he read to himself with a smile as he went through the outer room to his chambers and stood inside, looking around. "This is where I belong. This is why I worked so hard."

Rich, wood-paneled walls. A capacious wardrobe where his judge's robes always hung, ready for the week. The large mahogany desk standing in the center of the room, two leather chairs with wooden arms positioned in front of it and his comfortable, well-used desk chair that they'd brought over from his old office, placed precisely on the opposite side. In the corner, a seating area for two with a table, a lamp and a box of tissues. Tall bookcases filled with his reference books. Everything was arranged to his satisfaction.

He set his briefcase on the desk and began his morning routine. Walking over to the corner, he turned on the lamp between the chairs. The bright light flashed in his eyes – an image of Zoe, laughing, pouring drinks at the New Year's Eve gala, flashed across his mind. *She always knew my name. She was so full of life.* Taking a deep breath, he pushed away the intrusive memory.

Tracey opened the wardrobe doors wide to ensure that his robes had been cleaned and returned during his vacation. With a pleased nod, he carefully closed them again before returning to his desk. The leather-bound folder his clerk faithfully placed there each morning lay open, ready for him to check his calendar for the day. As always, his schedule was full.

Click. He turned on his computer and began to review the upcoming cases. As the screen flashed, another image. *Zoe, apologizing for not getting my change right, her worried "excuse me", grabbing her red hair and twisting it.* Tracey shook his head, brushing his hands against his face to wipe away the unwelcome images. He blinked several times and forced himself to focus on his calendar and the cases on the docket for that day.

And then it was time. He stood in front of the wardrobe, carefully fastening his robe, and then checked his appearance in the mirror on the inside of the door. Precisely on the hour, he walked into the courtroom.

"All rise for the honorable Judge Tracey Lauch," intoned the bailiff solemnly.

The morning had been unusually exhausting, and he struggled to stay focused on the work before him. After ruling on the third case, he raised his left hand to bring down his gavel. And finally, he was able to reach for his glass and take a drink of water. The curtains moved as people entered and left the courtroom, a sliver of sun flickered as the curtain returned to its original position. *Waiting outside the museum gala. Following her. The echo of Zoe's heels clicking on the cement floor of the parking garage.* He closed his eyes.

"Judge Lauch, are you okay?" The bailiff's voice pulled him back to the courtroom.

He rubbed his face with both hands and massaged the bridge of his nose. "Yes. I'm fine. I've just got a little headache."

"Would you like to take a break?"

"No, let's press on. We only have this last case before lunch."

Alone in his chambers, with the sandwich his housekeeper had prepared that morning in front of him on the desk, he sat, mulling over the flashbacks that had disrupted his morning. *What's going on? This has never happened before. Why now? She is the third one, but this time it was different. I'm not killing by chance any longer. Now, I'm planning, waiting, following them. What's happening? This isn't me. I have to stop.*

During the fourth case after lunch, a camera flash went off. Tracey froze, staring blankly into space. *Zoe drawing her last ragged breath. My heart pounding in excitement. My breath coming faster.* He breathed heavily and covered his face with his hands.

"No pictures allowed," the bailiff cautioned. "We have minors here, and we don't allow photos. If it happens again, your camera will be confiscated." He moved to stand in front of Tracey and whispered, "Judge, are you okay? It's happened again. Maybe you should take a ten-minute recess." Tracey nodded, steadied his voice, announced the recess and quickly departed the courtroom.

In the bathroom of his chambers, he splashed water on his face. He looked into the mirror and closed his eyes. *That's Zoe's earring in my hand.* Tracey gasped and gripped the edge of the sink. He walked over to the corner seating area and sat in one of the leather wing chairs. Leaning back, he closed his eyes. And the murder flickered through his mind like disjointed still photography.

Chapter Nine

January 2005 to September 2007

Lydia McKay of Paris

Dublin, Ireland

Lydia sat at the dining table with her much older sister, Fiona. They twisted and turned their cups, two sisters who had nothing in common and who didn't know what to say. Finally, Lydia broke the silence, "Why wouldn't the others come? They're her daughters too. They haven't seen Mam since before I was born."

"We all wish it was Da who had died," Fiona replied, her voice unsympathetic.

Lydia heard her sister's voice reflecting the emptiness she was also feeling. She had cried all her tears the day she'd found her mam in their dressmaking shop, lying lifeless on the floor next to her workbench and sewing machine. Now, there was nothing left, no tears, no feelings, just emptiness.

"Why?" she asked.

"Because he's a bastard," she hissed. Her voice grew heated. "Because he beat us, and he beat Mam."

"I never knew that until I found her diary after she died."

"How would you? You weren't even born yet. We all left home as soon as we could, to get away from him. And that's why the three of us have never come back."

Lydia's voice was toneless, "I was sad when I read in her diary about how Mam hid his beatings from me. I remember her having some bruises, but she always had an excuse for them. And a few years ago, when he broke her arm, she said she'd slipped and fallen."

"He was good at hitting us where it didn't show."

"It was like none of you ever existed. Mam didn't talk about you, and Da never did either. If I hadn't sneaked into their room after she died to see if there was anything of hers that I wanted, if I hadn't seen the picture tucked into her diary and read what she had written about you, I wouldn't have known about any of you. I found the photo you sent her. She'd left it in the envelope with your address, and that's how I knew how to find you. Until then, I didn't know I had any family left, except Da. For what he's worth."

"I sent that picture a couple of years ago. It was the first contact I'd made with her since I left. I wanted her to see my family. I'd hoped she would answer, but she never did. Was my letter there too?"

"It was. She must have read it a lot because it was falling apart."

"Why didn't she write back?" she asked angrily. "Why did she stay with him, Lydia? Did she say?"

"She wrote in her diary that she and Da agreed that if she stayed, he would stop beating you all, but it was too late and the damage was done. The three of you had already gone when Mam found out she was pregnant with me. That was when she wrote that she'd only threatened to leave to stop the beatings. She loved him so much, and she could never have gone through with it anyway because she didn't believe in divorce. Marriage was for life in her eyes. She was a good Catholic, you know." Lydia shook her head.

"Even so, I will never understand why someone would stay with a beater."

"What did the others say when you called them? Don't they care that she's gone?"

"We feel like it's her fault. We thought she should have left him when he first started to hit us. She should have left him then. Instead, she stayed, and we had to stay with her. We all hated him so much, even after he stopped. But she chose him over us. That's why they wouldn't come back." Fiona's voice had grown sharp and bitter, "A beater never changes. Didn't he beat you too?"

"No. Mam made the same deal with Da to protect me," Lydia replied in a hollow voice.

"Well, then you're lucky. I still don't understand why she didn't leave."

"It's a sad way to live, isn't it? But she loved him very much. She said that over and over again in her diary."

"I wonder why she never told you about us?"

They sat in silence before Lydia continued, "I guess we'll never know. The entries stopped about the same time your letter came. But I could tell that she still loved him, even after he started up with women from town several years ago. There was a sad look in her eyes, like the hurting was fresh every time. I think she always hoped he would change."

Fiona looked over at her father. He looked like an old drunk, with his shapeless body, his bloodshot eyes, his face tinged with yellow from years of too much alcohol. Other than his luxuriant silver hair, not a remnant of his earlier good looks remained. She watched him kissing and hugging a not very attractive, middle-aged woman.

"He's been chasing after her for the past few months. I don't understand why Mam still felt the way she did about him."

"Look at him over there, laughing and joking. No respect for our mam. He's drunk already, and it's barely past lunch. He makes me sick. He should have died, not her." Fiona's voice was bitter as she took a drink of her cold tea and made a face.

Finally, there was nothing more to say between them, and Fiona stood up. "Well, I've paid my respects. I've got to go home to my family. I have a four-hour drive ahead of me. Take care of yourself, Lydia," she said, her voice cool and detached.

Lydia stood up and hugged her sister. "Thank you for coming." Fiona gave her a stiff little hug in return.

"Will I see you again?" Lydia asked.

"Probably not," said Fiona. "The only thing we have in common is our red hair."

"Then why did you come?"

"It was my duty."

Once she had left, the other guests began to depart. Lydia saw her father stumble out with his arm around that woman. He said nothing to her. After everyone was gone, she mechanically cleaned up the cottage and put away all the food brought by the mourners. Standing alone in the middle of the kitchen, she thought, *There's no reason for me to stay here. Mam is dead, my sisters don't care enough to stay in touch, and my da is a drunk and a womanizer. He doesn't need me.*

With just a duffel bag over her shoulder and her handbag slung across her body by its long strap, Lydia walked through the living room and paused at the front door. She turned back and pulled the diary out of the pot on the bottom shelf of the kitchen cabinet where she'd hidden it and stuffed it into her bag. Then she closed the front door behind her. "I'm all alone now."

She walked to her mam's shop and set her bag in the middle of the front room. As she moved around the two rooms, running her hands across her small worktable, fingering the rolls of fabric stacked against the wall, she thought about her mam, about how she'd taught her to sew and how she'd helped her use her crayons to design dresses for her dolls when she was very little. And then her mam always helped her make the dresses. Early on, they turned out pretty badly, but she always smiled and said, "They'll get better. Creativity is all about trial and error."

She wandered around desolately until at last, she sat in her mother's sewing seat, touching her machine. *Why did you leave me, Mam? Now, I have no one.* She put her fingers on the controls on the large sewing machine her mam had saved so long to buy, adjusting them slightly, back and forth. "It's too bad I can't take this." In the small storeroom at the back of the shop, she picked up the portable machine that she'd often used when they had a lot of sewing to do at one time and put it in the middle of the room next to her bag. She stood in front of the rack where their customers' dresses hung, waiting for a final fitting or to be picked up, thinking about the fabric they were made from and selected several of the best ones.

"I mustn't forget the 'Lost and Found' that Mam hid away," she said. Hurrying back into the storeroom, she took a box off the high shelf and looked inside at the collection of jewelry. These were the pieces that, from time to time, customers had left behind in the shop when they came for fittings. If they hadn't come back looking for them, after a few weeks, with a smile, her mam would shrug her shoulders and put them in the box. The collection had gradually grown. "I can sell these to get a start." Lydia took the box and the portfolio containing her best designs and added them to the small pile of belongings she planned to take with her.

Finally, she looked around for her mam's favorite pincushion. It wasn't lying on the table where she usually left it at the end of a long day. After a futile search through the drawers at the side of the table, Lydia opened the large sewing basket that stood next to the stool where her mother had always sat, her back so straight, needing no support. She tipped the contents into a pile on the floor and sat down to look through it. There it was, the pincushion that fastened around her wrist with a wide piece of elastic, filled with sharp sewing pins, a few safety pins and a couple of threaded needles. Lydia sat with the pincushion in her hands and her tears came hot and hard. She cried – for the loss of her mam, for the times they'd never have again, laughing and talking as they designed and sewed dresses together, for her encouragement as she'd learned to create more intricate designs and for the sweet hugs she gave so spontaneously.

She dried her face with her sleeves and blew her nose in a scrap of fabric that lay next to the sewing machine. Then, rummaging amongst the tape measures, scissors and other sewing necessities she'd scattered about for anything else that she should take, her fingers touched a fat envelope with *"Lydia McKay of Paris"* written across the front in her mam's clear handwriting. She opened it and saw a thick stack of bills. *Mam knew about my dream, and she was saving this to help me on my way.* And she broke down and cried again.

§

Paris, France

Two days later, Lydia hopped off the train at Gare du Nord and ran down the platform to the baggage car to collect her duffel bag and the small case containing her sewing machine. Once she'd found the luggage lockers, she deposited all her worldly belongings and closed the doors of the two compartments she'd rented. *Those cost a fortune.* She walked back into the busy entry hall and stopped to look around. "Now I need a newspaper, a map and then food." *I'm exhausted and starving. Too many trains and buses from Dublin to Paris and no time for food or anything but little naps here and there.*

The man at the information booth handed her a map and directed her to a small kiosk to buy a newspaper. She decided to find a place outside the train station to eat. A few minutes later, she found a sandwich bar and bought coffee and a baguette sandwich, half with butter and ham and the other with butter and cheese, before continuing down the street to find a bench. The air was brisk, but since there was no wind, she found it was bearable as long as she stayed in the sun.

Lydia took a sip from the paper cup and, balancing her coffee beside her on the bench, she turned the newspaper to the right section with a prayer that her school-girl French would be enough to understand the ads and took a pen out of her handbag. She looked at the two halves of the sandwich, trying to decide which to eat first. *Cheese, because I like ham better, so it'll be nice to end with that.* She took a huge bite and sighed with pleasure. *I hadn't realized how hungry I was.* With the baguette in one hand, a pen in the other and the folded newspaper on her lap, she began circling ads for rooms to let. Once she'd finished eating, she took another sip of coffee and opened her map. As she located the addresses for the rentals, she realized the farther she was away from the central part of Paris, out in the double-digit *arrondissements,* the less expensive the rent. *That makes sense. But I guess I'll be staying much farther out than I had hoped.* Since a cluster of places were all in the same northwestern district of Paris, only a few kilometers from where she already was, she decided to start there. *This is the beginning of my dream. Mam, I wish you could be here to share it with me.*

After hours of tramping about the area to the addresses listed in the paper, looking at rooms and trying to negotiate prices with her small amount of French and a little phrasebook, Lydia chose a clean, cheap room in a boarding house. It was the only one that had a decent lock on the door and allowed her to opt out of meals. *I don't eat much, so I can probably get by on less than they charge.*

She had returned from the station with her bags and dropped them on the bed. *Small dresser, small wardrobe, small bed, and small table,* she took a mental inventory. *Good thing I'm a small person.* And then she unpacked and arranged her work area. Sitting on the bed, staring at the Lost and Found items and her remaining cash that she'd laid out in front of her, she said to herself, "How am I going to make this last until I can find a job?" With a sigh, she picked up the empty envelope that had held the cash. Flipping it over to the backside, she added up her expenses, the cost of her room for twelve weeks and what she thought she would spend on food. *And I'll need a French phone card for my Irish phone. Otherwise, it will cost a fortune to use it here. I'll need a phone when I start applying for jobs.* Lydia slipped the money back into the envelope and stuck that and the jewelry into her large handbag. Picking it up, she headed off to buy groceries. *Since I'm not allowed to cook in the room and there's no refrigerator, I'll have to shop almost every day. I'll need to be careful how much I buy at one time.*

Just over an hour later, she returned, having explored the shops in her neighborhood, the small bakery, that had the delightful smell of baking bread wafting out as the door opened and closed and so many tempting breads and sweets stacked in the showcases; the cheese shop, where the shop keeper had let her taste several cheeses before deciding which one she wanted to purchase; the produce market, with fruits and vegetables galore. Of course, she had compared prices with those at the small grocery on the corner. For the time being, at least, she'd opted for the individual shops, in hope that if she became a regular customer, she might get special deals, a little bit of something extra here and there, as she and her mam had back in their Dublin suburb.

She laid a roll, a small chunk of cheese and a few grapes on the paper bag that the roll had been tucked into. She picked up the small sharp knife she'd brought with her and sliced the roll and cheese. And then, seated at the table as she ate, Lydia pulled the phone card from its packaging, put it into her phone and confirmed that it worked. *One item off my list.*

She finished her meal and brushed the crumbs from the table into the paper bag, which she twisted up and dropped into the small trash can under the table. Picking up her handbag, she pulled out the envelope where she'd jotted down the figures that would rule her life for the next few months. She spread the dwindling pile of cash and the lost-and-found items on the table, counting the worn bills again and running her fingers over the pieces of jewelry, examining each one carefully. "Oh, it will be tight. After rent, food and the phone card, there's not much left." She caressed the lost-and-found items again. *I'll have to find a pawnshop to sell these, one at a time.*

With a smile, she looked over at her sewing machine, her sketchbook and her portfolio, arranged carefully on the table. *I can do it. This is where my dreams will become a reality.* She reached out and stroked her hand across them and then looked over her shoulder at the dresses from her mother's shop that she'd hung on the door to the wardrobe to inspire her. *I can redesign them to make a few stylish pieces by "Lydia McKay of Paris" to showcase my business and my skills,* she thought, and reached for her pencil and sketchbook, ready to capture the ideas already filling her mind.

After a minute, she said, "Oh, customers – I'll have to get business cards or something. That's another expense I can ill afford" She made a note on her envelope.

Her thoughts were interrupted by a loud voice yelling at someone down the hall outside her door. *I guess I'll have to get used to that type of noise, living here.*

§

A few weeks later, Lydia walked down a busy street in central Paris, replaying the conversation in her head. *Young lady, your French isn't very good. We need someone who can speak fluently.* She sighed deeply. *Without better French, I'll fail. I have to do something. I have almost no money and what I have will run out soon. I need to find a job, any job.*

She continued to think about her problem. *Brrr – it's so chilly today. If I were working, I'd be inside somewhere warm.* She looked around and saw a plaque on the face of the building in front of her. *"Bibliothèque Nationale de France". Libraries are good places to get out of the cold,* she thought. *Maybe there's a place I can sit for a while before I go back out looking again.* In the foyer, she saw a large corkboard with cards and notices posted on it. Lydia looked around surreptitiously and then pulled out an A4-sized poster with tear off strips along the bottom that said, *"Lydia McKay of Paris"* and her phone number. The poster showed beautifully drawn examples of her dresses, along with her name and information about her services. She'd had a number of them copied for a fraction of the price of business cards. It wasn't as classy, but she hoped they would do for now. She found a prominent space and tacked it to the board. *You never know, someone may take one and call.*

She ventured a little farther into the foyer and saw an information desk. Referring to her little phrasebook, she fumbled through a few halting phrases of French and then noticed the woman smiling broadly. It turned out, she was the French wife of an Australian diplomat and spoke fluent English. Relieved to find someone to speak to, Lydia explained that she'd recently moved to Paris but was having trouble finding a job because of her poor

French. Lydia asked the woman if it was okay that she'd put up a poster on the board by the front door. She asked to see the poster. Lydia held one up for her to see and then handed her one of her few business cards.

"Oh, is this you, this Lydia McKay of Paris? May I keep it?"

Lydia assured her that she was the very same Lydia, and sensing the woman was a good contact, said she was welcome to keep the poster as well to share with her friends. She asked if the woman had any recommendations about places where she could apply for work without knowing French.

"Why don't you take one of our free conversational French classes?" asked the woman.

After the woman had provided her with brochures about the class, Lydia left the library feeling like things were beginning to turn around for her. *The sun should burst through the clouds and illuminate the street,* she thought. *There should be beautiful female voices singing.* Instead, she pushed open the door to the library to find that heavy rain was falling.

Huddled under an awning, waiting for the heaviest part of the rain to let up, Lydia shook out her cheap black umbrella. The shop owner had pulled all the bins of fruit back under the awning to protect them from the rain, and she leaned against one, tired, cold and hungry. As she stood there, her stomach gave a long growl, and she slowly closed her hand around an apple and dropped it into her pocket. She shook her umbrella again, stepped boldly out into the rain and walked away, expecting at any moment to hear running footsteps and a shouted, "Stop, thief!" – or whatever the French equivalent to that was – from behind her and then to have a strong hand clamped on her shoulder. Around the corner, she pulled the apple out of her pocket. Straining her ears once more and hearing nothing, she relaxed and began to eat the piece of fruit. *At least, if I need to, I can steal food to survive.* She smiled to herself.

§

Mari quickly walked out of the pawnshop, pushing the button to raise her automatic umbrella as she exited into yet another April shower. There Lydia stood, just outside the door, one arm crooked over her face to keep the drizzle away, her red hair already turning to masses of riotous curls in the damp. "I wanted to thank you for supporting me in there. I've sold Shane a lot of stuff the past few months, and I've always felt as if he wasn't paying me enough."

Mari moved a little closer so the umbrella partially covered Lydia. "He seems like a real cheapskate."

"He is. He never pays a penny more than he can get away with, but you helped me get a lot of money out of him for that brooch."

Mari caressed the pomegranate flower brooch with the thumb of her free hand, "Actually, I owe you more." She slipped the brooch into her handbag and pulled out a folded bill.

"What are you talking about?"

Lydia's eyes opened wide in surprise at the hundred euros Mari had just tucked into her hand. "You deserve to get a good price for it."

I have almost no money left except what I've put aside for my rent. Maybe it means I won't have to steal food this week. Even though Lydia felt like jumping up and down for joy, she kept her voice calm and replied, "Are you sure? Thank you. Thank you. Thank you. You don't know what this means to me. But how do you know what it's worth?"

"I collect vintage jewelry, and I believe this is an original Schiaparelli. If it is, it's worth far more than I paid for it, even with that," she nodded at Lydia's hand where she still gripped the large bill tightly in her fingers.

Lydia slipped the cash into her handbag, "Oh, my goodness. Thank you!" Sticking her hand out, she said, "By the way, I'm Lydia McKay."

Mari took Lydia's slim fingers in hers, "I'm Mari Oliver." As their hands clasped, Mari felt an unexpected attraction to Lydia. *I'd like to get to know her better.*

"I wonder how many of the other things I sold Shane were originals?" *Some of Mam's clients were very wealthy, so it wouldn't surprise me that the things they left behind in the dressing area were valuable.*

"Do you work for him?" The drizzle had turned to light rain. "You know, I have some time before I have to go back to work. Would you like to go somewhere and get a coffee?" Mari looked around in appreciation at the eclectic old neighborhood, where jewelers rubbed shoulders with pawnshops and coffee houses stood side by side with kebab sellers and shoe stores, where the narrow streets, paved with cobblestones, all curved and wound around and across one another.

"Sure. There's a nice place just down here." Lydia pointed to her right. *Today, I'll splurge a little.*

They smiled at each other. "Here, share my umbrella," offered Mari, and Lydia stepped closer and tucked her arm through Mari's as they walked down the street.

This is nice, walking arm in arm together. I think she's the kind of person I'd like to be friends with.

As they went down the street, Mari asked, "McKay is an interesting name, where are you from?"

"Ireland. How about you?"

"Spain."

The small coffee house they entered was filled with plants and copper pots on shelves above the coffee machines. "This is charming," Mari said, her eyes searching for a vacant table, "How long have you been in Paris?"

"I moved here a few months ago. How about you?"

They found a table for three, and after throwing their raincoats over the extra chair, they quickly ordered two espressos. "I don't live here," said Mari. "I'm a concierge for the Spectrum River Cruise Line. Our cruise begins and ends in Paris, so my boat's docked south of here along the Seine. Today is my day off, and I come into the city whenever I can to poke around in little antique and junk shops. I saw the jewelry in Shane's window and went in. How fortunate for me. What do you do, Lydia?"

"I do a little of this and a little of that right now." *I wonder what she'd think...* "I'm saving to open my own shop."

"What kind of shop is that?"

"I'm a dress designer. As soon as I've made enough money, I'm going to open my own boutique. It'll be called 'Lydia McKay of Paris'. It's going to take me a while – a long while – to save up the money to do it. But I will – someday," she shrugged wistfully. *Whatever I need to do to make that happen.* Mari watched as she tugged a precious card from its little leather case and handed it to her.

"Meanwhile, I'm ready to take on individual clients."

"Wow, how courageous of you to come to Paris to start a clothing design business. I don't think I'd ever have the guts to do something so ambitious." Mari reached out and laid her fingers on Lydia's arm for a long moment, and Lydia's heart did a quick flip at the touch. "What is your background? What type of dresses do you design?"

The waiter set their espressos in front of them, each small cup on a little stainless-steel tray along with two sugar cubes and a tiny glass of sparkling water. They put the two cubes from the trays into their cups and reached toward the sugar bowl for a third. Their fingers touched, and they both laughed nervously. "What are the odds that two women from different countries meet in Paris and both put three cubes of sugar in their espresso?" asked Lydia as she stirred her cup, and they laughed again. "To answer your question, my training was very broad, and that means I can design any type of dress. When I lived in Ireland, I had to be flexible to meet the needs of my clients. They had wildly different budgets, and they would ask me to create wedding dresses, suits, day dresses. That meant sourcing a wide variety of fabrics, from cottons and wools to silks and lace and doing custom designs with multiple fittings. I've been in the business for many years. What about you?"

"I might work for a cruise line, but my real passion is flamenco dancing. I'm always looking for a unique dress for my competitions."

After a deep breath, Lydia blurted out, "I could make one for you. Do you have pictures of you in flamenco dresses that you especially like?"

Mari pulled up some pictures on her phone, and the two women scooted their chairs closer together to look at the photos and talk about the designs. Lydia pointed to one. "You look wonderful in that dress. But I know that you and I could create something even better – together."

"Do you have pictures of your work? Do you have a portfolio?"

"I don't have it with me." Lydia took a drawing pad and pencil out of her handbag, "Here, let me sketch something I think will look stunning on you. Just sit there and let me look at you." Lydia sat looking at Mari for a long time, running her eyes over her body, examining her posture as she sat very still. "Now, please, stand up and turn around very slowly. I want to see your figure, your proportions and how you move."

As Mari turned, Lydia's eyes lingered, and she said, "Again. Very slowly. You have a beautiful dancer's body, you know."

A thrill ran through Mari as Lydia looked at her so intimately, but she simply said, "Thank you."

Lydia gazed at her. *She takes my breath away.*

Mari sat and watched Lydia draw in her sketchbook that she'd propped against the table's edge. *Look how focused she is on her work. You can see her confidence in the way she holds her pencil, the bold strokes and intricate little marks she makes.* "Do you mind if I talk while you do that?"

Fully engrossed, Lydia didn't look up as she responded, "Of course not. I think this uses a different part of my brain."

"Did you make the dress you're wearing? How daring of you to choose that shade of pink. It's wonderful with your hair and coloring. One never thinks of pink for redheads, but it works on you. And I like the way you've chosen to make the bodice fitted and then the waist so trim and belted. It makes the skirt look fuller than it is without using so much fabric. You look so stylish, a tiny bit retro and totally unique. I know that those dreadful peasant cuts are coming back into fashion, but then, of course, slimmer cuts have never gone out of style. I think it's fabulous that you have a unique style, one that suits your figure, and I suspect, your personality as well."

Lydia looked up, startled at Mari's effusive praise. "Thanks. It is one of my designs. It's just a simple day dress."

When she'd finished the drawing, she sat back in her chair and pushed her sketchpad over to Mari, who studied it carefully and then leaned close to Lydia, "Oh, this is *exactly* what I want. If this and your dress are any indication, you definitely know how to showcase women's bodies with your designs. Flamenco dresses need to show our bodies to the best advantage while they accentuate our movements." She turned and looked directly at Lydia and let her hand rest on her arm. Lydia took a quick, sharp breath and then a sip of her coffee to cover her reaction. "I'd like to have you make this dress for me, please."

Lydia blushed, "Thanks. I'd be honored. You'll be the first customer of 'Lydia McKay of Paris'. I'm so excited. We have to make sure the color we choose complements those red highlights in your hair."

"Definitely. What do we do next?"

"I'll make a pattern. You're a size thirty-six, aren't you?"

Mari nodded her head vigorously, "That's exactly my size. Oh, this is so exciting."

"Once I have the pattern ready, I'll need to check your measurements so I can adjust it to fit you perfectly. When will you be back in Paris again?"

"Next month, on my break from work."

"Your break?"

"Life on a riverboat – I work six weeks and then get a two-week break. Anyway, I can't wait to see you. We can talk about fabrics and colors – and maybe about more designs?"

"Then when you come back, wear something you can slip out of easily," said Lydia, feeling a little bold.

Mari looked at her and then down at her watch, her eyes regretful. "I wish we could sit and talk forever, but I have to go back to the boat. Back to work." She dropped some money on the table and said, "My treat, Lydia. I feel so fortunate to have met you."

They stood and kissed each other on the cheek. Mari pressed her cheek against Lydia's for just a moment, perhaps a moment longer than new friends would. And Lydia's heart did that funny little flip again. *I'm so attracted to her. Is that wrong?* she thought but merely said, "It was so nice to meet you, Mari. Thanks for the espresso and thanks again for your help with Shane. I'm very excited about designing this dress for you."

"I'm thrilled." Mari reached for the pencil and wrote her number next to the design. "Call me," and she walked toward the exit. In the doorway, she paused to look back at Lydia. Lydia lifted her hand hesitantly, and Mari smiled and waved back and walked off briskly.

Lydia stepped out onto the sidewalk. This time, the sun was shining. She looked up and down the block and then did a brief twirl of excitement and the skirt to her dress flared just a little. *My first Paris design. And maybe a new friend – or more!*

§

When she entered the empty pawnshop a few hours later, Lydia saw the middle-aged owner standing at the counter, filling in some paperwork. He was bent forward, and she noticed his full head of grey hair had threads of a red similar to hers running through it. Before looking up at her, he grumbled, "What shite! People just quit without any notice."

Lydia approached with her eyes narrowed. "Shite? You're pure shite, Shane."

"Well, hello to you too, kid," he said, his bright blue eyes squinting back at her through the smoke of the Gitane that was clamped between his teeth.

Lydia waved her hand at the smoke, and leaning forward, she jabbed a finger at his face. "I think you've been ripping me off every time I've brought you something. And that brooch you sold Mari earlier? It was a Schiaparelli and worth way more than the hundred euros she paid for it."

"Hundred euros? I gave you seventy of that." Shane laughed. "Anyhow, do you want a job, kid? I just lost my office assistant."

"What? A job? Me? I just called you a shite."

"I like you. You've got sense. You're tough. You say what you think. Between that and your red hair and freckles, you remind me of the girls back home in Dublin."

"Assistant? I'm way better than that. What about your office manager? I can organize your business."

Shane named a salary.

Lydia thought about it and came back with a figure almost double his.

Shane laughed again and made a counteroffer.

"I'll take it."

Shane stuck his hand out to seal the deal.

What a pushover. I would have settled for his original offer. And she reached out to shake his hand.

§

High-end bank buildings have high-end bathrooms, Lydia thought as she exited the stall. Each one was a separate, elegant little room with a dark, mahogany door and inset panels, a coat hook on the inside of the door and a good-sized shelf for her handbag. *No metal dividers in this posh facility.* Lydia admired the slightly worn, grey marble floor that told her it had been there for a long time. And then the wallpaper, a Morris flower design in silvery greens and blues, its soft lines and curves chosen to reflect the high arches of the ceiling.

Lydia stood behind two women, carefully listening to them as they washed their hands and chatted about business and who they were meeting. The attendant handed each of them a fresh towel.

A beautiful ring with a large oval ruby, surrounded by diamonds, lay on the marble counter next to the soap container. *I wonder if it belongs to one of them. Otherwise, the attendant surely would have picked it up when she wiped off the sinks and counters.* One of the two women in the room had stepped over to the cosmetic mirror to repair her makeup. The other stood at the sink, carefully reapplying her lipstick. Lydia looked in the large gilt-framed mirror over the sinks and watched the bathroom attendant walk back to her stool.

Lydia smiled at the woman at the sink. "So, how long have you worked here?"

"Five years now." They continued to chat idly, and then the woman admired Lydia's dress – the intricate dart work that showed off her slender figure, the light black wool that draped so beautifully from her waist. "I adore it. It's like an upscale version of the traditional little black dress. It's suitable for the entire day, from work to cocktails and dinner. I bet you can take off that charming bolero jacket and go out for the evening. Would you show me?"

Lydia unfastened and shrugged off the jacket and hooked it over her shoulder like models on the runway. She spun around slowly, showing off the slightly asymmetrical cut of the neckline and the detailed tailoring of the bodice and skirt and then, with a shiver, quickly pulled the jacket back on over her bare arms.

"That really is very clever. A dress for all seasons. May I ask who made it?"

She smiled. "It's by Lydia McKay of Paris. You should try her some time. She's very talented." Lydia pulled a small leather case out of her pocket and handed the woman a business card.

"Thank you."

Shortly after, the two women left, gossiping about the party they were headed off to next.

Lydia turned back to the sink, washed her hands and rubbed some lotion onto them. The ring still lay on the counter. She raised an eyebrow. *Ah, well, one for the Lost and Found, I think.* She curled her fingers around it and slipped it into her handbag. *This is a long way from taking apples from a fruit stand.*

Then, after carefully touching up her lipstick and makeup, making sure her freckles were still covered and tucking a few loose tendrils of hair in place. She touched her earrings, *The first thing I stole. I couldn't bear to give them away.* She drew a deep breath and went back out to the reception.

Frank leaned against a big pillar in front of the entrance to the elevators, people-watching, a drink in his hand. He caught a movement out of the corner of his eye and turned his head toward the back of the room. A petite redhead came out of the hallway to the ladies room. Even before he registered any details, it was her confident demeanor that caught his eye.

She paused and surveyed the room. Her vivid red hair was pulled into a chic knot at the base of her neck, her black dress shaped her body impeccably, the jacket was just right for the reception they were attending. *The combination is striking. I wonder who designed her dress? No one I recognize.* Frank watched her walk into the middle of the lobby. As she got closer, he noticed her simple, square-cut emerald earrings. Understated. Elegant. No watches, no rings, nothing flashy. *There's something about her that I like – very much.*

She passed a group of women, who were standing, chatting and having a drink together, and he noticed how she discreetly dropped something into the purse of one of the women in the group without pausing as she continued toward the bar.

Mmmm, this is interesting.

He kept watching her as she arrived at the bar and spoke briefly to the woman next to her. The redhead ordered a drink and looked out across the room. *Everyone here is wearing dark clothes – black dresses, dark suits. But something about this woman is different.* She looked at him for just a fraction of a second, and then her eyes moved on. She turned to talk to a man at the bar. But he was called away by a colleague before they'd spoken for long.

She's confident. She dresses well. She appears to know how to make conversation. She blends in, but not too much. Maybe I can use her. I need to figure out what she was doing when she dropped something into that woman's pocketbook. What was it?

The redhead stood at the bar for a while, keeping an eye on the group of women she'd passed before. She observed one of them break away and walk to the chairs on the other side of the lobby, opposite the bar. *She's not joining the group of women, but she's watching them. Is she working with that woman who she passed something to? Are they friends?*

Lydia looked around the room, and then her eyes came to rest on Frank again. He lifted his glass to her and gave a little nod.

She paused a second, wondering, and then lifted her glass. *Obviously, he's interested in me. I'll have to be careful. Hmmm, he's very attractive and fit. I wonder how tall he is. He's very well dressed. A well-cut suit, most likely bespoke since I don't recognize the designer.*

She heard a woman call out to him, "Frank, I need to talk to you," and he looked away.

So, his name is Frank. Behind him, the woman who had caught Lydia's attention set down her purse on a chair and leaned against the wall. She slid her foot out of her shoe and rubbed it with her hand.

Lydia wandered over and set her handbag down next to the woman's. She took off her shoe to rub her foot. The two women chatted about high heels, what fun they were, but how brutal and how they made their feet hurt. As a male colleague approached, the woman slipped her shoe back on and excused herself. Lydia tipped her head and smiled as the woman turned toward him.

Frank saw the redhead lean over and slip something out of the woman's purse and into hers. *Hmmm. She's a natural. Is she going to deposit the item with her 'friend' too?*

Frank chatted with a man who had tapped him on the shoulder and maneuvered himself so he could see the friend. Out of the corner of his eye, he saw the redhead talk to a person here and there as she crossed the room. She looked down and shook the ice in her glass, as though she had just realized it was empty and strolled back over toward the bar for a refill. On her way, she slipped the item into her friend's purse. *That was quite good. She's very talented. Maybe I could use her.*

Frank turned away. He didn't want to be noticed watching the redhead or her friend. *She's bold.*

He wandered toward the bar to refresh his whisky and saw her friend leave the event, the doorman holding open the large doors made of rich wood and trimmed in well-polished brass. He heard the redhead order still water on the rocks with a lime. *I know that trick, ordering a drink that looks like vodka on the rocks.* Frank turned away slightly, appearing to let his eyes roam around the room so she wouldn't notice him paying attention to her again. And he watched her sip her beverage. After one last swallow, she set the glass on the bar and left.

Intrigued, he waited a few moments and followed her. Her pace was not too fast but not too slow as she covered several blocks. Frank kept a safe distance, making sure she didn't notice him. He stood in a doorway, his gaze intent as she embraced her friend and then as they kissed. *Definitely not interested in men,* he thought. One hand at the back of the redhead's neck, the friend appeared to be savoring the kiss, lingering, while the other hand came out of her purse and slipped something into the redhead's handbag. The redhead stroked her friend's cheek as she finally pulled away. Frank stepped back into a doorway and continued to watch as they exchanged a few words.

"I was so scared."

"You did a great job for your first time, Mari," said Lydia. "Welcome to the other side, love."

Mari grabbed Lydia by her forearms and shook her lightly. "I was so nervous. It was exhilarating to experience what you do, but I don't think I want to be involved in actually doing it again" Her eyes narrowed, "It's so dangerous, and I don't do dangerous well, Lydia. I know you're reckless and like to live on the edge, and that's one of the things I adore about you. How about you continue to do reckless, and I continue to do cautious?"

They kissed again, another long intimate kiss.

Lydia murmured against Mari's cheek, "We'll talk about it when I get home. I'll be there soon. After I walk around a bit, I'll take the ring to Shane." They went off in separate directions.

Lydia meandered a few blocks, pausing from time to time to look in a shop window before she finally entered a small bar, where she ordered a Pastis. She'd just added water and ice to her glass when Frank, the tall, dark, handsome man from the event, moved over and stood next to her at the bar. He placed his order for a large whisky.

They had both taken a first sip from their drinks when he said in French, "I saw what you did back there."

Startled, Lydia recovered quickly and replied, also in French, "What are you talking about? I don't even know you."

Frank frowned for a moment, thinking, and then asked, this time in English, "Where in Ireland are you from?"

"None of your business."

"You have a charming accent. Why don't we go somewhere for a drink?"

"I have a perfectly good drink right here."

"I have a proposition to discuss." He threw back the rest of his whisky. "I'll buy you a new drink and tell you about it." Frank dropped some money on the counter, took her by the arm and walked her out of the bar.

Lydia looked around. As nervous as she felt, she remained calm while tugging her arm to get him to release it.

"I'll scream if you don't take your hands off me," she muttered.

"Go ahead. Then I'll turn you in for what you have in your handbag."

Her voice was sarcastic, edged with the tiniest frisson of fear, as she replied, "Oh, aren't you the mysterious one? A proposition that you need to sneak away to make. Can't talk in there, eh?" She jerked her head back toward the bar they'd just left, trying to appear tougher than she felt.

Frank held onto her arm as they walked to a quiet bistro around the corner. He found an outside table and took the chair right next to hers. In a low voice, he said, "The *gendarmerie* know the owner at that other bar. They are in there often. I don't think this is a conversation you want to have in front of the police. Show me what you took." Lydia's heart did a double beat at the mention of the French police while she looked at him, weighing her options.

Frank ordered a Pastis for Lydia and another double whisky for himself. The waiter brought their drinks, and she made a show of adding the ice and water and then took a long, slow swallow as she stalled, trying to decide what to do. Casually, she glanced around at the people and traffic on the street. And then Frank repeated himself, "If you try to run, I'll call the police. Show me what you took out of that woman's purse." He gave a hard look at her handbag.

Still, Lydia said nothing. To gain her trust, he said, "It was a smooth move. You've got real skill. And you were quick too." He snapped his fingers.

"So, what is it that you want? I have to meet someone soon. What is this proposition anyway?"

Frank laughed at her and told her what he'd seen at the bank, in particular the smooth move on the woman by the chairs. "I need someone with your skills, your finesse. So, show me what you took."

"What made you notice?"

"The way you walk. The way you dress. You're attractive. I like women. So, you caught my eye."

She gave in and opened her handbag, tilting it toward Frank. He looked down as she showed him part of a wallet before dropping it back into her bag.

"What's in it?"

"I don't know. I assume there'll be some money in it. What do you want?"

"The two of you make quite a team. But I know it's all you."

Lydia was flattered but didn't let on. "Two of us?"

"It was pretty daring of you, right under the noses of all those people. Now, show me the first thing you passed to your girlfriend."

Lydia realized he truly had seen everything that had happened, and her stomach dropped.

"Like I said, I could turn you in. Show me. Maybe we can work together."

Her fingers were unsteady as she unfastened her handbag again and reached into the inner pocket, fumbling for a moment as she slid the ring onto her finger. "I got this too," she said, holding her hand toward Frank.

Frank pulled her hand up to take a closer look at the ring. "Where did you get it?"

"I – ermmm – picked it up in the restroom. Someone left it lying on the counter."

"How much do you think it's worth?"

"I can get three hundred euros for it."

Frank laughed at her and shook his head. "Three hundred, huh?"

"I know I can get that much. I've been selling my stuff to Shane for years. I know what I'm doing." *Oops, I probably shouldn't have said his name.*

Frank looked at Lydia, seemingly puzzled. She took another sip of her Pastis. "I might even get four."

Glancing around to make sure no one had sat down at the table behind them, he said, "I can give you twice that, even though it cuts into my profit."

"I'll take it." Lydia held out her hand.

"I'll only buy it if you go to work for me to acquire more. I'll give you a cut that's better than what you get from this Shane guy."

"We'll go fifty-fifty. I'll be taking the risk," *and not for long, I hope. Once I open my shop, I'm done.*

"I have the overhead. We'll do a split of eighty-twenty."

"I get more than that from Shane."

"Where does your Shane sell these things?"

"Like you do, at his pawnshop."

"Pawnshop?" Frank scoffed. "I have brokers. My twenty percent is worth way more than Shane's."

Lydia didn't reply. *He's so arrogant. But is he telling the truth? Maybe. Or he could be lying.* "Eight hundred now and I won't take less than thirty percent for anything else."

Frank took a drink and thought about it. "We can try it out for a while. We don't know anything about each other. This could work, or it could go terribly wrong. Before committing, we should try a few jobs and see how it goes, and I could teach you some more techniques."

Lydia looked away in silence. I don't know if I want to work for this guy. He could murder me in a back alley, or maybe he's the police. It could all be a setup.

Frank continued, "What made you choose the bank, and how did you get in?"

"I looked in the window and saw all the expensive clothing. I figured there would be some easy targets. We just walked in – not together of course. Once we were inside, we mingled and talked to people."

"You have a good eye." Frank opened his wallet and began counting out money. "You can keep the wallet and the headache of disposing of whatever you don't want from it. Here's the eight hundred for the ring as a gesture of good faith, and we can meet later to discuss our arrangement." They discreetly made the exchange.

"I'll give you my number. Give me your phone." He entered his name and number into it. "I'm Frank. Call me soon and let me know."

"I know your name, but you don't know mine."

"I call you 'the redhead', and I know your voice. That's enough."

"The redhead?" she scoffed. "I'm Lydia."

§

When Frank slipped back into the bank event, he went directly to the bar and ordered a double whisky, his mind still on the interesting encounter with Lydia. He leaned on the bar, sipping his drink and noticed many people had already left. Alan came up to him and began to scold him. "I don't ever want you to leave these receptions to chase after girls again. The people here are too important to our business. They are our priority."

Frank felt like he was ten years old again. "I wasn't chasing girls," he said, knowing it didn't matter.

"You're the European liaison for Tomas Brazilian International Bank. You can't just leave like that, whenever you please. The acquisition of this Paris bank is crucial to our European footprint.

For God's sake, you're thirty-two years old. You have a PhD from Georgetown. I paid to make sure you were well-educated, but sometimes, you behave like a spoiled child. Today, you neglected your responsibilities and left all the work to your colleagues while you were out, gallivanting around."

Frank lowered his voice, "Dad, stop with the lecture. Can't you drop this?"

"Just don't disappoint me when we go to dinner tonight. You're only invited because you're my son. Be ready to leave in thirty minutes."

"I thought you were going back to Brazil tonight?"

"Change of plans. I'm heading home tomorrow night. Tomorrow, I have more bank business."

Nice of you to let me know. I'm only your European liaison. Frank finished his drink and asked the bartender for another. Alan glared at him before stalking off. As his father walked away, Frank muttered, "Maybe I should have taken Uncle Victor's rug business after all instead of dealing with this fucking bullshit." *But Dad would have disowned me, and I would have lost my inheritance.*

Chapter Ten

December 20, 2007

Their Earrings

Raleigh, North Carolina

Obituaries

Sheila Kovacs, 30

It is with deep sadness that our community announces the loss of a treasure on December 20, 2007, Sheila Kovacs, beloved daughter of Jim and Rae Ann Kovacs and older sister to Victoria and Jaqueline.

After graduation, Sheila became an attorney at Buxton, Cranston and Wilson Law Firm in 2002, and poured her heart and soul into her job, treating every client she represented as a member of her own family.

Outside of work, Sheila was an avid quilter and founded a quilting club, a small group that donates materials and time to make lap blankets for senior citizens in retirement homes. She was well known for saying, "Every blanket is made with love, so every person is wrapped in love."

Sheila was born in 1977 and lived her entire life in Raleigh. She will be forever remembered by her parents, sisters, grandparents, seven aunts and uncles and thirteen cousins. She is sorely missed by her dog, Lucy.

A service will be held, and stories of remembrance will be shared at 2 p.m. on Sunday, January 13, 2008, at Eli's Point Baptist Church.

Please make any donations to Frieda's Schnauzer Rescue in Millbrook, NC.

Tracey finished his shower, toweled off, put on his robe and then chuckled while he watched Mrs. Whiskers go through her customary routine, daintily licking the water from the floor of the shower, periodically shaking her wet paws. He followed her into the dressing room where she jumped up to her usual spot at the foot of the chaise and began her evening grooming.

The top tray of the elaborately carved wooden box that sat on the chest of drawers was lined with sapphire velvet and filled with cufflinks, collar stays and his watches. Tracey lifted the tray out of the box and set it carefully on top of the chest. Below that, there was a second tray of small velvet-lined compartments. He took out a drop earring, a chain with two small diamonds attached to a slightly larger diamond stud, held it up and gently touched it and watched it swing, the stones sparkling in the light from the ceiling fixture. *When I was small, I used to sit on my mother's lap and play with her earrings. They always sparkled so. I was fascinated by them. And I thought she must be a queen or a princess, to have all those wonderful jewels. This one was hers. I guess she never lost her love for those sparkles, even when she could afford to buy the real thing instead of cheap imitations.* Carefully, he put the earring back in the box.

Then he picked up the gold, teardrop-shaped earring from the top of the chest to put it away in the section where it belonged, next to the other small compartments containing earrings from his three earlier victims. He paused and looked at it again and sat down on the chaise. Holding it gently in his fingers, he showed it to the cat. "Mrs. Whiskers, this is Sheila's earring. She had the richest red hair. She wore it over her forehead in thick bangs. I watched her in the bar tonight. I saw how she pushed them back from her face when she spoke."

He groaned at the memory, "And she said, 'Excuse me,' in that low voice of hers. She reminded me so much of my mother." A memory of Sheila flashed through his mind. Tracey sighed. Mrs. Whiskers sat and watched him. He looked down at the earring in his hand. His voice had become hoarse with desire. "Tonight, I killed Sheila. It felt good. It reminded me of when I killed my mother and when I killed Ruth and when I killed Zoe. But what makes me do this? Why can't I stop, Mrs. Whiskers?"

Tracey rubbed the earring between his thumb and finger. "I had my hand over her nose and mouth. I felt her moan against my fingers. She struggled against me. Oh, God, that aroused me so." His breathing grew thick and heavy, and he groaned and leaned back. He slipped his hand under his robe, and he groaned louder this time as he reached between his legs and stroked himself, remembering, all the while holding the earring in his other hand and rubbing it. At last, after a final sound of pleasure, he lay there with his eyes closed, breathing heavily, his heart pounding, satisfied for the moment.

When his heartbeat and breathing returned to normal, Tracey stood up, and gently placed the earring into its compartment in the carved wooden box.

Chapter Eleven

December 2007

We Have so Much to Catch Up On

Spectrum Cruise, *The Citron*

"Let's get some breakfast from the buffet over there and come back in here to find a table, Chloe Rose," said Isabelle. "It's a shame it's too cold to eat on the bow or the upper deck."

"That works for me. I prefer the light food they provide up here to the heavy breakfast down in the dining room."

"I do too, because I don't like to go to bed on a full stomach." Isabelle looked down at her very round stomach, grinned and rubbed it gently. "I love my job, even though working a night shift messes up my eating and sleeping patterns," she said and grinned again. "Doing night shifts is like having a baby – you never sleep properly, so you're always off kilter."

They stood looking at the selection laid out in the small area off the end of the lounge before serving themselves plates of toast with homemade jam and fresh fruit. "You hold the plates, and I'll get the drinks. Orange juice for you, Isabelle?"

"Yes, thanks."

They walked back into the lounge and found a quiet place by a window in the sun. They sat down, and Chloe shook her head slightly as Isabelle spread butter and then a thick layer of jam onto her toast. She laughed when Isabelle took her usual enormous first bite and closed her eyes in enjoyment.

"Oh, I brought you something." Chloe reached down and handed Isabelle a small gift bag. "I want to start Baby Rose off on – the right foot."

"The right foot? Seriously?" They both giggled as Isabelle peeked into the bag.

"You know, who better than their godmother to get these girls started early with their shoe collections. Like mother, like daughter, yes?"

"You know, Frankie and Lily take out the baby booties you gave them and talk about how tiny they were when they were babies, and they play with them and put them on their dolls. But I think Iris is going to be the real collector. Her first word was 'shoe'. And Victor has to drag her out of our bedroom screaming because she wants to play in the wardrobe where I keep my shoes."

"They each have their own personality, that's for sure. So, how do you do it? Almost eight months pregnant and all that family stuff, with three little kidlets still under five and all your responsibilities here. It's two full-time jobs. Mother and – what is your job now? What do you call it?"

"I'm the first mate. That's one step below captain."

"Ay, ay, mate," Chloe snickered. "Anyhow, I'm so glad that after all these years, I finally came on one of your river cruises. What a life you live. All the travel." Chloe tipped her head to one side and raised an eyebrow, mocking herself, "It's so *international*." The two women looked at each other and broke out laughing.

"Right, all the travel. Seriously, as I move up in the ranks, there're fewer and fewer women holding those same positions. There still aren't any female captains in Spectrum. I want to be the first. I've had to work harder than any man to prove that I can do all these jobs, even when I'm pregnant. I was thinking about it early this morning." She rubbed her stomach absentmindedly.

"You're always thinking." Chloe took a sip of her coffee and all of a sudden, started to chuckle.

"What?"

"I remember when you told me about your abortion and that you couldn't get pregnant. I guess Victor must have very potent sperm."

"Yeah. He and I joke about that all the time." Isabelle grinned at her.

"I've never understood how people with kids have more kids. Don't they cramp your style?"

"We drug them at night."

"Really?"

"Seriously, Chloe Rose? Seriously?" Isabelle gave her a funny look, and the two women both laughed. "Thank goodness he has such a competent assistant who's able to cover the periods when I'm home. Otherwise, we would never see each other." Isabelle looked at Chloe and gave a little laugh. "Without any help at the shop, there would be fewer of these," she rubbed her belly with a little smile. "You know, Victor's a very busy guy. What with running a business in two locations and being dad *and* mom much of the time, I'm in complete awe of him. But he says he loves it and wouldn't have it any other way, apart from having me around more, of course. It would be a lot harder for him without Tom in New York, his shop assistant in France, and Genevieve, she's such an amazing au pair – that's the only way I can do my job here without worrying about what's going on back home. But Victor runs a tight ship."

"Tight ship? Is he Captain Dad?" Chloe laughed. She looked out the window. "You're living your dream, Isabelle, a wonderful family and doing so well with your career."

"Yeah, and it's thanks to Victor being willing to raise our girls." Isabelle took another sip of her juice, "Hey, remember how disappointed I was that my first internship was going to be at Spectrum's headquarters instead of on a boat? All I did that summer was odd jobs. I thought I was just a gofer, but then I came back to school completely jazzed because I had learned so much about how the business is run." Isabelle popped the last of her toast into her mouth.

"Wasn't that when you worked for that guy…" she grimaced as she tried to remember, "…oh, what was his name… Oscar?"

"Oliver," corrected Isabelle, "Yeah, it was, and after I started working for Spectrum full-time, he called me. Did I ever tell you about this?"

"I don't think so."

"Well, Oliver was a great boss, and he knew how ambitious I was. He's had an impressive career, with over thirty years at Spectrum – he literally worked his way up from the mailroom to the boardroom. When he called, he told me he'd been observing me during my internships. He said he'd had a mentor who'd helped him with his career and asked me if I wanted to be his mentee. I was flattered that he'd remembered me. We talk regularly now about any issues I'm having, and he gives me solid advice on how to handle them, who to talk to, and he helps me figure out what I should say. As I've gained seniority, it's become clear to me that there are unwritten rules of etiquette and over the years, Oliver's been sharing them with me – giving me a heads-up, so to speak. He's never said so, but I also have a feeling he talks to management and other senior captains, checking in on how I'm doing, and he gives me advice based on their feedback."

"What a generous person to give you that much of his time. But enough about work. How're Victor and the girls? I miss those little babies."

"Little babies, ha! They aren't so little anymore. But I do miss my family. Victor's a wonderful parent. And even though things are going well with juggling our careers and childcare, I do still miss them terribly. Sometimes, I envy Victor, being with them all the time, and sometimes, I panic that I'm missing out on them growing up," she said wistfully. "But hey, you can't have it all, can you?" She swallowed a lump in her throat.

"I guess not," Chloe replied. "So, with that in mind, and with baby number four about to appear, are you rethinking your career plan – you know, putting it on hold for a while?"

"I've talked with Oliver about this a lot, and he told me to do what's right for me and my family. He said not to listen to what anyone else says. But it's so hard to decide, Chloe Rose."

Chloe put a supportive hand on Isabelle's.

"You know, I thought we would stop after three. And then along came this one. Baby Rose was unexpected, very welcome, but still, unexpected." She stroked her stomach. "I have been doing a lot of thinking about it. But I haven't had a chance to talk it through with Victor yet. I've wanted to be a riverboat captain all my life – you know, I could have pursued music, my piano teacher said I was good enough to get into music school. But this is what I've always wanted to do. I'm confused. I want to make it all the way to captain, and I'm so close now, but I also want to be with my family. Would I be happy to just stay home, to be a mother and a loving partner to Victor? We have enough money without me working, but I don't know if I'd come to resent giving up my dream when I was that close."

Isabelle thought about Victor, and a faraway, loving look crossed her face. "Speaking of family, have you heard anything from Frank?" she asked hopefully.

"No. I haven't spoken to him since your wedding. You know, we didn't break up because we weren't really dating, but it always makes me sad that he never called to end things. It all just stopped."

"Frank was just being Frank."

"You're right. But then again, I never called him either," said Chloe. "I'm sorry about what came between the two of you."

Isabelle's eyes filled with tears, and she looked out the window, blinking them away.

"I know you still miss him," said Chloe. "I'm sorry. I didn't mean to make you sad."

"Frank can be so stubborn. We still haven't spoken since I was pregnant with Frankie. He gets angry and refuses to speak to people, but he's never let it go on so long before. Chloe Rose, it's a shame, but he won't have anything to do with us or even with the kids. I don't think he knows we've had two more children since Frankie."

"That's so sad, but I'm sure his mom has told him."

"Probably."

"Oh, guess who I ran into when I was in Hamburg for my book signing last month?"

"Rick?" Chloe nodded her head and Isabelle continued, "How is he?"

"Can you believe he came up to me and asked me to sign a copy of my book?"

"He always liked you, Chloe Rose."

"He's a good guy. I went over to his house for dinner. You know he got married to a very nice German woman last year and has twin sons. He always wanted boys."

"That's wonderful. He deserves to be happy. We had such great times together in Texas, didn't we?"

"Those were the golden years – the four amigos. They asked me to come and visit the next time I'm in Germany." Chloe smiled at her friend, "Now, you both have families, and you're so happy." She reached over and stroked Isabelle's belly. "Who do you think she's going to look like?"

"That's one of the things with kids. You never know. Frankie and Lily are so fair, and they both have all that tight curly blond hair."

"Or she could look like Iris with her brown skin like your dad's and all her thick, wavy, black hair."

"Or she could be completely different from any of the other girls. I talked to my mom the other day about how each time one of our babies is born, that's part of the wonderful surprise."

"Bless your heart."

With a warm look at Chloe, Isabelle said, "I'm so glad you're here. It's nice to have someone who's family to spend Christmas with, and as much as I love all of my children and miss holidays with them, I'm glad we're getting to spend some time together without a passel of little ones clamoring for our attention." Isabelle quickly grabbed Chloe's hand and placed it on her belly. Chloe's eyes grew round in surprise, and she gave a huge grin as the baby kicked so hard against her hand that she could see it move.

She tickled the foot lightly with her fingertips. "I'll see you when you come out into this world to join us, Baby Rose."

§

Southern France

Gravel crunched under the tires as her car moved off the paved street onto the circular driveway. Two small blond heads were peeking out the living room window. As Isabelle got out of her car, the light snow caught in her hair, and she hurried to pull her bag and coat off the back seat. The front door burst open, and she heard the squeal of little-girl voices as they ran toward her. And then their arms were wrapped around her legs in welcome. Isabelle dropped her bag and threw her coat on top of it and squatted down to hug them.

"Mommy, I dressed myself today."

Isabelle touched her mismatched clothes, "And you did a fine job, Lily."

"Did you know that dragonflies eat mosquitoes?"

"We have so much to catch up on, Frankie,"

"Mommy, Baby Rose got so big!" Frankie touched Isabelle's large stomach, and Lily reached up to copy her big sister.

Isabelle covered their hands with hers. "It won't be long until she gets to meet you." The girls giggled in excitement, and Isabelle looked over their heads and smiled at Victor. He stood in the doorway, in his arms, a wriggling Iris, her arms stretched out toward Isabelle.

Frankie grabbed Lily's hand, "We need to get inside out of the cold and snow." She looked over her shoulder, "Come on, Mommy. You and Baby Rose too."

Isabelle hefted herself up and reached to pick up her suitcase and coat. "Leave those. I'll get them for you." Victor came over, brushed his hand across Isabelle's tummy and with a light kiss, handed her Iris, who was screaming, "Mommy," over and over. Iris wrapped her arms around Isabelle's neck and covered her cheek with big kisses.

Isabelle turned to follow the two older girls inside. Victor rubbed a hand across her back, "Izzy, you look exhausted."

"I'm more hungry than tired. I can't wait for a homemade meal." She glanced at him, "You're the one who looks exhausted, Old Man."

"Raising our little ones is a labor of love. I wouldn't have it any other way – well, maybe have Genevieve work a few more hours," he laughed.

Isabelle smiled and leaned her face against his shoulder.

Victor set the suitcase inside the door, closed it and dropped her coat on a chair nearby.

They all trooped into the kitchen, where Frankie stopped in the middle of the room and announced, "Mommy, I'm making dinner for us tonight."

Isabelle looked at Victor and back to Frankie, "Oh, really? I'm starving. What are you making?"

"The menu is spaghetti and meatballs with a salad on the side." She nodded her head for emphasis.

"Which side, the right or left?"

Frankie paused and rolled her eyes, "Mommmmmy, you say that all the time." She smiled, proud of herself, "Daddy let me make all the meatballs."

"I bet they are going to be so yummy."

Lily said, "I set the table, Mommy."

Isabelle looked over and saw silverware placed randomly on the table with napkins thrown onto each plate. She smiled. "You're such a great helper, Lily."

"Lily stirred the sauce too. Daddy helped."

Victor leaned over and gave Isabelle a kiss, and then he hugged Isabelle and Iris both. A little voice said from between them, "Squishing me, squishing me, Mommy."

Victor whispered in Isabelle's ear, "God, I missed you, Izzy, so much."

She nodded and whispered back, "Me too." She looked back at Frankie, "So, what did you put in your meatballs?"

"Well, Daddy had to use the big knife, but I mixed it with my hands. I had goop all between my fingers. It was icky, but you know, you have to mix it very well for them to taste perfect."

Isabelle smiled, *Being at home, all our routines, all this happiness.*

When dinner was ready, Frankie and Lily plopped down at their places on the bench on one side of the table. Isabelle put Iris into her highchair and pushed it close to the end before taking her chair across from the older girls. Victor set the bowl of pasta in front of her, and Isabelle reached out and stroked his leg, and they gave each other a smile. While she served the spaghetti and meatballs, Victor put the salad on the small plates that Lily had stacked precariously at one corner, just barely on the edge of the table.

Then everyone began to eat, and Isabelle asked, "What did you do for Christmas?"

"I gave all the poor people rolls."

Frankie corrected her, "Lily, not everyone was poor. Some people were at our church to celebrate Father Christmas like us and to help with dinner."

"I said 'hi' to everyone too."

"You're the best greeter, Lily," Victor chuckled.

Frankie stood up quickly and walked over to Isabelle, "When I met people, I shook their hands. I said, 'I'm Frankie Tomas. I'm very glad to meet you,' and they always told me their name." She stuck her hand out to her mom, showing her.

Isabelle shook her hand and smiled. "Nice to meet you too. I'm Isabelle Ronaldo."

"I'm older than Lily, so I shake hands." She returned to her seat.

"I'll shake hands when I'm almost five, like you."

"I bet you will, Lily."

"Will Baby Rose be able to see me shake?"

With a mouthful of noodles and sauce, Isabelle nodded, "Mmmhmm."

"Oh, goodie," Lily giggled. "Frankie, Baby Rose will see us shake."

They continued to talk about the soup kitchen and all the people they had seen again from the previous year.

Isabelle asked, "Did Father Christmas bring you a gift?"

Lily said, "We put on our new nightgowns, and then we slept under the tree. We had to close our eyes before Father Christmas could come. He brought us stockings. It snowed, and there were presents under the tree in the morning."

"Mommy, I'll show you my book from Aunt Chloe." Frankie started to get out of her chair and then thought again and sat back down. "After dinner. This year, we all got books from her."

"Why don't I read all three books to you tonight?"

"*Daddy* reads to us," Lily said, "after our baths."

Isabelle swallowed hard, and Victor took her hand in his and stroked it. "Tonight, you're so lucky. Mommy will do it," he said quietly.

"Yay!" shouted Frankie, and then Iris banged on the table and shouted, "Yay!"

While they continued to eat their dinner and talk, Victor leaned back in his chair watching his lovely, very pregnant wife and their three beautiful little girls. *What a wonderful family we've created.*

Frankie said, "Mommy, you also missed Saint Nicolas Day. That was before Christmas. Aren't you going to ask us about that too?"

"Thank you, Frankie. That slipped my mind. Did you put your shoes out?"

"The donkey came, and the carrots were gone in the morning," Lily answered.

"Did Iris put out the carrots, Lily?"

"She's not old enough. You're silly, Mommy. You have to be at least three, like me, to get the carrots. They're in the pantry, and the shelf is too high for Iris. She doesn't even know where they are."

Frankie sat up taller in her seat, "Lily did such a good job with the carrots. This time, I didn't have to help her at all." Lily smiled happily. And then Frankie went on, "Before we went to bed, we put our shoes out on the windowsill," and she pointed with her fork to the living room window. "In the morning, we found the shoes in front of the fireplace."

"So, Frankie, were they empty?"

"Of course not, Mommy," she replied. "They were filled with chocolate money, a cookie, nuts and a toy, like every year. Don't you remember? Doesn't Saint Nicolas come to your boat and bring you gifts? Maybe you need to stay home with us so you can see it too."

I hate missing the holidays. I hate missing my family. Missing seeing our children grow up, all our traditions. I hate that I can't share in most of them. Is missing out on all this what I want? This is the decision I have to make.

"He does find me on the boat, and he leaves me the best chocolate in the whole world," Isabelle said with a very serious look on her face.

"Saint Nicolas brings gifts to children. Mommy is too old," said Victor, a chuckle in his voice. "She only gets chocolate."

Isabelle laughed at him, "That's right, Old Man."

"All right, girls, let's clear the table and clean up."

Lily and Frankie cleared the table, and Victor washed up while Isabelle picked Iris up and sat on the bench, snuggling her.

When they were all done, Victor said, "Do you girls want to show Mommy your new nightgowns?"

Frankie said, "They aren't new anymore, Daddy. They've even been washed. Race you to the bathroom," she said to Lily, and the girls ran up the stairs as Isabelle followed behind them with Iris in her arms.

Victor listened to the chatter of the little girls as they had their bath and how they quieted down when Isabelle read to them. He heard her moving around upstairs, the old wooden floors creaking, the shower running. He sighed with contentment as he put a tray on the coffee table. *I'm so happy to have her back home again. She has no idea how very much I miss her every moment she's gone.*

When Isabelle came downstairs with her comfy, oversized

winter robe wrapped around her, she saw that Victor had lit a fire and some candles. He'd set their silver tray with a bottle of sparkling cider and two glasses on the coffee table in front of the fire.

Isabelle collapsed onto the couch with a long sigh, "And you do that every night without me? You're a saint."

Victor stroked the back of her neck as he walked behind the couch. "I'm not pregnant. Thank goodness for that. I'm sure everything feels much harder for you right now." He sat next to Isabelle and pulled her into his arms and said, "Let me welcome you home properly."

Their mouths met. "Maybe you should welcome me home improperly."

"There is time for that later, Izzy."

They kissed again, and then they heard a whisper from behind them, "Mommy, I'm not sleepy yet."

Isabelle turned around to see Frankie and motioned for her to come around the couch. "Are the other girls asleep?"

She nodded. "Mommy, what does 'improperly' mean?"

"Frankie, have you been eavesdropping again? What have we told you about that?"

She nodded again sheepishly. "Don't eavesdrop."

Isabelle patted the couch between her and Victor, "Five minutes."

Frankie smiled, "Only five?" She handed a brush to Isabelle. "Will you brush my hair, Mommy? I missed you so much."

"I missed you too, and I've missed brushing all your tangly little curls," and she took the brush and began carefully pulling at the snarls in her blond hair. "I'll be home for a while now, Frankie. Until after the baby is born and grows up a bit."

"Oh, goodie!"

Frankie placed her feet on Victor's lap and wiggled them. He tickled them, and she began giggling. Isabelle said, "Don't get her riled up, dear. It's bedtime."

Frankie opened her eyes with a wide-eyed, innocent look. "But tickling always helps me sleep. Right, Daddy?"

"Oh, I never would have guessed." Isabelle suppressed a laugh, "Okay, five minutes are up. Up you go to bed."

"Already?" Frankie pouted as Victor picked her up in his arms.

"Say goodnight to your mommy." He leaned over so Isabelle could kiss Frankie's cheek.

"Good night, Mommy." She reached down and touched her belly. "Good night, Baby Rose."

"Sleep well, my little one."

As Victor climbed the stairs, Isabelle heard him humming *Twinkle, Twinkle, Little Star* softly into the top of Frankie's head.

When he returned to the couch, she said, "Remember the first time we used this? On the porch when I told you I was pregnant with Frankie?" Isabelle ran her fingers fondly over the rim of the well-polished, old silver tray before handing him one of the glasses of cider, "Here's to us, Victor. This is the most wonderful part of coming home. I've been looking forward to this all day."

After they'd each taken a sip, Victor set their glasses back on the tray, and he slipped his hands into her hair, and their kiss went on and on.

"I cannot believe how our lives have changed. I'm so lucky," he murmured, with his cheek against hers.

"So lucky to have a pregnant wife every New Year's Eve?"

"Well, there was one year you weren't." They looked at each other in contentment and sat, leaning together, watching the fire and remembering.

Victor grinned as he turned to Isabelle, "You're the most beautiful woman in the world, especially when you're pregnant and wearing nothing."

"Nothing at all?" They both began to laugh at the memory.

"Izzy, would you like me to rub some lotion on your belly?"

"Only if you read your poetry to me afterward. There's nothing like the sound of your voice when you read to me to make me realize I'm finally home."

He leaned over and opened the drawer in the end table and pulled out a jar. Carefully unscrewing the lid, he scooped the thick cream into his palm and held his hands together, warming the lotion. Isabelle untied her robe, and Victor began massaging her belly, first gently, then gradually applying a little more pressure. Rose kicked him, "She's a mommy's girl, kicking me when I touch you."

"Oh, she does that all the time."

Isabelle sighed and leaned back with her head on the cushion, her eyes half-closed, luxuriating in the feel of his hands stroking her stomach. Victor looked at Isabelle, thinking about how very deeply in love he was with her.

Chapter Twelve

January 2008

A Drink and a Nod

Train from Paris to Zürich

Lydia stood in the Gare de Lyon at the foot of the stairs leading up to the restaurant, Le Train Bleu. She yawned. *I'm definitely not a morning person. Especially when I have to be somewhere when it's still dark outside.* While she waited for Frank to arrive, she looked around at all the stone, glass and ornate ironwork, watching the way the city lights sparkled through the glass, even at that dreadful early hour. *Designing a building is like designing a dress – if all the parts come together just right, it can be spectacular. And if not—* Her thoughts were interrupted by a family walking by, the father saying loudly, "Come on, kids. The train leaves in fifteen minutes."

Then Frank's voice caught her attention, and she whirled around. "Lydia, I haven't had any coffee this morning, so let's go get one up there before we board." He pointed up the stairs to the restaurant, "We've got plenty of time."

After they'd finished their coffee, not long before they were scheduled to depart, Frank strode ahead of her, weaving around people on the teeming platform. *My little legs can never keep pace with his.*

He waited for her at the door to their train car. When she finally caught up, she stopped in front of him. "This platform is a madhouse today," she said. Suddenly, she felt someone push hard against her back, and she grabbed onto her purse as she stumbled toward Frank. He caught her and steadied her. "Sorry about that," she said, looking up at him with a sly little smile.

He put his hand out to help her onto the train and followed close behind. Over her shoulder, Lydia asked, "What's our compartment number, Frank?"

At their first-class compartment door, he looked at the seat reservations posted outside. "It looks like we got lucky, and we'll have it all to ourselves." He gave her a quick little wink as they entered.

The steward knocked and came in. "Will you be having

breakfast in the café car this morning?"

"No. Just a plate of croissants in here," said Frank.

"With lots of butter and jam, please."

"Coffee or tea?"

"A pot of coffee."

"With extra cream too. Thank you," said Lydia.

After the steward left, Lydia picked up her stylish briefcase, set it on the table and slipped her hand into the pocket on the back. Frank watched her carefully. She pulled out his wallet and handed it to him. "You may need this back to tip the steward when he returns."

Frank looked at her closely. "Ah, the crowded platform outside the train when that guy pushed you."

"Nope, guess again."

"Really? Hmmm, so it had to be after we had coffee because I paid then. That's it. You brushed up against me when I leaned over to pick up my portfolio, just before we left the restaurant."

Lydia tilted her head to the right and raised her eyebrows ever so slightly, and the corners of her lips turned up just the tiniest bit in a self-satisfied little smile. "Good, then you don't know. You have no clue."

"Then when?"

"Your last guess was close. It was when I tucked my arm through yours coming back down the stairs after we'd had our coffee."

Frank raised an eyebrow back at her in approval, "Well done."

The steward tapped on the door and came into the compartment carrying a tray with their coffee and croissants, just as Frank was saying, "Then we are all prepared for this evening." They watched him as he flipped a white cloth onto the small table and carefully set out their breakfast. He gave a formal little bow as Lydia thanked him, and he closed the door quietly. She took a croissant, tore off a large piece and slathered on butter and jam from the small dishes between them. After her first bite, she sighed with pleasure and then set the remainder of the torn piece on her plate. She swallowed, wiped her fingers carefully and reached into the briefcase she'd set next to her chair.

"And then I have this. There were so many opportunities," she said. She lifted her hand, a diamond and sapphire tennis bracelet dangling from her fingers. "Just look at these stones, Frank. And I think the setting is platinum, not white gold, so it must easily be worth thirty-five hundred euros."

She's smart and a quick learner. Frank narrowed his eyes as he looked at the bracelet and nodded his head in approval. He reached out, but Lydia pulled her hand back. "Sixty-forty for this one."

He started to object, and Lydia said, "I acquired this without you, so I should get more." She squinted her eyes thoughtfully, "I often wonder about the people who we steal from. Do you think they miss the stuff?"

"It's just stuff. Just one piece in their huge collection, and they have insurance anyway."

"Do you think any of it has sentimental value?"

Frank touched his watch, "Well, I try to look for things that are expensive but not old."

They finished their croissants, piled the plates on one side of the table as they chatted and drank their coffee. Then Lydia set her cup back in its saucer and looked at Frank. "I'm all about practice until everything is second nature. I want to make sure we're totally prepared. Let's go through tonight's plan again."

After they had gone over it several more times, Frank asked, "Where did you learn so much about jewelry? I've only known you for a few months now, we've done a handful of jobs together in Paris, and I don't know much of anything about your background or training."

Lydia sat back and crossed her legs, swinging her foot, thinking about what and how much to tell him. Frank watched her face as she thought about her life in Ireland and how things had changed since she'd come to Paris, since she'd met Mari. Finally, he nudged her with his foot as he pulled his stretched-out legs back in, "Lydia, are you okay?"

Caught up in her thoughts, she jumped at his touch. "Yeah, I'm fine. Ahhh, it's just complicated."

Frank stared out the window, waiting, watching the countryside pass by, villages and farms barely visible in the diffused light as dawn broke. "God, I love trains," he said, his voice suddenly sentimental.

"Where did that come from?"

"Every chance I get, I take the train. Trains are my escape from everyday life at the bank. I don't like flying if I don't have to." Frank looked over at Lydia and then returned to staring out the window. "When I was a kid, my Uncle Victor and I would go to the station, pick, say, the third train from track ten. Then we'd buy tickets and go wherever it went, just to hang out. Sometimes, it was for the day, and other times, it was for a weekend. It was always an adventure with him."

Lydia finished her coffee while she listened, and then she asked him, "Have you ever taken the Orient Express? Like in the movies? It looks so romantic. All that wood and lamps and carpets – and tablecloths and flowers, and all the staff in their white dinner jackets—"

"It's very posh. Hey, maybe one of these days, we'll take that to a job. It would have to be a lucrative one. But wouldn't it be fun? We could pose as a couple on vacation. Like the thieves do in those old movies."

Lydia watched him, suddenly so boyish and carefree. "Frank, that would be such an experience." They both laughed.

Then the lighthearted moment passed, and Frank returned to his more serious self. "Okay, back to my question, where did you learn so much about jewelry?"

"I've learned some from Shane, my boss, but mostly I'm self-taught. I read about it at night. And I practice, practice, practice, taking things and then studying them to learn their real value. I have to be perfect. I want to steal only the best and only the most valuable. And I can't afford to get caught. So, I practice some more."

Frank looked at her with respect. "Is Shane your boss? I thought he was your pawnbroker."

"He's both now."

"And you work at a pawnshop?"

"I'm the office manager."

"That can't possibly pay enough to cover those fabulous dresses you wear."

Lydia looked down and smoothed the fabric of her dress. "I design and make all of them myself. So, they cost almost nothing."

He looked at her dress again, "You're very talented."

"I don't want to steal for the rest of my life."

"What do you want to do?"

"Lydia McKay of Paris. My own boutique, a couture business. I've designed and made dresses for over fifteen years."

"Fifteen years?"

Lydia blushed. "In the early years, they weren't very good. But I stuck with it and learned fast. By the time I was sixteen, I'd begun designing dresses for my mam's clients. They all thought they were her creations." She thought fondly of how they'd never let on that it was her work that had surpassed her mother's, and how they would laugh after the clients left.

"Tell me about Lydia McKay of Paris."

"Well, I've already started it, actually. I visit clients at their houses and discuss what they want. Then I make their dresses at home, in my room – I've got everything set up there. But eventually, I want my own studio to design custom clothes and a commercial space to sell them. By my calculations, it's going to take about eight years – at this point, I'm on track to save the money I need, I already have a small clientele, and I put up posters and hand out business cards at every possible opportunity. I've been working and living in that one tiny room and stashing away all my spare cash."

Frank was impressed by her ambition. "That's a lot of work. Making it in Paris is hard."

"Yep, after an opportunity presented itself and I realized I was actually good at stealing, I found I could make far more money than just from working for Shane. Now, I make my own opportunities." Lydia looked out the window, "But I never feel good about taking jewelry from these women."

"It will feel good when you open Lydia McKay of Paris."

"I know, and I'll make it. I know I will. I have to – for my mam." Lydia wished she hadn't mentioned her mother again because it was just too personal.

"Your mother?"

"Ugly story. I don't want to talk about it."

They fell silent and sat, watching the scenery flash by. The steward knocked, entered and cleared the dishes. "Would you like more coffee?"

Lydia shook her head, and Frank said, "No more for us."

Lydia looked up, "Thanks anyway."

After the steward left, Frank asked, "What if you could make this boutique of yours happen in four years instead of eight?"

"No way. When I first came to Paris, I thought it would be quick, but I've done the math over and over. I know the startup costs. I know what I make and how much I can save. That's impossible."

"Quit working for Shane. Come work for me at the bank, as my assistant. We can work and travel together so we can take care of this other business too."

"But you live in Brussels. I'm not moving to Brussels. I have to stay in Paris."

"That's a detail we can work around. You stay with me for four years, and then you'll be set."

"What's the catch? Nothing comes for free."

"We'll make a lot of money."

"So, how do you find these people, Frank, the ones you steal from, your targets?"

"I'm the European liaison for my dad's bank, so I meet wealthy people all the time all across Europe. I read the society pages in the newspaper, and then I find events they attend in various cities. And like you did at the bank reception and today on the platform, I take other opportunities when they arise."

"You must have quite a journal to track all these people and locations. I could never remember it all."

"I can remember conversations and names without writing them down. It's my gift. Although sometimes, it can be a curse."

"Why is that?"

"There are people and conversations that sometimes you want to forget. Another one of those ugly stories." Frank asked again, "So, do you want to work for me or not?"

"How much does it pay?"

"Twice what Shane pays you."

"That's not much. Three times."

Frank looked out the window and smiled at her boldness. He

watched her reflection in the window as he thought about how well they worked together. When he looked back, he said, "Deal." He leaned forward and stuck his hand out across the table.

"How can I refuse an offer like that?"

They shook hands. *Mari won't be happy about this, but it's only for a few years. It will be less time than if I were to stay with Shane and steal for myself on the side. I can save so much more so much faster this way.*

Lydia sat back, pleased with the offer. "Where did you grow up?"

"I lived in New York City until I was ten. Then my grandfather died, and my family moved to Brazil so my dad could run his bank from the headquarters there. My favorite part of growing up was with my uncle in New York. We were very close. And then, I met my best friend when we moved to Brasília."

"You said you and your uncle were close. What about now?"

"We haven't spoken for years. Another ugly story." He shook his head.

"I think you have more ugly stories than I do."

"Zürich Hauptbahnhof in ten minutes," called out the conductor as he came through the train, knocking on compartment doors.

§

Zürich, Switzerland

When they arrived at the Opernhaus Zürich, they went directly to the bar. While they stood waiting for their drinks, Frank looked Lydia up and down and noticed again how attractive she was, how the lines of her gown flattered her figure and how the color complemented her hair. The dress was raw silk in a deep, emerald green, matched by the same earrings she'd worn when Frank had first met her. It had a plunging neckline, outlined with a mink collar and long, fitted sleeves with mink-trimmed cuffs. It was perfect for the opening night. *Another Lydia McKay design, no doubt. She is extraordinarily talented.*

Frank reached out and ran a finger across her nose. "Your skin is so beautiful and creamy tonight, but I do miss your freckles."

"I always cover them when I dress up."

"The two sides of Lydia McKay. I like them both. The grown-up and the carefree young woman."

The bartender delivered their drinks. Frank stood, casually sipping his whisky, looking, confirming that his targets were there. And Lydia watched him, his eyes constantly moving as they chatted. *He wears that tuxedo well. He's handsome. And he's so smart.*

"Beethoven's *Fidelio* has always been one of my favorite operas. Are you familiar with it?" He broke into her thoughts.

Lydia shook her head.

"Fidelio is actually a woman named Leonora who has disguised herself as a guard to rescue her husband, Floresta, from a Spanish prison. It celebrates unrequited love and freedom and risk and triumph."

"Risk? That suits you."

Frank gave her an appraising look, "Ready?" With their drinks in hand, they began to work. They drifted through the crowd as though they were mingling with the other patrons. They passed each of the five targets, and each time, Frank signaled to Lydia by lifting his glass and taking a sip. Lydia took a small drink in return and gave a nod in acknowledgement. During this time, they never drank unless they were signaling to each other. They laughed and talked in a carefree fashion and took only the five careful sips each.

Once the targets were identified, Frank glanced at his Rolex and then over to the bar. "I see my clients have arrived," and he pointed with the hand that held his glass.

Lydia looked at him. "Clients? I thought you didn't mix bank business with—"

"Let's go." Frank slipped his hand under her forearm and led her to the bar. "John, Anne, this is my assistant, Lydia McKay. Lydia, John and Anne Gold are long-time clients of our bank. They are here in Switzerland to ski, and I thought we should try to meet up. Anne used to sing with the New York City Opera Company. In fact, Anne," he turned to her, "wasn't *Fidelio* the opera you sang in the first time I met you?"

"Yes, it was," smiled Anne, and she turned to compliment Lydia. "Your gown is fabulous. Who is the designer?"

"Lydia McKay of Paris."

"Lydia McKay? Is that you?" Anne asked.

"It is. Here, let me give you my card. I design gowns in my free time."

Frank scowled as he listened to Lydia conducting *her* business on *his* time.

"You're so talented." Anne turned to the two men, "Why don't you boys go off and talk business? I have so many questions for Lydia about her creations. Who knows, I may ask her to make an outfit or two for me."

Frank gave Lydia another scowl, and he and John turned away.

"Tell me about your clients," Anne asked eagerly.

"Living in Paris has reinforced for me the importance of designing for the individual rather than simply reproducing the latest trend. It's truly a partnership, and I learn so much about each woman as I complete our designs. The women I've worked with usually know what they need and what they want and the image they want to present. If they're not sure what they're after, I guide them through it, giving them ideas to get things started. But it's always a collaborative process. One of my clients works at a bank and needs a traditional look, but as soon as you see the dress, it becomes evident the outfit has unusually elegant details. I designed it after one of my own. She can wear it on many occasions, not just to work. The flamenco dancer I design for has danced since she was a child and knows exactly what she wants. I just guide her and make her vision come to life. Another woman I work with is a lawyer, and our focus was to design the right suit in the perfect color to frame her face so that when she is in court, the jury focuses on what she's saying and not what she's wearing. But still, the fit is exquisite, and when she changes the blouse, it turns into an evening outfit, or with yet another top, something she can wear to dinner."

As they approached their box, Anne said, "I could listen to you for hours. We'll have to talk more."

As the curtain went down for the intermission, Lydia turned to Frank. "I'm going to wander around and look at all the splendid gowns. They might serve as inspiration for some of mine." Then she looked at Anne, "Would you like to join me, Anne?"

"Of course. Honey, I'm going with Lydia while you two go and smoke a stinky cigar."

John patted Anne on the arm. "Okay. We'll see you back here at the box."

Lydia and Anne descended to the crowded bar level. As they walked around, Lydia pointed out gowns that were particularly attractive, and she saw the first of Frank's targets. She noticed the woman, constantly fidgeting with her diamond Cartier watch. *That's too bad. That was the best item on our list.* She passed her by.

Then they stopped to look at a painting hanging in a particularly busy area, while Lydia stood close to their second target. As they talked about the painting, Lydia quickly removed the woman's emerald bracelet. She pretended to adjust her purse and slipped the bracelet inside, and then she turned to Anne, pointing across the lobby to a woman wearing a slim-fitting scarlet dress with a plunging neckline and a slit almost to one hip. "Now, that is over the top. It leaves absolutely nothing to anyone's imagination." Anne giggled in response.

They strolled on, Lydia describing why certain gowns had a flair and style that others were missing, pointing out how some dresses moved and others didn't, while she raised one hand to touch her hair and removed an ornate necklace from a woman's neck. "I hope I'm not boring you. Frank teases me that I'm obsessed with clothes."

"Oh, not at all. This is so fascinating. It's like an inside look into the design business and how designers think."

On the way back to the box, Lydia and Anne chatted about the opera and Anne's life before she'd retired. "John always makes it sound like I was a diva or something. I only sang in the opera chorus for a few years before my so-called retirement. And then, one day, we just decided that we wanted to travel and see the world. I keep telling John that I'd like to do a round-the-world cruise." Anne chattered on about places she'd been and places she still wanted to go.

The chimes sounded to indicate the next act would begin in five minutes.

Once they got back to the box and settled, Frank asked Lydia, "How about an authentic Swiss fondue tonight?" If she agreed, that would mean that she had been successful in stealing one or more of the pieces they wanted. If she said she preferred Italian, then she hadn't been able to get anything at all.

"That sounds perfect, Frank."

"Anne, John, what do you think? Swiss? There's a charming little place a couple of blocks from here. I presumed and made a reservation, just in case," Frank said.

§

Back at the two-bedroom suite in the hotel, no sooner had Lydia closed the door than Frank was pouring himself a large glass of whisky. "Do you want anything?"

"No, I'm fine."

He turned abruptly, scowling at her, and snapped, "What were you doing there? This was about *my* business."

"What are you talking about? I did my job. I upheld my end of the bargain."

"Lydia McKay of Paris?"

"She asked a question, and I answered it. Am I supposed to lie or not answer her or do something else rude? Walk off and leave you with your clients?" Lydia walked over to the couch and kicked off her heels.

Frank followed her and sat down heavily on the chair at the end of the coffee table. "I thought you worked alone. It was risky taking Anne with you."

"What are you talking about? She was the perfect cover."

"What if she'd seen you?"

"Do you have any idea how easy it was to distract her? The artwork, the dresses, the idle conversation. I pointed out dresses and told her to watch how women move. She was hooked and spent her time watching them very carefully. She wasn't paying attention to me or anything else. Give me credit, Frank. It was brilliant."

Frank sighed in annoyance. "I just don't like it. It's too risky."

"You're wrong. Are you telling me how to do my job?" Lydia reached into her purse and pulled out two pieces of jewelry. "This is what me doing my job – my way – got us." *I hate that I stole from them. I know it won't make up for it, but if they ever come into my shop, I'll give them a really good deal.*

Frank took the bracelet and necklace and stood up, walking over to the bar where he flipped a switch and looked at the jewelry in the bright light. Nodding in approval, he slipped them into his right pocket. He poured yet another whisky for himself and a glass of champagne for Lydia and walked back to her. He sat on the couch next to her and handed her the champagne. "Good job." He lifted his glass and clinked it lightly against hers.

Lydia smiled to herself. *I told you so,* and she took a sip.

Frank set down his drink and pulled the jewelry out of his pocket. He laid the bracelet on the table next to his glass. Then he took the necklace and slowly leaned toward her. He clasped it around her neck, ran his fingers along the necklace and let them linger at the base of her throat. Then he stroked them along her collarbone. "You know, we could be good at more than just this."

"Frank, I'm with Mari. You know that. We're lovers. We're moving in together next month. And other than that, I'm just focusing on my business." Lydia unfastened the necklace and dropped it into his hand.

Chapter Thirteen

June 2009

Four Cold Cases

Raleigh, North Carolina

Eric glanced over at the open staircase tucked in at the back of the reception area. "What are you gonna do with the second and third floors, Em? Do you think Haypress Security'll expand so much that you'll need the space?"

"Business is great, and I've met all of my five-year goals – including buying my own building. It's the one I've always wanted." Emily sat back and looked around the open space, admiring the character of her new property, the old brick walls and uneven dark wooden floor, the heavy ceiling beams. "Now that I have contracts with those additional cruise lines to provide security systems and support, there's more than enough work. The good news is that it means most of my staff stay out on assignment and don't need permanent offices. I'll be able to lease the upper floors for the time being. Or maybe I won't. It's still too new. I just don't know yet if I want to share."

Penelope asked, "Any updates with Spectrum River Cruise Line? You've been talking about them for years."

"Nope, they keep saying, 'No thanks.' They don't seem to think they need help with their security. So, next year, I'm going to change my annual cruise to travel on Spectrum as a little fact-finding mission to get a feel for how they do business. Then I'll be able to present a very on-point pitch to them."

"You've done well, Em, since you retired," Penelope said, proud of her friend's success.

"I have, haven't I? You know, there's always a position for both of you here at Haypress. I'm not pushing, just reminding you."

Eric raised his beer and gave a brief nod. "Thanks. But Morgan doesn't want me away from home, traveling the world." *And I don't want a cushy security job.*

Penelope turned toward Emily and tucked one leg under her thigh. She sighed. "I know you think I should retire and come work for you. But I need to solve these four murders first." Her voice was impassioned as she said, "Those women need a voice, an advocate, and I'm determined to be that for them. I've been working on these cases for so long that their names and the dates they were killed are burned into my mind. I can't give up on them. I know that bastard is still out there." She rubbed her face in frustration.

"And that's why I've asked Edgar Spring to join us today," said Emily.

"The press? You keep pushing them on us, Em," Penelope complained.

"Because you need to be pushed. They're the only option we have left, and Edgar is the one who wrote the articles in the *Raleigh Weekly News.*"

Eric looked across at Penelope and said in annoyance, "For years you've been saying you'll figure it out without the media. 1998 – 2002 – 2005 – 2007. It's 2009 now. How's that goin'?"

Waving her hand to brush him off, Penelope said in a disparaging voice, "Look what happened when that guy wrote his first little news article about the 'Parking Lot Strangler'. Except for a bunch of scared citizens, what did we get from it? Nothing. Zip. Nada."

"We have to keep trying new things, Pens," Emily said quietly before she looked over at Eric. "So, E, what was your boss's objection to using the media to get leads?"

He leaned forward. "Remember, way back when the mayor was running for re-election, Em, and his campaign message included being tough on crime? And how worried he was that his opponent would spin it that he's a poor leader because the murder rate was so high? Well, Raleigh's index is still substantially higher than the national average. And he fought that same battle last year when he came up for re-election again. It's all politics, Em. They're more concerned with keeping their jobs than solving this series of murders. They just want it to go away."

"What finally changed your bosses' minds? Why is it different now?"

"It's been just over a year since the fourth murder, and we haven't made progress on that case either. Or on any of the other three. I told our supervisor that we can't wait for a fifth or sixth murder before doing something. That would look worse on the mayor's record than just confirming that reporter's story that we have a serial killer and using the press to try and get some new information."

Penelope broke in, "I've probably spoken to thousands of people over the last decade. What can anyone add?"

Eric ignored her and continued, "You have no idea the hoops I had to jump through to get our supervisor to agree to involve the press again. She was spitting mad about the first article last year and threatened to pull me and Pens off the case. I don't know if we ever convinced her that we hadn't leaked that information."

"Well, whatever you did, it worked," said Emily. "Too bad you couldn't convince your boss that nothing was leaked. All I did was call Edgar with the names and dates of the murder victims and told him to look into them. The information had already been in the papers. I just connected the dots for him, that's all, nothing more." She gave a little shrug. "We saw how resourceful he was. That article included a lot of facts I never told him. He did a lot of research." She glanced up at the Roman numerals on the large, round, antique clock that hung on the brick wall. "He should be here soon. Let's finish our beers and go into my office to meet with him."

§

What does she know about the Parking Lot Strangler that I don't? Edgar stood in front of the red brick building, its large windows and doorway encased in white stone and the old front door flanked by the original isinglass sidelights. *Nice place,* he thought. *They must be pretty successful. I wonder why I've never heard of them before.* He checked the name on the discreet sign beside the door. "Yep, Haypress Security. This is it." He walked in and stood uncertainly in front of an empty reception desk. "Hello?"

Emily poked her head out of her office located midway down one side of the large open space. "Hi, Edgar." She beckoned him in. "I'm Emily Bissett. Come on back here."

"It's you? I saw you at the Lauch gala. You gave me the lead?" Edgar said as he walked toward her.

Emily reached out and shook his hand. "Yes, it was me. Nice

to see you again, Edgar."

"I knew it. I told my boss it was probably someone from one of the events I covered."

She said, "There are a couple of detectives here to work with us. Let me introduce you."

Edgar stopped for a second. *Oh my God.* "Cops? Police?" he said under his breath.

As he followed Emily into her office, Eric stood up and stared at Edgar long enough to make him uncomfortable before he stuck out his big, meaty hand. "I'm Detective Eric Daniel, and this is my partner, Detective Penelope Huber."

He's so tall, look at those muscles in his arms. He could easily squash me. Edgar was proud of himself that he stayed calm as he said, "Edgar Spring, investigative journalist for the *Raleigh Weekly News*. Nice to meet you, sir, ma'am."

"Just call me Eric."

"Penelope is fine. I'm not old enough to be a ma'am."

Emily glanced at Penelope and suppressed a smile. "So, you're no longer the society reporter, Edgar?"

"No, ma'am. They offered me this new position last September after I wrote my first article about the Parking Lot Strangler."

"Congratulations," said Emily. "Take a seat here at the table with us. Would you like a drink?" He blinked at her as though uncertain about how to answer. "Water? Soda?" she prompted.

Edgar looked around at the bottles in front of each of them. "Uhhh, water – ma'am."

Her mouth twitched, "Emily will do."

"Yes ma'am – I mean Emily."

She tossed a bottle to Edgar. He put his hand out, and it bounced off his fingertips. Penelope snickered. He bent down awkwardly to pick it up, his face flushing with embarrassment. Emily sat down beside him at the small rectangular table adjacent to her desk. She laid a newspaper article in front of him, "We want to talk to you about this." She tapped on it gently with her polished fingernail.

Oh, my God, what did I do? I'm being called out on this by two cops and this security woman. Am I going to be arrested? What's going to happen to my friend at the police department who helped me? Oh, my God. Oh, my God.

Emily saw the panic on his face. "Edgar, your article last year was good, and so we want to work with you. But this recent article," tap, tap went her finger again, "all it does is restate the facts about the murders. It doesn't tell the reader anything new – except that there's nothing new."

"We want to work with you to get some additional information out there to the public," said Eric. "We think someone might know something that will help us. That's where you come in."

"But you'll need to show us anything you write about this case before it's published," Penelope added.

"Hey, that violates freedom of the press."

"Then you can step away right now and write another 'not report', where nothing's happened, where there's nothing new," she said in a withering tone. And again, Emily tapped her well-manicured finger on the article on the table. She gestured in a wide circle to include all four of them. "This," she said, her voice now stern and quiet, "this is how cooperation between the press and the police happens. We give you access to information, and you help us put the pieces together."

Penelope pressed her lips together hard and looked down to hide her smile. Emily normally liked to win people over with kindness. *Em always says, 'With honey.'* In all their years of working together, Penelope rarely saw this side of her friend. She'd usually played the good cop and Penelope the tough one.

"So, are you in, Edgar, or out?" Penelope pressed him.

Edgar cleared his throat and sat up straight, "I'm in." He cleared his throat again.

He reached down and took his notepad from his backpack. Then he pulled out his chewed-on stub of a pencil that was tucked into the notepad and looked around at them eagerly.

Penelope continued, "Edgar, if we're going to do this right, there's one thing I have to make very clear."

He nodded, his face solemn and his eyes blinking rapidly.

Penelope leaned toward him, holding his gaze to emphasize her point. "Until we agree on what can be released to the public, nothing we discuss can be leaked. It cannot be leaked to another soul. Not to your friends, not to your girlfriend or boyfriend, not to your mom or dad. Not. Even. To. Your. Boss. Nothing – not even the smallest detail – can be leaked. Not. A. Thing. Do you understand?"

Wow, she's scary. "I understand and – and in the – the interest of full disclosure, I need to let you know that – that my roommate works in the files room at Raleigh PD. He – he made copies of the four files for me, and I used them for the first article."

"So, you're throwing your roommate under the bus?" Emily chuckled.

Edgar's face turned white. "No, no! That wasn't my intention. I just wanted to let you know." His voice cracked a little as he spoke.

Penelope gave Edgar her most intimidating stare. "You can't tell your roommate anything more. Nothing. As we talk through what we know, there will be some things that we will decide we want you to put in your articles, and some we'll tell you to leave out."

"I completely understand." Edgar slid down in his chair. He stuck his pencil back into his notepad and leaned over slightly to tuck it into his backpack. Then he looked straight at Penelope, trying to look confident and not stumble over his words. "I completely understand – understand the sensitivity of the information. I won't take any notes. Once – once we agree on what's to be included, I'll write everything from memory. We'll review the article together, so you can make sure it sends precisely the message you intend."

"Good. Edgar, you can take notes, but they have to stay in here."

Emily looked back and forth between him and Penelope. *This will be interesting to watch.*

Eric pushed his chair back slightly and leaned forward, resting his elbows on his knees as he spoke. "Let me give you some background, Edgar. The three of us have been involved with all these cases, in one way or another, since the beginning."

Edgar set down his water bottle and leaned forward and propped his chin on one fist.

"Pens found the first body, and Em and I worked the case. That was Maggie Wilson. We pounded the pavement for months, talking to her customers, acquaintances, friends, looking for that additional little piece of evidence that would lead us to her murderer."

"Right."

"With the Ruth Sampson case, we did the same thing. That time, Pens worked it with her former partner, and they went through the same routine. And, again, there were no connections to Maggie that they found in their discussion with Ruth's acquaintances. It was Pens who linked Maggie's and Ruth's crime scenes. It was simply good analysis on her part."

Penelope held out her left hand with the palm up and said, "Maggie had red hair and was missing an earring, right? She was strangled." Then she held out her right hand with the palm up. "Ruth was strangled, had red hair and was missing an earring too."

"And the third case was the bartender, Zoe," Edgar jumped in, eager to show he knew the cases.

Eric nodded, "Yep. Zoe Abrams. At that point, Emily had retired, and Pens and I became partners. The two of us worked Zoe's case and Sheila Kovacs's too. Same routine, same lack of results. This guy is literally getting away with murder."

"They were both redheads too," Edgar said knowingly.

"Yes." Penelope looked at him and went on, "By the third victim, I was convinced we had a serial killer. Eric thought we might have a copycat murder, but I knew it wasn't."

Eric smiled and shook his head. "The first three murders are now cold cases, and Sheila's is well on the way to becoming one too. Our supervisor finally threw more manpower at it, but that's turned out to be too little too late."

"I care so very much about these cases. I want to catch this guy more than anything in the world. These women deserve justice – all of them. I'm sure the killer lives and walks among us – God, we might see him every day! I can feel it in my bones," Penelope added passionately.

Emily placed her hands on the table in front of her. "So, with that background, we're ready to begin. Let's go next door to my small conference room. I've had several whiteboards installed there, so we'll have lots of room for notes."

She stood and picked up her water. They followed her through the connecting door as Emily said over her shoulder, "There are no windows in there. I'll lock the door between our meetings to keep the information confidential."

"I'll leave my backpack and cell phone here, outside the conference room."

"That's not necessary, Edgar. We trust you. That's why you're part of the team." Emily smiled at his youthful eagerness.

Eric sat down across from Emily and Edgar. Penelope walked over to switch on the ceiling fan and then picked up a handful of dry erase markers and drew five columns on the whiteboard. "We'll use a column for each murder." Starting on the right, she wrote the victim's name and date of the murder at the top of the column. "2007 was the last murder." Then she moved to her left. "Before that was 2005, 2002, and 1998."

Edgar interjected, "What's the empty column on the left for? And if he is a serial killer, why haven't you left any additional columns in case there are new murders?"

Penelope turned away from him and rolled her eyes. "First, Edgar, we are working to solve these four murders." She rapped a marker impatiently on the board. "If there are any more, we'll adjust our chart." He slid down a little in his seat at her tone. "Now, to answer your second question, in the left column, we'll list the type of information we have for each murder." She began at the top of that column and, as she continued, she wrote, "Time, location, job, DNA, crime scene photos…" They talked about the four cases.

Once they were sure the matrix on the whiteboard contained everything they knew, Penelope walked over to the wall on the other side of the room. "We want plenty of room as we continue to develop the killer's profile. Right now, we don't know much," she said as she wrote in large, bold letters at the top, "*Criminal Profile*" and began to list what they did know on the board, with Eric and Emily adding bits to help her fill it in.

Penelope finally flopped down on a chair with a sigh.

Eric said, "Edgar, the vast majority of homicides are committed by people known to the victims. We figured that whoever did this was someone the victims either knew, or they weren't threatened by because of his position—"

"Like a police officer or a teacher or a priest?" asked Edgar.

"Precisely," Eric continued, "and by the time they figured out he was strangling them, it was too late to fight back. Based on the autopsy, the marks on their throats and the postmortem bruising around their noses and mouths, we concluded that whoever it was was quick and very strong. At least they didn't suffer long." He waved his hand at the board filled with data about the murders. "But after years of trying, we haven't found a social or professional connection between the women. An artist, a dental hygienist, a bartender and a lawyer. Based on our interviews with family and friends, all of them had very different personalities and interests, and they each moved in different social circles."

"That's right, E. These women knew a lot of folks. Maggie had a large following through her gallery. Ruth knew hundreds of patients where she worked. The bartender, Zoe, I can't even imagine the number of people she encountered in her job. Sheila was born and raised in Raleigh, and her family has lived here forever. It's like looking for a needle in a haystack." Penelope shook her head in frustration. "Every time we think we've found an overlap, it vanishes with the next case."

Edgar stood up, pushed his glasses up on the bridge of his nose and walked over to the board with the evolving profile on it. Trying to appear confident, he put his finger on a line in the profile and tapped it lightly. "Penelope," he said, "I don't understand why you think the murderer is not intelligent?"

Emily smiled at his tapping. *Mirroring my finger tapping to fit in. Clever young man. And he's not afraid to stand up to Pens.*

"These aren't complex robberies that took time, energy and brains to plan and execute. They're random, depraved acts of violence," replied Penelope.

"I think you may be making two bad assumptions."

"What? Why? How can you say that, Edgar?"

Raising his index finger, he said, "First, we all agree that these are ninety-nine-point-nine percent for sure the actions of a serial killer. The physical similarities make it highly unlikely that the murders were random. Anyone can act violently if they are angry or sufficiently provoked." Edgar looked around the room. The other three were quiet, listening to him. Encouraged, he raised a second finger and continued, "Next, the shoe print you found with the last victim—"

"That victim was found between her car and a building at the edge of the lot. Right next to the wall was where we found it. Some snow had accumulated, and we found the impression of a man's shoe there. How can you judge from that one footprint that it may or may not belong to our killer?" asked Penelope sarcastically.

Edgar walked over and looked closely at the photo taped to the board. He tapped on it gently. "You are right, we can't. But we can't discard it either. I assume that's why you included it. That print looks like it was made by an expensive dress shoe, not a sneaker or some casual shoe. If he left that print, it tells me that the murderer is probably someone with money, who dresses up for work or to go out. And that indicates he may be a professional, an *educated* person, a person of higher intelligence. Additionally, the murders all occurred in the downtown commercial district, surrounded by office buildings, small businesses and nice restaurants, not out in some remote country setting or impoverished neighborhood."

Emily encouraged him, "Ahh, a new set of eyes sees things differently, and a few overlooked clues shake loose. According to your impromptu analysis of this little piece of the crime scene, we have someone who is possibly well off enough to buy expensive shoes and who may have strangled each of these women in cold blood." She turned her head to look at Penelope. "I agree with our young reporter on this one, Pens. We'll need to follow up on that." Emily looked back at Edgar. "If you ever want to become a detective, let me know."

Edgar blushed.

Penelope rolled her eyes again. *What's going on here?* And then she scooted her chair over to the board, added a question mark next to "*Low Intelligence*", and then, with a scowl, she noted "*well-to-do*" and "*planned the murders*" with question marks beside each.

Edgar sat down, proud of himself for contributing to the investigation. "Also, a hair was found on the third victim. You said there were no DNA matches to it?" he said to Penelope.

"Correct. My crime lab submitted a sample from the crime scene and inputted it into the state database, and no match was found. Then it was uploaded to the national databases, and again, no joy. The process is very thorough."

Edgar's voice was bright with excitement at his first real involvement in a police case. "Did you canvass pawnshops or antique jewelry shops for the earrings that were taken?"

"We keep checking, but so far, nothing has surfaced," Penelope replied, an edge of impatience in her voice. "It's very unlikely anyone would be interested in single earrings anyway."

"Do you suppose that the killer suffers from objectophilia and keeps them? I wonder what he does with them, anyway?" Edgar mused out loud. "And, what about camera footage from businesses around the areas of the murders?"

"Hate to burst your bubble. We had nothing that could help from the few surveillance cameras we even found. Poor quality video with incorrect timestamps."

"But did anyone look at the footage to see if someone who looked similar was at all four murder scenes? I know they all occurred in the wintertime or, at least in cold weather, so they may have worn the same coat or hat. I don't know. I'm just curious."

"That's several good ideas, Edgar. Maybe you'll be useful after all. Maybe we won't need to vote you off the island," Penelope snickered. "We'll have to consider that. But all these places were using analog systems. The pictures weren't very good quality, even when we first looked at them. Hopefully, the tapes haven't degraded too much. Believe it or not, none of the store owners had switched to digital security cameras. That 'don't fix it if it ain't broke' mentality."

The four of them sat staring at the information. For a long time, no one said anything. Then, Eric broke the silence with his deep voice, "So, we desperately need somebody to come forward with new information. And that's where you come in, Edgar."

Killer is Still at Large

The Parking Lot Strangler – Special Appeal to the Public

by EDGAR SPRING

In an unprecedented manner, the police are collaborating with this reporter and a private security firm to solve the case of the Parking Lot Strangler who we believe is responsible for killing four women. The cases remain unsolved.

Maggie Wilson, local artist, strangled April 2, 1998
Ruth Sampson, dental hygienist, strangled January 17, 2002
Zoe Abrams, bartender, strangled January 1, 2005
Sheila Kovacs, lawyer, strangled December 20, 2007

Investigations are being conducted across the United States to see if there are any similar cases. So far, they have yielded no results.

Four redheads, all apparently the victims of the same killer. We ask you to come forward if you have any additional information. Contact the police, Haypress Security or The Raleigh Weekly News using the numbers below.

This is a plea for help from the public. If you know anything, however insignificant it may seem, please don't hesitate to come forward. You will be treated in strictest confidence and offered protection, if needed.

Here's what we know so far:

- All victims were strangled at night in secluded areas around parking lots
- Except for Maggie Wilson, forty-seven, the victims were in their late twenties to early thirties
- All victims had red hair
- All victims were missing their right earring and it is believed the killer took them
- The killer is believed to be around six feet tall, or taller
- The killer is probably of professional or higher social standing

Chapter Fourteen

July to December 2010

I Never Said I'm Sorry

Brussels, Belgium

Frank sat in the back seat with Lydia, rambling on about how horrible his dad was. "He's messed up my life. He's messed up my business. He's never supported me."

I can't wait to get back to Paris, but Mari won't even be there. It's still another four weeks until she gets home, and I'm always so lonely when she's gone. And babysitting Frank when he's drunk is no fun. I'm just glad he waited to have that extra drink until after the bank clients left. "Frank, maybe we shouldn't have stopped for that last drink."

"Lydia, I had to have another one to relax. I'm so mad at my dad. He foisted those clients on me at the last minute. Thank goodness you were here to help me."

"I know, Frank." Lydia patted his knee and leaned forward to talk to the cab driver. She pointed, "Thanks. Over there on the right is fine."

"He's just a bastard."

"Come on, Frank, we're at your apartment. Give me your wallet so I can pay the driver."

After they climbed out of the cab, they stood together on the sidewalk. She tucked his wallet back into the inside pocket of his suit jacket. "I have to figure out what to do now," he muttered.

"We're not deciding anything out here. Let's go inside. Where's your lobby-door key?"

"In my pocket." He fumbled and was unsuccessful at removing it. "I can't go to my uncle. He already told me no."

"For God's sake, Frank, just let it go."

She reached impatiently into Frank's pocket. "Just move your hand over a bit, and you'll find the real thing down there."

"Shut up, Frank. Don't be obscene. If you weren't so drunk, you'd be able to take your key out of your pocket."

She opened the door from the street, and Frank leaned on her. "What am I going to do, Lydia?"

"Come on, Frank, in you go." She gave him a little push. *I'm so tired, and it's exhausting listening to him go on and on. But I had to make sure he got home okay. And maybe I can learn something about the other side of our business.*

When they arrived at his floor, she opened the door, and Frank pushed past her. "I gotta go." He headed down the hall. "I gotta see a man about a horse."

Lydia closed the front door and wandered around while she waited for him to return. She hadn't seen his new place yet. *This is so modern. The open, sleek style suits him. And all these shades of tan? I didn't think I liked browns, but this is quite attractive. It has just a touch of masculinity that is so Frank. Oh, it's so much nicer than what Mari and I have. It must be nice to be born with a silver spoon in your mouth.* She continued her assessment of his apartment. *Now, those abstract paintings with all the bright splashes of color* – she paused to admire one – *they keep it from being just another slick, high-end bachelor pad.* She walked over and looked out the window. *Standing here, you can see the whole city. These tall floor-to-ceiling windows are nice too, especially on a beautiful summer evening like this. Too bad they don't open so we can enjoy it.*

Frank came out, stood beside her and put one hand on her shoulder. "My uncle has big windows like these in his brownstone. But he doesn't have a view like this. His windows just look out into his little courtyard." He went over to the wet bar where he poured two drinks. He set them on the coffee table, sat down heavily on the couch and patted the seat next to him.

Lydia shrugged, walked over, picked up her glass and sat in the chair adjacent to him.

Frank continued to carry on about his dad until Lydia interrupted his ranting, "What happened with your dad today? I know you two don't get along, but you're not normally like this."

"He's a fucking bastard."

"What does that mean?"

Frank raised his voice, "I've been using the bank's inter-office mail to ship our goods to brokers around the world. It's so much easier that way, but now, my dad has effectively shut down my business. You should be mad too. Now, I have no way to get rid of my stuff in the States that doesn't cost me an arm and a leg to ship. I've just bought this apartment. I'm tapped out. I can't survive on just my bank salary. He pays me peanuts." He groused for several more minutes, finally muttering, "He's such a bastard."

"So, you send what we steal to the States? Is that where your broker is?" Lydia asked.

"But of course. He's the one I prefer to use. Where else would I send it?"

That makes sense. That's why he gets so much for each item. I need to find out who this broker is. "Who do you deal with in the States?"

"My broker." He looked at her, annoyed that she didn't seem to understand, and then he got up to get another drink. He stood there and propped one hip against the bar as he turned around to ask, "Are you ready for another?"

"I'm okay for now. So, tell me, what is it your dad did to stop our business?"

Frank took a big swallow before he came back to the couch. "He put in stricter bank mailing procedures. Now everything has to be screened before it goes out, 'for the safety of the employees'. Such corporate bullshit. He's just spying on us."

"Oh. That stinks. What did you do before you used the bank to ship goods?"

"That's what I've done – ever since I started my business. Ever since I had that big fight with Victor."

"Is that your uncle?"

Frank sipped steadily at his whisky, "Yeah, my so-called uncle. My whole family are assholes."

"Oh, I'm sorry – but you have more than just your U.S. broker. Right?"

"Of course, I do. I'm not stupid. It's important to keep your options open. But the guy in the States is the best, and that's the most lucrative market. The other brokers are harder to work with, and I never make as much money when I use them. So, I always send the best stuff to my guy in the U.S. Or I did," whined Frank.

Lydia picked up their glasses and went to the bar. *If I keep giving him more drinks, maybe he'll tell me more. At some point, I might have to sell all the jewelry I've held back from him and Shane – for my business or to live on. Who knows? It's my insurance policy.* She refilled Frank's glass and poured water for herself. "Tell me about Victor," she asked as she handed him a generous drink.

"He lived in New York City, and we were close, we were so close. I love that man. He's like a father. Or he was. It turns out he's just another bastard like my dad."

"So, tell me again. How do you do it? Who is this broker you use in the States? What about the other brokers?"

"Victor was more of a father to me than my real dad. That is, until he fucked that up completely." Frank stared morosely into the dregs in his glass. Abruptly, he stood up to get another drink. When he turned to walk back, his hand was empty and tears were running down his face. "Can you believe he's sleeping with my best friend? He's living with her. They have a fucking happily-ever-after family together, and I'm not part of it."

"Tell me about your best friend."

Frank lowered his voice and said sadly, "She's beautiful. She's tall and slim. She has long, curly, beautiful, dark blond hair. We did everything together when we were young. We didn't have any secrets. She married Rick. He was my other best friend. But she betrayed him with Victor. I love them all. This is just so wrong."

"Wow. That's terrible." *I have to get him back to talking about his brokers.*

"They haven't bothered to speak to me for years. I love him. I love her. We never talk. I miss them so much, but I can't call them." He put his face in his hands and began to cry drunkenly.

Lydia stood up and went over to sit beside him. She put her hand at the base of his neck and rubbed his shoulders. He pulled a handkerchief out, blew his nose loudly and stuffed it back into his pocket. "I'm sorry, Lydia."

He's so sad. He's such a mess. I feel so bad for him. She put her arms around him and hugged him. He hugged her back. *Wow, I really miss hugs when Mari's away.*

"My darling Lydia, you're the only friend I have. Would you help put me to bed?"

She stood up. *He's acting like a kid, and it's so late. I might as well get him to bed. I'm certainly not going to learn anything from him tonight.* She helped Frank stand, pulled his arm around her shoulder, and together they went to the bedroom. She started to help him undress when he threw his arms around her, grabbed her behind and squeezed it as he gave her a drunken kiss.

Lydia started to pull away. He tightened his arms, and suddenly, his kiss went from awkward to seductive, and she moaned. *Oh, this feels good. Sooo good.*

"You are so sexy, Lydia McKay of Paris." He took her face in his hands and pulled her into a lustful kiss, and she slipped her arms around his neck. When at last he drew away, he looked into her eyes. "You have such beautiful hair. All those wonderful curls. Such beautiful skin, and your freckles. You're enchanting." His eyes never left hers while he ran his thumbs ever so slowly along her jaw, down the sides of her neck, pausing at that point where her pulse fluttered rapidly and teased their way over her collarbone. They never left hers when he slipped his fingers under the fabric at her neckline and stroked her skin until he reached the curve of her breasts.

"Undress for me."

Lydia moaned with pleasure. *I feel so wanton,* she thought, *so desirable.* She undressed very slowly, pausing from time to time to watch his reaction, to hear his sharp intake of breath. *I've never done this before. It's fun.* His eyes gleamed in appreciation. And she stood naked in front of him.

"You have the most beautiful body." His hands roved over her torso, caressed her, excited her while she finished undressing him. Then he pulled her down onto the bed.

Lydia gave a sharp cry of pleasure. Frank groaned in satisfaction and rolled off her. He whispered, "I love you. I love you, Isabelle," and passed out, snoring loudly.

That was phenomenal. But what is it with him and this Isabelle?

§

Paris, France

Isabelle crossed the lounge of the boat. She pulled out the piano bench and sat down. As she began to play, Sasha ducked under the bar flap and approached her. "Hello, Captain Ronaldo. Would you like a beverage while you play?"

Her hands continued to move effortlessly across the keys, and she glanced up at him with a smile. "No, thanks, Sasha. Today, I won't be long. I just wanted to relax for a few minutes."

Sasha returned to the bar. *It's always so relaxing to listen when she comes in like this and plays whatever inspires her at that moment. She has so much talent. I hope she'll still have time to indulge herself like this now that she's been promoted.*

He was seated on a high stool behind the bar, polishing glasses when Gia walked in and waved to Isabelle. "Sasha, may I please have a lemonade? We cleaned every last room on the boat today, and I'm exhausted."

He slid a slice of lemon onto the edge of her glass and set it on a napkin in front of her. "It was a busy cruise, wasn't it?"

Just then, Isabelle finished the jazz piece she'd been playing and came over to the bar. "Hi, Gia. I've heard that you know international sign language."

"Captain, hello. Yes, I do. I've taken several classes in ISL, just as something different, while I've been working on my online architecture degree."

"We have an entire family who is hearing impaired joining us tomorrow for our next cruise. I would like you to help translate for them and serve them their meals."

"That would be so much fun," Gia said as she signed the words.

"I'll clear it with your manager. Thank you. I need to run. I'll see you two later." The sliding doors opened with a swoosh as Isabelle hurried through and out into the lobby.

Gia climbed onto a stool near Sasha, and with a heavy sigh, she kicked her foot gently against the boat's bar and then back against the brass footrest on the barstool. She pulled a brooch out of her pocket and stroked it lovingly. "Sasha, I've been agonizing over this forever. I'm so embarrassed that I've never given her my condolences. I was so wrapped up in my own grief that I never called or even sent her a card. But I have to go there, Sasha. I have to tell her in person how sorry I am. I can't leave it open-ended," she held out her hand, "and I have to give her this." The brooch gleamed on her palm. "I'm going while you guys have the party for Captain Ronaldo."

Sasha stopped polishing glasses for a moment. "So, you're

ready then, Gia? It's kind of you, thinking that Lydia might need closure too."

"I don't know how kind I'm being. I just want to get it done. I've been talking about it and thinking about it. The longer I drag it out, the more I find myself dreading it."

"And your jealousy – of Lydia, of her relationship with Mari?" He continued working.

"I was jealous – maybe. Just a little. She was my best friend, but she spent all her free time with Lydia. Lydia took that away from me. Time I could have had with Mari. If she hadn't been with Lydia, she wouldn't have gone to that store to buy fabric for another dress. We would have spent that morning together, and maybe, that murderer wouldn't have killed her. Maybe, she would still be alive." In a small, squeaky, almost crying voice, she said, "I still can't believe she's dead."

"Gia, you have to let that go. We can't control other people's destinies. It'll eat you from the inside."

She sniffled and gave a little half-grin. "You're always so wise, Sasha."

"I know you're still hurting. It's only been a few months. I know how that is. Even though it's been much longer for me, I'm still hurting over my partner's death." Sasha's face grew sad with memories of his loss.

"I know you understand where I'm coming from."

"You had a special relationship with Mari." Sasha walked over and put his hand on hers and looked into her face. "But you'll always have your memories. They are what get you through."

Gia sniffled again. "Stop it. Don't make me start crying."

"You know Mari loved you. Even in the beginning, when she first met Lydia, she told me how difficult it was to juggle her friendship with you and her relationship with Lydia. She loved you both very much."

"When did you find out about them?"

"When they first met, Mari came to me. She needed to talk about living openly in a same-sex relationship."

"I didn't know about Lydia until a few years after they started dating. Mari was such a private person. She talked with *you* about that? Why?"

"She *was* very private, but she needed someone to talk to. Someone who would understand. Someone who's been there."

"Oh. I hadn't thought about how lonely that could be. I'm glad you were able to help her." Gia took a sip of her lemonade, stroked the brooch again and thought about how Mari had always pinned it onto the lapel of her uniform first thing in the morning. "Sasha, I'm so nervous about going, about having to talk to Lydia about Mari's murder. But this belonged to her before Mari bought it. She should have it back."

"What does your heart say to do? That's your answer."

§

Gia looked up as she walked toward the entrance to the fifteen-story, grey building. *Not an attractive place at all. In fact, it looks like something from the Soviet Union in the communist era, a typical housing development. I'm sure this was built in the fifties – gosh, I hope Lydia is home.*

She got off the elevator and walked down a narrow hallway to the apartment at the end, her footsteps echoing on the hard floor. *This linoleum isn't very nice. It hasn't improved any since I helped her and Mari move in.* Gia stopped in front of the door. *This is going to be hard.* She lifted her hand to knock and dropped it. *Talking about Mari is going to hurt her badly.* She lifted her hand again and paused before knocking, three slow knocks.

Lydia opened the door, and her face lit up.

"Hi, Lydia."

"*Coucou.*" Lydia leaned forward to kiss her on the cheek.

She looked behind Gia. "Where's Mari?"

Of all the possible reactions to seeing her, Gia had not been expecting that. *Oh, my God,* her stomach dropped, *how can she not know that Mari is dead?* "Can I come in so we can talk?"

"Uh, sure." She stepped back to let Gia in. "Where's Mari?" Lydia looked down the hall again and then slowly closed the door. "Did she send you?"

Why do I have to be the one to break this news? After all these months, hasn't anyone called her or told her? I'm going to have to do it. "May I get a glass of water?" And before Lydia could answer, she went through the living room, into the kitchen. On the way, she dropped her purse onto the couch. "Let me get you some too."

"Okaaay?"

Gia turned on the tap and filled two glasses, walked over to the table and motioned to Lydia to join her. Lydia watched her set the water very carefully and precisely on the table before she sat down.

What is Gia doing here without Mari? Lydia sat. "What's going on? Why are you here? Mari left me months ago. She stopped texting. She stopped calling. She left me. She didn't even come back for her stuff – or to say goodbye. Why would you come instead? Did she send you to get her stuff? Why didn't she come herself?"

Gia played with her glass. *I don't know where to start.* Tears welled up in her eyes. She dashed them away with her hand and blurted out, "Mari's dead – she was murdered."

"No, she was going to work. She was on a boat."

"She did go to work – on the riverboat, on *The Krasnyy*."

"But why didn't she come home?"

"In August, we were together in Ukraine – when she was murdered."

"What?"

"We had coffee. She was so excited about your fifth anniversary. She talked about all the plans the two of you had. And she was so excited to go buy the fabric for her next flamenco dress, the one you'd designed together. She'd been waiting the whole cruise to go to that store in Zaporizhzhya." Gia began to cry, "But she never came back to the boat."

"Where did she go?" Lydia's voice was thin and high-pitched in fear.

"She was murdered. She's gone, Lydia. She was my best friend, and she's gone." Gia gave a heart-rending sob.

Lydia's eyes grew wide with shock. Tears hung on her lower eyelashes and then poured over, streaming down her face. "Murdered? How? What happened?" she said, her voice catching, breaking.

"The Ukrainian police haven't released much information because it's still under investigation. All I know is that she was strangled."

Lydia stood up, backing away, trying to distance herself from Gia's horrible news. "No. No. No. That's not true. It can't be." She stopped, leaned against the wall for support and lifted her hands to her face and sobbed.

Gia went to her, wrapping her arms around her, holding her tightly, rocking her, stroking her back, the way Sasha had comforted her not so long ago. Lydia buried her face in Gia's shoulder. "She was mad at me. That can't be true."

"I'm so sorry, Lydia," she whispered hoarsely. "I know how much you loved each other."

Lydia looked up, her face flushed, tears still pouring down, "She has to come back – so I can say I'm sorry." She sobbed harder. Gia took her hand and led her to the couch.

"We'd put down roots. That's what Mari wanted, to put down roots together. We were going to celebrate our anniversary, but she never returned. We loved each other. We were there for each other. We'd made a home here, together."

Gia began to cry. "Lydia, she's gone."

Lydia broke down completely, and Gia held her again. Once she had cried herself out, Gia said, "Tell me about it. Tell me why you think Mari was mad at you. She never mentioned it. I'm sure she wasn't really mad. She would have told me. I'm sure she knew you were sorry."

Sniffling, Lydia began to tell the story. Gia dug in her purse and pulled out a small packet of tissues and handed it to her.

"Before Mari left, I told her I'd slept with Frank."

"Your boss?"

"Yeah," she said sheepishly. "I couldn't keep it a secret from her. It was just that one time. We'd drunk a lot. I screwed up. I was so sorry the next day." Lydia hiccupped before continuing. "It just happened. And then Mari and I had a big fight about it. But I liked it. I told her I liked the feeling of a man. And it broke her heart, I could tell." She broke down again.

"No, you didn't break her heart. I'm sure it must have hurt her when you told her about being with Frank. But she'd forgiven you. I know she had."

"She turned her back on me all night, and then she wouldn't

kiss me goodbye in the morning. She said we would figure it out after her next trip. I thought when she didn't return, she had decided she was done with me. Fed up with me." Lydia continued to cry. "I was so lonely. I went back to Frank – but only because she never returned. I had nobody else. He's been here for me, to comfort me. I like the way he makes me feel. But I would give him up in a heartbeat to have her back. Mari was the love of my life."

"She'd never have abandoned you. She talked about you all the time. I could hear in her voice how she felt." Gia paused for a moment at the memory, and then she went on, "But she would want you to have someone to comfort you. She would have forgiven you. You need to forgive yourself, Lydia. You need to forgive yourself."

Gia reached into her pocket. "Maybe this isn't important right now, but I know Mari would want you to have this back. She wore it every day," and she handed Lydia the pomegranate flower brooch.

Lydia took it and held it to her heart and cried even harder. Caressing the brooch, she said, "It was her favorite flower. It was my mam's too. This was her brooch before she died." Through her tears, she said breathlessly, "Everyone I love dies."

Gia reached over and gently squeezed her knee. "I didn't know that. So, it's very special." *I'm so glad I decided to bring it to her.*

Lydia nodded and sniffled.

After a pause, Gia said, "She loved you so much and wanted to support you with Lydia McKay of Paris."

Lydia looked up with wet eyes. "I can't believe she's dead – murdered?"

"Tell me some of your memories of her."

The two women sat and reminisced, laughing and crying, as they talked about the Mari they had each known, the best friend and the lover.

Finally, Gia glanced at the clock. "I have to get back to the boat. I was only able to get away for these few hours. The staff is having a surprise party, and I skipped out on it because I had to come and tell you, to bring you the brooch. I'm so sorry I can't stay with you. Can I do anything for you before I go?" *I'm glad she has Frank and won't be completely alone.*

"No. I just need to be by myself. Thank you for coming to tell me about Mari." She took a shaky breath before going on, "And for bringing this back to me." Lydia cradled the brooch in her hand.

Gia laid her hand along Lydia's cheek. "I know this won't mean much now, but a dear friend of mine told me that, even though time never heals the wounds left by someone's death, it does make them easier to live with."

After Gia left, Lydia put on Mari's Frank Sinatra recording for the first time since she'd left. *She couldn't get enough of Old Blue Eyes, but she played his songs so often, sometimes, I just wanted to break all those CDs.* She wandered aimlessly around the apartment, humming to the music and crying a little as she touched Mari's things. She lifted the elaborate skirt to the flamenco dress she'd almost finished and stroked it before she let the fabric slide through her fingers. *I'll never design another dress for her.*

The phone rang. Lydia looked at the number and picked it up. She cleared her throat before she spoke. "Hi, Frank."

"Are you ready for our trip tomorrow?"

"Sure."

"What's wrong?"

Lydia broke down again. "I just found out that Mari is dead. She was murdered."

"What? Are you sure?"

"Yes. Gia came to tell me."

"I'm already here in Paris. I'll be right over."

Frank arrived a few minutes later, saw her miserable face and immediately took her in his arms. "My darling Lydia, let's get you calmed down." He walked with her to the couch and tucked a fluffy throw around her shoulders. He went to the kitchen where he poured them each a glass of brandy. He brought the glasses and the bottle into the living room. He sat down and handed Lydia a glass. Her hands shook as she took a long swallow, breathing unevenly, as though she was about to break down again. She slumped against him, and he took the glass from her and set it on the table.

"Sorry, but I'd better take this call, Lydia." Frank held her close with one arm as he pulled his phone out of his pocket. "Hello?"

"Hi, boyfriend."

"Is that really you, girlfriend? Your number's changed."

§

When Isabelle entered the dining room of the Spectrum riverboat, *The Topaz*, for the crew's meal, she was surprised as someone shouted out, "Captain on deck!"

Everyone stood up and sang *For She's A Jolly Good Fellow* as Isabelle stood, rooted to the spot, with a giant grin on her face. *This crazy crew is my responsibility now.* Clapping, she said, "What a wonderful beginning." She looked around at her crew and then noticed Victor standing at the back. She felt a little shiver of happiness run along her spine. He blew her a kiss and gave her a thumbs up, and she touched her fingers to her lips and held them up toward him in reply.

She walked over to where her senior staff were standing. "So, which one of you sneaked that man on the boat?" Still grinning from ear to ear, she pointed at Victor. "You know we don't allow guests on board while we're preparing for our next cruise."

Sasha gave a mock salute, "Captain, guilty as charged."

Someone else added, "Be careful, she'll make you walk the plank or wash the dishes or both."

Isabelle laughed, "Let's break out some champagne to celebrate." Before she had even finished saying it, she saw the bar staff bringing in glasses, already filled, and handing them out to everyone in the room.

Sasha's eyes twinkled, "Great minds think alike."

Once everyone had a glass, Isabelle tapped hers with her ring to get their attention. "There is only one first time, and this is my first cruise as the captain. I'm honored to be working with a crew as dedicated as you all are. This is the fulfillment of a childhood dream. A family friend told us about his career as a riverboat captain. You would have thought that this would be rather dull for a little girl, but for me, it was inspirational. Shortly thereafter my parents took me on a riverboat cruise through southern France. And I was hooked. I've worked my tail off to be where I am now. So, you're celebrating something that has been very near and dear to me for a very long time. Lift your glasses in a toast, so you can celebrate this first *with* me."

Sasha added, "We are so pleased for you. Here's to Captain Isabelle Ronaldo. The first female captain in Spectrum's history!"

Everyone raised their glasses toward her and took a drink. The pastry chef entered with a sheet cake, and Sasha said to Isabelle, "And when you're celebrating, what goes better with champagne – than chocolate cake!"

The chef set it carefully on the small table next to where she was standing, and Isabelle read out loud, "Congratulations, Captain Ronaldo!"

After the champagne was drunk and only crumbs remained from the cake, Isabelle led Victor to her cabin, and as soon as she shut the door behind them, he wrapped his arms around her and kissed her enthusiastically. "I'm so proud of you, Izzy," he said, his voice full of love and warmth. And he kissed her again and again.

Isabelle broke away with a wistful look on her face. "I told Chloe Rose about my promotion, and she was ecstatic for me. Oliver called me to congratulate me. But besides you, the person I want to share this with most of all is Frank. He's had to put up with me going on about my ambition all through our childhood. I miss him so much, Victor."

"It seems like everybody has been missing everybody, but nobody has done anything about it. Just call him. This has gone on long enough. It needs to stop."

She sat on the edge of the bed, straightened the stack of books piled on the nightstand and twirled her phone in her hands a few times before selecting Frank's number.

"Hello."

"Hi, boyfriend."

"Is that really you, girlfriend? Your number's changed."

He remembered my voice. I was so worried he'd have forgotten me. "I finally got my French citizenship and a French phone number."

"That's fantastic," Frank replied. She heard the tenderness in his voice.

"It's been a long time."

"I was so mad when I found out about the two of you."

"I know."

"You sound good."

"The reason I called is because…" She held the phone away and shook it excitedly before putting it back to her ear. "…I had to

tell you – I'm a captain, Frank – I'm a captain – it finally happened!
I'm doing the thing I've always wanted to do, and I've made it to the
top."

"Wow! Oh, I am so proud of you, girlfriend. I knew you would
do it. I'm so glad you called. I've picked up my phone to call you so
many times, but then I didn't. I don't know why." *I've missed her so
much.*

"That's okay. I've thought about calling you millions of times
too. And then I didn't. But I knew one day we would reconnect. And
now we have." Her face lit up.

"When did it happen?"

"I just got promoted a couple of days ago, and I'm starting my
first cruise as captain. We leave tomorrow morning. And I had the
most wonderful celebration with my crew. I'm overjoyed, and I
wanted to share it with you."

"Congratulations!" She heard the excitement in Frank's voice.

"Where are you these days? Are you still working for your dad's
bank?"

"Yes, I'm still here in Europe, working for my dad. I'm in Paris
right now."

*He's pretty mellow. He used to sound so angry whenever he talked about
his dad. I wonder what happened. Things must have changed.* "Hey, so am I.
Darn, I wished I'd called you sooner so we could have gotten
together. But there's no way I can do that before we depart
tomorrow."

"It would have been great to see you. Let's plan to meet up. I've
missed you a lot. I've got so much to tell you, girlfriend."

"So, what are you doing in Paris?"

"I'm with Lydia."

"Who's Lydia? Is it serious? What about work?"

"She works for me at the bank. We're discussing a business trip
we're going on tomorrow. Hey, do I have to call you Captain now?"

"As a matter of fact, yes. That would be Captain Girlfriend."
They both laughed, and it felt just like old times. "Frank, someone's
knocking on my door. But Victor's here, and he wants to talk to you
too. I'm sorry, I have to run. Let me pass you over to him. Bye, bye,
boyfriend."

"Congratulations again. I'm so happy for you. Bye, bye – Captain Girlfriend. I love you."

"Love you too." Isabelle handed the phone to Victor, beaming from ear to ear.

"Hello, son."

Frank choked up, and he had to pause a moment and clear his throat, "Hello, Uncle. It's been a while."

At the same time, they both said, "I'm sorry."

"I could have handled things better," said Victor.

"Me too," said Frank, his voice still choked with emotion.

"Izzy's coming home for Christmas at the end of this cruise."

Izzy? When I called her that, she punched me.

"It's the first time in years she's had Christmas off. Would you like to join us? We have a small farm in southern France. You could come and stay. I know it's a last-minute invitation—"

"That would be fantastic. I can hardly wait to see you both and meet the girls."

"So, you know?"

"Mothers. You know how it is. They can't stop talking about Mrs. Ronaldo's grandgirls."

"Ah, yes."

"Hey, would you all mind if I bring a friend? She just lost her partner, and I don't want her to be alone for the first Christmas."

Frank looked down at Lydia, curled in a desolate ball beside him, her eyes sad and swollen.

"Of course, your friend is our friend."

Once they'd hung up, Lydia sat up and asked, "Who's this 'girlfriend' anyway? You sounded like you're close." *Mari is dead, and my boyfriend has a girlfriend. Can this day get any worse?*

"We were, but we've been – out of touch – for a long time."

"Oh, why did she call?" *Maybe she wants him back?*

"She's always been hell bent on having a career on riverboats, you know, traveling, cruises, that sort of thing. She just called to say she's been promoted to captain."

He's confusing sometimes. "I didn't know you had a girlfriend."

"No, no. That's just silliness left over from when we were younger. Isabelle's been with my uncle for a long time now. For years. They have four little girls."

Ah ha, that's who Isabelle is. "Big family. Four girls, just like mine."

Frank knelt down in front of the couch and took Lydia's hands in his. "Would you like to go away to southern France for the holidays? We can spend Christmas with Uncle and Isabelle and spend New Year's in Nice."

She gave him a wan smile. "It would be nice not to be here, not to be alone, not this year."

Frank hugged her around her shoulders. "I think you could use a distraction, my darling Lydia."

I can't believe he's inviting me to spend the holidays with his family – and with his old girlfriend?

Frank wrapped his arms around her and held her tightly. "Something new would be good for you."

Chapter Fifteen

December 2010

At the Farmhouse

Southern France

Frank reached over between the seats to where Lydia sat in the middle of the back seat and caressed her knee. She put her hand over his and pressed it lightly. *Hmmm, I thought she worked for Frank.* Isabelle looked in the rearview mirror to talk to Lydia. "You know, Frank and I have known each other forever. Once you're settled in, I want to get to know all about you."

"That would be nice. I'd like to get to know you too."

Isabelle pulled the car into the gravel driveway and around the circle to the side of the house. "I'm sorry you weren't able to arrive any earlier today. It'll be dark in about an hour, so there won't be time to give you a tour of the farm tonight. Victor and the girls and I walk the land every morning when we can. We'll have a nice walkabout tomorrow after all the excitement of stockings and gifts. It'll calm the kidlets down before we go off to serve Christmas dinner."

They got out of the car, and Frank took hold of Lydia's hand. Isabelle glanced quickly at them before she opened the trunk. "So, we made up the guest room upstairs for Lydia. But now I'm thinking you two are together." She looked pointedly at their hands. Lydia blushed. "I'm so happy you've found someone, Frank."

"Yes, it would be better if you put us together. Otherwise, you'd hear me sneaking around at night trying to find her. Oh, let me get that, Isabelle." Frank began to unload the luggage. "Where should I put this?"

"See that stone building off to the side of the kitchen?" She pointed toward it. "Back in the day, it was used for storage. Anyway, we've just finished renovating it, and now, it's our guest cottage. It's so serene. I think it's the nicest place on the farm."

She led the way to the cottage, and as they entered, Isabelle said, "Let me give you a quick tour. It won't take long. This is obviously the sitting area, and that sofa turns into a bed." Huge windows looking out over the orchards caught Lydia's eye. Isabelle waved toward the other side of the room, "And there's the kitchenette. Victor will be doing a lot of cooking, as always, so you probably won't need to use it. But it's there, just in case." Isabelle turned toward Lydia, "I saw you eyeing our orchards. Those trees out there are filled with the most delicious pears in the fall. They've all been picked now and sent off to market. But we traditionally hold back a few bushels, and I think you'll find Victor makes a mean pear clafoutis. In fact, I believe it's on the menu for dessert tonight." She rubbed her stomach.

She walked across the room. "Back here is the bedroom and bath."

"This is like a spa," said Lydia as she looked around the bathroom, at the tall, narrow window, at the floating vanity with two sinks and the oversized shower. "Frank, there's so much room for your lotions and body wash." Lydia smiled when she heard Isabelle snicker. Fluffy towels were stacked on open shelves below the vanity, and a bowl of scented soaps sat on the counter between the sinks, alongside a huge bouquet of lavender in a cut-glass vase. Lydia leaned over and drew in a deep breath, "From here?"

"Sadly, no. It gets a bit too cold in the winter, but there is a florist in the town who likes lavender as much as I do, so he imports it from Spain when we can't get it locally."

Finished with his luggage duties, Frank came into the bathroom. "You did this up nicely, girlfriend." His hand reached out to stroke Lydia's back.

Out of the corner of her eye, Isabelle noticed Lydia stiffen slightly at the term of endearment. She hurried on, "Lydia, Frank and I have always been like this with each other. The 'girlfriend' and 'boyfriend' thing are just nicknames left over from when we were kids. We've never dated. That would have been too weird." She gave a light shudder, "We're too much like siblings for anything like that."

Lydia relaxed under Frank's hand. And then she leaned back against him as he slid his arms around her.

Isabelle stood watching from the doorway. "Through there is the bedroom. There's a king-size bed. I'm sure the two of you'll be quite comfortable here. Well, dinner should almost be ready. Come on in through the kitchen door after you're settled in." She pointed to the house.

Frank kissed Lydia's neck. "Let's christen the cottage later," and pushed himself against her from behind.

Isabelle turned away as she joked, "Frank, I'm still here, remember?"

Embarrassed, Lydia reached back and gave Frank a little push away from her.

"Hey, we're all adults," he protested.

§

Lydia opened the door from the courtyard. In her hand, she held a box wrapped in dark blue paper and tied with a silver ribbon. Victor was drying the last of the dinner dishes that they'd stacked up in the kitchen earlier that evening. "Done already? I was coming back to help you."

"I'm quick. I get lots of practice." They both laughed companionably.

She looked through the open kitchen to the dining area where Frank and Isabelle were sitting at the table, talking in low voices. As she crossed the open space toward them, Lydia glanced at the huge room to her left, furnished with tall bookcases, comfortable couches and easy chairs and paused to look at the girls, three little blond heads and a dark one, all sleeping soundly under the Christmas tree that was centered between the front windows. The lights on the tree twinkled, and colorful glass balls glinted in the flames from the low fire burning in the living room fireplace. Small stockings were hung on the mantel, waiting for Father Christmas to arrive. "It's so cozy. Wow, they've gone out like lights."

"Thank goodness." Victor hung up the towels.

Lydia looked back over toward the dining room table that had another fireplace in the wall behind it. A fire was crackling away there too. Isabelle waved her hands, beckoning her to the table with a welcoming smile. Victor turned out the kitchen light and followed Lydia. He looked over at the girls. "I think we're in luck tonight. It looks like they're all asleep."

Isabelle was perched on the end of the bench, and Frank straddled it, facing her. She said to Lydia, "I love having this second fireplace here in the dining room. Why don't you take that chair right next to it? You'll be nice and toasty. It's my favorite seat at the table."

Before she sat down, Lydia stopped beside Isabelle. "This is for you and Victor." She handed her the lavishly wrapped box. "It's just a little something from me and Frank to thank you for inviting us to share Christmas with you. He's so excited, and it's rubbed off on me." She walked around and took the chair by the fire.

Isabelle ripped open the package. "Oh, my God! I love Belgian chocolates. And so many of them! Thank you so much."

She popped an entire white-chocolate-covered truffle into her mouth and closed her eyes, savoring the rich flavors that exploded on her taste buds. "Mmmm. Mmmm," she groaned in ecstasy and took one more before she passed the box around.

"Those chocolates will go well with our wine." Victor poured two glasses of local red wine and handed one to Lydia before he sat down in his chair at the end of the table. "More, anyone?" He held out the bottle, and Frank immediately reached over to take it and fill his glass. He tipped the dregs into Isabelle's with a grin.

"He, or she, who hesitates is lost," he snickered, setting the empty bottle on the table.

Frank watched Victor reach out to take Isabelle's hand between his and lift it to kiss her fingers. *They certainly are touchy feely, even after four kids. It's so different from the way she and Rick were after they were married.*

Isabelle looked at Lydia. "How do you like the cottage? Are you comfortable?"

"It's beautiful. We're in the lap of luxury out there – in our own little house."

Frank poked Isabelle's shoulder. "I'm glad you continued our tradition." He gestured with his head toward the girls.

"Of course, even though it was mine to start with."

Victor watched his wife and his nephew – *I'm so happy to see them back together, just like before. Isabelle missed having him as part of her life. And I've missed him too.*

"As a kid, I always slept under our tree on Christmas Eve," Isabelle said to Lydia. "We shared this tradition with Frank and his family when they moved to Brasília. We were ten, but we still loved the smell of the tree and falling asleep under the lights. It was such a magical time."

She smiled at Frank, as she recounted the story. "Every year, we invited Frank's family over to celebrate Christmas Eve. After dinner, our parents would sit, drinking their cocktails and chatting, and Frank and I would go and lie under our tree. We'd talk for hours and hours, looking up into the branches, enjoying the scent of the pine, because we always had a real tree. We pretended we were in a private forest, in our own secret world. And then, at some point, we'd fall asleep."

Frank reached over and put his hand on Isabelle's knee. "Those were special times, girlfriend."

"When Isabelle told me about that wonderful tradition, I knew we had to raise our girls the same way," said Victor.

"Why don't we sleep under the tree tonight, girlfriend?"

Isabelle laughed at him, "Not when I've got a soft, warm bed and this old man to snuggle with."

It sounds so natural – girlfriend, boyfriend. They really were close, I guess. And Victor isn't fazed by it, so I suppose it's okay.

After a couple of hours of drinking wine and laughing and talking quietly, Victor got up, took the stockings from the mantel and brought them over to the table. Lydia watched Isabelle pull a box out of the storage closet beneath the stairs. They filled the stockings, first a tangerine in the toe, to fill the space where nothing else would fit. Then small toys that were carefully wrapped, one for each stocking, just the right size for little fingers. And a big gingerbread man to go in the top. Isabelle looked at Frank and Lydia and said, "These stockings are from Father Christmas."

"All this is to keep the girls busy, so they won't wake us up too early," Victor told them.

"Victor, we're all set." They stood up and took two stockings each and placed them next to the girls.

When they returned to the table, Lydia said. "Let me go get my gifts. I brought something for each of them."

Minutes later, she tapped at the kitchen door, her arms piled with four boxes, wrapped in bright paper with elaborate bows. Victor jumped up to let her in. "Thank you, Lydia. You're spoiling the girls. But they'll be thrilled to have another gift to open."

"Normally, they only have one gift from their godmother, Chloe Rose, that they open on Christmas Eve, and two others. One from us and another from my parents that they open in the morning," added Isabelle, "So this will be a big treat for them."

"Chloe, from Texas?" asked Frank.

"Yep. She's so successful." Isabelle said, happy to brag about her dear friend.

"What's she up to?"

"Working on her fourth book covering the results of her research. Traveling. Giving lectures. Loving life. You know Chloe Rose, the world is always full of excitement for her. And she's very involved with the kidlets, Frank. She's their godmother. When I told her you were coming, she was so disappointed she couldn't be here to celebrate and see you again."

"That's great. We lost touch after you guys finished at Texas A&M. It would have been great to see her again. She was always good fun."

There's so much I don't know about him.

Isabelle touched the gifts on the table. "What's in these beautiful packages, Lydia?"

"I bought dolls and made three outfits for each one."

"Lydia is an incredible dressmaker."

He's so sweet. "Frank told me you had four little daughters. I made dresses that I hope they'll like."

"That's so thoughtful," said Isabelle. "I can't wait to see them. They'll be thrilled. Let's put these under the tree with our gifts."

Victor poured the last of the wine into their glasses. "Tomorrow morning, we'll do a walking tour of the farm and then all go down to the soup kitchen at our church to serve Christmas dinner. We'll eat there too. I used to do that when I lived in New York, and it's become another of our family traditions. Would you like to join us?"

"Yes, of course. Frank and I would enjoy that."

Isabelle turned to Lydia, "It must seem like we have a lot of traditions."

"I like traditions. And yours are nice." *I'd like to have traditions like that someday, to ground me, to bind me to someone,* she thought, her eyes resting on Frank.

The conversation slowly wound down, and finally, Lydia said, "I'm going to head off to bed. What time is breakfast? Do you need help?"

"Probably nine o'clock by the time the girls calm down," replied Victor. "But there'll be coffee and fresh rolls in the kitchen at about seven. Come on in and join me."

Frank looked at her, "I'm going to stay on a little and catch up with Isabelle." Lydia walked around the table and gave Frank a quick, self-conscious kiss on his mouth. As she turned to go, Isabelle pulled her in for a warm hug, and then Victor hugged her too.

"Good night. I'll see you all in the morning." Lydia walked briskly to the guest cottage in the cold. After getting into her pajamas, she lay in the king-size bed, looking at the ceiling. *I didn't think I would like them, especially Frank's "girlfriend", Isabelle. But now, I understand, and I like them both very much. And Frank is so happy to be here with them, with her. It's obvious they all missed one another.*

§

Lydia stepped through the back door and heard someone playing the piano on the other side of the house. She followed the sound through the kitchen and on through the living room to the music room doorway. Two of the little girls were sitting on the bench in front of the enormous grand piano. She stood quietly and watched Lily playing *Joy to the World* while Rose mimicked her motions.

In the middle of the room, Victor was focused on the other two children. Dressed in comfortable old sweats, he'd squatted down to talk to them. He lifted his head and gave Lydia a quick nod of welcome. Iris asked, "Daddy, is it time yet? Can we open our gifts under the tree now?"

Frankie stood behind Iris. "Daddy, I told her we have to wait for Mommy and Cousin Frank."

"And Lydia too," said Victor. "But look, she's already here."

The two girls squealed and ran over to hug her, "Merry Christmas! Merry Christmas!"

Lydia was caught by surprise, but then she put her arms around them and held them tightly for a moment and whispered, "Merry

Christmas."

The other two girls slid off the piano bench and joined in, hugging and kissing Lydia. They were so preoccupied with her that they didn't hear Isabelle come down the stairs, still in her robe and slippers, or see Victor slip out of the music room. Isabelle went over to Victor, rested her hands on his shoulders and then pulled his head down to give him a quick kiss. "Merry Christmas, Old Man."

He responded with a warm kiss. "Merry Christmas, Izzy," and he pulled her back to him for another quick kiss. "Sit, and I'll make coffee."

Lily took Lydia's hand, and they went to sit under the Christmas tree together just as Frank came through the kitchen door. He went directly to the table where he sat down next to Isabelle. She turned to Frank and touched his face. "I'm so happy you're here, boyfriend," and she gave him a quick peck on his lips. "Merry Christmas."

"Merry Christmas, girlfriend."

Lydia heard their voices and looked up in time to see the exchange. *That whole thing is just strange. This mouth kissing between unrelated adults is so odd to me. Even my parents barely touched each other.*

Victor handed Frank a mug of coffee. "American-style coffee. I hope you still take it black," he said with a warm smile and a gentle clap of his hand on Frank's shoulder.

"I'm hungry. What's for breakfast?" asked Isabelle.

"A Great American Breakfast. Sausage, eggs, and pancakes."

"I haven't had one of those since I was at Georgetown, when I would come visit you," Frank chimed in. "Do you use the same pancake recipe? They were the best ever."

"Of course." Victor raised his voice, "Lydia, do you like American breakfasts?"

"I don't know what that is." She began to unwind herself from the girls.

Frankie explained to Lydia, "Daddy is American, from New York City. He cooks all the time. He always makes sausage, eggs, and pancakes for Christmas. He makes the best pancakes in the whole world. He calls it the Great American Breakfast."

"Well, I never had one of your daddy's breakfasts, but I'll

certainly give it a try."

Frankie yelled across the room, "Lydia's never had one, but she'll certainly give it a try."

All the adults at the table laughed. Isabelle looked at Frank and whispered, "Frankie is always helpful."

Iris ran past Isabelle to Victor, "Daddy, Daddy. Can we open our gifts *now*?" Isabelle winced slightly as Iris deferred to Victor.

"Let's do that before I start breakfast," Victor suggested.

They went into the living room to join Lydia and the other girls. Victor followed last, his camera in hand, to catch this first Christmas celebration with Isabelle since the children had been born.

Isabelle's stomach rumbled loudly, and the girls giggled. "I'm starving." Isabelle grabbed her stomach, pretending to be in pain. "Got anything I can munch on?"

Frankie picked up the remnants of her gingerbread man from the coffee table and held out her hand, "Here. You can have the rest of my gingerbread man, Mommy."

Isabelle took the torso of the man. "Thank you, Frankie," and she broke it in half and popped one huge piece into her mouth and closed her eyes in enjoyment. "Mmmm."

Frank asked, "You still do that?" Isabelle nodded, as she crunched on the crisp cookie.

Frankie looked over at Lydia. "Mommy always takes enormous bites to fill her mouth with flavor. That's the way you do it," and Isabelle tried to laugh without spitting out the cookie.

After the girls had opened their gifts, they scurried around excitedly to each adult with a "thank you" and a hug. Victor stood up. "Time to make breakfast. Frankie, will you help me?"

Frankie carefully set her new doll down on the couch and instructed her sisters, "Lily and Iris, you have to set the table. That's your job," and she skipped into the kitchen after her father.

Lydia thought, *It's so sweet how Frankie instructs the younger ones and helps her dad without complaining.*

"I'll race you, Lily," yelled Iris, and she popped up from the floor, leaving her doll and its clothes scattered under the tree.

"Girls, when you set the table, you don't race. You'll have sharp knives and forks and plates that might break," Isabelle admonished them and pulled Rose onto her lap. Rose giggled and squirmed as her mother blew raspberry sounds into her neck.

Iris pouted because she loved to race. She looked at Frank. "Will you help us?" She glanced at her mother. "Please, I mean."

"How can I refuse you?"

Frank stood up, and the girls each grabbed one of his hands and led him into the kitchen.

On the way to the kitchen, Lily told him, "Cousin Frank, you have to hand us the plates. We aren't tall enough. When I'm eight, I'll be tall enough, because Frankie can almost reach, and she is nearly eight. She's more than seven and a half."

Isabelle and Lydia sat under the tree sipping their coffee. They laughed at the kids' obsession with their ages. Isabelle said, "Lily started it when she was little and wanted to do everything that Frankie did, and for some reason, now it's extremely important to all of them. They use age as a marker for acquiring certain skills and being allowed to do things." She paused. "Lydia, you're so good with kids. Do you plan to have a family someday?"

"I never thought about it." She glanced toward Frank. *Wouldn't it be nice if Frank and I got married? Then I could be part of this family too.*

Isabelle noticed her look. "I hadn't either. I got pregnant with Frankie accidentally. I thought I couldn't have kids, and then they just came – one after another."

Iris and Lily ran in together and interrupted their conversation. "Daddy said breakfast is ready, and you should come to the table." Lily grabbed Isabelle's hand, pulled her up and led her over to the table.

Iris grabbed Lydia's hand, "You too, Lydia."

She started to stand up. "Pull me up, Iris."

"But you're too big."

Lydia let her pull a little, and suddenly she was on her feet. "See how strong you are, Iris."

"That's because I'm almost five."

§

It was a couple of days after Christmas, and Victor had just checked on the girls upstairs. As he was coming back, he looked into the living room and saw Isabelle and Frank lying on the floor with their heads under the tree, gazing up through the branches. Isabelle giggled when Frank whispered something to her and then poked her in the side.

Victor shook his head and murmured, "They couldn't resist doing that – just like old times."

When Frank realized Victor was there, he quickly stood up and helped Isabelle up from the floor.

"Where's Lydia?"

"She's packing in the cottage. Uncle, before we leave, I need to speak to you – outside."

"Let me get a refill. Do you want more coffee?" Victor filled their mugs and then pulled on his heavy sweater.

Isabelle sat at the table, and Victor leaned down and put his cheek against her hair and touched her shoulder. She reached up to caress his hand before he walked out the dining room door onto the side porch.

Frank noticed the intimate exchange, *They're so right for each other. I never would have imagined it.*

Outside, Frank put his mug on the table. "One second, Uncle," and he jumped off the porch and dashed over to the cottage for a jacket. Victor stood still for a moment, squinting against the late morning sun, looking over their property and enjoying the crisp air after the warmth of the house, and then he walked over and sat at the small table. He took a sip of his coffee and waited for Frank.

§

Lydia came in the kitchen door, and Isabelle said, "The guys are talking on the porch."

"Yeah, Frank zipped into the cottage for a jacket and told me." Lydia smiled and poured herself another cup of coffee. "This gives us time to chat a little more."

Isabelle took a final sip, giving Lydia an admiring look as she walked to the dining room table in her knee-length, slim-fitting black dress. "It looks like you're all ready to travel. Your dress is gorgeous. It fits you so beautifully. Did you design it?"

"Thanks." Lydia sat down next to her. "I make all my dresses.

I can get exactly what I want that way. This one was made for traveling. It's comfortable, it's dark, so marks won't show, and it doesn't wrinkle."

Isabelle looked down at Lydia's shoes. She clasped her hands over her heart, pretending to be ready to faint. "Oh, look at those darling, black booties! They're divine. The intricate stitching all spiraling toward that big button at the ankle – *magnifique*. But you're brave to wear suede and high heels in the winter."

"Probably, but I have such a passion for shoes. I don't always think about whether they are appropriate for the weather. I have an entire wall of shoe boxes in my bedroom. You have to have precisely the right shoes for every dress. I justify it by telling myself that they are part of my business. I'm saving my pennies, and so I shouldn't spend so much on them, but they are my guilty pleasure."

"I adore shoes too. I call them my secret shame. Victor teases me about them. I can't wear them to work, and we live on a farm, but still, I have an entire wardrobe filled with boxes of shoes that I hardly ever wear. Hey, do you want to see *my* collection?"

"Of course."

Isabelle carried their empty cups to the sink, and they went up the stairs, chattering happily.

§

Convinced that this time, his uncle would agree to help him, Frank plunged in immediately, "I need your help."

"What's that, son?"

"You know I was using the bank's internal mail to transport my goods because there's no way I'm shipping valuables in the mail – that would be too risky."

"What are you talking about?" Victor asked slowly, hoping it wasn't what he suspected.

"My business, the one I have outside of working for my dad. You know, we talked about it at my apartment in Geneva."

"You're not still doing that, are you?" Victor shook his head. "I'd hoped, when you didn't mention it during this visit, that you'd given up all that nonsense."

"Why would I want to do that? I make great money. Far more

than I make working for my dad."

Victor frowned, *It's still all about the money for him. I wonder where that came from? Alan, I'm sure.*

Frank took a deep breath and then sipped his coffee before continuing, "It's so exciting. It's the only thing that's held my interest for my entire life. I've been thinking about quitting working for him and doing my business full time. I'm very good at it, you know."

"But you could be good at anything, Frank. You just need to put your mind to it," Victor said in exasperation.

"I've tried the whole corporate thing, and it's a bore. So, I'm thinking, I could use the money from my business to branch out into real estate."

Victor shook his head. *What is he thinking?* "What do you know about real estate? Have you ever bought or sold any property?"

"I bought my new condo in Brussels. Come on, it can't be that hard. This would be a whole new career for me. But money is tight for me right now. In July, Dad put in new security measures where the bank scans all internal mail, and I have a backlog of jewelry I need to get to my brokers in the States and elsewhere. I just need a little help."

Victor set down his empty coffee cup very slowly and carefully as he tried to contain his anger. "Frank, so let me make sure I understand what you're doing. You are still stealing jewelry, and you've been using your dad's bank mail to ship these stolen goods to America, and now, you're in a bind because he's put in this new system. Please, just give it all up, Frank. You're a damn fool. You've got Lydia. You've got your whole life ahead of you. You can sell your condo and fund your real estate business with the proceeds. Just rent for a while until you get on your feet again. I can lend you some money."

"I'm not selling my condo. And I don't want a hand-out from you. What I need is help with my business."

What the hell is he getting at? Victor thought in frustration. But he just raised his eyebrows.

Frank cleared his throat, "So, I have this proposal for you."

Victor sat and stared at Frank – waiting. Frank took a final swallow of coffee, and he set down his cup in the same meticulous fashion his uncle had. He spoke slowly at first and then more quickly as his excitement grew, convinced that his uncle would see how brilliant his idea was. "Now that we are both in Europe, why don't we use your Turkish rug business over here to ship merchandise to the States, hell, all over the world. You'd earn good money, and of course, you'd get a healthy cut from moving the other stuff as well. Don't you see, it's the perfect solution to my problems."

His temper rose again as Frank laid out his proposal. He opened his mouth to reply, but Frank went on, "And it would solve your cash-flow issues too. That's why I want to bring you in on it. I'm sure you can use the money. I honestly don't know what you're living on."

Victor's face suffused with color. "You don't know what you're talking about, Frank. You don't know anything about my lifestyle. You don't know anything about our finances or my business." Victor sat for a moment, angry and breathing hard. *He doesn't get it, even after being here with us. Even after seeing the life that we've built here on our small farm. Even after he's seen how happy we are.*

"It's obvious you need cash. You spent a load of money renovating the cottage, and the rest of the place could use some work." He looked around at the porch, the uneven floorboards and paint that needed to be refreshed. "You probably aren't making much from your business in New York since you aren't there to oversee it. There's no way your tiny shop here, in the middle of nowhere, can be making any money. And Isabelle's salary can't possibly take care of your property or your family, a family of six, in a fashion you're accustomed to."

"What *I'm* accustomed to? *This* is a work of love." Furious at Frank's insinuations, he swept his arm around at the house, the yard, the orchards. "We own this farm outright, and we are doing the work on it ourselves, on *our* schedule, because *this* house, *this* land, *this* life is part of who we are, not just something we bought." Victor clenched his jaw. *For someone so smart, he's an idiot.*

"And Isabelle told me you want to send Frankie to ballet school in Paris. That'll cost you a pretty penny. Oh, and piano lessons for Lily. It all adds up."

Victor's eyes narrowed, and he spoke in a slow, measured tone,

"How dare you imply that I cannot take care of my family without *your* help? I don't need *your* money. We don't need *that kind* of money. How dare you suggest that I participate in this criminal scheme of yours? How dare you suggest that I put my family and our lives at risk?"

"Come on, Uncle. Don't overreact. It'd be easy money for you guys. Lydia and I do really well. It would be great to work together."

Don't overreact? His face flushed redder still. Victor stood up abruptly, and his chair fell back onto the floorboards with a crash. He turned his back to Frank and walked to the door. His voice was full of pain and sadness, "I'm so disappointed in you, Frank. So disappointed. This life isn't about money." Victor swept his hand around again at all those things that made up his life. He stopped before he opened the door and looked back at Frank, "What an absolutely stupid suggestion. And in case you didn't understand me, my answer is *NO*. After Isabelle takes you to the airport, Frank, don't ever come back." Victor shook his head sadly, *I should just turn him in and be done with this, but he's my family, and I could never do that.*

§

Victor came downstairs. "Frankie is completely out. No eavesdropping tonight."

Isabelle pulled Victor down to the bench beside her and wrapped her arms around him in a hard hug. "You look worn out tonight, Old Man. The visitors? It's been a very busy few days."

"Well, yes. Kind of."

Isabelle handed him a big glass of red wine. "You look like you need this."

Victor sighed and turned to face her, bending one leg up and tucking his foot under his other thigh. "I had a most disturbing conversation with Frank before they left."

"I thought things were off when you came back in from the porch."

"I'm done with him, Izzy, I'm done," he said, his voice despondent.

Confused, Isabelle asked, "What do you mean?"

"We need to keep our distance from him." He took a gulp of

wine without even tasting it.

"But he's only just come back into our lives. What do you mean? I don't understand."

"I'm afraid he's going to find himself in over his head. I'm concerned. I don't want you or me to be accidentally caught up in his criminal activity."

Her voice was puzzled as she asked, "Criminal? Victor, what are you talking about?"

"And I think Lydia's in it with him – she's part of his scheme."

"Scheme? I don't understand, Victor. I feel like I've come into a movie partway through. Start from the beginning. Please?"

"Okay." Victor took a deep breath and let it out slowly. "Frank is stealing jewelry – expensive stuff – and fencing it. He invited me to be part of it that day in Geneva, and then he asked me again today."

"Oh, shit. I thought he stopped stealing after the incident in Texas."

"What?"

"He stole some earrings and got arrested. I helped get the charges dropped. I thought a couple hours of jail time would frighten him and make him stop. Especially when I told him I was going to call you."

"I wish you had."

"Actually, I did, but you didn't pick up. We weren't on speaking terms then, so I didn't call again. Victor, he's been doing this for as long as I've known him. All the time we lived in Brasília. But it was small stuff then. Kid stuff. He always said he wanted to be a jewel thief when he grew up, but just now I realize he was serious."

"Oh no – no, no, no, no. I thought it had stopped with the watch." They sat silently for a moment, and then Victor turned toward the table and stared at his hands folded in front of him, one thumb rubbing the other. "He stole that Rolex a little while before they moved. This has been going on for far too long. It's not a hobby or a – a game or a – for fun anymore. It's serious criminal activity that he's involved in. And he's doing it for real."

Isabelle touched his arm and put her other hand flat on his back between his shoulder blades. She began to rub it in slow comforting circles. "What are we going to do?"

Victor scrubbed his hands over his face in frustration and disappointment. "Damn Alan. He never paid any attention to the kid except to criticize him and tell him he needed to do better. I'm sure this started as a child crying for attention. If they had stayed in New York, maybe I could have helped." His voice cracked, "I can now see it was such a bad move, me selling their house."

He took a deep breath. "I should have been tougher on Frank when he gave me the watch. Instead, I gave it back to him – engraved, for God's sake. I should have turned him in when we were in Geneva, when he asked me to join him. Maybe that would have stopped this. Now, he's an established criminal. I feel as if I've played a part in this."

"Victor, you can't hold yourself responsible for Frank's behavior. He's an adult. His choices are his decision."

"I loved that kid like a son. I still love him. I thought this visit would bring us back together. When he was growing up, I wanted to be the fun uncle and let Alan take care of the discipline. I wanted to be the one he liked. But instead, I was too easy on him."

"But look at how you've raised our girls. You've set boundaries. You discipline them in a loving fashion. You have rules. You're a wonderful father – and mother when I'm not here."

"Oh, Izzy, I'm sick over this. Frank's going to get caught one day. I know he will. It'll be the ruin of him. And if we join in, we'll be ruined too. I sent him away. I told him we can't see him again."

"Oh, Victor, it was one of those hard conversations, wasn't it?"

He simply nodded and folded his hands on the table again, rubbing his thumb, the lump in his throat choking off any words.

He stared out the window at the barren trees in the orchard and turned back to Isabelle with a bleak face. "But we can't have anything more to do with Frank – we can never see him again." His face crumpled, and he dropped his head into his arms, and his shoulders rose and fell in heartbroken sobs.

Isabelle wrapped her arms around him, "Oh, my dearest darling, I'm so sorry." She pressed her face against him.

Victor turned and laid his head on Isabelle's shoulder and clung to her while he continued to cry. Isabelle rested her head on his, and tears sheeted down her cheeks too. "You're right. But the thought of life without him hurts so much. I can't bear it. Oh, Victor."

Chapter Sixteen

August 2011

Flash Mob Convergence

Rotterdam, The Netherlands

"I'm famished. That was quite a workout last night, my love." Charlotte gave Tracey a lascivious wink. "I'm going to need some breakfast, and soon. The place where we had drinks last night isn't very far from here, and I noticed that it serves breakfast. The food looked delicious, and I heard lots of compliments from the patrons."

"That sounds good to me." Tracey gave her a rousing kiss before they set off toward the restaurant.

When they arrived, they found the tables were all taken, and there were only a few seats left at the bar. The two stools where they'd sat the night before were vacant, and with a raised eyebrow and a grin at memories of the night before, Tracey led her over to them. Charlotte laid her guidebook on the bar top before draping the strap to her large handbag over the back of the barstool.

As they settled into their seats, the attractive woman behind the bar approached them. "Good morning. What may I bring you?"

"Menus, please. We're in desperate need of food," said Charlotte.

The bartender pointed to the large chalkboard over the bar. "The menu is there. We try to cater to many different tastes. We have some American dishes, light European breakfast fare and some heavier meat and cheese plates such as we eat here. While you decide, what may I bring you to drink?"

Tracey looked at Charlotte. "Two Bloody Marys?"

She nodded and said in her faint British accent, "That would be brilliant. Please make mine extra spicy."

The bartender turned around to make the drinks, and Tracey leaned over close to Charlotte's ear and murmured, "You were *extra* spicey last night." He rubbed his nose along the edge of her ear.

Charlotte giggled and asked softly, "Is that right?"

He chuckled, "Oh, yes indeed. But all that extra spice has given me an extra-large appetite this morning."

Charlotte chortled, and Tracey continued, "For breakfast, of course."

"Of course."

They studied the board while waiting for the bartender to return with their drinks. Tracey decided on an herb omelet and some warm crusty rolls, and Charlotte made her apologies for ordering avocado toast instead of something more local. After they had placed their orders, the bartender said, "You were here last night, weren't you? We were very busy with the wedding out on the patio, in addition to all our regular customers. But I remember seeing you. You were in these same seats, right?"

"We were, and we did sit here." Extending her hand for a shake, she said, "I'm Charlotte, and this is Tracey. Thanks for remembering us."

Tracey smiled and reached over to shake the bartender's hand.

"Nice to meet you. I'm Johanna Visser. My husband, Piet, and I own this restaurant. We are always grateful to see our customers come back again." She pointed toward a large table in the dining room where the guests were discussing food choices with the waitress and said, "Excuse me while I put your order in ahead of that big party. They're regulars here, lovely people, but as you can see, a lot of them — I wouldn't want you to be waiting behind them."

After she'd disappeared into the kitchen, Tracey said, "Let's figure out what else we're going to do while we're here." He pulled a small moleskin notebook from his jacket pocket and opened it to a fresh page. With his fountain pen in his left hand, he leaned over Charlotte's shoulder as she flipped through the guidebook she'd laid on the counter.

"I know, let's go see the Dutch Pinball Museum! It isn't too far from here. See, here we are in Dijkzigt, and there's where the museum is." She traced a line on the map. "It's right on the other side of the river. We could take a water taxi or the metro."

"I used to play pinball with my granddad when I was a kid," said Tracey, a fond look on his face as he recalled those childhood days.

"I didn't know that — so did I! But with my father."

They relaxed and savored their cocktails, and Charlotte showed Tracey the pictures of the machines in the museum. "Look at this.

They have ninety playable machines. What fun! We'll have to play a game or two. We can see who's better. I'm sure there's some kind of penalty the winner could assess against the loser."

Tracey waggled his eyebrows as he leered at her in response.

Johanna set their breakfasts down in front of them. "Is this your first time in Rotterdam?"

Charlotte tucked the book into her handbag, watching Tracey as he took a bite after sprinkling pepper lightly onto his omelet. "Yes, it is," he said. "We took a river cruise from Basel to Amsterdam and came here as an add-on. Yesterday, we joined a bus tour of the city to orient ourselves. We had just a quick glimpse of the seaport. Oh my, it's massive."

"Today," said Johanna, proud of her native city, "we are a major logistic and economic center with the largest seaport in Europe. There are only a few larger ones in the world, and they are in Asia. But tell me, what did you think of our city center?"

"Downtown Rotterdam is so modern, much more contemporary than I thought it would be. I had envisioned an area dense with quaint, old buildings," replied Tracey. "I particularly enjoy religious architecture, so it was intriguing to visit the Grote of Sint-Laurenskerk. The guide said the church had been restored and it's all that's left of the medieval buildings that once stood in the middle of the city." He shook his head sadly, "It was very reminiscent to me of the center of Berlin with the Kaiser-Wilhelm Gedächtniskirche, another beautifully restored ruin, standing among all the modern, post-war buildings."

"Yes, unfortunately, our city center also was demolished in World War Two," Johanna told them. "After the war, between the nineteen fifties and the nineteen seventies, it was gradually rebuilt. And now, look at it today. What a miracle!"

"It's very impressive," said Charlotte. "But the district I liked best was Delfshaven. You know, it has such a village-like feel with all those eclectic old buildings lining the Nieuwe Mass. It's hard to believe it is so close to the city center. The houses look like the little porcelain ones that KLM airline gives to their passengers. I think it would be fun to live on the water, even just a small river like that. Imagine, boats docked out in front of your house, right there."

"Our dear friends, David and Raul, whose wedding you saw being celebrated here last night, live in Delfshaven in one of those old houses on the river. They are pediatricians – their clinic's in the area also. When they return from their honeymoon, they're going to start renovating it – but excuse me, you aren't here to listen to me go on about my friends. While you were in Delfshaven, did you have a chance to visit the Pilgrims Church? You know, where they went to pray before beginning their journey to the New World in 1620?"

Charlotte turned to Tracey, her eyes dancing. "We should go there, my love, after we visit the pinball museum. To atone for our gambling. And then we could rent bikes and spend the afternoon exploring the canal pathways and the farmers' market."

"If you are going back there, let me recommend a splendid seafood restaurant for dinner. You can have fish caught today by their own fleet of boats." Johanna jotted a restaurant name and address on the back of one of her business cards. "Tell her that Piet and I sent you." She handed the card to Tracey, who tucked it carefully into the pocket in the back of his notebook.

"Johanna, I must say, the herbs in this omelet are superb. How do you find such fresh ingredients?" asked Tracey, laying his fork and knife on his plate for a moment.

She replied, delight spilling over in her voice, "Those are our secret ingredients. We grow them in an herb garden, in a plot that our children once planted. It's just off the rear patio, alongside the building."

Charlotte picked up a piece of her toast. "So, the basil on this is from there too? It's so aromatic." Johanna nodded as Charlotte continued, "I peeked out back last night. I didn't see the garden, but I saw the party. It looked like a beautiful, fairy-tale wedding. Do you have a lot of them here?"

"We do. You could say Piet and I are a pair of old romantics – we both love to create the perfect settings for couples on their special day. But enough of my talking, I'll let you eat in peace."

Before she could leave, Charlotte quickly wiped some avocado off of the corner of her mouth with her white linen napkin and said, "No, no, please don't leave on our account – it's nice chatting with you."

Johanna looked around to make sure no one needed her and then back at them. "It's a pleasure talking with you too. I just didn't want to intrude."

"You're not. Talking to locals is one of my favorite parts of traveling." Charlotte smiled at her.

"And talking to customers is my favorite part of owning this place." Johanna smiled back happily and then picked up a glass of water from behind the bar and took a sip. "The wedding yesterday was a beautiful, happy occasion for our two friends. How long have you two been married?"

"Oh, we're not married," Tracey corrected her. "We've been dating for a year."

"I'm sorry for jumping to conclusions. You look so comfortable with each other, I just assumed." She took another sip of her water. "I meet a lot of people and would have never guessed you were still in the early stages of your relationship. How did you meet?"

Charlotte put down her toast and sat back. "On a river cruise in Ukraine. One evening, in the lounge of the boat, we started talking about the toilet museum in Kyiv, and well, we've been together ever since." She chuckled to herself at the memory of that night. "Funny isn't it, that we had to travel halfway around the world to meet. But then again, we probably would never have met any other way. Tracey lives in North Carolina, and I live in Washington state – on opposite sides of the country."

"What a story. That's certainly a long-distance relationship. Do you need anything else?"

"I'm good," replied Tracey, "Charlotte?"

She swallowed a bite of her toast before answering. "Your food is fantastic, Johanna. Wherever we go, Tracey and I try to find places that serve great food. This is some of the best I've had on this trip."

"Thank you. I'm glad it pleases you. I haven't traveled much outside of The Netherlands. Where are you off to next – home, or some other place?"

"In a few days, we fly to Russia," Tracey replied. "We'll spend several days there. Charlotte belongs to a flash mob performing in St Petersburg." He paused, noticing the puzzled look on her face.

"Flash mob?"

Charlotte turned toward Johanna, "A flash mob is a group of people who assemble in a public place and suddenly start dancing. It's all choreographed. But they only dance for a brief amount of time. Then they disperse as quickly as they appeared."

"Oh, a *flitsmeute!* What fun!"

"Charlotte has worked really hard with her Seattle mob. They've won a spot in the first ever flash mob convergence in St Petersburg next week. So, we're traveling there a couple days ahead of time so she can meet up with them and practice for the big event." Charlotte noticed the pride in his eyes as he spoke.

"That's a lot of work. I take Zumba classes for exercise. I know what hard work dancing is," Johanna smiled at Charlotte.

"I take Zumba too. I love it."

"You're both more energetic than me. I'm looking forward to a lot of sightseeing and watching the flash mob from the sidelines."

An employee approached them and said quietly, "Sorry to interrupt, Johanna. There's a customer who would like to speak with you."

"Excuse me, Charlotte, Tracey. It was very nice to meet you. I hope you have a great time sightseeing, and if you have the opportunity, please come back."

"We will," Tracey tipped his glass toward her.

After Johanna walked away, Charlotte said, "I get such pleasure from sharing our story with others."

"I know. You like to share everything with everyone, in person or on social media. That's just the way you are."

"I hope you don't mind."

"That's one of the things that makes you special, Charlotte. You're the opposite of me."

Charlotte turned to Tracey and kissed him on the cheek. "Ohhh, your face is a bit rough today. I don't know why I didn't notice that before," she said in surprise.

He raised his hand and rubbed his chin with his thumb and forefinger. "I've decided to grow a beard. My dad shaved every day, and I've always followed his lead. Because of my job, I've never felt comfortable having a beard. But this morning, while I was getting ready, I decided I might give it a try. Do you mind?"

"I'm certain you'll look even more distinguished with a salt-and-pepper beard to match your hair."

§

St Petersburg, Russia

Tracey and Charlotte pushed through the revolving door, squeezing into one section, laughing hysterically at a story that Charlotte had just shared about one of her students. *I've been extraordinarily happy with her the last few days. Ever since that strangely wonderful night in Rotterdam.* The bellhop followed through the other door with their luggage piled on the brass cart.

"While you check us in, my love, I'll go over and register and find out where we are assigned to practice and what the schedule is."

Tracey looked around at all the people standing about in the lobby, signs that indicated gathering spots for different mobs, and hotel staff wending their way through the crowd to deliver luggage to guests' rooms. A group of children had discovered that they could take off their shoes, run and then slide in their socks down the marble-floored hallways, at least until their parents or nannies stopped them. "Better you than me," he said. "Once we're checked in, I'll need to find the bar and escape all this madness."

Charlotte raised her face and gave him a warm kiss, "I'll meet you there." She looked around the lobby and spotted the sign, *The St Petersburg Flash Mob Convergence – Seattle Mob* and headed off in that direction. As she approached the registration table, two women from her group came toward her, and she gave them an enthusiastic wave.

Cheryl hugged her, "I almost didn't recognize you. Your hair. That's a gorgeous red, but why did you dye it? When did you do it?"

"I didn't feel I was old enough for all the grey I was getting. When I found a fabulous hair salon at our hotel in Rotterdam a few days ago, I thought I'd try something completely different."

Amanda gave Charlotte a hug. "It's wonderful," she gushed as they pulled apart. "How was your trip?"

"The flight from Rotterdam was uneventful. Just the way I like it."

Cheryl chimed in, "But how was the cruise?"

"Oh," Charlotte's face grew animated, "it was fantastic. We had a wonderful time, and then in Rotterdam, we saw some people from the cruise we took last summer – the cruise where Tracey and I met. They were all there for a wedding. What a complete coincidence – we'd stopped at a little local restaurant for drinks, and the wedding and reception were going on in the back garden. It was charming. And we went back there the next day for breakfast, and I even learned how to say flash mob in Dutch – *flitsmeute*. I could go on and on. But I'm sure you don't want to hear all those details."

"Oh, I love hearing about all the exciting things you've done. You're so lucky," said Amanda with an envious sigh.

"I am. We had such a great time."

Cheryl stepped aside to let someone go by with a cart full of luggage. She looked around. "Is Mr. Wonderful here with you?"

"He is. He's very excited to explore the churches here, particularly if they have been adapted for other uses. And he's developed a new fascination with iconography. His mental foot is already tapping. He's so impatient to see some of them here. We're cruising off to Moscow after the convergence, and then we'll spend a week at a resort on the Black Sea."

"Oh, my gosh. I wish I could afford to travel like that. This is my one trip for the year."

"It's all about good divorce settlements," Charlotte grinned at her friend, "and having a flexible teaching job where I can take a semester off now and then."

Cheryl playfully bumped against Charlotte with her hip, "You take your first cruise in Ukraine, and you meet this tall, handsome, wealthy judge who loves to travel. Now, you're off to a resort on the Black Sea? You're living the life."

"Some people have all the luck," Amanda said.

"I know, Amanda. I'm one lucky woman."

She looked at Charlotte for a moment. "Check out the look on her face, Cheryl." Turning back to Charlotte she said, "This is getting serious, isn't it?"

"You know, it is. I think our relationship has changed during this trip, and I'm liking it."

Cheryl reached over and shook her arm. "Is that really you speaking, or has someone taken over your body?"

Charlotte smiled, "Yeah, that 'I never want to be tied down again' person? So, we'll see how it goes. It is pretty nice, I have to confess. We're compatible in a lot of ways." She thought about their lengthy conversations, their similar humor, the astonishing sex they had a few nights ago. "You just have to find the right guy."

They moved back toward their registration table to let a loud group pass. Cheryl handed Charlotte a packet of information. "We're already registered. Our practice is scheduled for tomorrow morning at seven. We'll be in the north room." She pointed down the hall.

"How have the practices been going while I was away?"

"Much better. Things finally came together. And you'll be happy to know I haven't changed any of the moves."

"The third part is so much better," Amanda raved. "We've all practiced hard. It's really spectacular now."

"Whew, I'm so happy the choreography hasn't changed. I'll definitely have to work hard the next couple of days during practice to catch up to you gals. But right now, I'm off to the bar for a drink with Tracey."

"I need to get the group together, and then we'll go have a glass of wine in the bar too. But right now, Amanda and I have to wait for some of the others to arrive."

"Do you need any help?"

"No, today'll be pretty easy. We're just checking people in, maybe we'll see you in the bar later. We're going to run through the initial scheduling over our drinks." Cheryl tapped her pen on the stack of folders on the table in front of her.

"I'll join you. I need to get back in the loop. Tracey and his sudoku puzzle can survive without me for a while."

"Or he can come sit with us?" Amanda said with a sly grin.

"He won't want to get in our way. But I'll make sure to introduce you all to him. See you in a bit."

When Charlotte finally entered the bar after her meeting with the girls, she saw Tracey sitting there, his summer jacket draped over the stool next to him. She stopped for a moment and watched him as he worked through his sudoku puzzle, gin and tonic in one hand

and pen in the other, sporting the beginnings of what was shaping up to be a very sexy-looking beard. *He's so attractive. So sure of himself. Amanda is right, I am one lucky woman.* She climbed onto the stool next to him and pulled his jacket onto her lap, took a sip of his drink, nodded in satisfaction and ordered one for herself. She shared her schedule for the next day.

Then Charlotte took a St Petersburg guidebook out of her handbag. "Okay, we only have four days in St Petersburg before we board the riverboat. Let's get serious about what we want to see." Tracey smiled at all the pages she had already marked with tiny Post-it notes. Ready to make a list, he flipped to a fresh page in his small notebook and pulled the cap off his fountain pen.

"A full day at the Hermitage, of course." He scooted closer to her and flipped to the corresponding section, pointing out image after image, "...and then, I want to see this wonderful statue of Voltaire that was commissioned by Catherine the Great." He circled his forefinger several times around the illustration. Then he said, in an impassioned voice, "But most of all, I want to see that sixteenth-century icon of the Archangel Michael. And the late fourteenth-century double-sided icon of The Savior and The Virgin. My God, Charlotte, I want to try to step into the artists' shoes, you know, stand in front of these creations and appreciate the process, if I can, to feel the prayer the way the painter did as he put brush to wood. Because they *are* a way of praying – through painting rather than with words, of transforming nature's raw materials into images, into icons, the way a gardener does when he works in the soil. It's an offering of artistically transformed matter as a prayer."

Tracey stopped suddenly and glanced up to see Charlotte watching him in astonishment. "I don't think in the year I've known you that I've heard you talk about anything or any place we've visited as emotionally as that. Of course, we must visit them, and you can tell me more about the creative process as prayer. And speaking of prayer, while we're there, I want to walk down the Jordan Staircase. I'll imagine it's Epiphany, and I'm part of the Tsar's entourage on our way to bless the waters of the Neva River."

"We'll do all of that and more. That's why we're going to spend an entire day wandering through all the buildings that make up the

Hermitage. And we also have to visit the Church on Spilled Blood."

"Russians have such a graphic way of naming churches." She searched for the page that described the former Russian Orthodox church and began reading. "Oh, interesting. We shouldn't have any problem getting in to see it since it's also a secular museum and open to the public."

"Look at the pictures of the religious mosaics on the interior and exterior." Tracey sighed and traced his finger reverently across the photographs of the brilliantly colored interior. "All those different minerals and materials that were used to create them. Astounding, aren't they?"

"They must be magnificent when you see them in person. No wonder it's on your must-see list. I'm excited to experience them with you."

Tracey took a sip of his gin and tonic and took the book back from her.

"But we won't be in Russia long enough to take a trip to Veliky Novogorod, and see the iconostasis there," he continued. "It's one of the oldest in Russia. Charlotte, just think, it's made up of icons from the eleventh to the seventeenth centuries. Look at this little diagram. I've seen many pictures as they've been working on it but imagine actually standing in front of those six tiers of icons. Oh, my, now there's definitely a reason to return."

"I've never thought of you as a religious person," she said.

"Not religious, no. But I do consider myself spiritual. Icons touch something deep inside me," he said, laying a hand against his chest. "Not because they are pictures of saints and other religious figures but because of the process and the dialog they represent. The discipline involved—"

Tracey frowned as a loud group of women came into the bar, the noise interrupting his train of thought and that moment between them. Charlotte peeked over her shoulder at the noise and grinned and waved, "Yes, that's my mob." She pointed over her shoulder at the women pulling chairs up to a large round table and tucked the book into her bag. He drew a deep breath. She turned to him and with an apologetic look, said, "Tracey, I have to go sit with them for a bit. Probably twenty minutes or so. Then would you come over and rescue me?"

"It will be like jumping into a pool of sharks," he replied, quirking an eyebrow at her.

"They will gobble you up, my love."

He laughed and leaned sideways to kiss her.

She walked over to the group of women who had their registration packets open and sheets of paper, covered with diagrams, spread across the table. Cheryl was showing them the map of Palace Square and Charlotte dragged a chair over next to her. "This is where we are going to converge. It's a perfect place to meet. On the ground, there are already squares, and the organizer has put markings on each one. We're meeting in F-five." She pointed it out on the map. "We'll be using this whole surrounding set of squares as well, so we'll actually have a lot of space."

For the next thirty minutes, Cheryl continued to go over the practice schedule, time and logistics for the day of the convergence. "That's all, unless you have any questions."

Charlotte blew Tracey a kiss. Glancing at his watch, he shook his head with a smile and gathered up his belongings, wandered over to their table and put his hand on her shoulder.

"Hey. Want to sit down, my love?" she asked.

"Thanks, but remember we have a dinner reservation. I just wanted to drop by and say hello to everyone."

"Ladies, this is Tracey Lauch." Charlotte reached over her shoulder and took his hand. "Tracey, this is the Seattle Mob." She gestured at the group.

"Nice to meet you all. Palace Square is huge. How many groups are going to be there?"

Cheryl answered, "There will be about a dozen of the best mobs from all over the world."

"So, this is a big thing. I'm only familiar with flash mobs who sing or play music."

"Tracey, this is Cheryl. She's the brains and choreographer behind our wonderful group. If it weren't for her, we wouldn't be here."

Cheryl continued, "Instead of the usual pop up of a group that dances and then disappears back into the crowd, this is going to be like a dance-off. Each group dances to short extracts of different songs, and at the end, we all come together in one final dance. It's going to be the first event like this ever held."

"Holy smokes. It sounds fascinating." Tracey looked at his watch and then down at Charlotte, "Our dinner reservation's in less than thirty minutes. We should be on our way. It was nice to meet you all. I'm looking forward to seeing you at the convergence."

Before leaving the group, Charlotte said, "I'll come find you after dinner. Will you still be here?"

The group laughed, and Cheryl quipped as she raised her glass, "Where else?"

As they left the bar, he said, "You never told me about the scale of this thing."

"I was hoping you'd be surprised by it. Besides," she gave him a sly, flirtatious look, "we've been busy with other things," and she rubbed his arm affectionately.

Cheryl leaned back in her chair. "Oh – my. Tall, handsome, salt-and-pepper hair. Do you think he's growing a beard?" She fanned herself. "He's gorgeous. I've always been attracted to men with beards."

Amanda added, "What a catch. If only I'd seen him first – She's so lucky."

§

After two days of practice and a couple of sightseeing tours into the surrounding countryside, Tracey and Charlotte entered Palace Square. "Look, there's the Winter Palace and that's the General Staff building behind us. I'm glad we've waited to "do" St Petersburg together, Charlotte." Tracey made air quotes with his fingers. "This square is enormous. How are you going to dance with all these people around? It's so busy."

Charlotte looked up at Tracey, using a hand to keep the sun out of her eyes. "We'll hang out in our numbered squares. We're number F-five." She pointed to the ground, "Somebody marked all of these for our event. Once we hear the introductory music for our mob, we gather together and start dancing. With the other flash mobs we've done, people step back to watch and that gives us plenty of space."

"How do you know when it's your turn to mob-out?" He chuckled at the word he'd made up.

"When we hear our music?" She grinned, "You'll see. The mobs will go in order. We each have a different piece of music. When we see the group ahead of us start to dance, we need to be ready because there's no break between songs. We have forty-five seconds each for our individual mob dances, and then the finale, when we all dance together, is about two minutes. It's going to be a lot of dancing. It'll be a spectacular sight."

"It's pretty warm. Do you want me to bring you a bottle of water before I disappear?"

"No, I have several in my backpack." She tapped her shoulder strap.

"Do you need anything else before I wander off? I think I'll explore the area around here and then watch the whole shebang from several different spots."

"Nope, I'm all set. Oh, just remember, it starts in two hours. So, that gives you a good amount of time before you need to be in place to watch us. When it's all over, I'm sure the square will be a madhouse, so should we meet at that entryway to the Winter Palace?" she pointed to one of the gated doorways to the building.

"Sounds good to me."

Charlotte pressed against Tracey and teased him with a passionate kiss. He felt a surge of desire and responded with equal fervor, his hand in the small of her back holding her to him. *I'm so carefree around her. She brings out things in me I didn't know were there. She makes me so happy.* He gave Charlotte a little swat on her bottom. "I'll see you later. Go break a leg."

She laughed and smacked his hand gently before giving him another quick kiss, turning and walking off. Tracey admired her as she moved away into the crowd to join her mob. Her trim figure, her confident walk. *She has so few inhibitions. That excites me too.*

He walked away from Palace Square to explore the area along the Nevsky Prospekt and then angling his way to his left, knowing that if he kept going, eventually, he'd run into the Neva River again. American fast-food places were scattered along the way. *The best of America has made it to St Petersburg, I see. The things we want to see together are within easy walking distance of the Hermitage.* Tracey meandered on and saw signs for the Russian Museum and the Mussorgsky Theatre and the Philharmonic. *Ah, now I'm beginning to get a good feel for the way it all fits together.* He left the main avenue to wander through an old neighborhood. *This is better. Less crowded. Less touristy.*

When an attractive woman approached Tracey, he tried to go around her, but she blocked his way, stepped closer and said something in Russian. With a puzzled look on his face, he said, "Excuse me, I don't speak Russian."

The woman parroted his words in a thick accent, "Excuse me? You English?"

"No, American." He tried to walk around her, but she blocked his way again.

"Excuse me?" She pulled her thick red hair back, holding her arms up, pushing her breasts forward.

Tracey felt that first tug of arousal and shook his head, *No! I don't want to do this. I don't want her. I have Charlotte now. I don't need to do that anymore.*

In her thick accent, she said, "You want company, American?" and she came close and grabbed his crotch. "Oh, you're a big boy. I feel you want me."

He thought of Charlotte, "No. No." He pushed her hand away. *I don't want her. I don't want this.*

The woman huffed, turned around and stalked away. Tracey watched her walk down the street, how her hips swished back and forth. *She could have been a model, the way she walks. She's certainly good-looking enough.* A picture of his hand around her throat flashed through his mind, and he felt his body respond again. *I want to pull her against me and strangle her.*

"Hello. Wait. Some company would be nice."

The prostitute turned around and flashed a smile before walking back toward him. She tucked her arm into his. "Buy me drink, American. I know good bar." She led Tracey down a sidewalk near the river, and she chattered on. They entered the bar, and she led him to a table in a dark back corner. "Best seat in bar." She turned to Tracey and ran her hand along his face and down the front of his shirt. "Mmmm, nice body. You want sex here, American?"

"Good lord, not here! What will you have to drink?"

"I want – New York."

Tracey looked puzzled for a moment and then grinned, "Ah, a Manhattan?"

"Yes, Manhattan. Like New York City."

Tracey went to the bar, and his shoes made sticky sounds as he walked across the floor. The lights were low, and the room smelled of old beer and alcohol. *You wanted local color. Here you have it. This is an authentic dive.*

He returned with her drink and beer in a bottle for himself and set the drinks on the less-than-clean tabletop. She patted the bench seat next to her, but he shook his head and sat in the chair across the table.

"You from New York? Tell me about America." Tracey talked a little about North Carolina, the beaches, the landscape, the heat and humidity.

When they finished their drinks, she stood and stepped close to Tracey. She took his hand and pulled. "Come, American." He stood up, and they walked toward the door.

Outside, she turned to him. "Drink make you relax. Now sex. Have good place."

Tracey followed as she led him down to the river and under a large bridge. *Will I have sex with her before I kill her?*

Under the bridge, the prostitute led him to an isolated area between the abutments. It was dark with shadows. She stood very close to Tracey, running her hands over his torso, sliding her hands lower, touching him, arousing him. "Sex or blow job, American?"

And at that moment, he decided. Tracey gulped, "Blow job." *My God, I haven't called it that since I was in college.*

She slowly knelt down and unfastened his trousers. Afterward, she walked over and spat into the river and wiped her mouth with the back of her hand. When she returned, Tracey was tucking his shirt back into his waistband.

The prostitute held out her hand. "You pay now."

"Turn around, I have a surprise for you."

The prostitute smiled, "Ahhh, you want more? Big spender."

Tracey's breathing began to quicken again as he reached around her. He put his right hand over her mouth and nose. She giggled under his hand and murmured, "You like rough?" She squirmed against him in anticipation of what would come next until he tightened the hand covering her face and wrapped his other hand around her throat. But by then her scream was muffled. He squeezed tighter and tighter. *I love this feeling. The way she moans. The way she grinds against me. It excites me.* He thought of Charlotte. And for the first time, he groaned with pleasure and began to thrust against her.

Finally, she stopped resisting and was just a limp weight in Tracey's arms. He gently put her in a corner, deep in the shadows. He looked around and saw no one, and he unfastened his zipper again and ejaculated against the abutment. *What just happened to me? I've never been that aroused before.* He stood there as his heartbeat returned to normal.

He looked at the woman, pushed her hair off her face. "You could have been so much more," he said and reached down to take her earring. He put the earring in his pocket and took out his wallet and dropped a one-hundred-euro bill on her lap.

§

He watched the grand finale as all the mobs danced together. *That was remarkable.*

Tracey rubbed his thumb over the earring in his pocket, still astounded by what he'd just done. *In such a public area. With a prostitute.* He continued to rub the earring gently. *Edgar Spring, you were right. I am a serial killer. I can't go back. Even if I never kill again, I'll always be a serial killer.*

Charlotte came bouncing up, exuberant, hot and sweaty. She threw her arms around him and lifted her face to his. She was astonished at the intensity of his kiss.

Chapter Seventeen

Valentine's Day 2012

The One Who Got Away

Strasbourg, France

"Enjoy the cathedral tour this evening, Tracey. I wish I'd been able to join you on that cruise. I'm dying to spend some more time exploring France. And the Rhine, with all those castles and vineyards." She sighed, "It must be so romantic."

"It is, but it would be even more so if you were with me. I miss alone time with you. But family has to come first. Your mom needs you right now. We'll have other cruises together in the future. Maybe we can take that Seine cruise that goes from Paris to Mont St. Michel, and we'll visit Monet's gardens in Giverny and then Rouen, where we can see the cathedral that inspired some of his paintings. Would that be romantic enough for you?"

"Oh, my love, that would be magnificent."

"It's a deal, then. I've sent you a surprise, so be on the lookout for a little package. It should arrive sometime this afternoon."

"That'll brighten my day. I love you."

"I love you too, Charlotte. I'll call you tomorrow. Say hi to your mom for me."

Tracey glanced at his watch as he walked into the lobby of *The Marigold. Plenty of time to make it to the tour.* He could see the Spectrum crew directing the passengers through its lobby and across a wide, carpeted ramp which connected to *The Sunglow,* the boat they were anchored alongside. He followed them across into its lobby. *If you'd never been on a Spectrum riverboat, you would still know they belonged to the same cruise line by the layout and furnishings of the reception areas. They are very elegant, but — I wonder if someone's ever gotten onto the wrong boat and only discovered it when their cabin key didn't work?* He chuckled to himself as he took the idea further and imagined the person's embarrassment as they discovered that not only had their key worked, but they had awoken in an absolute stranger's bed and were now heading to a totally different destination.

Tracey paused to let a handful of passengers from *The Sunglow* move ahead, and then he put his foot on the gangplank that led to the wide walkway along the river. He'd taken just a few steps onto the gangplank when the wake from a large boat traveling past rocked the two riverboats violently. The woman immediately in front of him swayed and lost her balance. Tracey grabbed the elbow of her black coat to steady her.

"Wow, that was a close one. Thank you."

The boats moved abruptly, and she wobbled again as though she might pitch over the side into the river. Tracey continued to hold her elbow, "Steady now."

"Excuse me. I'm so sorry." Her red hair whipped around in the wind, and she grabbed it with her free hand and pulled it out of her face, tucked it under her coat collar, and pulled up her hood.

He felt his reaction to her words. *It's Valentine's Day. Maybe I'll kill her tonight,* flashed suddenly through his mind.

"You'd think I'd been drinking or something. I'm afraid these shoes don't help." She balanced on one foot, still leaning on Tracey's arm, *He smells of pipe smoke. I've always like that on a man.* And she lifted her other foot to show off her red, patent leather, platform stilettos.

Tracey looked down at her very high heels. "Shoes like that could be the death of you."

When they arrived on the embankment, she turned to Tracey, "You probably saved my life back there." She looked at the device in his hand, "I see we are on the same tour this evening. Can I buy you a drink to say thank you when we're done?"

"That would be nice. I'm traveling on my own this trip, and I'd welcome the company."

The woman put out her hand. "I'm Mimi. I'm traveling with thirteen girlfriends on *The Sunglow*. We're supposed to go bar hopping tonight. I'd welcome the chance to duck out of that."

"I'm Tracey. I'm traveling solo on *The Marigold*."

Tracey and Mimi listened to the tour guide point out sights as they walked through the narrow, cobblestone streets filled with black-and-white timbered buildings on their way to the cathedral. "Strasbourg was originally a Celtic village. Yes, just imagine that. The Celts all the way down here. Most people associate them with the British Isles, but remember, they were originally spread across much of Europe. Under the Romans, Strasbourg became known as

Argentoratum. And when it was captured by the Franks in the fifth century, they named it Strateburgum. Strasbourg derives its current name from that. Our port is one of the largest on the Rhine River. And two of the significant modern organizations headquartered here in Strasbourg are the European Parliament and the European Court of Human Rights. You might want to know that in 1988, the Grande Île was designated a World Heritage site by UNESCO. So, as you explore the island after our tour, look for the brass plaques showing that designation.

"Now, we are approaching our destination, our own Notre-Dame, here on the Grand Île. The cathedral was once described by Victor Hugo as 'a skillful combination of monumental size and delicateness'. It is the sixth-tallest church in the world. Just look at it," the guide said, her voice filled with pride. She stopped the group on the narrow Rue Merciére so they could appreciate the grandeur of the building before moving closer. They paused again at the arched entryway with its massive red door surrounded by stone carvings of saints. "This cathedral, known as the Cathédrale Notre-Dame de Strasbourg, or the Cathedral of Our Lady of Strasbourg, is considered to be one of the finest examples of mid-thirteenth to mid-fourteenth century Gothic architecture, which is also known as Rayonnant Gothic. A team of architects from Chartres actually suggested this style. It is interesting to note," she went on, "that this entrance, with its thousands of figures, is a renowned masterpiece of this style of architecture." The guide continued to point out things of particular interest around the west entrance. "Along with the one in Chartres, our cathedral represents some of the earliest uses of architectural drawing to envision and design the building. And now, if you'll follow me," she led the group through the enormous red door into the interior.

"As we walk through, take note of these magnificent stained-glass windows. They date from the twelfth to the fourteenth centuries. Here, ahead of us, on the western facade, is the enchanting rose window. This is a wonderful time to enjoy it when the evening sun lights it from behind. Just look at the beautiful colors." Tracey stood, admiring the window as the guide spoke. He rested his hands on Mimi's shoulders and then he slid his left hand up to caress her throat. Under his thumb, he felt her pulse quicken.

And then the guide was herding them toward the organ with its case of animated figures. Their final stop was in the south transept, where the splendid Renaissance astronomical clock stood eighteen meters tall. "Every day, at solar noon, when the life-size cock crows three times, a procession of eighteen-inch figures of Christ and the Apostles moves across the front of the clock. It's a magnificent mechanical work of art," she said. "This is the end of your guided tour, but please, take your time and enjoy the many treasures of our cathedral."

As they walked back out the red door, Mimi trailed her fingers across it as she said to Tracey, "I've always wondered why so many churches have red doors, even ones that aren't Roman Catholic. I'm not very religious, so I'd always assumed it was something to do with symbolizing the blood of Christ. But the fact that, back then, red paint was one of the few paints that were easy to make and lasted a long time, now, that I find fascinating." She touched his arm and fluttered her eyelashes at him ever so slightly.

"Interesting." He glanced over at her, thinking about putting his right hand over her mouth to stop her talking, and then he could put his other hand on her neck—

§

On the embankment near the boats, Frank called out, "Isabelle, wait—" She slammed the door, and the cab left.

"That was weird. Do you think there is something bothering her, Frank? We haven't seen her the last couple of days since we boarded *The Sunglow*."

"She's just busy, being captain and all." Frank hailed a cab for them. *I bet Victor's turned her against me too.* When they arrived at the hotel and got out of the cab, Frank stopped Lydia and pointed, "See the cathedral up the street?"

"It's breathtaking."

Frank took Lydia's hand. "I registered us for the sunrise service and tour tomorrow."

"Thanks for arranging that, Frank. Sunrise services always bring back fond memories of Easter Sundays with my mam."

They entered the Hotel Le Fleuve and walked over to the coatroom. Frank helped Lydia take off her black coat and then removed his and passed them both to the woman behind the counter. Tucking the two small receipts in Lydia's hand, he asked, "Would you put these in your handbag?" He leaned over and gave her a sensual kiss that promised more later.

As they walked through the doorway of the ballroom, they paused for a moment, watching the other guests. Frank put his arm around Lydia and pulled her in close against him. "Happy birthday, Lydia. I can't wait until we can celebrate it alone and naked. But first we're going to dance until dawn, my darling Lydia. Until the stars go out and the sun rises." He took a curl and lifted it to his lips.

She giggled, turned toward him and, standing on her tiptoes, she kissed him. "How romantic. Let's do that."

Frank led her toward the long bar, the ornate wood front carved with flowers and woodland creatures. Above it, gauzy crimson-and-white material was swagged in a tent-like effect, mimicking the lines of the red-and-white chiffon draped from the glittering chandelier in the center of the room. The tables, short and tall, were covered with crisp white tablecloths, and elaborate arrangements of red roses in crystal bowls had been placed in the center of each. The band sat on a raised dais with roses mounded in front of it.

Lydia looked around, and then, as they reached an empty table, she whispered to Frank, "Very festive, but I think it's a little overdone for my taste."

Frank looked down at her and burst out laughing, "No doubt, Lydia. But don't you think it's fun anyway? It *is* a Valentine's ball after all."

She picked up the red brochure on the table. "Look, Spectrum River Cruise Line is one of the sponsors of this ball. I bet Isabelle had to come since she's a captain."

"I'm sure that's why she came, even though Victor couldn't be here." He turned toward the bar and ordered a glass of champagne for her and two double shots of whisky for himself. He threw one back directly and then carried their drinks over to the table where Lydia stood, watching the couples on the dance floor, her foot tapping in time to the music.

Lydia murmured to Frank, "There's a lot to offer here. Take a look at that woman in the raspberry dress with black piping." Lydia nodded ever so slightly to her right. "She has no taste in dresses but makes up for it with her jewelry."

"Let's take the night off," he said quietly. "I want you by my side tonight, not running around collecting things." They stood looking around, people-watching, listening to the music, making comments about the couples on the dance floor and the ones who were mingling. Lydia leaned against Frank in contentment, her thoughts straying to a life with him. She jumped when he suddenly asked, 'Would you like another champagne?"

She looked down at her drink, "Sure, why not? We aren't working tonight."

Lydia watched as he sauntered over to the bar. *He looks so handsome in a tux.* She saw him slip his hand into his right pocket, the way he always did when he'd stolen something. *Frank, Frank, Frank. I thought we weren't working tonight.*

Frank ordered two more double shots. Again, he threw one back in a single gulp before bringing Lydia her champagne. Setting her drink on the table, he immediately took a quick sip from his glass.

She tipped her glass and took a long swallow, and setting it down, she held a hand out to him. "Would you like to dance, handsome?" she vamped.

He looked over his shoulder, "Who are you talking to? Oh, me? Why, thank you." He flashed his smile and gave a little snap of his fingers before leading her to the dance floor.

As they danced, Lydia asked, "So, what's in your pocket, Frank?"

"Mmmm, a little bling. This one made me think of you, and so I had to take it."

Lydia reached up and caressed his face, "Ahhh, Frank Tomas, you're such a romantic."

Suddenly, he twirled her around and pulled her in close. He stepped to one side and executed a perfect lunge. His hand slid firmly against her lower back, the other supporting her neck. *We've done this a million times, and it's just as exciting every time. It makes me feel so elegant,* thought Lydia with her hands on his shoulders. He lowered her toward his knee, his eyes never leaving hers, and she pointed her leg and foot. She threw her head back, laughing in delight. He pulled her back upright and then bent his head to her, pressing his lips to her neck. Lydia sighed with pleasure.

As they walked off the dance floor, she fanned herself.

"Another round to cool off?"

"Why yes, kind sir," and she gave him a curtsy. He returned it with a bow.

Watching him with a smile as he came back toward their table, Lydia suddenly noticed that he was a little unsteady on his feet. *Oh no, not tonight, Frank. I wanted tonight to be sweet and romantic. Now, we'll make love, and then you'll grunt and roll off me and fall asleep snoring. No sweet talk afterward, no loving little touches.* When he returned, she took both their drinks and set them on the table, and then she pointed across the room. "Look, there's Isabelle standing all alone. Let's go talk to her." She walked off ahead of him. He tossed back half of his drink, set the glass on their table and followed.

"Hi, Isabelle."

"Lydia."

"You look marvelous. Oh, those are the shoes I was admiring at Christmas. That tiny bit of a platform – and the shiny red matches the satin underskirt of your dress. They're perfect."

"Thank you. You look very attractive. I assume that's one of your creations. Where's Frank?" said Isabelle, her voice cool and remote.

"Thank you. It is. Frank was right behind me." She glanced back over her shoulder. "Oh, look, here he comes now."

"Excuse me, Lydia." Isabelle's voice went from cool to cold. "It was nice seeing you. This is work for me. I'm here representing Spectrum, and I have to go over there to talk to Captain Lionel." Abruptly, she walked away.

Wow, that's twice now. I wonder if I did something to offend her at Christmas. I wrote a thank-you note right away, but I never heard back from her.

"Where did she go?" asked Frank.

"I don't know. She barely spoke to me. And as soon as I said that you were coming over, she had to leave to go talk to someone else."

"That's my girlfriend. Always busy." *Now I know Victor has poisoned her against me.*

Frank took Lydia's hand, and they walked to their table. After they had each taken another sip of their drinks, Frank pulled Lydia into his arms and kissed her passionately. As the kiss finally ended, with her heart pounding, Lydia looked into his eyes, and for the first time, she said, "I love you, Frank Tomas, I love you."

Love? Frank was caught off-guard. *Love?* He stared at her with a panicked look on his face.

The guests clapped loudly as the band ended its number. Lydia thought Frank hadn't heard her, and she laid her hand on his lapel over his heart and repeated, "I love you, Frank."

He shook his head. *Love? This isn't casual for her anymore. We work so well together, and the sex is fantastic. But obviously, I haven't been paying attention to what's been happening with her.* "Lydia, I'm just a rebound from Mari."

Devastated, she drew in one sharp breath and then another. And then in a tiny voice, she said, "But I've fallen in love with you. I thought you felt the same. The way you treat me. You're so good to me. We're so good together. And we've been with each other for such a long time now. It's not a rebound. It's not."

"Lydia, time doesn't change these things. And that's just the way I am with women. I cherish them. I bring them gifts and flowers. I flirt. I make them happy. And I enjoy them while I'm with them. But it doesn't mean I love them." Frank gave her a chaste peck on her cheek, and then he pulled away, his eyes nervous, darting around, unable to meet hers. "I can't love you, Lydia. Not the way you want me to."

I should have known since that first night, when he said, "I love you, Isabelle." I should have known, with all those kisses on her mouth, with all the touching, with the way he looked into her eyes. I should have known, with the girlfriend nickname that wasn't a nickname in his heart. I should have known. Her eyes brimmed with tears. "No, not the way you love Isabelle."

Frank simply nodded, shocked that Lydia recognized his feelings for Isabelle, that she understood for him those feelings were more than friendship.

"I'd hoped you'd have let her go. That I would be enough for you and that we could have a life with each other, together. You can't have Isabelle, Frank. She and Victor belong together. You've seen how they are. They love each other. They have a family. But we could have a family like that too." Her voice quivered in one last desperate attempt, "I could love you enough for both of us."

"I just realized, I've always wanted Isabelle," Frank tapped his chest, "for myself." He was desperate to escape and looked down at his glass. "I need another drink. Do you want more champagne?"

"I'm fine." She watched Frank go to the bar. He ordered a double shot and slammed it down. Then he ordered another and downed that too. And then in a moment of clarity, she realized, *He's a drunk. Just like my father.* She stared blankly at her glass of champagne that sat nearly untouched by her hand. *Now, what will I do? What will I do?*

Frank carried a big drink in his hand past Lydia without a word or a glance. Isabelle stood at a table all alone. He went to her. Lydia watched Frank take Isabelle's head in his hands — *like he used to do to me.* She blinked back tears and walked away toward the exit. *I won't let him see me cry.* She took a deep breath. *He betrayed me. He used me. He used me to steal for him, and he used me in bed. And all the time, he was probably imagining I was Isabelle. How could you be so stupid, so blind, Lydia McKay? How could you be so stupid?*

§

Tracey and Mimi walked down the street, side by side, after their drinks. She stopped in front of the Hotel Le Fleuve. "Excuse me, I'm just going to pop in here. I need some postcards, and I want to look around for some trinkets for my family and friends back home. It's hard to do that with thirteen women hanging around."

"The tour, the drink. It's been a very pleasant evening. Thank you."

She held her hood up against the wind. "It has. Thank you." She put her hand on his arm, bright red nails against his overcoat sleeve. "But this doesn't have to be it for tonight." Over his shoulder, she spotted a little bar across the street, and she pointed.

"Why don't you wait in that quaint little bar there? After I'm done, we can have another drink or something more..."

"Mmmm. Come find me when you're ready." *I'm going to do this. I'm going to wait for her, and then I'll do it. I've been aching for it all evening.*

She reached up and touched his beard and went into the hotel to the gift shop.

Turning around, he looked at the bar opposite the hotel. *I'll sit there and watch for her.* He went in and found a table where he could see out the window. And while he waited, he ordered a drink from the young girl who bounced over to serve him, "A simple glass of scotch, single malt, no ice." While he sat, he thought about how he'd killed the prostitute in St Petersburg. About her face and how she'd turned her back for him, about how it had felt to put his hands on her throat and feel her press and writhe against him. He thought about his arousal again afterward. And the prostitute's face turned into Mimi's.

It had begun to rain softly while he sat, staring out the window, and he watched the drops hit the glass and run down, blurring his view. *I'll wait, and when she comes back, we'll make love and then I'll strangle her. I've never done that before.* He felt that familiar frisson of excitement, which seemed to get stronger every time, every time he killed.

Lydia left the hotel, pulling on her coat, and Tracey leaned forward, squinting through the wet glass as the lights from the lobby caught her red hair. His mouth grew dry as he watched her look his way, preparing to come to the bar where he waited.

She looked at the bar, pulled her coat up over her head as the rain came down harder and sprinted across the street. *I can never be with him again. I have to get back to Paris. Tonight.*

It wasn't Mimi, he realized when she came through the door.

Lydia pushed the wet curls off her face. *Maybe I should cut this all off. That would show him.* Sitting down at the table next to Tracey, she began to cry quietly. *I'm going to have to do everything on my own. Thank goodness I have all that jewelry tucked away and the money I've saved working for him. I have enough, just like he promised I would the day he hired me. I don't need him anymore. I don't need anyone. I can open Lydia McKay of Paris without him. He's just a worthless drunk.* And then, out loud, she said, "What a shite!"

Tracey was staring out the window, lost in his thoughts and anticipation, but when he heard Lydia's voice, he turned to her. "I beg your pardon. Do you need something?" *Oh, this is the woman from across the street. Oh my – look at that beautiful, curly red hair and creamy flawless skin. She's quite attractive, but oh, so young.*

She sniffled, "No, it's my birthday, and I just broke up with my boyfriend." She cringed as she said it, thinking of Isabelle. *That is, my boyfriend that never was.*

"That's too bad." Tracey nodded absently and looked back out the window as the rain continued to come down.

§

Under the soft light of the chandelier, Frank held Isabelle's head between his hands and pressed his mouth on hers. She pushed him away. "No, Frank. Stop. You're drunk. It's me. Isabelle. We're not like that."

"You're so beautiful, girlfriend. I haven't seen you in so long," Frank slurred as he tried to kiss her again.

Isabelle shoved Frank harder. "No, Frank. This is wrong. I'm with Victor. You're with Lydia."

"I love *you*, Isabelle. I've always loved you."

"Frank, stop this. You're drunk and confused. You're my best friend. You were like my brother. You can never be my lover, not now – or in the future. Please try to understand that and move on. You'll be wasting your life if you don't, as well as your chances of finding your own happiness." *I wish Victor were here. Then I wouldn't have to deal with this by myself.*

Completely drunk, Frank held her arms tightly and shook her hard enough to frighten her. "You don't understand. *We* were meant to be together. Fuck Victor. It's supposed to be you and me. Always. Always been that way. I can take care of you. I know you better than anyone. I've always loved you more than anyone."

"Frank, stop. You're hurting me. You've changed. You're not a nice person anymore. You're a criminal, and you're drunk."

"I'm not a criminal. I'll quit stealing for you."

"You're DRUNK."

"I'm not drunk, Isabelle. I've only had a few, to take the edge off. Please, give us a chance. I've always loved you, and I've always wanted you. I just realized it tonight. Even Lydia could see it. She told me I love you. We're meant to be together, girlfriend. Not you and Victor. You and me. I want you." Frank pulled Isabelle into his arms, and again, he tried to kiss her.

Isabelle wrenched herself away and slapped him as hard as she could. "Quit it, Frank. Get off me. You're a piece of crap. Total crap. Just go away! Now."

"But I want you. I'll do anything to have you."

Isabelle shook her head, "No, Frank. No. Stay away from my family. Stay away from Victor. Stay away from me. Just stay away. I need to get away from you. I need to get back to *The Sunglow*. I need to call Victor."

"Fucking Victor. He's ruined everything." Frank stumbled off to the bar.

§

Back to staring out the window, Tracey saw Mimi come out of the Hotel Le Fleuve. *Shiny red shoes with very high heels. Black coat with its hood up. Leaning over to keep the rain out of her face.* He stood to go out and meet her, but she turned down the alley directly across from the bar. *Hmmm, she must have changed her mind. That's unfortunate.*

Tracey jerked on his coat and thrust his hat onto his head, dashing from the bar and into the alley to catch her. With his right hand over her nose and mouth and his left hand around her throat, he strangled her – in the dark – in the alley – in the rain.

Through the light rain on the window, Lydia watched. She saw the back of the man from the bar and a woman in front of him. She saw the way his elbows pointed outward, the way he stepped to one side and leaned over. She saw the red shoes and realized the woman was lying on the ground. She saw the man pause for a moment, bending, reaching toward her. *Maybe she's hurt and he's helping her. I should go see if I can help too.* And then she saw the man put his left hand in his pocket the same way that Frank had earlier that evening, and she watched as he walked briskly down the alley and turned behind the hotel. The woman lay still in the dark alley in the rain.

Lydia rushed across the street, not even bothering to button her coat, as she hurried to see what had happened to the woman. As she got close, she recognized the shoes and saw the familiar dress beneath her open coat. She put her hands over her mouth and stumbled back, staring in shock.

She backed into someone, and suddenly, hands were grabbing and shaking her, and she heard a familiar voice, "Isabelle. Isabelle. Have you seen Isabelle?" Frank was asking her, his voice frantic. "I don't know where she went. She left me, and I need to find her."

Lydia screamed and pointed down the alley, toward the woman's body, Isabelle's body, on the ground, her hair and dress soaked by the rain.

Frank knelt down beside her and called to her, "Girlfriend, oh, girlfriend." He cradled her in his arms and pushed her hair back from her face. "Isabelle. Isabelle. What's wrong?" Then he yelled over his shoulder, "She's not breathing. Help! Help!"

People gathered around the entrance to the alley, and Lydia found herself surrounded by the crowd. She continued backing away in shock.

Tears ran down Frank's face as he screamed, "She's not breathing. Call somebody. Call an ambulance." He continued to rock her in his arms, "I love you, Isabelle. Don't leave me."

While Lydia stood and watched, it continued to rain. And then she heard a vaguely familiar voice beside her, "Do you think he did it?" She turned to look at the man from the bar.

Chapter Eighteen

February 2012

The Aftermath

Strasbourg, France

"Hello?"

"Rick, I need your help."

"Frank? Is that you? I need to put you on speaker. My wife had to leave early for work today, so I have to make lunches for the boys and get them off to school."

Frank scowled. *Boys? I don't have time for your family-life shit.* "I only have a few minutes."

"It's been a long time. Chloe is here, visiting." Rick beckoned her over, "Say hello, Chloe."

Flirting a little, she said, "Well, well, well, Frank Tomas. It's been a long time. You sound—"

"Rick, I don't have time for that," he snapped.

Chloe raised her eyebrows and shook her head. *He hasn't changed one bit. We've all grown up except for Frank.*

In a curt voice, Rick said, "You stopped returning my calls five years ago. And you're calling me now because—?"

"Shit, just listen!" Frank's voice rose, "They've only given me five minutes."

"They? Frank, slow down. Take it easy. Tell me who you're talking about." Rick deepened his voice and spoke slowly as he tried to calm him down, the way he always had when Frank got agitated.

He took a deep breath and spat out, "They've fucking arrested me."

Hearing Frank's desperation, Rick stopped what he was doing, took his phone and pulled out a chair to sit at the kitchen table. "Where are you, Frank?" he continued, in the same soothing tone.

"I'm in Strasbourg, Rick. In fucking Strasbourg."

"France?"

"Yes, France. Where else? Rick, I need you to get me a lawyer. I need a really good lawyer."

"Can't you get a lawyer through the bank or use your family's lawyer?"

Chloe came over to sit next to Rick and chimed in, "What were you doing? What were you arrested for?"

"Murder."

In unison, Chloe and Rick responded, "What? When?"

"Last night. They arrested me at eleven o'clock. I didn't do it. There's a witness. You know I can't go to my dad. Rick, please help me get a lawyer. I don't have anyone else to go to. I don't have any money. I'm broke." Frank's voice trembled as, for the first time, he put words to his predicament.

"What? Slow down, Frank, tell us what happened," said Rick, wishing he could reach out to his old friend and put his hands on his shoulders like he used to when he became unreasonably angry.

Chloe whispered in his ear, "Even for Frank, this is weird. He's gone round the bend." Rick nodded.

"Fuck, don't you get it? I need a lawyer. A criminal lawyer. They think I killed Isabelle."

§

The door opened with a slight screech of its hinges, and the gangly young policeman gently pushed Frank into the interview room. The grey walls, the usual scarred wooden table, two chairs and—*Uncle Victor.* Frank's eyes lit up in relief. *Maybe Uncle can get me out of here,* and his emotion nearly caused his knees to buckle.

The policeman removed Frank's handcuffs. "No shaking hands, no hugging. Take your seat and stay in it. You have ten minutes," he said in a gruff voice and stepped outside, letting the door slam closed. He leaned against it, watching the scene inside the room through the narrow window.

Frank walked over to the table, snapping his fingers lightly, and pulled out the nearest chair. "Uncle—" He looked at Victor's face. His jaw was clenched, his eyes puffy, bloodshot and angry, his expression unforgiving. Frank's mouth went suddenly dry, and he swallowed several times, and then he took a long breath, let it out and continued, "Thank God, you're here. I have to get out of this place. They think—" He stopped as he looked at his uncle again.

Deep lines of exhaustion and profound loss etched Victor's face. He hadn't slept since he'd heard about Isabelle's murder. Slowly

he turned red, "How dare you?" His voice was hoarse with pain and
fatigue.

"Wha—?"

Incandescent with grief, Victor's voice, his hands, his body all
shook. "You murdered my friend, my partner. You murdered the
love of my life. You murdered the mother of my children."

"But I didn't—"

"This was to be Izzy's last cruise. She was going to be home
with us – all the time. She was going to teach piano. We all have
nothing now. Because of you. Because you killed her. And now, I
have to go back today and tell our little girls that their mommy won't
be coming home – ever." His voice broke for a second, "That she'll
never use the new bathroom we built to surprise her. That she won't
be there to bathe them or brush their hair. That she'll never snuggle
with them or read them another story. We had ten years together,
only ten years. We should have had a lifetime. You've taken all of
that from us."

"But—"

"How dare you?" He put his hands flat on the table as he stood
and leaned menacingly toward Frank. Frank cowered back in his
chair. "You're just an entitled, spoiled brat. You only think of
yourself. I had hoped for so much more from you. If I could, I would
reach across the table right now and put my hands around your neck
and strangle the life out of you. I would strangle you, just like you
did to my Izzy." Victor's voice broke on the last words, and he
walked to the door, tears streaming down his cheeks, and banged for
the policeman to let him out.

"But I didn't do it. She was the love of my life too," Frank
whispered as he put his head down on the table and wept. *My life is
fucking shit now. My best friend is dead. My dad is going to disown me. My
uncle thinks I murdered Isabelle. Will Rick get me that lawyer? Will Lydia
clear me? She has to. She found her body. She knew I was searching for Isabelle.
She knows I couldn't have killed her. Is she so angry at me? The last thing I
told her was that I didn't love her. But maybe I do love her. She put up with me
and never judged me like all the others. Maybe I do love her.*

§

Paris, France

She watched the puffs of white her breath made in the night air as she pounded on the door to the small apartment above his shop. She hoped he wasn't out drinking somewhere. If that were the case, she'd be stuck on this rickety landing in the freezing cold until he came home, hours from now. "Shane, answer the door. Answer the door, you shite," called Lydia as she continued to bang with her gloved fist.

She heard the locks turn, and then he opened the door a crack. "Lydia?" Pungent smoke from the Gitane in the corner of his mouth greeted her.

"Let me in, Shane. I'm freezing out here."

He opened the door a little wider, and she pushed past him into the smoky room. Coughing, Lydia waved at the smoke and looked around. The sparsely furnished room still managed to look as cluttered as his shop had been before she'd become his office manager. Newspapers were piled on the table in front of the sofa. His folded laundry was balanced precariously on a seat cushion. The TV blared away in the corner with one of the ridiculous game shows that he watched non-stop in the evenings when he wasn't down at the corner bar, nursing a glass or five of his favorite Armorik blended whisky.

"I need to stay with you while I figure out what to do – is that okay? I can sleep here on the sofa."

He walked back over to the table in the center of the large front room, sat down and poured himself another glass of whisky from the half-empty bottle.

Lydia dropped her bag on the floor near the small table – *I have to keep an eye on my jewelry. I don't trust Shane that far* – and she sat down heavily across from Shane. "Thank God you were home. I didn't know where else to go."

"Where's Frank? Why not go to your apartment?"

"I stopped by my apartment to pick up some clothes and stuff, but I couldn't stay there. That's where they'll look for me. We were on a cruise together, working. Frank was arrested. He's in jail."

"Did he get caught stealing?" Shane sat back and took a drag on his cigarette.

"No, for murder."

The Gitane nearly fell from his lips, "Hold on, what are you talking about?"

Her story spilled out. "Frank and I have been splitting our time between Paris and Brussels, staying together at his apartment there and mine here in Paris. And we went on a cruise. Isabelle was on it too. We were working." *Thank God, when I left Strasbourg, I took all the jewels we'd stolen so far on that trip.* "As part of the cruise, we went to a Valentine's ball. I thought he loved me, but it turns out he's always been in love with Isabelle. He told me, there, at the ball. And then she was murdered in an alley, and Frank was arrested for killing her. But I saw the murder. And I know who did it, and I know it wasn't Frank. The murderer came back and stood next to me in the crowd. He asked me if I thought Frank did it. I'm scared he'll find me – the murderer is out there, Shane."

"Wow, you've been busy. It sounds complicated. But why can't you stay in your apartment, here in Paris?"

"I have to figure out what I'm going to tell the police. If they discover that Frank is a jewel thief, that might lead them to me too. Frank'll tell them I was with him that night, and that I saw the murder. And they'll come looking for me. They could arrest me for being a jewel thief. And if the police can find me, the real killer might too. Please, Shane, can I stay with you while I figure it out?"

Shane poured Lydia a drink. "Here, drink this."

"Thanks," she said and drank it down in one long swallow.

He continued smoking and drinking until his glass was empty. Then he picked up the bottle and poured another drink for himself and one for Lydia. He pushed it across the table to her.

Lydia reached over, took a cigarette from Shane's pack and grabbed his lighter. As she fumbled to light it, Shane said, "This must be bad, kid. You hate smoking."

§

Spectrum Cruise, *The Marigold*

Mimi sat on the bow of *The Sunglow* under the outdoor heaters, enjoying the morning air. She and her thirteen friends had taken over most of the area to sit and gossip while they ate breakfast. The women were all laughing and talking, oblivious to the noise they were making or the passengers whose breakfasts were being disrupted by them.

Tracey stood on the bow of *The Marigold* with his mug of coffee in his hands, alternating between watching Mimi engrossed in conversation with her travel companions and the crew of both boats preparing for their departure.

Tracey thought about that night and the woman he'd killed by mistake. *But it was just as exciting. Just as satisfying. The unknown woman.*

The Marigold pulled away from *The Sunglow*, and the crews put away the ropes. The movement caught Mimi's eye, and she looked up. She waved when she saw Tracey and said something to her girlfriends.

Tracey lifted his coffee cup in acknowledgement. *The one who got away.*

We hope you enjoyed this book.

You know, we really love the characters in our books. We discuss them endlessly, and when we have to decide who will die, we agonize over it, changing our minds multiple times before we finally decide. No matter whom we choose, we are always very sad when we read the scenes about the murder and about the characters who have to live with that loss.

And, by the way, we hope we left you wondering – what's happening with Tracey? Well, stay tuned, there are more books to come.

When we published the first book, *The Killings Begin*, readers like you thanked us for writing a book that took them away from home, with characters they loved, to places around the world. They wanted to know if Tracey killed Charlotte or not, and what happened to Gia and Sal. Your questions and comments are critical to fine tuning our series. You're the reason we included the prologue in this book, to answer the question about Charlotte up front. And don't worry, we'll explore Gia and Sal's future too – in book three.

So, tell us what you liked, what you loved, even what you hated. Please do us a favor and post a review of *Death in a Dark Alley*. We'd like to hear your feedback. Reviews can be tough to come by, and you have the power to make or break a book - **https://amzn.to/3tRa0yx**

Thank you for reading our book,

A Body Washes Ashore

Available on Amazon, October 31, 2022

Physical cheating or emotional cheating – which is worse?

Paris, spring 2012, and the Spectrum riverboat *The Indigo* is embarking on another luxury trip. On the first night, cousins Remy and Frannie are introduced to seasoned cruisers, Lee, Fong, Charlotte and Tracey, and along with Sasha the bartender, they quickly become firm friends.

As the year rolls on, the group – often joined by old friends, Gia, Lydia and Sal – meets up regularly for parties, fun and friendship.

Sometimes, they gather in smaller groups.

And sometimes, it's just two…

Meanwhile, Tracey continues his struggle to tame his inner urges – why do red-headed women make him lose control? And all the time, Emily, Edgar and Penelope are hot on his heels with their investigation, desperate to identify the Parking Lot Strangler before he strikes again.

This third novel in the series follows the story started with *The Killings Begin* and continued with *Death in a Dark Alley*. In true Spectrum style, it teases the reader with a crime story while sensitively addressing the moral dilemmas surrounding infidelity.

The Killings Begin

THE FIRST BOOK IN THE SERIES is very well written and well-paced. I like the way the characters are being introduced, I feel like I'm really getting to know them! I read it in two days, you know you have a good book when you can't wait to get back to it. My husband is reading it now and enjoying it very much. You always hate to see a good book end, but we have the whole series to look forward to. The suspense is building!

OBSESSED STRAIGHT AWAY! Such an easy read and couldn't put the book down. Found the story gripping and so excited for the second! Never wanted it to end, truly talented authors!

THIS IS A UNIQUE TALE and I enjoyed how strong of a character Gia Delgado was…I don't know that I've ever read another book with this sort of arrangement…

THE KILLINGS BEGIN **IS A CAPTIVATING READ.** I couldn't wait to get back to reading it. Now, I look so forward to reading the next book in the series. It couldn't come too soon.

I BOUGHT THE BOOK IMMEDIATELY, and once I received it, I was hooked. I give books the first chapter to hook me before abandoning [them]. This book hooked me before the first page was over… I bought the physical book so that [my husband] can read it to me out loud, but then I had to get the kindle edition to keep reading throughout my day no matter where I was.

MY WIFE BOUGHT THIS BOOK. Because of the lockdown, I decided to read it. I was skeptical because it is called a romance, but I really enjoyed the story. It is very well written, a quick and easy read. The romance is not too heavy or sappy and is more than offset by the suspense, making it a great read, even for someone who would not typically read a romance story. I also enjoyed the focus on the geography and culture of the various cities visited in the novel.

Acknowledgements

Writing this book was so hard. We keep saying that – because it was. It spanned more than two decades and played out across three continents. Keeping the characters' lives intertwined but not entangled challenged us to use a range of creative tools, from timelines and character bios to the "killing list".

But even with all of those aids, *Death in a Dark Alley* wouldn't have made it to publication in this final form without the help, thoughtful recommendations and encouragement from our beta readers: Rae Ann Dilks, Jan Erkes, Pam Hays, Alyssa O'Neal, Gavin Pay, Mallory Paxton and Judy Zaller. Our gratitude has no end.

We'd like to say a special thanks to Alyssa who, in addition to all her other comments, called out a handful of words that we had developed a particular fondness for – and used prolifically throughout this book. What an interesting task that was – searching for other words and equally or more effective ways to say the same thing. And, along those same lines, our thanks to Mark Maves, who challenged us to find other ways to say how much a character appreciates something besides "loving" it. That made us smile.

Eric McCaleb's and George Bell's assistance with the chapters about the murders, the police detectives and our security firm owner was invaluable. Understanding how a murder scene is "worked" and how an investigation might proceed was critical to make those chapters feel real.

Our advance readers were fabulous. They all jumped in at the end and read our pre-publication draft. Not only did they write wonderful reviews for which we are so grateful, but their eagle eyes also found little errors which we'd introduced as we made final changes to the manuscript. Thanks to each and every one of them: Julia Barugel, Vicki Costello, Jennifer Cranston, Dona Dinkler, Cheryl Engen, Diane French, Jessica McCaleb, Sarah Pay, Ken Pitz, Maureen Sollitto, Jim Tully and Melissa Watson.

And finally, to our copy editor extraordinaire, Miranda

Summers-Pritchard, who is so much more than just a copy editor – her insight and suggestions about our plot and those characters that needed just that extra bit of backstory helped us give this book additional depth and texture. And again, the back cover write-up was spot on.

Thank you, each and every one. We look forward to seeing you back for book three.

About the Authors

Robin Bradley grew up in a home where they had no TV, and so everyone read voraciously and played with words. She is often known to say things like "Speaking is one-way; talking is two-way, a conversation," or "Passive voice? Really?" She loves a good story, whether it's reading, hearing or telling it. She inherited her love of writing from her family - her mother was an English teacher and published poet, and her uncle was a reporter for the San Jose Mercury. Robin also writes poetry, although she hasn't published any yet. Besides writing, Robin keeps very busy as the president of her condo board and loves wine, cooking, and reading.

Jody Leber-Pay loves writing because she gets to be a collaborator, an inventor, a researcher, a storyteller, a problem solver, a writer, an editor, a marketer, and a techie. She finds the process of going from an idea to a published book fascinating, and that's what keeps her motivated. Before writing fiction, Jody authored technical documents for work and published a technical book. When she's not writing, Jody enjoys the great outdoors - walking, hiking and golfing.

Robin and Jody met in 2016 on a European riverboat cruise from Budapest to Nuremberg. As a way to pass the time while they traveled through the series of locks from the Danube to the Main River, Robin, Jody and a handful of friends sat around in the afternoon, drinking Chianti, laughing and making up silly romantic stories.

The development of those stories into the Spectrum Series began with an email from Jody to Robin: "By the way – You still interested in the Lock Series? … it will be fun."

And so began their unusual, long-distance friendship and their collaboration on the Spectrum Series.

Working as Bradley Pay, they found that their unique interests and skills were complementary, but it was their enjoyment that kept the process going. Creating the first book and outlining the remainder of the series was hard work but far more fun than they had imagined at the outset.

Some of the original characters remain, albeit much evolved, and many new characters have appeared. These stories are no longer the bosom-heaving romances of our river-cruise days. Instead, although the love interests remain, they are now haunted by an international serial killer who changes the course of the characters' lives.